THROUGH STREETS BROAD AND NARROW

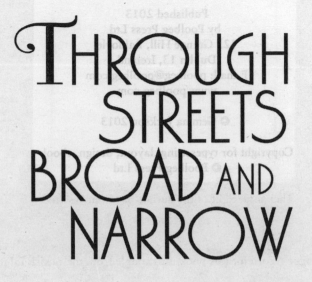

THROUGH STREETS BROAD AND NARROW

GEMMA JACKSON

POOLBEG

The moral right of the author has been asserted.

1

A catalogue record for this book is available from the British Library.

ISBN 978-1-84223-597-3

Typeset by Patricia Hope in Sabon 11.5/15.5

Printed and bound by CPI Group (UK) Ltd, Croydon, CR0 4YY

www.poolbeg.com

About the Author

Gemma Jackson, a Holy Catholic Irish girl from Dublin, left home for the first time at seventeen – to see what was out there. With no money and the best education the nuns could give, she set off on her worldwide 'adventures'. To a great extent, she's still adventuring.

Gemma has worked her way around the world, taking whatever work was legal and available. She has herded sheep in Devon, been air hostess to the Shah of Iran and written speeches for a TV evangelist.

Gemma's motto is: 'I'll try anything once. If I don't like it I won't do it again.' She has one child.

Through Streets Broad and Narrow is Gemma's debut novel, a fictional amalgamation of the stories she grew up hearing of the The Lane in Dublin.

Acknowledgements

I have to give thanks to the people who populate my world, starting with me da Patrick Jackson who convinced me as a child that the Dublin Horse Show was put on to celebrate my birthday. Sure what did I want with a present when the biggest event of the year was put on just for me?

Me ma, Rose Jackson, who taught her children the world was their oyster – get out there and look for the pearl and light a candle while you're about it.

My daughter Astrid, who got the short end of the stick having me for a mother. Thanks for the oceans of tea you've brewed and served to me. Thanks for shouting at me to "stand and stretch". I got a good one when I got you.

The strangers I've met on my travels who took me in, educated and nurtured me until I left on the next stage of my adventure. I've passed through so many lives and learned so many weird and wonderful things on my travels. The world is a great place.

The people at Poolbeg. Thank you from the bottom of my heart for allowing me to tell my stories and see them in print. You can have no idea of the wonder and joy you've brought to my life. Paula Campbell and Gaye Shortland, two ladies who have earned their places in heaven having to deal with me.

Words of wisdom for my daughter Astrid McCorkle
without whom this book would not have been possible.

As you pass through life pain is inevitable.
Suffering is optional.

ANON

Chapter 1

The sound of her own teeth chattering woke Ivy Murphy from her uneasy sleep. She had a crick in her neck and every bone in her body wanted to complain. Ivy didn't know if the aches she felt were the result of her uncomfortable position in her battered fireside chair or her shenanigans in the street earlier. The Lane had celebrated the brand-new year with a lively street party.

Ivy didn't drink alcohol but she'd been the first to start dancing and singing. To someone unused to celebration it had been a wonderful way to greet the year 1925. She'd been giddy with happiness until she'd returned home.

Ivy stared in the general direction of the battered clock ticking away on her mantelpiece. She had no idea how long she'd slept. She'd been waiting for her da to come home, praying he had a few coppers left in his pocket.

"Stupid woman," Ivy muttered, trying to stand.

It was pitch-black and cold, the fire in the grate having died completely. She couldn't see her hand in front of her face. By feel and familiarity she found a couple of matches and pulled the chain on one of the glass-covered lamps situated on the side of the mantel. She struck the match off the mantelpiece and held the tiny flame to the gas jet. The light flickered weakly. The gas supply coughed and sputtered. A sure sign indicating the need for more money in the gas meter.

"Da, are you home?" She kicked the black knitted shawl she'd used to cover her knees away from her. The darn thing was wrapped around her ankles. She stumbled, shivering in the cold predawn air. "Da, where are you?" She held her arms in front of her as she made her way to the second of the two rooms they called home. She pushed the heavy wood door ajar.

"Da, it's black as pitch in here." She sniffed the air like a hound. Her da smelt like the bottom of a barrel after a night on the tiles. "Da!" she shouted again even though she knew the back room was empty of life. "Where in the name of God did yeh get to, Da?"

Ivy longed to collapse on the floor and scream like a banshee.

"It's past four in the morning. Where can he be? The pubs are all closed," she sobbed.

Last night, not for the first time, Éamonn Murphy had cleaned out the jar she kept her housekeeping money in – the rent-money jar was empty too. Thanks to her da's two-finger habit, Ivy always checked her cash before she went to bed. There wasn't a penny piece to be found in the place. Her da had waited until Ivy joined the street party before stealing the money and disappearing with his drinking cronies.

The sound of footsteps coming down the entry steps had Ivy spinning around towards the window of their basement flat. It wasn't her father: the footsteps were steady. Ivy froze for a moment. Should she blow out the gas lamp and pretend she was asleep?

"Miss Murphy! It's Officer Collins, Miss Murphy." The soft words were accompanied by the rap of knuckles on the entry door. The Murphys were fortunate in that their basement rooms had a private entrance, a luxury in the tenements. "Miss Murphy!"

"Officer Collins!" Ivy opened the door, trying to make out the features of the man standing in the concrete cage that framed the iron steps leading down to the doorway. Officer Collins was a familiar face to the residents of these tenements. "What in the name of God are you doing at my door?"

"Could I come inside, Miss Murphy?"

Barney Collins wished he was anywhere but here. He'd walked the streets of this tenement block known locally as "The Lane" for years. Ivy Murphy was a well-known local figure. She'd pushed a pram around the high-class streets that existed only yards away from the squalor of The Lane from the time she was knee-high to a grasshopper.

Ivy stepped back and watched the tall police officer remove his hat and bend his head to enter the tiny hallway. "I can't offer yeh a cup of tea," she said, leading him into the front room. "It's a bit early for visitors."

"I wonder if we could have a bit more light on the subject?" Barney Collins couldn't see a thing in the flickering gaslight. With Ivy's pride in mind he held out a copper penny and offered it to her with the words: "Saves you searching in the dark." Barney well knew everyone in these tenements squeezed every penny until it screamed but right now he needed to be able to see the woman.

"Give me a minute." Ivy was glad the dim light hid her burning cheeks.

She hurried into the hallway and quickly pulled the door of the cupboard that hid the gas meter open. The strength went from her legs when she noticed the broken seal on the money-box of the meter. Her da had nicked the gas money as well. Ivy passed the penny through. Might as well be hung for a sheep as a lamb, she thought, catching the penny in her open palm and passing it through the meter again.

"Thank you, Officer," Ivy said, returning the coin to the policeman. "I had several coins on top of the meter." She lied without a blush but she was mortified at being forced to play penny tag with a police officer.

She quickly lit the second gas lamp on the mantel. With very little fuss she raked the fire and in minutes had a blaze climbing up the chimney. When you came in freezing from the winter conditions you needed to get the fire going, fast. Paper, sticks and small nuggets of coal were kept close to hand.

Ivy wiped her black-stained hands on a damp rag hanging by the grate, before turning back around to face Officer Collins. To give her father his due, he was a dab hand at finding nuggets of coal spilled around the docks. He sold some for drink money but always made sure there was enough at home for his own comfort.

"What's going on?" Ivy sank down into one of the chairs flanking the fireplace. She gestured towards the chair on the opposite side of the fireplace.

"I'm afraid I have bad news." Barney Collins perched on the edge of the chair, staring at the woman opposite.

Ivy Murphy was a good-looking young woman. In the proper clothes she would stand out in any company. Her blue-black hair pulled back into an old-fashioned bun suited her face. The starvation diet of the tenements gave her face a high-boned patrician appearance. Eyes of brilliant blue framed by thick black lashes stared across the space between them.

"Just get it out quick, please." Ivy forced the words out. Her lips felt frozen and her teeth wanted to rattle, but she sat stiffly upright. "What has me da been up to now?"

"There's no easy way to tell you this, Miss Murphy." Barney Collins swallowed audibly. "Sometime during the early hours of this morning, in what we believe was a drunken stupor, your father Éamonn Murphy fell into the cement horse trough outside Brennan's public house and drowned."

"Me da is dead?" Ivy fell back against the chair, her hand going to her incredibly narrow neck, almost as if she needed help holding up her head. "That's not possible. I'm expecting me da home any minute."

"I'm very sorry for your loss." Barney Collins wondered if he was going to have a hysterical woman on his hands.

"He's really dead?" Ivy whispered. "You're sure? It's not some kind of mistake?"

"I'm sure, Miss Murphy. I know your father well enough to make a positive identification."

"Yes, I suppose you do." Ivy wanted to float away, disappear. What on earth was she supposed to do now?

"Ivy, Miss Murphy, is there anyone I could call to be with you?" Barney Collins couldn't just leave the poor young woman here alone.

"There's only me and me da," Ivy whispered. "All the others left." Her three younger brothers had taken the mail-boat to England as soon as each turned sixteen. Ivy hadn't seen or heard from them since.

"I could knock on Father Leary's door if you like," Barney offered. "I pass his house on my way home."

"He'd only be round here with his hand out!" Ivy blurted out before slapping her hand across her mouth. It didn't do to badmouth the clergy in Holy Catholic Ireland.

"I see." Barney Collins was astonished to hear anyone dare to voice a negative comment on the clergy. The poverty-stricken families living in this slum were devoted Catholics. The people of The Lane accepted the decisions of the priest before the law of the land. Every family gave pennies they couldn't afford to the Church each Sunday and every Saint's Day. It was a wonder the local church didn't burn down with the number of candles these people lit.

"I'm sure you don't see." Ivy grinned in spite of herself. "I have a problem . . ." she paused, wondering how much to say, "with the Church. It's a well-known fact in these parts."

"I'll have to leave you to it then," Barney Collins was unsure what to make of this situation. "The death certificate and your father's body will be waiting for you at the morgue in the basement of Kevin's Hospital. Because of the time of year," he shook his head – it was a rotten start to 1925 for this woman, "it will be a few days before the body is released into your care."

"Thank you for coming in person to tell me." Ivy stood waiting for Officer Collins to push himself upright, then slowly walked the police officer to the door. She wanted a cup of tea and time alone to think.

"I'll keep in touch if you don't mind," he said.

"Thank you." Ivy held out one pale, cold, shaking hand, offering a handshake as a token of her gratitude. It was all she could afford.

"Let me know if I can help in any way." Barney Collins stepped through the open door and replaced his uniform hat on his head. "It seems almost insulting to wish you a Happy New Year," he shrugged, "but I don't know what else to say." He began to climb the iron stairs leading up to the street. When he reached street level he turned with his hand on the iron railings to look down. The door was closed tight, the gas lamps extinguished.

Ivy wasn't even aware of turning off the gas lamps – the habit of saving money by any means possible was bred into her bones. She dropped back into her chair, staring without seeing into the fire.

"What in the name of all that's good and holy am I going to do now?" she croaked aloud, tears running down her cheeks unnoticed. Her da had left her without a brass farthing to her name. There was no way she could give him the send-off he would want, the kind of send-off his friends and drinking cronies would expect. Her body began to shake as she tried to grasp the situation she found herself in. What would she do? Where could she go?

Ivy finally gave in to the sobs she'd been forcing back since she heard the news. Her big, tough, rascal of a da was gone. She'd never see him again. She'd never again scream at him for the trouble he never failed to bring to her door.

"Tea, I need a river of tea." Ivy wiped her hands across her wet cheeks, her eyes sore from the ocean of tears that had poured from her shaking heart.

She grabbed the heavy black kettle from the grate and without conscious thought picked up the galvanised water bucket. She hoped she could get down the back of the tenement building to the communal outdoor tap without anyone seeing her. She didn't want to talk to anyone. All she was capable of thinking of at this moment was her desperate need for a cup of tea. She wanted to think, plan, try and find some way out of this nightmare.

While the heavy stream of water slapped against the bucket a smoky rasp issued from the half-open door of the outside toilet.

"Jesus, would yeh have some mercy for the suffering of others!"

Ivy raised her eyes to heaven, praying she'd have all the water she needed before Nelly Kelly came storming out to see who was out and about at this hour. Nelly made no secret of her admiration for Ivy's da. She'd try to barge her way in to see him. Ivy knew enough about the mating of animals to know what the noises coming from her da's room meant whenever Nelly closed the door that separated the two rooms. Nelly was the last thing she needed this morning.

The kettle and bucket filled at last, she scurried away and back to the basement.

There she sat for hours at the table under the window of their front room, moving only occasionally to tend the fire and add hot water to the tea she sipped through pale lips. She held the chipped enamel mug to her mouth with two hands, trying to force her mind to settle into some useful train of thought. She listened to children scream in the street and barely flinched when the steel rim the boys were playing with fell down the basement steps with an unmerciful clatter. Even Nelly Kelly's screamed curses and shouted abuse failed to penetrate the daze she'd fallen into. She had to think.

She'd visit her da. That was the Christian thing to do. Her head almost wagged off her shoulders as she nodded frantically at the first solid idea that had come to her. She'd go and see her da – then she'd be able to think.

She stood and stared around the sparsely furnished room, wondering what she should do first. She banked the fire with wet newspaper, causing clouds of grey smoke to fill the chimney breast.

Without thought she picked up the threadbare old army overcoat one of her brothers left behind. She pulled the coat over her shaking body. Throwing the black knitted shawl over her head and shoulders, she wrapped the belt of the coat around her waist to hold the long ends of the shawl in place. Without a backward glance she let herself out of the only home she'd ever known.

Ivy ignored the shouts of the children playing in the square cobblestoned courtyard. She was aware of the women leaning in the open doors of the block of twelve Georgian tenements at her back but didn't respond to their shouted greetings. She stared without seeing across the courtyard at the local livery, a long barn-like building that snaked along one complete side of this hidden square. Mothers yelled at their children from the row of two-storey, double-fronted houses that marched across the furthest end of the square but Ivy didn't hear them.

She bowed her head, covered her face with her shawl and walked quickly across the cobbles towards the tunnel that was the only entry and exit point to this hidden enclave. The square sported the official name of Verschoyle Place but the inhabitants, for no apparent reason, never called it anything but The Lane.

Ivy wrinkled her finely formed nose at the stench that seemed to reach out of the tunnel and choke her. The wide tunnel was cut into a high wall that formed the fourth section of the square. The wall protected the rear entrances of the prosperous Mount Street houses from their impoverished neighbours.

One wall of the tunnel stretched along the side of the last house on Mount Street. The wall on the opposite side formed the side wall of the public house that occupied the rest of Mount Street and backed onto the livery. The drunks who fell out of the pub daily used the tunnel as a public toilet. The women of The Lane battled constantly with the odour of stale urine, but no matter how many times they scrubbed the tunnel out, it still stank.

Ivy stood for a moment with the rank-smelling tunnel at her back. She ignored the shouted comments of the drunks standing outside the public house as she gazed around at a world that had suddenly become alien to her. She knew this area like the back of her hand. How could she suddenly feel so lost?

The Georgian mansions that marched along both sides of Mount Street blazed and sparkled in the sharp icy-cold air. Snow-white steps leading up to impressive doors with polished brass fittings lined both sides of the street. One row of Mount

Street mansions elegantly hid most of the poverty-stricken world mere steps from their rear gardens. Mount Street was a different world entirely from the world Ivy and her friends inhabited.

Which way should she go? If she had a ha'penny for the charabanc she could walk through Merrion Square towards Grafton Street and public transport, but it would be Shank's mare all the way for her. The biting cold of the stones under her feet ate through the paper covering the holes in the soles of her shoes.

Ivy turned towards the Grand Canal. She'd follow the canal, walking along the pathways worn bald by the constant passage of the horses that pulled the barges travelling from Dublin to Kildare daily. Following the canal would take at least twenty minutes off the hour-long walk. The bare earth should be warmer and softer than the stone pavements.

Ivy felt invisible, a lost soul no-one could see, moving along the river path without friend or family to comfort or console her. Her da was gone. The big noisy laughing rogue that broke her heart once a day and twice on Sunday was dead. What was she going to do without him?

Ivy had been looking after her da since her ninth birthday. Ever since her ma had taken the mail-boat to England leaving her da alone with four kids under nine to raise. Ivy covered her mouth with her hand, pushing back the laugh that seemed disrespectful under the circumstances. Her da raise the kids? That was a joke. Ivy had become the mother and chief earner of the family from that day to this. It was Ivy who walked the streets pushing a pram, begging clothes and unwanted items from the wealthy houses that encaged her world. It was Ivy who sat up all night cutting and stitching at the discarded clothing, turning rags into money-making serviceable items she'd sold back to the servants of the houses she frequented.

She stepped off the path to let a horse-drawn barge pass her by. She waved to the people on board, wondering what life would be like living on one of those floating homes. Was it any better than the life she led? She shrugged and turned to walk on.

A sudden thought almost brought her to her knees. The rent book – had her da changed the title-holder like he'd promised? Sweet Lord, was she about to lose her home as well as everything else? She thought back frantically to her twenty-first birthday – hadn't her da boasted to his cronies about being a modern man and changing the rent book to her name now she was a woman grown? Whose name was on the rent book? If it was still in her da's name she'd be evicted. Her ma had shouted often enough, "You can eat in the street but you can't sleep in the street!" Dear God, was she about to become homeless? She could end up in the poorhouse.

Ivy tried to think back – late last year, when she turned twenty-one, had the name on the rent book been changed? She'd check as soon as she returned home. It would be the first thing she did. Ivy shook herself like a wet dog. She couldn't think about that, not now that she was at the back end of Kevin's Hospital. Garda Collins said the morgue was in the basement. She'd visit her da and pray for a miracle, some kind of a sign.

Ivy stared at the large signs with pointing arrows in despair. How she longed to be able to read the words! She could follow the arrows with her head held high then. A sigh that seemed to start at her feet shook her slender frame. It wasn't to be. She was ignorant, stupid. The pretty squiggles meant nothing to her.

Ivy ignored the tuts of disgust she received from the people she asked directions from. She was used to that. She just wanted to see her da. Make sure it was really him. Maybe the police had made a mistake. Her big laughing da couldn't be dead. Not her da, the larger-than-life Éamonn Murphy.

It took a lot of time and effort but finally Ivy was outside the cold grey doors that led to the morgue. She was shaking, unaware of the tears that soaked into the part of the woollen shawl she'd wrapped around her face. Her hands were blue, frozen, but she forced herself to apply pressure and push the heavy doors apart.

Chapter 2

Ann Marie Gannon watched the wide double doors of the morgue open slowly. She wondered who else was on duty this New Year's Day. Ann Marie had drawn the short straw yet again. Everyone knew she lived with her uncle and was a soft touch. Every holiday or feast day, here she sat filing reports and shivering in the badly heated small office attached to the morgue, her only company the dead.

"Can I help you?" Ann Marie came out of her office and into the frozen stillness of the morgue. She walked slowly over to the visitor. She didn't judge the strangely dressed figure standing frozen with her back to the double doors of the entryway. Death didn't distinguish between social classes. She saw all sorts down here.

"Me da," Ivy croaked, pushing the shawl away from her face, being careful to leave her head decently covered. "They said me da was down here."

"What's your da's name?" Ann Marie asked gently. There were corpses in here with more colour in their faces than this poor woman.

"He's me da." Ivy stared at the woman, seeing only the white coat. She couldn't be a doctor – everyone knew that was impossible.

"What's his name?" Ann Marie repeated.

"Éamonn Murphy," Ivy forced out through chattering teeth. "They told me me da would be in here."

"Ah yes . . ." Ann Marie turned her head towards the sheet-shrouded tables that lined the cavernous space, then turned back in time to see the woman sink gracefully to the floor.

Ann Marie wasn't surprised. This happened a great deal in here but normally there were more people around to lend a hand. She didn't try to catch the woman. She was taller than Ann Marie. It was difficult to judge her size in the bulky clothes she wore but at a quick glance she outweighed Ann Marie by several stone.

"My goodness!" Ann Marie put her hands under Ivy's arms and began to pull her along the floor out of the path of the slowly opening door.

"Another one overcome by your stunning beauty, Ann Marie?" Austin Quigley, one of the hospital porters, stuck his face through the opening gap.

"Give me a hand here Austin, please." Ann Marie ignored his lame remark. The man was a joker but now was not the time. "She must have bird bones because in spite of her size she's light as a feather."

"It's all bulky clothes I imagine," Austin grunted as he picked Ivy's unconscious form up from the floor. He stood holding the inert body, waiting for his instructions. "I'm surprised you didn't recognise the signs of slow starvation in her face. The Good Lord knows it's a common enough sight where I live."

"How in the name of goodness would I be able to see anything under all those rags? Bring her into my office please, Austin." Ann Marie hurried back in the direction of her private kingdom. She held the office door open for Austin to pass through with his burden. "Listen, Austin – could you sneak a bowl of soup and a couple of buttered rolls from the doctors' kitchen?"

"Her table manners will probably upset your stomach." Austin wasn't joking. Ann Marie had a heart of gold but her weak stomach was a standing joke. Bad table manners had been known to cause her stomach to revolt.

"Austin, you would try the patience of a saint! Would you please put her down here?" She indicated the visitor's chair in front of her desk. "If you could bring this poor woman a bowl of soup I'd appreciate it." Ann Marie knew the porters helped themselves to the food in the doctors' kitchen. She didn't see why this poor creature couldn't have a little something. No-one would miss it.

"If I get caught stealing I'm blaming you, Ann Marie Gannon!" Austin put the woman in the chair and turned to leave. He walked swiftly back out through the office door, pulling the door closed quickly to keep the heat inside where it was needed. The poor sods in the main part of the morgue didn't need heating. Austin pulled the morgue's main doors open and hurried away to see what he could finagle from the well-stocked doctor's kitchen.

"Oh me aching head, what happened?" Ivy held a shaking hand to her head. Her stomach felt sick. "Where am I?"

"Just sit still a moment, dear." Ann Marie walked over to sit behind her desk. "You fainted."

"I've never fainted in me life!" Ivy snapped, struggling to find an inner balance. "Oh, I remember . . ." she sighed. "I prayed it was a dream."

Ivy made a concentrated effort to force her eyes to focus on the woman sitting behind the desk. The pretty face, with its peaches-and-cream complexion, was framed by hair the colour of toffee and pale-blue eyes beamed goodwill from behind wire-framed glasses. To Ivy's befuddled eyes the woman looked as if she hadn't a care in the world. Working in a place of death, how could she look so at peace?

"I'm sorry," Ivy said. "I didn't mean to snap at you."

"No need to apologise to me," Ann Marie said and smiled. Before she could add anything else the phone on her desk rang. To her complete amazement the young woman almost jumped out of her skin. Ann Marie grabbed the phone, wanting to stop its strident demand before the woman fainted again.

Ivy watched, her eyes hurting they were open so wide. This must be one of them telephone things she'd been hearing about. Wasn't that a wonder? Without a pause the woman put something against her ear and spoke aloud into the black thing she was holding up to her face. As Ivy watched in stunned admiration, the woman took a paper out of a nearby huge grey drawer and read from it into the phone, unaware of the genuine awe and envy of her audience. The woman was obviously well educated, Ivy thought and sighed. What would that be like?

Ann Marie completed her phone call and returned the file to its drawer. "I'm sorry about that," she said, smiling at Ivy. "I don't know your name." She waited, the smile still curving her pale lips.

"Ivy," Ivy croaked, unable to believe this superior being was actually speaking to her, asking her name. "Me name is Ivy Murphy."

Ann Marie's little office had a long glass window to allow her to see into the morgue at all times. Now she spotted Austin pushing open the main mortuary doors with his back, while carrying a tray in his hands. "Well, Ivy Murphy, here's Austin with the soup I asked him to bring for you."

Ivy wanted to refuse but the smell coming from the bowl on the tray had her mouth watering. She couldn't remember the last time she'd eaten. She definitely couldn't remember the last time she'd been served and never by a man.

Without a word being spoken Austin placed the tray on the desk, then with a quick nod of his head towards the two women he left the office.

Ivy waited until the man had left the office before allowing herself to examine the tray. It held a bowl of soup, a plate with two buttered rolls and, holiest of holiest as far as Ivy was concerned, a pot of tea steaming gently, surrounded by two cups and saucers, a milk jug and a sugar bowl. A feast fit for a king.

"Would it bother you to answer some questions while you eat?" Ann Marie had expected Ivy to attack the food in front of her but Ivy surprised her by eating slowly and elegantly. She was fascinated by this young woman who appeared, to her eyes, like a creature from a fable. The total and complete shock Ivy had experienced when the phone rang could not be feigned. Obviously she had never seen a phone before. In this day and age how was that possible?

"What do you need to know?" Ivy wanted to close her eyes and groan at the first taste of the food in her mouth. The rolls had actual butter on them. She vaguely remembered her mother buying butter but it had been years since she'd tasted it. She, like everyone else she knew, used the drippin' from any meat she was lucky enough to fry. She bought drippin' from the butcher when she had the pennies, drippin' from the meat the butcher roasted – that was the stuff of legend.

"I don't mean to appear indelicate," Ann Marie shrugged, "but why are you here alone? Surely your mother or some other member of your family could have accompanied you?"

"There's only me." Ivy couldn't believe the richness of the soup she'd been served. She'd never tasted soup with so much meat in it before. It was delicious.

"You don't want your parish priest or perhaps a nun from one of the local convents to come?" Ann Marie saw the figure in front of her stiffen. The reaction surprised her. She was of the Quaker faith herself but generally the people of Dublin were Catholic. "Have you no-one to share this burden?"

"Like I said, there's only me." Ivy savoured her soup and rolls with a blissful sigh. She was conscious of the ticking of a clock somewhere but she refused to rush. Who knew when she'd get to eat again? She wanted to lift the bowl up in her two hands and slurp, but she remembered enough of the lessons on manners her mother had drummed into her to know that was unacceptable.

"Do you have a local funeral home I could telephone for you?" Ann Marie offered. She really wanted to help.

"Lady, I don't mean to be rude or ungrateful but you have no idea, do you?" Ivy hoped she hadn't sounded too sharp – she didn't want to repay this woman's kindness with rudeness.

"Please, explain to me while I pour us both a cup of tea." Ann

Marie busied herself setting out the cups and saucers and pouring from the pot of tea.

"I don't have a brown penny to me name." Ivy was tired of always being the strong one. She didn't have to protect her da any more. Her da was dead and nothing on this earth could hurt him now. And she'd never see this woman with the kind eyes after today.

"Me da, the man who fell into a horse trough and drowned, the man out there on one of your tables, he took the last bit of food in the house and shared it with his drinking pals. Not satisfied with that, he cleaned out every penny of my hard-earned money and blew it celebrating the New Year with his cronies." Ivy bit back a sob. She was damned forever now for speaking ill of the dead.

"Oh, my goodness!" Ann Marie had no experience at all of something like this.

"If I fail to give me da the send-off his drinking cronies and all of the neighbours think he deserves I'll be shunned," Ivy continued. "People will cross the road to avoid me." Her sigh came from her tired soul. She'd carried the weight of her family for so long. "I don't know if I have a home to return to. I can't remember if me da put my name on the rent book or not. I have no money for the rent anyway – me da took that too and the rent man isn't exactly understanding."

"Today is the first day of a brand-new year." Ann Marie believed every word out of this young woman's mouth. Those blue eyes clouded by tears could not lie. Ann Marie believed in fate. This woman, this Ivy Murphy, was the answer to her prayers. She believed Ivy had been sent by a higher power – she was a lost soul in desperate need of her help. She would do everything in her power to aid this woman in her hour of need. "We are two women who find ourselves in a very unusual situation." Ann Marie refilled Ivy's teacup. "Will you allow me to assist – to help – you?"

"I know what 'assist' means." Ivy was bone-weary now. How could anyone help her?

"Ivy, without taking anything away from the pain and loss you are suffering," Ann Marie spoke softly, afraid of offending "would you agree your greatest problem at the moment is a lack of funds, of money?"

"The story of me life," Ivy sighed.

"Then let us put our two heads together and figure something out." Ann Marie slapped her two hands on her desk, shoved her chair away and stood up. "First let us visit your father. Then, with a fresh pot of tea, we will begin to try and find a solution to your problem."

Ann Marie had an idea but she didn't wish to share it with Ivy just yet. First she needed to see Ivy's father. She wasn't sure which body belonged to Éamonn Murphy. If it was the emaciated, wizened old man she'd seen earlier in the day her idea would not be feasible.

"You'll come with me?" Ivy had seen dead bodies lying in the street or laid out in the tenements but she'd never seen the dead body of someone she loved.

"Of course. We're in this together now."

Ann Marie quickly checked Éamonn Murphy's details and with the slab-number fresh in her head, she led the way out of her office.

"This is it." Ann Marie stopped before the third table from her office. "Are you ready?" She waited for Ivy's nod before pulling the sheet away from the rigid form.

"Ah, Da!" Ivy stroked her fingers through her father's mane of rich auburn hair. Someone had washed it recently and it felt like silk under her fingers. "Da, look what you've done to yourself! Yeh auld eejit!" Ivy's tears dropped onto the waxen features.

Ann Marie stood with her arm around the sobbing woman's shoulders. She was shocked and appalled by this man's appearance. He was young, his heavily muscled chest and full-featured face showing no sign of the starvation that was written so clearly on his daughter's face.

Ann Marie promised herself she'd pull the sheet back later just to check but it appeared to her the man was taller than average with all the hallmarks of a rich life written into his skin and bone. She was honest enough to admit that if she'd seen this man on the street she'd have turned around to get a second look.

"Da, what am I going to do without you?" Ivy pressed her trembling lips against the ice-cold skin. There was no reaction. Her da didn't open his laughing blue eyes and grin at her. He was really dead – not here – gone away without her. She should be used to it by now – all of her family left her behind one way and another.

"Would you like some time alone with your father?" Ann Marie was familiar with the crippling grief the death of a loved one brought.

"No, thank you." Ivy pulled her shoulders back and straightened. "This is his body but me da is not here. He always told me the body we wear is just an old overall, nothing special. He was religious me da, never doubt it, and he always said that when we died we left our old worn-out overall behind and went on to a better place." Ivy wiped her shaking hands over her tear-stained cheeks. "His overall is not that old but he's left it here anyway."

"Come away then, Ivy." Ann Marie slowly covered Éamonn Murphy's handsome face. "I have the makings of tea in my office. I'll make us a fresh pot and we'll talk."

"I'll be grateful for any advice you can offer." Ivy was so tired, so emotionally bankrupt she didn't seem to be capable of making a decision for herself. It was seldom anyone offered her help. She'd listen to what this woman had to say.

She sat silently, grieving, while the tea was being made.

"Believe it or not, Ivy, there are several options open to you," Ann Marie said as she poured the tea.

"I'm glad you think so."

Ann Marie sipped her tea with a grateful sigh. "If I understand correctly, in order for you personally to survive you need to find money for food and rent, urgently." She waited for Ivy's nod. "A big send-off for your father is out of the question. I don't for a moment mean to be disrespectful to the deceased but wouldn't you agree that by taking the last of your food and all of your money your father has already had his big splash?"

"I hadn't thought of it like that!" Ivy laughed. Her da would be tickled pink to think he'd danced at his own wake.

"I know of a way your father can earn a few pounds." Ann Marie grinned, delighted to have some way of helping Ivy.

"Would yeh go way!" Ivy gasped. "Me da never earned a pound in his life!"

Chapter 3

The two women locked eyes and without a word spoken began to laugh like idiots. They laughed until tears rolled down their faces.

"Thank you!" Ivy smiled through her tears. "I thought I'd never laugh again in me life."

"I must say I didn't think today would hold a great deal of laughter for me either," Ann Marie admitted. "However, time is passing and we need to talk seriously."

"Tell me what you meant?" Ivy couldn't imagine how her da would earn more in death than he ever had in life.

"Before I go into detail . . ." Ann Marie was stalling. She wasn't sure how Ivy would react to her proposition, "could we first discuss all of your options?"

"It surprises me to hear I have options." Ivy's voice broke.

"Oh, yes, my dear." Ann Marie beamed. "With my help you do indeed have options." She pushed up her sleeves and leant forward across her desk. "Now, let us think about your situation."

"Me da is dead." Ivy almost snapped. She couldn't seem to think much past that horrible fact.

"Yes, indeed he is. However, you've given me to understand

that every decision from this point and indeed every problem entailed rests firmly on your shoulders. Would you agree?"

"It usually does." Ivy sighed.

"Right, what do you want to do with your father's remains?"

"His remains," Ivy sobbed. "Is that what he is now – 'remains'?"

"I'm not trying to distress you but we need to make some decisions and I'm afraid time is against us." Ann Marie glanced at her wristwatch, sighing. It was almost time for her to return to the place she called home. She would willingly invite Ivy to join her but she wouldn't dream of subjecting the young woman to her aunt's censure and snobbery. "You need to answer my question."

"I'd like to give me da a send-off that would make the angels weep but that's impossible. Once again it's a case of 'Want must be my master' – that's nothing new to me." Ivy bit back a sob. She was holding this woman back and she knew it. "I'm sorry, I know I'm stupid but I don't understand my options."

"Ivy, you are far from stupid!" Ann Marie said, horrified to hear this woman denigrate herself. "You are perhaps uneducated, through no fault of your own, but you are far from stupid." She slapped both hands on the desk, disgusted at her own shilly-shallying. "Right, your options." She had been thinking hard about this and now put her thoughts into words. "You are currently penniless. Your father is dead due to an accident of his own making." She was being deliberately harsh. "We must discuss the matter of the disposal of his remains – his old overalls if you will. A burial of any nature is an expensive undertaking. There is no getting away from that unfortunate fact, I'm afraid."

"What about the money you mentioned?" Ivy couldn't understand how this woman thought her da could earn money in his present state: dead.

"Your father is . . ." Ann Marie gulped. She could hardly call the man Ivy obviously loved a fine specimen. How on earth could she voice her thoughts delicately?

"Dead."

"Undoubtedly." Ann Marie sighed. "Ivy, this is a teaching hospital. The surgeons have a need, that is to say, they use . . .

Oh, for goodness sake!" She slapped the desk in frustration. "What I'm trying to say is that you could sell your father's body – his old overalls – to the College of Surgeons."

"Mother of Jesus, you want me to become a grave-robber!" Ivy yelled, horrified.

"Your father doesn't have a grave, that's the problem." Ann Marie knew this would be difficult but she was determined to persevere. "Ivy, your main problem leads on to all others. You have no money – a grave site and coffin is expensive. You could have your father buried in a pauper's grave . . . ?"

"Never."

"Right, I thought that and understand but your delicacy of feeling will cripple you." Ann Marie thought of her own parents' gravesite and understood Ivy's reluctance. "There is a cart that travels from hospital to hospital in the city – it removes the dead in the dark of night."

"No."

"I agree because even then you need to pay the drivers. I doubt they can read but you must show them a death certificate and the colour of your money before they'll agree to take the body." Ann Marie shuddered at the thought of that grisly cart.

"I thought you said I have options," Ivy muttered.

"I did and you do but you're not listening. As I said, you can sell your father's body to the College of Surgeons." She held up her hand when Ivy opened her mouth. "There are rich people who offer their own bodies and those of their children to the college."

"What, rich people sell their dead childer?" Ivy was horrified. She'd known the rich were different, but selling their dead childer – that was evil.

"Ivy, the surgeons study the dead to help the living. It's a wonderful gesture. Your father would help young doctors understand so much about the human body."

"What would I tell people?" Ivy felt sick to her stomach but it struck her that her da would be killing himself laughing at all this, wherever he was now.

"Why do you need to tell them anything?"

"Me da is kind of hard to miss." Ivy gave Ann Marie a look of disgust. "I'll have to tell people something and I couldn't lie about something like that to save me life."

"I don't suggest you lie," Ann Marie said softly. "You tell the truth, just not all of the truth. Your father is dead, drowned, there is no body for burial. He wouldn't be the first person lost in the Liffey or indeed overboard at sea."

"I don't know what to do," Ivy dropped her aching head into her hands. She pushed at her shawl, suddenly feeling smothered by its weight. She was mortified when the wooden comb she used to hold up her hair got caught in the shawl and came off too, her hair tumbled down her back.

"My goodness, how long is your hair?" Ann Marie gasped.

Ivy's hair belonged in a fairy story, all blue-black curls that trailed down almost to the floor.

"I don't know." Ivy shrugged, her hair the last thing on her mind. "Me da wouldn't let me cut it."

"You could sell it," Ann Marie whispered. The money Ivy could receive for the sale of her hair wouldn't pay for a fancy funeral but it increased her options.

"In the name of God, woman, who'd be mad enough to pay good money for the hair on someone's head?" Ivy shouted. "How many mad people with money do you know?"

"Quite a few." Ann Marie smiled. "There's a shop on Parliament Street – Iverson's – they pay good money for healthy clean hair. You should be able to demand a good price for that magnificent head of hair."

"Me head's aching. I can't think." She gathered her hair and with a quick experienced twist of her wrists, knotted the hair before pushing in the comb to hold it in place.

"Let me make a suggestion," Ann Marie offered. "We can do nothing today. While not officially a holiday, few people actually work today if they can manage it. Let me loan you some money."

"No!" Ivy shouted. "Thank you but I couldn't take your charity!"

"I'm not offering charity," Ann Marie said. "Take the loan, Ivy, buy yourself something to eat. Buy yourself some time to think. I'm sure any money I loan you is safe."

"You're a lovely woman but you're not the full shillin'."

Ann Marie stood and pulled a file cabinet open. She took out her leather handbag and, with a shy smile at Ivy, opened it to take out her matching purse. "Take the loan I'm offering. No, don't refuse. I know my money is safe with you."

"I could do a runner."

"I don't think so." Ann Marie held a coin in her hand. "Take this money, go home, think about your options. We'll meet tomorrow and discuss your situation some more."

Ivy held out her hand, her pride almost crippling her. She couldn't see how she could survive the day penniless on top of everything else. If she could believe this woman, the money she was offering now was only a loan and she would pay her back.

"A half crown!" Ivy shouted, trying to force Ann Marie to take the coin back. "Jaysus, there's men don't earn that much in a week!"

"Take the money. Believe me, your hair alone is worth more than that. I know." Ann Marie had never appreciated the life she led more. "Let us both go home and after a night's sleep we will both feel refreshed and able to think more clearly."

"I don't know how to thank you." Ivy had never been treated with such kindness in her life.

"No need to, my dear." Ann Marie wanted to suggest that Ivy should visit the multi-denominational chapel in the grounds but as she was dressed now she'd be chased away from the premises. "Would you like to spend some time with your father before you leave?" This at least she could offer. She waited for Ivy's nod of acceptance before crossing to hold open her office door.

Ann Marie held her office doorknob in a white knuckled fist while she watched Ivy almost visibly pull herself up from her bootstraps. With a stiff nod the woman walked out of the office. Before closing the office door Ann Marie watched Ivy walk alone to the sheet-covered slab holding the remains of her beloved da.

Ivy pulled the white sheet back, still expecting her da to explode from the table laughing and shouting 'Boo!' She'd never seen him so still. "I've never seen yeh so peaceful neither," Ivy whispered, staring down at his handsome face. The priest preached pride was a grievous sin. Ivy didn't care – she'd always been proud of her three handsome brothers and her tall laughing prince of a da.

"This is probably the last time in me life I'll see yeh, Da. How am I supposed to do that? I love yeh, yeh auld eejit. We never say things like that to each other, do we? I do love yeh though, for all the times I screamed and shouted at yeh. Oh, yeh made me so mad at times!"

Ivy fought the sobs shaking her body. She couldn't allow them to escape. In this great big room the sound would show her up as a cry baby. Her da would be disgusted with her.

"Da, do you know what I'm going to do with your body?" she whispered. "Where yeh are now, do you know what I'll have to do? Do yeh mind, Da?" Ivy could almost see him rubbing his hands together, his broad shoulders shaking with delight – 'Take the money, daughter, it'll be a few bob for your auld da to treat his mates.'

"I'm not treating your mates!" Ivy snapped aloud, the words echoing around the room. She hunched her shoulders, giving a quick glance behind her at the woman sitting behind the long glass window of the nearby office. The woman was staring at something on her desk, more of those important papers maybe.

"Yeh treated yer mates to everything in the feckin' place on New Year's Eve, Da."

Ivy patted the waxen cheek. She felt bristles under her fingers and felt her knees give. With massive effort she remained on her feet, remembering all the times her da used to rub those bristles against the skin of her face and neck. He'd chase her screaming around the room until she was almost sick laughing. Her da always told her it was as easy to laugh as cry.

25

"I don't feel like laughing now, Da," she choked. "If I don't do what this woman is suggesting I'll end up in the poorhouse. I won't do that, Da. I'm not going in there and I'm not selling me body neither. God, Da, you'd love the joke. I'm selling your body instead!"

Ivy wanted to crawl on top of her father's body and just drift away with him but she couldn't do that. She had to survive as best she could.

"I love yeh, Da." Ivy took the sheet in her white knuckled hands. "I'll never forget yeh. I'll try and make yeh proud of me so keep an eye on me, will yeh?"

Shaking with silent sobs Ivy replaced the sheet over her father's face. She straightened her shoulders and turned to walk away.

With a lump in her throat, Ann Marie Gannon watched Ivy say goodbye to her only relative. The sheer strength of character the raggedly dressed woman displayed impressed and shamed her. Ann Marie gave generously to charity and thought herself a fine Christian woman. Meeting with this woman had changed that.

"Ivy!" Ann Marie came out of her office and stopped her leaving with a gentle hand on her shoulder. "Tomorrow is another day and unfortunately your problems will be waiting for you. My advice, for what it's worth, is to get some rest, get something to eat, and think about the options I've mentioned."

Ann Marie would have liked to make Ivy understand the effect this meeting had had on her but this was not about her. Ivy was in the kind of straits Ann Marie had difficulty understanding. She was determined to help in any way she could.

"Will you agree to meet me somewhere tomorrow?" she asked.

"I'll have to come back here anyway, won't I?" Ivy nodded in the direction of her father's body.

"Yes, you will, my dear. I'm afraid that's unavoidable." Ann Marie had so much she wanted to say to Ivy but not here and not now. "But I want to see and speak to you before you come in here again."

They discussed places they could meet. Ann Marie was surprised to discover Ivy lived not far from her own home in Merrion Square. They quickly agreed on a time to meet the next morning outside the park on Merrion Square.

Ivy would have agreed to anything. She just wanted to get away from this house of death. She needed to breathe fresh air. She needed to be alone. She knew the place where this woman wanted to meet her tomorrow. It wasn't that far from The Lane.

"I'll see you tomorrow," she said.

Ann Marie watched Ivy walk through the double doors of the morgue. Then she walked over to the still figure of Éamonn Murphy and for the first time in her life visually examined and talked aloud to the dead.

"Just as I thought!" Ann Marie nodded her head in great satisfaction. "You really are a most impressive figure of a man, Éamonn Murphy." She felt the colour burn her cheeks. If anyone caught her examining the naked figure of a man she'd be the talk of the College. For once in her life she didn't care.

"I don't think you were much of a parent to the young woman who just left here."

Éamonn Murphy had been the kind of man any woman would be proud to call her own. With all signs of social status stripped from him, naked in all his glory, he was a truly superior example of a human male. Ann Marie intended to see that Ivy, for perhaps the first time in her life, profited from her parent's superior breeding.

"I'm going to help your daughter in all the ways that I can," Ann Marie said as she pulled up the cover until it reached his chin. "If she'll let me I'll be there for her from this moment on. I make you this promise, Éamonn Murphy. I'll watch over your daughter. If she'll allow me. I'm going home now – I have a lot to think about."

Ann Marie removed her white lab coat and gave the office

space a quick visual check before taking her coat from the tall coat stand. Then she collected her belongings from her desk, locked the office door and left the building. The morgue would remain unstaffed until the morning. The people in here were going nowhere.

Chapter 4

While Ann Marie talked to the dead Ivy struggled to remember the way out of the twisting hallways. She was panting by the time she finally reached a door that opened to the outside world. With a glad cry she pushed the door and almost fell into the cold wet evening air. She stood for a moment trying to figure out exactly where she was, then with a nod of her head started to walk in the direction she knew would take her to the canal.

Ivy was empty of emotion. Like an animal seeking its cave, she just wanted to get home and lock the door behind her. She put one foot in front of the other, heading in the direction of home. She wanted to curl up in a ball and die, but she'd do it in the privacy of her own home. She was all alone now. Everyone she loved had left her, gone away.

A hearty shove in the middle of her shoulders almost sent her to her knees. Ivy turned, fists raised, ready to protect herself from her attacker. A big black head shook up and down – the horse tossed her mane and her neigh sounded a lot like laughter.

"Rosie, you frightened the life outa me!" Ivy approached the horse slowly, her hand out in front of her, just like her da had taught her.

"I'm so sorry, lady!" Jem Ryan jumped down from his perch

on the driver's seat of his carriage. He didn't know what was going on. Rosie had attacked someone – what was he going to do?

"It's all right, Jem," Ivy said into the evening gloom. "It's only me – Ivy."

"Ivy, I didn't see you there." Jem felt weak with relief. His horse, his livelihood, hadn't gone crazy. "Rosie knew you right enough. What are you doing around here? It's a damp, dark, cold aul' evening to be out taking a stroll."

"I'm heading home." Ivy raised her head from Rosie's neck and smiled at a man she'd known since she was eight years old and he was fifteen. "Did you have a fare over here?"

"There's nothing much doing today." Jem Ryan had the livery across The Lane from Ivy's block of tenements. Rosie the dray horse was a favourite of Ivy's. "Hop in and I'll take you home."

"I will not." Ivy was sincerely shocked. In all the years she'd known Jem Ryan he'd never allowed anyone from The Lane into his pristine carriage. The carriage was his bread and butter. He went out in all weathers, picking up fares around Dublin. Jem was very particular about the kind of people he allowed into his carriage. "I've never been in a horse-drawn carriage in me life. That's for the quality," Ivy stated a fact of her life, "not the likes of me."

"Well, climb up on the seat with me then. If you're not ashamed to be seen with me, that is."

"Really? You'd let me come up there with you?" Ivy was amazed. She'd never had a carriage ride.

"Come on! I know I don't have to show you how to get up on the seat." Jem laughed. "How many times did I have to lift you and your brothers off me driver's seat?"

"Rosie was never in her traces then." Ivy hadn't waited for Jem to change his mind. She was sitting up, proud and excited, before Jem had walked around the back of the brougham.

When Jem took the reins in his hands and shouted his familiar "Walk on!" Ivy wanted to scream with delight. She wished her da could see her riding high like this – but the thought of her da brought her crashing down to earth.

"Isn't this a bit early for you to be going home?" Ivy didn't want to think about her da. Not now.

"It's a miserable aul' day with not a sinner out and about." Jem clicked his tongue at the horse. "Poor old Rosie is getting a bit long in the tooth for this work." He sighed.

"It's the New Year has yeh down in the dumps, Jem. The first bright day you'll feel better." Ivy automatically slipped into her role of lifting a man's spirit.

"It's not just the New Year, Ivy. Times are changing. Look around you," Jem waved one of his hands at the world at large. "This country and everything Irish is changing and fast. We'll soon have our own government and how is that going to affect us? The likes of you and me, Ivy, how will all the changes affect our lives? We have to be ready or we'll be left behind."

"I've never heard you speak like this before, Jem." Ivy said.

"We've never had what I'd call a real conversation, Ivy." Jem nudged Ivy gently with his shoulder. His teeth showed white against the bush-like flaming-red beard that covered most of his face. Wisps of his chestnut-brown hair escaped from the sacking he used to protect his head and shoulders.

"I pulled you and those three holy terrors you called brothers out of danger more times than I can count." Jem didn't mention the number of times he'd kicked her father out of his livery. Éamonn Murphy saw the stables, empty through the day, as a prime site for setting up his roving gambling club.

"There's a shop up here I need to stop at, Ivy." Jem pulled gently on the reins. Rosie knew the way as soon as she felt the signal. "There's not a thing to eat in my place."

"Don't you shop in Brennan's?" Ivy had never given any thought to Jem Ryan's life before.

"No, I don't." Jem left it at that. It wasn't his place to tell people that Brennan's charged over the odds for their goods, a lot of which was old, fit only for animals.

"I need a few things meself," Ivy said. "I won't shame you by coming in with yeh – yeh can drop me off by Brennan's if you would."

"In the name of God, Ivy," Jem turned to her as soon as Rosie had come to a stop. He tied the reins around the side hand-bar of the driver's seat, making sure the brake was firmly in place. "Why would you think I'd be ashamed to be seen with you?"

"Look at the state of me," Ivy said simply.

"Have you looked at me with me sacks wrapped around me head, shoulders and lap?" Jem laughed. "I'm not exactly a figure of fashion meself. Anyway, old Hobbs is glad of the custom. Come away in and get what you need. It'll save you a trip later." Without waiting for permission Jem reached up and with his hands around Ivy's waist pulled her from her perch. "By God, girl, yeh don't weight much more than yeh did as a tiddler!"

Ivy brushed down the old coat she wore and made sure the shawl covered her head decently. Her da would never allow her to accompany him into a shop. He said she'd make a show of him. Ivy sucked in her breath. Her da wasn't around any more. She would have to do everything for herself now. This could be her first big step on her own. She straightened her shoulders and walked over to where Jem held the door open for her. This unaccustomed gallantry almost caused her to trip over her own feet.

At the sound of the bell hanging over the shop door, a voice shouted from the back of the shop. "I'll be out in a minute!"

"Take your time, Hobbs. It's only me, Jem Ryan." Jem began to gather the items he'd need for a meal.

Ivy stood frozen inside the doorway. She'd never been inside a fancy shop like this before. She did all her shopping at market stalls and Brennan's, the only shop inside The Lane. This place was spotless, with sawdust spread over the floor thick and evenly. Glass-fronted boxes stood on the floor, openly displaying their goods. The articles for sale on the counter were under glass domes, for goodness' sake! Ivy wanted to slink back out through the door. She watched Jem examine items, impressed by his ease in these circumstances.

"What did you need, Ivy?" Jem turned to look at her. "Living on me own as I do, a fry-up is the easiest thing for me to make of an evening."

"A man needs more than a fry-up to eat after a day's work."
Ivy was afraid to touch anything.

"I have a hot meal during the day in one of the working men's
clubs down by the docks."

Jem could see the sheer terror on Ivy's face. He felt his fists
bunching, longing to punch Éamonn Murphy in his handsome
face. Did the man never take his daughter, the one who made his
style of living possible, anywhere?

"What do you need?" he asked again, deliberately looking
away from Ivy.

"I just need a bread cob, a few strips of fatty bacon and milk
for a cup of tea." Ivy was still staring around at the attractively
arranged items in the shop. She wanted to examine everything in
the place. "I've nothing with me for the milk." Ivy had a tall tin
mug with a handle that Brennan's filled with fresh milk when she
could afford the luxury item.

"Hobbs will give yeh a glass bottle." Jem watched as the door
from the back room into the shop opened. Hobbs struggled
through, carrying a large cheese in front of him.

"There yeh are, Jem – not much business around today for
man nor beast, ay," Hobbs greeted one of his regular customers
cheerfully. He ignored the well shrouded figure standing inside
the door. He'd soon deal with the likes of her when Jem Ryan
left.

"I have what I need on the counter." Jem noticed the man's
reaction to Ivy. Did the poor soul have to put up with this kind
of attitude regularly? No wonder she hadn't wanted to come
inside. He was sorry now he'd insisted. "What did you say you
needed, Ivy? Bread, bacon and milk, wasn't it?"

Ivy nodded.

Jem turned and gave the order to Hobbs.

The man took the hint and quickly filled the order. The man
was a well-known soft touch – but if Hobbs got on his bad side
he'd lose his custom.

"Here," Ivy tried to pass her half crown over to Jem.

"We can settle up later." Jem wanted to get Ivy out of the

shop. Slapping a florin onto the well-polished wood of the counter, he waited while Hobbs took care of his order. He snatched the change from Hobbs hand, took the two brown-paper-and-twine-wrapped packages Hobbs passed to him and without a word led Ivy from the shop.

"I told yeh I'd make a holy show of yeh," Ivy whispered, her cheeks red.

"You didn't embarrass me, Ivy." Jem almost threw her up onto the high seat of the brougham. "I'm angry that you should be subjected to that kind of attitude. Your money is as good as anyone's."

"That's not how everyone sees it." Ivy shrugged, well used to being insulted.

Jem wanted to curse at her for her acceptance of her lot in life. Ivy Murphy was a paragon as far as Jem was concerned. He'd watched through the years as she'd pushed that pig-ugly old heavy pram through the streets.

Her father and brothers should have hung their heads in shame. They'd allowed her to keep them all comfortably situated while she worked herself to skin and bone. The lot of them needed a good kick up the arse and Jem would love to be the one to deliver the kick. He wasn't the only one who felt this way either.

"I want to get old Rosie home and give her some hot mash." Jem picked up the reins and clicked to the patient animal.

"Why do you keep calling Rosie 'old'?" Ivy asked, oblivious to Jem's fury.

"She is old, Ivy. She's earned a bit of rest. I don't know what I'll do without old Rosie." Jem sighed deeply. "The day of the horse is going, Ivy. The motor car is going to replace the old horse."

"Never!" Ivy loved watching the horses working around the city.

"I'm afraid you can't stop progress, Ivy." Jem wanted to ask her what she'd been doing out in this area but was afraid she'd be offended.

"You really think change is coming, Jem? Really?"

"Bound to, Ivy." Jem shrugged. "We fought for our freedom. The end of all of that is in sight. That's going to change everything. If we don't buck ourselves up we'll be pulling our forelocks for the rest of our days. I'm not willing to do that."

"Nothing changes for the likes of me." Ivy shrugged. "It doesn't matter who is ordering yeh around or kicking yeh. There's always someone at the bottom of the pile. That's my place and I'm reminded of it every day of me life."

"Don't be so bloody defeatist, Ivy." Jem could hear all the people through his life telling him to know his place. Well, he was going to make a place for himself and the devil take the hindmost.

"I don't even know what that means, Jem." Ivy wanted to cry. "I'm stupid."

"'Defeatist' means someone who lies down without a fight!" Jem snapped. "We've fought for the freedom of our country. Now those of us left have to fight for our rights."

"That sounds good – impossible, but good." Ivy was aware of The Lane coming closer by the minute. She wasn't really paying attention to Jem and his words. She was wondering if she should ask to be let down before they went into the tunnel.

"Ivy, will yer da be waiting for yeh?" Jem couldn't imagine Éamonn Murphy having a warm home waiting for the shivering woman on the high seat beside him.

"No," Ivy answered simply. She wasn't ready to make the announcement of her da's death. She wanted time alone to think about everything that had happened since this morning. She'd tell people her da was dead – just, not yet. She'd keep that information close to her heart until she figured out what the heck she was going to do.

"Let me down here, Jem," she said when Rosie slowed to turn into the tunnel leading into The Lane.

"I will like heck, Ivy Murphy." Jem loosened the reins. Rosie knew her own way home. "You just sit there like . . . what did you call it when you climbed up on this seat when you were little? Queen of the World, wasn't that it?"

"Yes," Ivy whispered. "I always loved sitting up so high. The world is a different place from up here."

"Well then, Ivy . . ." Jem pulled on the reins as Rosie cleared the tunnel – he was aware of the street kids shouting and pointing at his companion sitting up proud and tall now. "It's the first day of the New Year. Maybe it's the first day of your new life?"

Jem jumped down and turned to help Ivy down from her perch. Ivy allowed him to put his hands around her waist, well-padded as it was with her coat and shawl. The man was more right than he knew. Ivy just had to think and study her new position. Who knew what the future held for her now? She was a woman alone with responsibility to no-one but herself. Why did that make her feel like crying?

Chapter 5

"Don't forget the bottle of milk and your messages!" Jem shouted when Ivy turned to hurry away.

"Thank you." Ivy blushed brightly, accepting the package and the glass bottle of milk she hadn't even noticed Jem pack away safely at the side of his seat. "I'll bring the money I owe you over later," she whispered. "Unless you have the change for a half crown on you right now, do you?"

"I do, as a matter of fact." Jem didn't want to let Ivy go but Rosie needed to be put into her stall, brushed and fed. The animal was his livelihood. Rosie came before Jem's own wants and needs.

"Thank you." Ivy was aware of the many interested glances they were attracting. She moved her body to hide the coins being exchanged. She had no intention of being hit up for a loan by anyone. She'd enough problems without visits from neighbours on the cadge. She didn't check to see what money was in her hand but, with a nod, left Jem and hurried to her own home.

As soon as the door closed at her back Ivy put the package and milk on the table under the window. The room was completely black. She lit the gas lamps and stood with her back to the cold fireplace, checking around the generously sized square room with her eyes, trying to remember where she'd thrown the rent book. She clearly remembered flinging it away from her when she'd discovered her da had done a runner with the rent money.

She was desperate to check the tenant named on it. She couldn't think or do anything until she'd seen if she'd still have a roof over her head.

The little book was on the floor just outside her da's room. Ivy bit back a cry and hurried over to pick up the precious document. She hurried back to the light and ran her finger slowly over the written name. Ivy could recognise and write her own name. She'd insisted her brothers teach her to do that at least.

Ivy collapsed to the floor, all the strength leaving her body. Her name, Ivy Rose Murphy, was clearly written on the front of the little book. She was safe, for the moment anyway, she was safe.

Ivy shook the big black kettle – there was barely enough water to make a pot of tea. Ivy dropped to her knees to check under the table for the fresh water bucket. She couldn't remember filling the thing before she left the house. Ivy groaned aloud in relief when her fingers dipped into water close to the rim of the galvanised steel bucket. Keeping that bucket full was so much part of her routine she must have done it automatically. With a grateful sigh Ivy filled the kettle. Outside of an emergency the neighbours wouldn't knock on her door but if she was out in the yard she was fair game.

Ivy wasn't hungry but she needed something to warm her up. She felt blue with the cold. She raked out the cold fire, sighing at the mess the damp papers she had used to bank the fire had left in the grate. She cleaned the fire out completely, shovelling the ash into the ancient biscuit tin she used for household rubbish. Ivy used her fingers to check the ash – it was nice and clean. Without thought she reached to the top of the mantel for the cracked milk jug she kept there. Ivy poured a generous amount of ash into the jug. Her da had a tin of paste he used to clean his teeth but he insisted ash was the best tooth-powder for young teeth.

Ivy decided to light a generous fire for the first time in her life. She wasn't going to worry about the supply of coal nuggets. God knows her da had begrudged every nugget Ivy put on to burn when he wasn't around to enjoy the heat. She was going to sit in front of a roaring fire and try to think. She needed to make plans and decisions about her future.

"First things first." Ivy dropped back to sit on her heels, holding her frozen dirty hands out to the struggling blaze. The sound of her own voice made the empty room seem less lonely. "Your one at the morgue said I could sell me hair. Isn't that enough to make the cat laugh? I wonder how much the hair on me head is worth. Doesn't matter – whatever I get it will be welcome money."

Ivy filled the small fire-blackened metal teapot she kept in the grate with fresh water. Still on her knees, she pulled paper from the supplies she kept to hand and made a plug for the spout from tightly rolled newspaper. The tea got too smokey when you forgot the plug. She put the pot directly on the fire. The nuggets were not really red yet but she couldn't wait. The flame from the sticks and papers should be enough to heat the small amount of water in the pot. Ivy didn't move from her position in front of the fire as her eyes begged the water to boil, quickly.

Ivy almost fell off her heels when the teapot sitting on the fire began to spit boiling water from under its rattling lid. She'd fallen into a daze, a stupid thing to do in front of an open fire – she should know better. She hunched her shoulders, expecting a clip around the ear. When nothing happened, she relaxed and quickly spooned some of her precious tea leaves into the pot.

"What'll I do now?" she said aloud as she sat in one of her fireside chairs sipping her cup of tea, enjoying the luxury of fresh milk in the brew. She glanced at her hands holding the cup and saucer on her lap. "It's amazing what you can do without thinking," she murmured – her hands were spotlessly clean. She rubbed her fingers together. She had no memory of moistening and using the rag she kept hanging from a hook by the fire. From the feel of her skin she'd obviously used the special cream Granny made from goose fat. She had to snap out of this daze. She was alone now. She couldn't be doing things without thinking. What if she'd damaged her hands? Granny Grunt would kill her. You couldn't do "white work" with rough dirty hands.

No-one remembered the old lady's real name. Ivy supposed it was written in her rent book but Granny Grunt was a title of respect within the Dublin community and that's what she was known as. The old woman lived in the back room of next door's basement. She'd offered Ivy a helping hand when she'd been too young for the burdens placed on her shoulders. Granny made a living repairing delicate lace and expensive fabrics. She worked on a cash basis for the posh shops and some of the ladies of Dublin.

From the time Ivy first waddled into Granny Grunt's room, the old woman had taken the little girl in hand. Granny had trained Ivy in the handcrafts it had taken herself a lifetime to learn. They helped each other out. Granny Grunt needed Ivy's young eyes and nimble fingers. Ivy became the old woman's apprentice.

From day one Granny ruled Ivy with a rod of iron. Granny had a system. Ivy was allowed into the corner Granny used as a work area only after the old woman performed a daily inspection of Ivy's hands. A touch of roughness, a spec of dirt, and Ivy got a heavy-handed box around the ear. Granny knew what she was about. She wouldn't allow Ivy to take her white wraparound apron home with her. Granny kept the apron bleached, starched and ironed. The old woman knew the apron wouldn't stay long in Ivy's hands. Éamonn Murphy would pawn it as soon as the girl's back was turned. The apron covered the wearer from neck to ankles and was an essential item of equipment as far as Granny was concerned. Under Granny's harsh tutelage, handcare became an automatic reflex – a part of Ivy's day-to-day life.

The two females sat for hours chatting while they repaired

exquisite lace garments and household trimmings. After Ivy's mother left Granny used the time they worked together to instruct Ivy in the running of a household. Granny taught Ivy to cook, bake and do laundry. It was Granny who'd taught Ivy to shave soft soap into the tin bathtub filled with hot water and walk on the clothes to get them clean. Ivy knew she would be lost without the old woman.

"This must be what a lady of leisure feels like," Ivy whispered while refilling her teacup. "I can't say I care for it much."

For the very first time in her life she had time on her hands: no-one would be coming in demanding a meal, a few pence to buy the first pint – what her da called his entrance fee to the pub – a shirt pressed to perfection in a hurry – nothing.

I've managed to pay the rent on this place since I was nine years old, she thought. Me da never had any money, at least none I seen.

Ivy began to tidy the room she thought of as hers. After Petey, the last of her brothers, left home, the front room became Ivy's domain.

Éamonn Murphy had insisted he and his wife use the back room as their private area. When his wife left the family, Éamonn had kept to the back room, coming and going through the back door. Ivy and her three brothers had never been allowed into that room without permission. Éamonn allowed Ivy to enter his domain only when he was present. Under his watchful eye she was allowed to clean the room and empty his slop bucket.

Ivy spent every evening, and the days when she wasn't walking the streets or working with Granny, repairing and improving the clothes she begged from the houses she visited weekly. Ivy's mother, Violet, had started using the heavy well-sprung pram to push first Ivy then all of her children from house to house collecting discarded items. When Violet left, Ivy had taken over the route.

Ivy had expanded the business. She'd never bothered to apply for a street trader's license. It hadn't seemed worth her while. She had enough to do. She had a list of women with stalls in the various markets who took her work, and the multitude of second-hand clothing-shops that riddled the Dublin backstreet warrens were also a source of income. If she was lucky enough to get a torn sheet she bleached the fabric and made handkerchiefs and baby nappies to be sold for a handsome profit.

I can keep on working and doing what I've always done, she thought.

She worried about the neighbours. She knew some of the families would want this space. The basement had a door you could lock front and back, a luxury. The lower ceilings made the rooms easier to heat. A pram could sit comfortably outside the back door, safe from thieving hands. Would any of the families living in the big, high-ceilinged, draft-ridden rooms of the tenement houses try to have her, a woman alone, moved out of this prime location? She could worry about that another time.

"I could have a bath!" Ivy jumped at the sound of her own voice. "Jesus, I could have a bath in peace without worrying someone might come. The fire is high enough. I'll have a bath and wash me hair." She stood and began to spin around the room, delighted with the idea.

"I'll have to haul in the old tin bathtub. Oh, I never thought! I can put the tub in me da's room and just empty it out the door and down the drain. I'm going to do it."

Ivy sat down suddenly, breathless. She had . . . what had that woman at the morgue called them? Yes, options – she had options she'd never had before. She'd lived her life surrounded by males, always trying to save and protect her modesty. Well, there was no-one to see her now.

Ivy fell to the bare floor and cried. She shook so much that the force of her sobs made her body travel across the cold floor. She wailed and cried but had no idea why she was crying. Was it the loss of her da or the wonder of her sudden freedom?

Ivy was subconsciously waiting for her da to nudge her, none too gently, with the steel-capped toe of his boot and tell her to stop being such a stupid bitch. "That's enough of that." Ivy stopped herself. She had things to do. She was going to have that bath and the devil take the hindmost.

"Ivy Murphy, where have you been all day?" Granny Grunt shouted as soon as Ivy appeared in the large paved area that formed the backyard of the tenement block. The lamplighter had been around – the tall gas lamps dotted around the back yard hissed and gleamed, illuminating the cracked paving slabs where stalks of dried grass pushed up between each one.

Granny had cracked open the door to her room, trying to keep the heat inside.

"You're lucky I had no work for you or I'd be boxing the ears off you! What in the name of heaven are you doing now?"

"Hello, Granny!" Ivy shouted at the old woman. "Can't stop – I'm having a bath."

"Yeh're what?" Granny Grunt was astonished enough to step outside her doorway. Pulling her shawl over her head she waddled out into the yard. "Have you lost your mind? You disappear for the day and now you're telling me you're having a bath. Yeh'll catch your death of cold, girl."

"Did I hear someone mention a bath?" Pegleg Wilson put his head through the window of the room he rented over Granny's basement. Pegleg didn't have a wooden leg – his nickname came from his childhood passion for a stick of rock called a pegleg. He could still be seen sucking on the gold-coloured sugar-stick even now.

"Never you mind, yeh dirty old man!" Granny Grunt shook her fist up at the face hanging from the window over her head.

Ivy ignored them both. She had things to do. She pulled the old tin bathtub from its nail and dragged it into her da's room. She closed the door behind her with a key. She didn't want visitors. She stood for a moment, panting, trying to figure out how she was going to have the bath she was determined to have. She became aware of a rank odour in the room.

"Well, Da, looks like you left me something to remember you by after all." Ivy went and got her tin of disinfectant, putting the

Jeyes Fluid in her skirt pocket after she'd shook it to be sure there was something left in the tin then adding her bar of Ivory soap. She held her nose closed with her fingers while she searched for the bucket her father used to relieve himself. The stench was vile. Her stomach heaved when she found the slop pail – obviously someone besides her da had used the bucket.

"Thanks very much, Da! Not only do I have your shite to clear up but your woman friend's too." Ivy regretted opening her mouth.

She carried the bucket out into the yard, locking the door behind her. She held the slop bucket in front of her, walking swiftly but carefully over to the outside toilet. Thankfully the toilet was empty. She emptied the bucket and pulled the naked chain to speed up the disposal. She had to fight the urge to fling the smelly bucket down the yard. She used the Jeyes Fluid liberally before adding cold water from the outside tap.

Ivy left the bucket standing soaking outside her back door. She didn't care if someone 'half-inched' – pinched – it. They were welcome to the darn thing. She went to wash her hands at the tap and then returned to the rooms that were hers alone now. Ivy wished she could leave the door standing open. The room badly needed to be aired out.

Ivy was breathing through her mouth, holding her nose closed, while she stood looking around the space that had been her da's private quarters since the day her ma ran away. She'd have to clean the place up – it stank. The big brass bed stood in the middle of the room, taking up most of the space. Ivy wondered if she should keep the bed for herself or try to sell it. She'd keep it until she needed extra money. That would be the smart thing to do.

"What am I going to do without you, Da?" Ivy's body shook but she refused to cry any more. "I won't know what to do with meself now. I loved you all me life, Da. You were always my hero – but you have to admit, Da, you were a demanding bugger!"

Ivy laughed and walked through the smelly room. She closed the door at her back. She was going to have to think about that

44

bath she wanted. It wasn't a simple procedure. She'd plan it out carefully before she started anything.

Jem Ryan was settling Rosie into her stall for the night. He'd eaten and was looking forward to his pipe in front of the fire. The nightly ritual soothed him after a day of sitting freezing on top of his brougham. He used the time to think about the day behind him, plan the day ahead.

Jem was feeling all out of sorts this evening. Perhaps it was simply the date. It was the beginning of a new year and he'd been so busy New Year's Eve he hadn't taken any time out for himself. Jem knew he needed to take stock of his life. He'd been drifting along aimlessly for too long.

"Have you heard?"

Jem stopped brushing the horse and looked over his shoulder. He'd heard Pegleg Wilson speaking to him but the man was nowhere in sight.

"Heard what?"

Jem froze. That voice he knew. Pegleg hadn't been talking to him but to someone else. The two men must be standing just outside the stable door, their voices carrying to where Jem stood. Jem had never liked Tim Johnson – the man was a nasty piece of work – a married man with a bad reputation with the women.

"Ivy Murphy is having a bath." Pegleg snickered. "Heard her meself telling old Granny Grunt all about it."

Jem imagined he could see Pegleg licking his lips.

"So?"

"Well," Jem heard the sly delight in Pegleg's voice, "you're always talking big about how you have a key to Éamonn Murphy's place."

"What's that to you?" Tim Johnson sounded slightly drunk. The man was a disgrace sober, drunk he was dangerous.

"Well, old Éamonn is nowhere about – leastways I haven't seen him." Pegleg snickered. "Why don't you let yourself into his place? Ivy Murphy will be all naked and wet. You could offer to wash her back."

"Maybe I will," Tim Johnson laughed. "It's hard to reach your back. She'd be real grateful for the help, I bet."

Rosie whickered in dismay when Jem's fist tightened on her mane.

"Sorry, girl," he whispered, soothing the animal with a quick caress. He didn't want that pair to know he'd heard them. He'd like nothing better than to teach the pair some manners but they were known for getting their own back. He didn't want a fire at the livery. He wouldn't put anything past Tim Johnson, and Pegleg was simple – he'd follow along.

Jem waited until he heard the men move off. Then he risked cracking open the stable door. He could see the backs of the two men heading towards the tunnel and the pub. He had time.

Jem lived in a room over the stables. He shot the bolt home on the livery door before hurrying up the ladder to his home. He grabbed his jacket from its peg inside his door. He kept his cap in the jacket pocket. He had to warn Ivy. What the hell was Éamonn Murphy thinking, giving the key to his place to a lowlife like Tim Johnson?

Jem rapped on the Murphys' front door.

"Miss Murphy!" he called out for the benefit of those listening and he was sure there were people watching and listening. "Miss Murphy, you dropped something in my carriage!" He figured everyone in the lane knew by now he'd given Ivy a lift home.

"Jem Ryan, is that you making that racket?" Ivy pulled open the door and stared. This was a red-letter day: two eligible men calling on Ivy Murphy in one day.

"Invite me in quick, Ivy," Jem whispered with a quick glance over his shoulder.

"What's going on?" Ivy stepped back and opened the door wider. She knew Jem Ryan was an honourable man. There was many another one she wouldn't allow past the door.

"I'm sorry to bother you, Ivy." Jem pulled off his cap and followed her into the front room. "I overhead something I think you should know." He could feel the colour flooding his face – he hadn't thought about being alone with Ivy.

"Tell me." Ivy thought the man was blushing but it was hard to tell with the amount of red hair that exploded around his chin and cheeks. The beard was the wonder of the kids in the lane – the thing hung down his chest. Jem reckoned it kept his face warm.

"Did you know Tim Johnson has a key to your place?" he asked. Maybe there was no need to mention everything he'd heard.

"Sit down, Jem. I'll make a fresh pot of tea." Ivy gestured to the table standing in front of the window. She pulled the curtains open. "With the gas lamps shining and the fire roaring we'll be backlit. That'll give people something to look at." She half smiled and shrugged. "I imagine there's more to the story than you're telling me."

"I didn't mean to barge in, Ivy." Jem, nevertheless, sat down. Anyone who looked down from the street would see him clearly, sitting fully dressed and exposed to every passing pedestrian.

"You didn't, Jem." Ivy was glad of Jem's company – it kept her from her own thoughts. "Tell me how you know Tim Johnson has a key to this place, please." She put her two best china cups and saucers on the table. She had only two matching cups and they were her pride and joy. "I can't offer you a biscuit, I'm afraid."

"That's okay." Jem smiled. "A cup of tea in good company is a rare treat for me."

"That's your own fault, Jem. You don't mix much and you're not a drinking man which is almost a mortal sin in these parts."

Ivy had a pot of tea made in minutes. She'd kept the big black kettle filled with water and hanging from a hook over the fire. With real pleasure at this unexpected opportunity, she served the tea. Then she returned the teapot to the grate. She liked her tea piping hot.

"Now stop stalling," she said, "and tell me how you know Tim Johnson has a key to this place."

"Okay, it was like this, I was brushing Rosie down, getting her ready for the night and I heard Tim Johnson talking to

Pegleg outside . . ." Jem repeated everything he'd heard the two men say.

"Tim Johnson did have a key to this place." Ivy stared into Jem's eyes. She'd never before noticed how attractive his very green eyes were. When you looked at him you only saw the flaming-red beard. It had been so many years since she'd seen him without his beard she'd forgotten what he looked like with a clean-shaven face.

"How in the name of God did that come about?" Jem almost shouted.

"Me da." Ivy shrugged – nothing more needed to be said.

"Does he not know what a . . . a bounder he is?" Jem was trying to be polite – after all, he was in mixed company. "I could call Tim Johnson a lot of other things but 'bounder' will do for the moment. The man's not to be trusted."

"I know." Ivy stood to fetch the teapot. "Here, empty your slops in there." Ivy brought a cracked sugar bowl to the table. "I'll pour you a fresh cup."

"What do you mean 'you know'?" Jem watched Ivy pour the tea. She had the most elegant hands he'd ever seen – how had he never noticed that before?

"Me da gave that key to Tim in case he ever locked himself out." Ivy was being discreet. Her da had given that key to Tim Johnson so the man could open the door and throw her father into the place when he was too drunk to stand up. He'd given it to him after a drunken night when he'd fallen down the iron steps and almost frozen to death in the entryway to his own home.

Ivy couldn't believe she was sitting in her own room, sharing a pot of tea with a man not related to her. She was actually enjoying the experience

"Your father should have given the key to Granny Grunt." Jem was still thinking about any father handing a key to his daughter's home to a well-known womaniser. Jem had to fight to keep his hands from fisting. Was there no-one to protect Ivy?

"You don't have to worry," Ivy whispered. "Me da wised up.

He changed the locks himself. He even put bolts inside the doors and windows."

"What happened?" Jem knew that something had – Éamonn Murphy wouldn't make work for himself. The man was a handsome specimen of useless space in Jem's opinion. He could have made his fortune as a bare-knuckled fighter. He'd the body for it and the women seemed to love him. God knows he was the pride of the public house but, where it mattered most, in his own home, Éamonn Murphy was a disgrace. Jem would never utter his opinion aloud but he was entitled to his own thoughts.

"Tim Johnson," Ivy almost spat the name, "used the key one day when he knew me da was out. You know how it is." She shrugged. "It's not hard to check the coming and goings of everyone in The Lane. There's only one way in and out of here after all. The so and so knew I was here on me own."

"Did he hurt you, Ivy?" Jem wanted to kick something, shout streams of abuse on the absent head of her useless excuse for a father but he kept his voice soft and his eyes gentle.

"No." Ivy shook her head. "At least not in the way you mean. It was just after Petey, the last of me brothers, left. I was nineteen that summer." She sipped her tea, proud the hand holding the cup didn't shake.

"Ivy?" Jem was only across the courtyard from this place but he'd been so busy minding his own business he'd seen and heard nothing. Ivy could have been raped while he sat with his feet in the fire smoking his pipe. He'd been going around for years with his eyes closed – it was about time he woke up to the world around him.

"Tim Johnson planned to do me the honour of making me his wife." Ivy gave a harsh bark of laughter. "Not for anything like love or even liking, you understand. The man has buried three wives already. He was full of himself that night. He really thought I'd be willing and able to provide for him and his brood of motherless childer."

"That bastard!" Jem shouted. "Excuse me language."

"I told him even if he managed to rape me I wouldn't marry

him." Ivy held back the memories of her fear that night. Tim Johnson had made his intentions known with his fists. She'd been battered and bruised but she'd refused to let him see her fear. "I told him even if he impregnated me I'd never agree to marry him. I'm not that much of a fool. I'd sooner raise a bastard child than have anything to do with the likes of him. I've supported four men, thank you very much. I have no intention of adding to that count."

"That didn't stop him though, did it?" Jem could imagine what Ivy wasn't telling him. There was a world of horror in her brilliantly blue eyes.

"No, by the grace of God me da forgot something. He came back from the pub to find his friend wrestling around the floor with his screaming daughter." She remembered her da's fury. He'd almost beaten Tim Johnson to death. "Me da made Tim Johnson cry for his mammy that night. Then he changed the locks. He gave me that hockey stick . . ." She nodded to the long-handled wooden stick standing by the window. "That's the only bit of wood me da would never throw into the back of the fire."

"So I didn't need to come over here to warn you after all?" Jem didn't regret his visit. He and Ivy hadn't spent any real time together before. They knew each other and always passed the time of day but that was all.

When he'd arrived in Dublin from his home in Sligo he'd thought himself a man at fifteen. He'd come to take up a job at the livery owned by his mother's brother. Ivy must have been about eight then, an enormous age gap at that stage of their lives. Sitting here with her in her cosy room the age gap didn't seem so much. He'd enjoyed this time with her.

"I appreciate your coming over here to warn me more than I can say, Jem," Ivy said softly. "I thought Tim Johnson had given up all ideas about me. He's a married man again. I pity that poor cow he married. She's aged a hundred years since he got his hands on her. Tim and his load of motherless childer will bury her before she's very much older."

"He has a bad reputation around women, Ivy." Jem pushed

his chair back, preparing to stand. "You should never turn your back on him. Keep that hockey stick close to hand when you're here alone."

"Stay a minute, Jem." Ivy didn't want him to leave. "It's not that late and we're in full view of anyone interested in what we might be getting up to."

"I know," Jem laughed. "Have you not noticed how many people have strolled past your railings since we've been sitting here?"

"Yes, it's amazing how many of the neighbours have decided to take an evening stroll." Ivy's laugh turned to a startled sob.

Jem looked at her, dismayed. "Ivy . . ." He paused. "I saw Officer Collins come up your stairs this morning." He waited, wondering if she'd tell him what was going on. "I was coming back from my night's work. Last night was a busy night for cab drivers."

"I thought someone would see him." Ivy shrugged. "It's hard to keep a secret around here."

"Is your da in jail?"

"No!" Ivy snapped. "How could you think that?"

"Ivy, whatever you tell me will go no further. You know that. I'm no gossip."

"I know, Jem." Ivy wasn't ready yet to tell anyone her business.

"I need to be on me way." Jem stood. "Lock the door behind me, Ivy."

"Thanks for calling, Jem." Ivy stood to open the door at her back. It was impossible to get into the small hallway with her sitting in the way.

"Happy New Year, Ivy Murphy," Jem said as he stepped through the outer door. "Ivy, about that bath, I know it's none of me business but are you still planning to haul in the water yourself?" Jem knew the amount of work involved in hauling in buckets of cold water.

"I'm thinking about it." Ivy shrugged.

"Why don't you go to the public baths in Tara Street?" Jem

didn't like to offer to pay for Ivy's bath but he'd willingly pay to save her from the hard work.

"I'll think about that too," Ivy promised. She'd never been to the public baths for herself but she'd thrown the boys in there when she had the pennies to spare. "Now be on your way, Mr Ryan. I thank you for the pleasure of your company and wish you a Happy New Year."

Ivy shut and locked the door.

Chapter 6

Ivy checked on Granny, making sure the old woman had everything she needed for the night. She listened politely to the lecture the old woman delivered without saying a word in her own defence. She wasn't ready to share the news about her da with anyone, not yet.

Ivy had used the back door, for the first time in years not having to walk around the tenement building when she checked on Granny. She sighed with satisfaction at the short return trip from Granny's to her place.

As soon as she'd locked the door at her back she began checking the locks on the door and windows of the back room, her da's room. Then she left the room as fast as her legs would carry her. She couldn't bear it. Her da's unique scent and the lingering stench of bodily functions were all around her.

How could you feel so numb yet hurt so much? Ivy couldn't believe she'd never see her big handsome da again. She'd never see his smile, hear his laugh, listen to him say 'I'm off to see if me ship's come in,' as he went out the door.

"You're being stupid, girl." Ivy leaned with her back against the door separating the two rooms, crippled by indecision. "You've a brain in your head. It may be a small practically useless female brain but it's there, girl!" Ivy wasn't aware she was parroting her father's favourite expressions but the slagging worked.

Ivy grabbed the enamel basin she'd used for years to wash dishes, clothes – herself. The large basin had originally been white but years of hard wear had chipped the enamel so much that there was more of the blue base showing than the white enamel. But it served its purpose.

I may not be able to have me bath, Ivy thought – she had returned the tin tub to its nail outside the back door before going to visit Granny – but I can strip meself down and wash. She poured hot water from the kettle into the basin. After adding cool water from the bucket, she put the wash basin on a small table tucked into one corner of the room.

She could feel a blush travel from her toes to her forehead. She'd never been naked for as long as she could remember. I'll go to hell for sure now, what with speaking ill of the dead and now thinking about getting naked and touching me own flesh. Yes, indeed, Ivy Rose Murphy – her head jerked back and forth in agreement with her thoughts – you'll be going straight to hell.

She pulled the chain to extinguish the gas lamps. If she was going to hell there was no need to light the devil's way for him.

"What am I going to wear tomorrow when I go to meet your one from the morgue?" Ivy was speaking aloud to distract herself from what her own hands were doing. She was removing her clothes, every stitch. Like everyone else in The Lane, Ivy slept in her clothes. The rooms were so cold you awoke of a morning with ice on your lips, and any bed coverings you were lucky enough to have had ice crystals on them. The crystals were formed from the breathing of the bed's inhabitant. It was a lucky family who could afford to light the fire first thing of a morning.

"I can't go to meet the one from the morgue in me old rags . . ." Ivy stood naked in the firelight, afraid to look down at her own body. This must be one of those 'occasions of sin' the priests talked about, she thought. "If I put the word out I was going visiting I'd soon have some kind of an outfit."

She wet an old rag and lathered it up with her bar of Ivory soap. She ran the rag over her arms and torso. With closed eyes and a silent prayer she ran the rag over her bosom. A relieved gasp left her lips when no occasion of sin occurred. Wetting the rag as needed she struggled to reach as much of her back as she could. Satisfied she'd done as much as she could she prepared to wash her legs. She chanced a quick peek, just to see what she was doing, and was amazed at the lack of flesh on her bones. Had her legs always been so skinny?

"Maura Flynn has that skirt she bought from me last week. There was a lovely bit of material in that skirt." She continued to wash her long legs. "If Maura hasn't pawned it yet she'd loan it to me."

Ivy was shaking as she rinsed the rag and prepared to wash between her legs. What if she felt some pleasure? She'd know then she was a depraved sinner for sure.

"Sheila Purcell, her that does for the priest . . ." Ivy was almost faint with relief. She'd washed her private parts, and received no pleasure from the action. Maybe she wasn't cursed to eternal damnation. "Of course Sheila smells herself – she thinks she's special. Just because she works in the priest's house!" Ivy stood with both hands in the water. "Still, she does have that lovely pair of shoes she wears on Sunday. Not a hole or a scratch on them. I wouldn't know meself wearing shoes like that. They'd be a bit wide and long for me but I could fix that."

"It's such a pity I don't know anyone with a decent coat to their name. A good coat would be just the ticket – a good coat covers a multitude of sins – it wouldn't matter what I wore underneath it." Ivy tried to get a picture of her neighbours in her head, trying to remember if anyone had appeared wearing a decent coat recently. She came up blank. A good coat would be taken to the pawn shop almost immediately. The amount of money you received for a decent coat guaranteed you'd never be able to afford to redeem it again, no matter how much you told yourself otherwise.

"So if I put the word out I'm going visiting I'd have all the neighbours coming over here to offer me something or other. Even those with nothing to lend will be over to see what's going on. So that puts the top hat on that idea. I'll be lynched if I tell anyone I'm selling me da's dead body. . . I'll hold me whist, sing dumb for the minute. It's not the first time me da has gone missing for days. I've a bit of time yet." Ivy rinsed out the rag, before throwing the water from her basin into the slop bucket. She'd do her face and neck in the morning.

"I'll have to rummage through me tea chests and see what I've got on hand. There must be something in one of them that I can cobble together into a decent outfit."

Ivy shivered. She wasn't cold – the fire was still roaring up the chimney. She was standing naked as the day she was born in her own room. The heat that flamed over her skin was almost as hot as the flames from the fire. She shoved her chin into the air and like a soldier walking towards the firing squad she marched over to the tea chests stacked in the nooks on both sides of the chimney breast.

Éamonn Murphy had a contact in Boland's Mill, a man who regularly could be trusted to find anything that 'fell off the back' of the delivery wagons. Éamonn sold the tea chests to Ivy at a fair price. The tea chests were viable income as far as Éamonn Murphy was concerned and were a constant temptation to him. Every time he was short of a few bob he tried to sneak a couple of the chests out from under Ivy's nose. Ivy had had to threaten him, claiming she'd stop going on her rounds if he even thought of taking the chests out and selling them to get his entry fee for the pub.

The eight tea chests with the board Ivy paid one of Éamonn's mates to cut for her formed a sleeping platform for the three lads. Éamonn had sold the big brass bed his children slept in, claiming sleeping on the hard floor would do them no harm. Ivy didn't agree.

The chests were used for storing Ivy's pickings, her stash. They were her treasure chests. During the day they stood in several stacks by the side of the fireplace. At night, with the board across the chests and a thin pad Ivy made of rag strips and flour sacks, they were a bed. The four children of Éamonn Murphy huddled together. The three boys slept at the top, Ivy alone lengthwise at the foot. They'd slept that way for years until one by one the males left home leaving Ivy in sole possession.

Ivy pulled an old hand-knit jumper from one tea chest. The thing was man-sized and full of holes. Ivy planned to one day rip it apart. She'd wash and stretch the wool then knit something she could sell. Ivy put her newly cleaned legs through the arms of the jumper and pulled the body up around her. She couldn't bear to put her dirty old clothes back on. She used a rag strip from a different chest to secure the loose jumper around her waist. With a shiver of relief, she covered her nakedness by pulling another man's jumper over her torso.

"The working man's pyjamas!" Ivy laughed aloud. "I wonder what I look like?" She didn't own a mirror. Her da wouldn't allow a mirror in the house. He said it would lead to the sin of vanity.

Ivy dropped into one of the fireside chairs, wondering what she should do now.

"Right, I'm washed and decently covered. What next?"

She couldn't sit still. She jumped up and with efficient movements lit the gas lamps. She shifted the top chests down to the floor, revealing the open top of each chest to her eyes and hands. She dropped to her knees and with the chests all around her glanced from one to another, wondering what she'd put into them and when.

"I'll have a rummage in these and see what I can find to wear. There might be something I've forgotten. It's been a long time since I had the time and space I need to pull these apart."

She was looking forward to emptying the chests. She jumped to her feet. She was sure her da had chalk in his room. He used it to mark the streets for his ha'penny toss school.

I'll mark each chest as I empty them, she thought. She was delighted by the idea. But I wish I could write down what is in each chest. She pulled one of her da's boxes out from under the bed – a crime that would have brought her a severe beating from her da. Without really looking she grabbed the chalk head of a statue sticking up from one of the boxes. Nobody used store-bought chalk. A shattered chalk religious statue worked a treat.

Ivy gleefully pulled items from one of the chests she knew she rarely used. The top item she recognised – a vibrantly pink expanse of fabric. One of the Morgan twins' ball gowns. She vividly remembered Mrs Morgan's housekeeper at Number 12 passing the two ugly big dresses to her. It had been a long time ago.

The Morgan girls must have looked like an explosion in a paint factory in the ugly great dresses. They were as wide as they were tall, not an attractive sight wrapped in yards of pink satin and lace.

Ivy might dress in rags but she could recognise something extremely ugly when she saw it. She'd been hoping to find a use for the yards of expensive material but the darn ball gowns had been buried in the chest for years. Ivy had fond thoughts of the Morgan twins. It was a good day's work when she received anything they discarded. There was always loads of really superior fabric in their clothes and she was sure of a good profit from anything she re-fashioned from them.

With a sigh Ivy continued her search.

Chapter 7

While Ivy searched through the discards of others Ann Marie Gannon – "your one from the morgue" – was being served a meal by her aunt's servants. She watched the butler, Foster, carry the soup tureen into the room and place it on the mahogany sideboard with great precision.

"Is something the matter, dear?" Charles Gannon asked his niece. "You seem unusually sombre. Did you have a busy day at work?"

"I have said it before and will repeat myself incessantly if necessary but I really believe you should give up that awful position, Ann Marie," Beatrice Gannon said before Ann Marie could answer Charles.

"Mother is in the right, cousin." Charles Junior, the pride of his mother's heart, chipped in. "There are plenty of people out of work. You should allow one of them to take the position. You would be better served helping Mother with her charity work." He smiled absently in his mother's general direction.

"I couldn't imagine anything more ghastly than working for one's living!" Clementine Gannon, the daughter of the house, tittered. "But you really take the biscuit, cousin, working with the dead. How perfectly dreadful!"

"Clementine, we are at table." Beatrice forgot herself enough to rap her knuckles on the table top.

"Perhaps you are right." Ann Marie spread her hand-embroidered Irish linen napkin over her lap. "I believe I will give your opinions serious consideration."

"I wish you would, niece." Charles Gannon picked up his solid silver soup spoon and began to eat.

Ann Marie lowered her head and glanced surreptitiously around the table from beneath her eyelids. How had she allowed this situation to continue for so long? It seemed such a short space of time since her beloved parents had been carried off in an influenza epidemic. Yet it was easily five years. Where had that time gone? Indeed, what had she achieved in that time?

Ann Marie stared across the expanse of table. The Irish linen tablecloth was practically invisible under the vast quantities of silver, crystal and china that spread over it. A magnificent display of hothouse flowers seemed to sprout from the tall silver and rose-pink glass epergne resting in the middle of the table. Two footmen and a butler stood by in case of need. Was all of this really necessary for five people?

Ann Marie allowed the conversation to float around her. She was vaguely aware of the subjects under discussion – titbits of news and gossip about their social circle. It all seemed so unimportant to Ann Marie. She couldn't work up the least interest. These people were her family but she felt removed from them.

She was beginning to realise that at the death of her parents she'd withdrawn almost completely from the world around her.

Ann Marie couldn't get Ivy Murphy's face and situation out of her mind. Who ordained that she should live in luxury, attended by servants, her every need met, while Ivy had to consider selling her father's corpse to make ends meet?

Ann Marie wanted to ask her cousins if they knew how very fortunate they were. She knew they wouldn't understand the question. It was simply the way things were. Why question one's own good fortune?

Ann Marie leaned back and allowed Foster to remove her

empty soup bowl. She had no memory of eating the soup. She stared fascinated at Foster's hand encased in pristine white gloves – heaven forfend that the family should be offended by the sight of naked hands.

She stared at the salmon in dill with white wine sauce and wondered what Ivy was eating that evening. A brief smile flickered on her lips. She imagined the servants' horrified expressions if she requested they pack up her meal for a poor person she knew. Did the servants eat the same food as the family?

Ann Marie rented two large comfortably furnished rooms in her uncle's house. Her suite consisted of a large bedroom with the almost unheard-of luxury of a private bathroom, and a sitting room to allow her a level of privacy. Nothing so crass as rent was ever mentioned of course but Ann Marie made a monthly contribution to the running of the household.

Doctor Charles Gannon, a noted physician, became head of the Gannon family upon the death of his brother George, Ann Marie's father. It had seemed the most natural thing in the world for Ann Marie to move in with her uncle's family.

"My dear, you haven't touched the salmon," Beatrice Gannon's voice cut into Ann Marie's thoughts. "Was it not to your liking?"

"I'm afraid I have one of my headaches coming on, Aunt." Ann Marie pressed the napkin to her lips. "Would it be terribly rude of me to withdraw?"

"Not at all, my dear," Charles Gannon was using his calming physician's voice. "Do you need me to prescribe a little something to help you sleep?"

"That won't be necessary, Uncle." Ann Marie stood as Foster pulled her chair away from the table. "I thank you for the kind thought but I'll be just fine. It is a mild annoyance only."

She swept through the doors being held open by the vigilant footmen. Holding her white satin evening gown away from her matching satin slippers and with her hand clutching the highly polished banister, she practically ran up the Aubusson-carpeted staircase.

When did I become such a competent liar? Ann Marie had to

make an effort not to slam the door at her back. She stomped into her living room, glad the fire was burning brightly. Someone had turned the gas lamps on, the soft light adding a cheerful glow to the furnishings.

Ann Marie didn't know what was wrong with her. Rip Van Winkle, the man in the popular story, had slept for twenty years. It would appear she'd been sleeping for five. What had caused her awakening?

Ivy Murphy. An image of the young woman formed in Ann Marie's mind. What would she look like without the mountain of rags that swaddled her? How would she have fared if she'd had Ann Marie's advantages? Something about meeting that young woman had awoken Ann Marie. What was it?

Ann Marie brushed tears from her cheeks, unaware of her actions. Mama, Papa, what would you make of your little girl now, she thought. Mentally she compared the people she'd just left to her parents. In her parents' home dinner conversation had been of world affairs, human rights – sometimes the conversation had become extremely heated with both of her parents beating the table to underline a difference of opinion.

Ann Marie had been encouraged to think for herself and express her opinions aloud. What would her parents think of the ghost she'd become? She'd drifted through life making no waves, taking the easy road.

She had spoken as an equal to her brilliant father. George Gannon had been a noted surgeon, a recognised leader in his own field. Her mother Elizabeth had been an extremely outspoken supporter of women's rights. They'd be ashamed of their daughter if they could see what she'd become.

She'd thought she was being so liberated, working outside the home. She'd simply been hiding, going from one day to the next without thinking. Her mother had a favourite saying and, thinking of it now, Ann Marie cringed: "A mind is a terrible thing to waste." Elizabeth Gannon had used that expression at least once a day. How much more terrible was it to waste a life?

Ann Marie walked over to one of the tall windows that

graced her room at the front of the Georgian house. She pulled back the heavy drapery and, holding the drape in one hand, stared down into a practically deserted thoroughfare. The lamplighter pushed his cart before him, checking on the many gas street lights. A horse-drawn carriage passed under her window.

How many service people did she pass daily, without ever noticing their existence? She'd once read that the longest journey begins with one simple step. Perhaps her meeting Ivy Murphy was the first step in her journey.

She had impulsively suggested meeting Ivy Murphy the following day. She'd had some vague idea of changing the woman's appearance before taking her personally to Iverson's shop. The woman in her ragged outfit would be disdained and ignored by the staff at Iverson's no matter how fine a head of hair she might possess. Ann Marie knew too that Ivy, in her rags, would not receive the full monetary value of her sacrifice. She would be judged on her appearance and found lacking. She would be cheated out of the money she so desperately needed. The same situation would apply at the morgue. Ivy would be cheated and scorned by those who considered themselves so far above her socially and financially.

Ann Marie tried again to imagine Ivy Murphy without her rags. The woman was tall, taller than she was, that much at least she knew. Ivy appeared to have a well-padded figure but her face and neck showed signs of starvation, so unless she was truly bloated by her lack of nutrition, she couldn't be overweight.

Ann Marie dropped the drape back into position over the window. She crossed to the mantelpiece and pulled the tapestry cord hanging there, summoning a servant.

"You rang, Miss?" Mary Coates, the upstairs maid, bobbed her knee and waited. It was unlike Miss Gannon to ring for a servant after dinner. Mary had had to leave her own meal cooling on the table in the servants' hall.

"Mary, I have a problem." Ann Marie wasn't exactly sure who in this household would be best able to help her.

"Yes, Miss." Mary wouldn't mind having a few of this woman's problems. Talk in the kitchen said this woman's money paid all the household bills.

"I wish to consult with Mrs Reilly, our admirable and very efficient housekeeper, on a matter of some delicacy." Ann Marie hesitated. "Perhaps you could advise me."

"Me, Miss?" Mary was flabbergasted. She'd never been asked for advice by the quality before. Wait till she told them about this below stairs!

"Where and when would it be best to consult with Mrs Reilly?" Ann Marie had no idea of the woman's duties. "Should I invite her to take tea with me here, in this room, or should I arrange to meet her below stairs?"

"I believe Mrs Reilly would prefer to meet with you here, Miss Gannon," Mary managed to get out through numb lips. The old battle-axe would skip up the ruddy stairs and be impossible to live with afterwards. She didn't mind really. Mrs Reilly ran the house with skill and experience and Mary was learning a lot from just watching the woman. Mary had plans to improve her own situation.

"Would it be improper to suggest you ask Mrs Reilly directly?" Ann Marie was very aware of the proprieties. It would not do for her to upset a valued servant in her aunt's domain.

"I'll speak with Mrs Reilly," Mary said. "Would that be satisfactory, Miss Gannon?"

"Thank you, Mary." Ann Marie bowed her head gracefully. "I'd be much obliged."

"Thank you, Miss Gannon." Mary turned and in her best black uniform and spotlessly white apron and mob cap she practically floated from the room.

Mary made her way slowly and quietly towards the servants' stairway though she wanted to kick up her heels and run. She couldn't wait to reach the servants' hall. This little bit of excitement would rattle the dishes right and proper. She'd better be careful how she went about it or she'd be in deep trouble. She'd have to inform Mr Foster, the butler first – that would be the right way to go about the thing.

"Aggie, get the plate out of the warming oven!" said Iris Jones, the cook, as Mary entered the kitchen.

The cook's young helper jumped to her feet, leaving her own meal.

"I put your dinner in the warmer, Mary," Iris said. "You weren't away long so it won't be ruined."

"Thanks, Cook," said Mary. Then she stepped forward and addressed the man at the head of the table. "Mr Foster, Miss Gannon has a request for Mrs Reilly."

"You may pass the message along." Foster bowed his head of magnificent grey hair in the housekeeper's direction. "If the matter is not of a private nature."

"No, Mr Foster." Mary was enjoying her moment in the spotlight.

Agnes Reilly wanted to box the girl's ears. She'd do it too if Mary didn't hurry along and pass on the message.

"Mrs Reilly," Mary took a deep breath, "Miss Gannon requests that you meet with her in her drawing room. Miss Gannon wishes to consult you on a private matter." Mary watched every member of staff lean in closer and stare at the stunned housekeeper.

"Blimey, Mrs Reilly, you're coming up in the world!" Davy, the young bootblack, grinned.

"Don't be impertinent, Davy!" Foster snapped.

"Did Miss Gannon mention a time for this meeting?" Agnes Reilly pressed her napkin to her lips. It helped to hide the pleased grin that crossed her face. A change in routine was always welcome.

"Miss Gannon asked for my suggestion," Mary stated daringly. She revelled in the gasps of astonishment that sped around the servants' table.

"I beg your pardon?" Foster was horrified by this breach of etiquette.

"She did, Mr Foster."

Mary's dinner was sitting ignored on the table. For once Cook didn't care – she was enjoying this little drama. "I hesitated to make any suggestion and asked if the Miss would allow me to consult

65

with Mrs Reilly before returning to inform Miss Gannon of Mrs Reilly's feelings on the matter."

"Servants don't have feelings!" Foster snapped.

"Yes, Mr Foster, but I'm just passing along Miss Gannon's request." Mary stood proudly, bosom erect.

"What is the world coming to when our betters ask for our opinion?" Foster snapped. "Mrs Reilly, take care of this matter yourself. At once if you'd be so kind."

Mrs Reilly stood, giving every impression of calm competence. Inside she was giddy. She brushed needlessly at her skirt. She knew the superior quality of her black uniform dress and the keys hanging from her waist screamed her importance to the world – she need do nothing to improve her appearance.

"In my absence you may carry on with your duties." Agnes Reilly glanced around the table. "You all know what to do."

She sailed out of the servants' hall, leaving a table filled with frantic whispers and avid listeners. For once Mr Foster allowed the servants to offer conjectures. Such a situation had never occurred before.

"You had better finish your meal, Mary," Foster ordered.

"Yes, Mr Foster." Mary delighted in her sudden rise in importance.

When the bell from Miss Gannon's room rang out Mary jumped to her feet. Foster examined her appearance personally. Such an unusual event had poor Mary almost swooning with the honour being bestowed upon her.

"Mrs Reilly . . ." Ann Marie had no idea of the commotion her simple request had stirred up below stairs.

"Yes, Miss Gannon?" Agnes Reilly was seated with Ann Marie at a small circular table. The table had been pulled out to stand adjacent to the glowing fire.

Mary Coates had delivered tea for two.

"I'm not quite sure how to go on." Ann Marie poured the tea from the silver teapot into two exquisitely fine china cups. "I've met someone."

"A gentleman, Miss Gannon?" Agnes Reilly was taking mental note of everything. Imagine the Miss pouring tea with her own hands for a servant! She'd have to work that little matter into conversation in the servants' hall.

"No." Ann Marie smiled, having no idea how much her private life fascinated the people below stairs. She'd be astonished to discover her every move and utterance was discussed and mulled over by the house staff. "A young woman." Ann Marie offered Mrs Reilly a plate of sugared dainties. The woman was so overcome by the honour paid her she accepted a tiny cake with shaking fingers. "Someone I sincerely want to help."

"Help in what way, Miss Gannon, if you don't mind my asking?" Agnes Reilly felt as if she was standing outside herself watching her own image taking tea like a lady of leisure.

"That's just it, Mrs Reilly." Ann Marie sipped her tea slowly. "I have no idea how best to help this woman. I was hoping to consult with you. I thought if I explained the situation to you, you might be a better person than I to work something out."

"I see." Mrs Reilly said having no idea whatsoever how she could be of help to one of the gentry. "Would you care to tell me about this young woman?"

"What I wish to share with you, Mrs Reilly, must remain strictly between ourselves." Ann Marie had no idea where Ivy Murphy lived but she had no wish to make the young woman the subject of servants' gossip, should they know of her.

"That goes without saying, Miss Gannon." Mrs Reilly was insulted by the suggestion she might gossip.

"Thank you." Ann Marie bowed her head. "Let me lay out the situation for you and when I've finished perhaps you could make some suggestions?"

Ann Marie first made known her wish to help someone in difficult circumstances. She wished to offer her advice and assistance without offending the dignity of the woman involved. She then gave Mrs Reilly a brief rundown of her dealings with Ivy.

"You wish to offer this person money?" Mrs Reilly couldn't

see the problem. Most people would almost break your fingers taking the money out of your hand.

"No, not at all," Ann Marie said. "In fact I think Ivy Murphy would be mortally offended if I offered her money. The woman was insistent that she'd accept no charity. I admired her attitude."

"Ivy Murphy?" Mrs Reilly felt faint. She could actually feel the colour leaving her face. It couldn't be the same person. Surely Miss Gannon wasn't talking about the ragamuffin that begged for cast-offs and throwaways from all the servants' entries around this square of prosperous Georgian mansions. "Is this woman you wish to help tall, badly dressed in filthy layers of clothing, with an enormous black bun sitting on the back of her neck?" She wanted to cross her fingers. She hoped very much she was mistaken.

"You know her?" Ann Marie was surprised. Where would their very upright housekeeper have met Ivy?

"If it's the same person, then yes." Mrs Reilly forgot herself so much she held out her cup for a refill.

"Without being indelicate or revealing something you wish to conceal," Ann Marie poured the tea, excited at the thought of learning more of Ivy Murphy's circumstances, "would you tell me how you came to know her?"

"Ivy Murphy, merciful heavens, I've known her all of her life." Mrs Reilly was feeling very important. Miss Gannon was hanging on her every word. Without giving the game away she'd be sure to mention that little fact below stairs. "I knew her mother."

"Would you tell me about Ivy?" Ann Marie couldn't believe her luck. She stood, walked over to her concealed liquor cabinet and removed a bottle of cognac. She added the brandy to her own tea before offering Mrs Reilly the same fortification. With satisfied smiles the two women settled in for a good gossip.

Chapter 8

Ann Marie left her uncle's home early the next morning. In her handbag she had one of the large brass keys used to open the locked gates of the private park the square was built around. She'd telephoned the hospital and informed them she would not be working that day. Ann Marie intended to take Ivy into the park.

Ann Marie was so wrapped up only her eyes were visible. Her winter fox-fur hat and shawl-like fur collar kept the wind off and the heavy tweed fabric of her coat covered her from neck to ankles. To the best of her ability she was dressed for the weather. She walked briskly around the park, having no idea which direction Ivy would come from.

The tale of Ivy's life, as much as Mrs Reilly knew, horrified Ann Marie. She'd had difficulty sleeping thinking of a nine-year-old girl being the sole provider for her father and three brothers. How had such a thing been allowed to occur? There were agencies set up to prevent child slavery. Ann Marie believed Ivy had been a slave to the male members of her family.

How Ann Marie's mother would have revelled in the opportunity to right this social wrong! Well, Elizabeth Gannon was dead but her daughter was determined to see justice done.

Thankfully Ann Marie hadn't mentioned Éamonn Murphy's demise to Mrs Reilly. That would have been unforgivable since it was obvious Mrs Reilly knew the family. It was imperative no-one should know Ivy intended to sell her father's remains. Ann Marie felt faint at the problems she'd almost brought upon Ivy's head.

Last evening the housekeeper had been able to tell Ann Marie a great deal about Violet Burton, a woman who'd married so far beneath her own social station her family had cut her off without a penny. How could any woman, any mother, leave four children at the mercy of a man like Éamonn Murphy? Granted Ann Marie had seen that even in death Éamonn Murphy was a handsome devil with mouth-wateringly tempting physical attributes. If life with the man had been so unbearable that Violet Burton had run away, how could she believe her children would be safe?

Ann Marie sighed, making another circuit of the park. It was really none of her business. She couldn't change the past but perhaps she could make a difference to Ivy's future. Ann Marie needed a project, a reason for living. She needed to justify her exalted position in society.

She had mistakenly believed her position in the morgue would allow her to help people. When she'd accepted the position at the hospital she had imagined herself consoling and counselling the bereaved, serving a purpose. She'd spent the last three years sleepwalking through life. Ivy Murphy had kicked her awake.

She huddled into the thick fur collar she pulled up to frame her face, finally admitting she'd taken the position at her father's old teaching hospital to remove herself from her uncle's house. The family were not unkind but their constant twittering on about their social engagements and pleasures had driven Ann Marie to distraction.

Charles Junior and Clementine, through no fault of their own, were completely useless individuals. They had no purpose to their lives. Charles Junior fainted at the sight of blood so a career in medicine had never been suggested for him. He seemed content to drift from day to day, posing a constant danger to any attractive housemaids his mother might employ.

"You must like white." Ivy had come unnoticed to Ann Marie's side. "Although the white fur is more attractive than that white doctor's coat you wore in the morgue." She smiled shyly.

"Ivy!" Ann Marie almost groaned. The woman was wearing the same atrocious old army greatcoat and moth-eaten wool shawl. "I brought the key to the park gate." She took the key from her handbag and held it high. "I thought we might talk inside – it should be more sheltered."

"Fine." Ivy hadn't come far but she was frozen.

"I don't know why they insist on keeping these gates locked." Ann Marie was embarrassed. "A park like this should be for everyone." She smiled over her shoulder. "You've probably never been in here before?"

"You'd think that, wouldn't you?" Ivy looked out of the corners of her eyes, amused at Ann Marie's assumption. She'd spent a lot of her childhood behind these gates keeping an eye on her brothers and picking daisies with her mother. Two or three of the iron railings had been loosened, allowing the women of The Lane and their children to enjoy the fresh air and sunshine in pleasant green surroundings. They were careful never to be caught by the residents of the mansions. The children of the families that owned the mansions were taken for strolls with their nannies, none of whom were a match for any of the ferociously protective women of The Lane. Both parties turned a blind eye to each other and no harm was ever done to the park.

"I wanted to speak to you in private," Ann Marie said as she locked the park gate behind her. She knew she was missing something but had no idea what it could be. She had the impression Ivy was laughing at her.

"We could talk in that little three-sided hut by the bandstand. We'd be out of this wind anyway?" Ivy smiled innocently.

"That would be ideal." Ann Marie left it at that. She was

flustered enough by the thought of the conversation she hoped to hold with Ivy. She didn't need to complicate matters.

They approached the bandstand and stepped into the hut that was used by the groundsmen and visitors alike. The back of the tall hut protected the two women from the biting cold wind.

"Ivy," said Ann Marie, "I have something I wish to discuss with you and I'm heartily terrified of insulting you. I don't want to hurt your feelings."

"Why don't you tell me your name before you start insulting me?" Ivy suggested.

"Oh, my dear Lord!" Ann Marie closed her eyes, horrified at her breach of etiquette.

"That's an unusual name." Ivy had no intention of kowtowing to this woman. It was obvious from a casual glance that they came from totally different ends of the social ladder. Ivy didn't intend to allow that to bother her.

"I'm so sorry!" Ann Marie held out a hand encased in a buttery soft beige leather glove. "My name is Ann Marie Victoria Gannon and I wish very much to be a friend to you."

"Ivy Rose Murphy." Ivy held out a hand encased in a discarded sock folded back to form a thumbless mitten. "You can never have enough friends in my opinion."

"Thank you," Ann Marie said sincerely.

"What did you want to say to me?" Ivy didn't know why this woman was bothering with her but she'd go along with it and see what happened.

"I wanted to advise you." Ann Marie blushed bright red. "We talked about visiting Iverson's with regards to selling your hair." She was choking on the words but she had to say what needed to be said.

"You said I could get some money for it. Have you changed your mind?" Ivy had known it was too good to be true. Who in their right mind would buy hair?

"No, I haven't changed my mind!" Ann Marie almost snapped. She was disgusted at her own cowardice. "The truth of the matter is, Ivy, and I do beg you to forgive me if my words sound harsh, but attired as you are Iverson's won't let you past the door."

"I see." Ivy had made an effort with her appearance. She'd sat up late into the night making a dress she was really proud of. However, she knew the old coat and battered shoes ruined everything.

"I'm sure you do," Ann Marie said sadly. "However, I'm hoping you will allow me to help you."

"How?" Ivy couldn't afford to allow her pride to get in her way. She was in a desperate situation and she knew it.

"I live just across the road."

"What number?" Ivy knew all of these houses. Well, she knew them from the back alley entrance anyway.

"Number 8." Ann Marie wondered why the number of the house mattered.

"Mrs Reilly's place?"

"I suppose, yes, in a sense I suppose it is Mrs Reilly's place." Ann Marie laughed softly, wondering what her aunt would think of that. "Anyway, what I wanted to suggest to you . . ." She paused, wondering if she dared go on. Mrs Reilly had advised her to tread carefully. "What I wanted to suggest was . . . if you would care for it, that is . . ."

"Ann Marie, will you stop beating around the bush and spit it out, whatever it is!" Ivy was frozen and wanted to get to this hair place and see how much she could get for the hair on her head. She was very much aware she owed Ann Marie a half crown. Would she get as much as that for her hair?

"I want you to come over to Number 8 with me and allow Mrs Reilly and I to try and find something that will fit you," Ann Marie said breathlessly. "Mrs Reilly thought my uncle's daughter Clementine might be of a size with you. We can put an outfit together that will allow you to stroll into Iverson's with your head held high."

"Old Foster would lay a duck egg if you took me into his house!" Ivy laughed until her sides ached. Every time she'd almost caught her breath the image of Foster's face would pop into her head and she'd be off again.

Just then Ann Marie heard the sound she'd been waiting for: her aunt's chauffeur cranking up the automobile. Mrs Reilly had mentioned, in passing, that the chauffeur had received orders to have the automobile outside the door early that morning. Beatrice Gannon and her two children were driving to Kildare to visit friends for lunch.

"Let's go." Ann Marie took a sniggering Ivy by the elbow and almost towed her from the park.

"I can't go in there." Ivy pulled back when they approached the house, staring upwards at the four floors of the redbrick building in front of her.

"Of course you can. The family have left for the day so we'll have the place to ourselves." Ann Marie considered the house empty once the family members had left – it didn't occur to her to count the servants.

"All right." Ivy couldn't wait to see Foster's face when he opened the door. She hoped someone had smelling salts on hand – the old fellow would likely faint dead away.

"Miss Gannon, I wasn't aware you had left the house this morning." Foster held the door open for Ann Marie, then attempted to shut it in Ivy's face, glaring his disdain.

"This is my friend, Miss Murphy, Foster." Ann Marie opened her coat. "Have the breakfast covers been removed?" She waited for the butler to remove her coat, passing her hat and gloves to him automatically.

"Not yet, Miss Gannon." Foster clicked his fingers in the direction of the hovering footman. He would not deign to touch the upstart's ragged coat and shawl. How dare she come into his home in this fashion? Someone should point out the correct way of doing things to Miss Ivy Murphy, and Foster felt he was just the man for the job.

"Wonderful!" Ann Marie watched Ivy peel away her layers, unaware of the little drama taking place around her. Her jaw dropped when Miss Ivy Rose Murphy stood in front of her in all her glory. Where on earth had she found the dress she was wearing? Ann Marie would be proud to have the garment hanging in her own wardrobe. What was going on here? She forced her jaw closed with effort. "Ivy, do you prefer tea or coffee?"

"I've never tasted coffee, Ann Marie." Ivy bit her lips. She'd given her shawl to the footman. Was it decent to be standing here with her head uncovered? Ann Marie didn't seem to mind, so it must be okay. Ivy shrugged, the rich were different.

The shocked gasp at her effrontery from Foster and the footman echoed around the enormous entryway. Ivy wished she could just stand here and take it all in – how the other half lived. She'd never get a chance like this again.

"Please ask Cook for a pot of tea and one of coffee, Foster." Ann Marie opened the door to the dining room herself.

Foster and the footman were standing, horrified, unable to move or function at this unacceptable turn of events.

"Bring an extra cup if you would," said Ann Marie. "I'm sure Ivy would appreciate her first taste of coffee." She entered the dining room, leaving the door open for Ivy.

"Suck it in, Foster, me auld flower!" Ivy almost skipped towards the dining room. "I'm an invited guest."

"What will you have, Ivy?" Ann Marie had lifted a silver dome that covered one of the many dishes on the sideboard.

"Miss Gannon, please, that is my duty." Foster hurried into the dining room, determined to protect his home from all ignorant intruders. It wasn't Miss Gannon's fault – she was a trusting soul – but that Ivy Murphy, that beggar girl, she was taking advantage.

Foster sniffed loudly – expressing his displeasure. This was not how things were done.

The footman returned quickly from the kitchen. Brian Sarsfield didn't want to miss a moment of this unusual event. Under Foster's watchful eye, he began to organise the table settings.

"I'll have a taste of everything." Ivy watched the footman hurry to pull out a chair for Ann Marie. Was the woman incapable of seating herself? What a load of pretentious rubbish! Ivy had caught a brief glimpse of the mountain of lean bacon under the dome Ann Marie had held in her hand. Her mouth watered at the scents that drifted around the large room.

"Thank you, Foster," Ann Marie said as soon as the man had placed a plate laden with food before her. "If you could bring in the tea and coffee, we will serve ourselves."

"Yes, Miss Gannon." Foster wanted to throw the food at Ivy Murphy but he restrained himself. He had his dignity to consider. He placed a brimming plate in front of the woman with exaggerated care. He knew the beggar had never seen so much food in her life. Highly indignant at his dismissal, he then signalled the footman to follow him from the room.

"Stand by that door and don't move," he said. "If that one," meaning Ivy, "makes a move you don't like, come and get me."

"Yes, Mr Foster." Brian Sarsfield turned his back to the dining-room door. What a turn up for the books! This palaver would be the talk of every house in the square. He'd be treated to a few pints tonight at the pub – everyone would want to know about these goings-on.

"Ivy, I don't wish to offend you . . ." Ann Marie picked up the correct tableware, conscious that Ivy was waiting to see what she would do.

"Ann Marie, can we agree that the two of us come from completely different worlds?" Ivy copied Ann Marie's movements. Her mouth was watering. She'd never in her life had a plate of food like this just for herself. She wanted to dive in and devour everything. They'd be lucky if she left any pattern on the feckin' plates. "If we worry about offending each other all the time we'll be afraid of opening our mouths." She bit into the bacon and egg she'd placed on her fork. She wanted to groan – it was the best food she'd ever tasted. "Let's agree to say what we mean and if either of us takes offence, well, it can't be helped."

"You're very wise, Ivy," Ann Marie was saying just as the footman opened the door to allow Foster to enter. He was followed by another footman carrying an enormous silver salver laden with the accoutrements of a formal tea and coffee service.

"If you'd place the tray on the table, please," Ann Marie said over her shoulder, "we will tend to ourselves."

"Yes, Miss Gannon." Foster's spine was in danger of snapping.

"Thank you, Foster," Ivy said just to get up the old goat's nose.

Foster and the footman withdrew.

"I can't help noticing," Ann Marie had seen Foster's reaction to Ivy's daring and wanted to laugh – this was turning out to be a lot of fun, "that your accent is a great deal less broad this morning."

"My mother insisted on her children learning to speak clearly and distinctly." Ivy shrugged. "My mother claimed there was no need for us to sound like little savages. After she left, my brothers and I continued to practise speaking posh, but only when my father was absent." She giggled, delighted with herself.

"That should make things a great deal simpler for you on our travels today." Ann Marie was astonished. It was as if Ivy had two different personas and could switch from one to the other at will.

Ann Marie longed to ask Ivy where the dress she wore had come from. The lacework on the white high-necked, long-sleeved top was exquisite. The black drop-waist skirt of the dress was beautifully cut and the fabric superior. Where had this woman come by a dress that was fashionably up to the minute and so obviously expensive?

Ivy would have gladly told Ann Marie that the lace top was her own handiwork. Granny Grunt was an acknowledged master lace-maker. The woman had taught Ivy everything she knew. The black skirt Ivy had attached to the top in a drop-waist style had come out of Ivy's tea chests, compliments of the Morgan twins. Ivy was thrilled with how the dress she'd laboured over all night had come out.

"I'm still having a hard time believing someone will pay good money for the hair on my head." Ivy felt she had to say something. She'd been taking in the furnishings of the large room. The high ceilings with beautiful plaster fascia of fruit and vines, the heavy dark wood panelling covering the walls. The marble fireplace alone must have cost a fortune. God alone knew how much the coal for heating just this room cost. It really was a different world.

"I'll be with you all the way. If you'll allow me I'll bargain with Mr Iverson for the most amount of money we can squeeze out of the man." Ann Marie watched Ivy's eyes roam around the room. She wondered about Ivy's reaction to her uncle's home. She'd love to demand that Ivy should tell her her every thought. "We'll travel down town in my automobile."

"In your what?" Ivy couldn't believe all of this was happening to her. She, Ivy Murphy, was going to travel in an automobile. What was the world coming to?

"Yes, if you don't mind." Ann Marie grinned. "I prefer to drive myself around the city."

"I'd be delighted to accompany you, Miss Gannon." Ivy grinned like a bandit.

"Okay, hurry up and eat your food." Ann Marie stood to serve the tea and coffee – she found it difficult to lift the heavily embossed silver coffee pot from a seated position.

The meal became a party. Ivy tasted coffee for the first time. She didn't really care for it, preferring her cup of tea. She'd be able to say she'd tasted it anyway.

The two women laughed and chatted in such a familiar fashion that Brian Sarsfield, standing outside, wanted to open the door and have a look. How could Ivy Murphy have so much to say to her betters?

"We should really be getting about our business, Ivy," Ann Marie said eventually. She couldn't remember a time when she'd enjoyed herself so much. "I think we need to find only shoes, stockings, gloves and a hat and coat for you to borrow."

Mrs Reilly had suggested they make use of the taller, slimmer Clementine's clothing. Ann Marie wasn't concerned about her cousin's reaction to the disappearance of her outer wear. Clementine shopped incessantly. She'd never notice items missing from her wardrobe.

Ivy couldn't imagine the luxury of being all decked out. Why was this woman doing this for her?

"Does your foundation garment have attached stocking-holders?" Ann Marie couldn't understand why Ivy started to choke on her tea at the question. It wasn't that embarrassing.

"No, I'm afraid it doesn't." Ivy wondered what Ann Marie would say if she told her that the only 'foundation garment' she wore was one of her da's vests pulled down and pinned between her legs.

"Well, never mind, we'll soon sort you out." Ann Marie was looking forward to the day ahead.

Chapter 9

Da, are ye there? Da, it's me, Ivy.

Ivy was in a side aisle of the Westland Row church. She'd made her devotions and paid for two candles in her da's name. She was kneeling in the empty church, staring at the flickering flames from the multitude of burning candles stuck in the iron stand.

I wouldn't wonder if you didn't recognise me, Da.

Ivy's thoughts were almost shouting from her head. She'd so much to tell her da. I've had me hair all chopped off. I've had such a day, Da. You'd never believe it.

The huge church stood silent around the single figure kneeling in a posture of devoted piety. Ivy wasn't feeling pious though. She was still reeling from the events of the day and had to tell someone. The safest someone she could think of was her da. Who was he going to tell?

Your one from the morgue, her name is Ann Marie, Da. Well, you wouldn't believe the things she had me do today.

Ivy thought for a moment. She wanted to be sure to mention all the wonders of the day.

First and foremost, she had me come into her house. By the front door no less. Da, can you believe it? Me! Auld Foster almost had a heart attack – you should have seen his face! Well, I didn't care – I put me nose in the air and made like it was nothing unusual for me to be going in the front door of one of those mansions.

Ivy was glad of the heat from the candles. The church was cold she could see her breath in front of her face.

Then your one had Foster serve me breakfast.

Ivy imagined her da, wherever he was, roaring with laughter, his handsome blue eyes sparkling as he beat his hands against his knees. That was a good one. Honest to God, Da. Foster and that Brian Sarsfield that serves as footman. You know him, Da. The two of yeh drink in the same pub.

Anyway, Da, after breakfast Ann Marie took me upstairs to her bedroom. Mrs Reilly was there and between the pair of them they soon had me decked out. Honest to God, Da. I was the cat's meow.

The two women had shown Ivy her image in a long mirror but Ivy didn't like to mention that here. Her da would think she was being vain.

So, there I was, Da. Dressed to the nines and looking like someone else. Then, didn't your one take me out to her automobile. I ask your sacred pardon, Da. I mean, me, I climbed into that automobile like I was the queen of the land and Ann Marie drove us into the town centre. I wish you could have seen me, Da!

It was a different Dublin to the one you and me know, Da. I was dumbstruck. I know you always told me we were as good as the next man but really, Da, this was different. I understand now why you insisted on having your good suit to hand. Remember that time you almost killed me for pawning your Sunday suit? We hadn't a bite to eat in the house but you leathered me good for that. I understand now, Da.

I was treated like Lady Muck. Honest to God, Da. You should have seen it. These fancy fellas falling over their feet to open the vehicle door. That's what the posh call their automobiles – vehicles. Put that in your pipe and smoke it, Da.

Anyway Da, the best part – your man Iverson, he almost fainted when he seen me hair.

Ivy looked into the flames of the candle, wondering if there was any possibility her da was really looking over her from heaven. If he really was looking down on her he'd have seen all the wonders of the day that she was trying so hard to tell him about.

Your man Iverson was a bit of a limp wrist, Da, but you can't hold that against the man. Anyway, Da, he gave me more money than I've ever seen in me life for me hair. Honest, he tried to pay me by cheque – imagine me taking a piece of paper instead of real money! I almost said something to put a flea in his ear but Ann Marie handled it like the real lady she is.

Anyway, Da, I hope you're sitting on a white fluffy cloud because you'll faint when I tell yeh. Da, I got a big white paper fiver, more than a year's rent money, for me hair. I know that's paper as well, Da, but it's real money as everyone knows. Ivy nodded her head frantically to underline the gravity of her words.

I won't have to worry about the roof over me head for a full year. Da, do you have any idea what that means? I don't mean to be cheeky or anything, Da, but you never had to worry where the rent was coming from, did yeh? First me ma and then me, we took care of that.

I was floating by the time we left Iverson's. It wasn't only that me head felt like an elephant had just been cut away from it but, Da, I was rich. I couldn't sit still. Ann Marie, she seemed to understand. So me in all me glory and her, we strolled around the fancy shops.

She'd felt such a toff in her finery. It was her dress – well, it was the blouse she'd made attached to a skirt belonging to one of the Morgan twins but that didn't matter, it was still her dress – everything else belonged to Ann Marie or her cousin.

Ivy had been dizzy with the different sights that opened up to her. The shops Ann Marie showed her were places of wonder and amazement, everything was so bright and clean. Ivy might have lived in Dublin all of her life but she lived in the back lanes. The fancy shops and wide clean streets of the city were for the quality.

The Dublin Ann Marie knew was very different from the dark alleys – the poor people and places Ivy knew. In Ivy's world, when you went shopping, you'd be lucky to get a botched-together table leaning against some buildings with things thrown any old how on the table top. The stall holder would sit in his or her open front door and keep an eye on the goods.

And then, Da, I got the shock of me life.

Ivy closed her eyes, desperate to tell someone about the horrendous shock she'd got today. She hadn't been able to tell Ann Marie. The woman was kind but she hadn't a clue about real life. She buried her head in her hands, remembering. Her fingers ploughed through the feathery soft curls that covered her head like a skullcap.

Ivy had been amazed and embarrassed to see a selection of the lace knickers and camisoles she and Granny Grunt made sitting proudly in the window of one shop. She couldn't believe her eyes, right out in the window for God and everyone to see. Well, the quality were funny, that's all she'd say.

Da, I asked Ann Marie how much was written on the ticket that sat in front of one set of frillys. I nearly passed out, Da. They were priced in guineas, Da – guineas. Me and Granny get pennies for the backbreaking hours we spend making those things. I asked Ann Marie the name of the shop and I know the old biddy who owns it well. Anyway, Da, the old bat is charging guineas for stuff she pays us pennies to make. It's not right, Da. There is a whole lot not right with our world, Da. I never noticed that before. What do you think of that then, Da?

Ivy wasn't aware of the people coming into the church to say a quick prayer. She was lost in another world having the kind of conversation with her da she'd never been able to have with him when he was alive. He wouldn't have sat still for it. Was having a dead da to listen to her going to be better than having a live one?

When we went back to the big house I gave back the stuff I'd borrowed. It mostly all belonged to Miss Clementine, the daughter of the house. So I'm back in Eamo's old green army coat, me broken-down old shoes and me shawl but I've seen something different now, Da.

Ann Marie wanted me to keep everything but I wouldn't. I have me pride. I did keep the shoes because they fit me a treat . She even said I should keep the lisle stockings and the thing that holds the stockings up. They belonged to Ann Marie anyway. They're all in the pocket of me coat, even the shoes. I was thinking of washing the stockings and selling them at the market. You should see the state of the shoes, Da. I'd get a pretty penny for them. I've had second thoughts though. I think I'll keep the shoes and stuff handy. Just the way you kept your Sunday suit, Da. You never know when you might need something decent to wear.

Da, do you know what I've done with your body?

Ivy almost cringed in the pew. She raised her head from her hands and stared at the statue of Our Lady, her with the snake and what seemed like hundreds of candles burning at her feet.

Ann Marie had taken Ivy by the morgue to sign the papers.

I had to do it, Da. I'm really sorry but there is no way I can give you the kind of send-off you'd like. Da, I need the money. Life is for the living and I'm still here, still breathing. I'd begrudge every penny I'd have to put out to entertain your drunken friends. I bought their drinks for years, Da. I'm not doing it any more.

Ann Marie is going to get me the best price she can for your corpse. I'm that sorry but, Da, truthfully, it will be the first time in your life – or your death – whatever – it'll be the first time you've ever given me anything except a thick ear.

I'm heartily sorry, Da, but that's the way it's going to be. I'll have to tell the neighbours something. I'll gladly make sandwiches and a few pots of tea for the women but I am not standing for buying rounds of drinks for your cronies.

"Ivy Rose Murphy, what are you doing there?" The voice

echoed around the church with no respect for the sanctity of the place.

"I've been praying, Father Leary." Ivy stood slowly. She'd known she'd have to speak to this man.

"Praying? You have a right cheek, Ivy Rose Murphy!" The obese figure of Father Leary waddled out from the sacristy. The priest's jowls jiggled while his face settled into its habitual expression of bitter disgust. "I've been watching you there, young woman, and you'd think butter wouldn't melt in your mouth. How dare you come in here and pray? I never see you at Mass or Confession, do I? Yet you feel at liberty to come in here and pray as if you have a right!"

"I thought everyone was welcome in God's house!" Ivy snapped.

"How dare you talk back to me?" Father Leary rattled the loose money in his pocket. A habit, if he did but know it, that made Ivy want to punch his fat face in. "I am a man of God and as such you will show me respect."

"I thought we were all God's children." Ivy stepped out of reach. The priest had a knack for catching you by the ear and twisting until you yelled.

"What would the likes of you know about God? You are a heathen, Ivy Rose Murphy, and everyone knows it." Father Leary wished he had his walking stick with him. He'd soon rap this cheeky article around the legs with it. "Your blessed father Éamonn can be seen in here every Sunday large as life. I've never seen you here with him."

"I need to talk to you about my father." Ivy used her posh voice just to annoy the priest. Father Leary didn't like the ragged members of his community to get above themselves.

"Why didn't your father come to see me himself?" Father Leary snapped. "Your father is a God-fearing Christian and I'm always happy to advise him."

"Yeah, I remember." Ivy bit her tongue. This man's interference in the private lives of his congregation was nothing short of catastrophic.

"My father, Éamonn Murphy, can't come to see you." Ivy

wouldn't give this priest the satisfaction of seeing her cry. "He's dead. I planned to see you about adding his name to the altar list of the dead this Sunday."

"Impossible," Father Leary glared. "I would have been called to his side to offer the last sacraments. You will surely go to Hell for lying about something so grevious, Ivy Rose Murphy."

"My father is dead." Ivy swallowed the lump in her throat. "He drowned in the early morning hours of New Year's Day. There were witnesses – there is no body for burial." Ivy expected the church ceiling to come tumbling down around her head. She was looking into the face of a man of God and lying through her teeth.

"I would have been contacted by the proper authorities if something so heinous had affected one of my flock!" Father Leary snapped. "I doubt your word, Ivy Rose Murphy. You'll need to furnish proof of this claim. If indeed there is truth in your words, see Father Massey about paying for a Requiem Mass for the repose of your blessed father's soul!" Father Leary glared. Really, did this chit think he was a clueless cleric?

"There will be no Requiem Mass for my father," Ivy stated, staring boldly into Father Leary's avaricious eyes.

"Shame on you, Ivy Rose Murphy! You're an unnatural daughter. Your sainted father deserves nothing less than a Requiem Mass! A Mass performed by myself, the parish priest."

"I have no intention of paying you to get dressed up in a fancy costume and say a few words into thin air." Ivy wasn't giving in. "I'll see Father Massey about adding my father's name to the altar list of the dead. That is all I'm willing to pay for."

"You will go straight to Hell, Ivy Rose Murphy!" Father Leary tried to hit Ivy across the face but she jumped out of the way. The priest lost his balance and was forced to catch onto the back of a pew.

"I'll be sure to save you a place, Father." Ivy was getting out of there. Her da could sort himself out from Heaven. "By the way, thank you for your offer of condolences for my grievous loss. It was very Christian of you."

Ivy walked down the long aisle, the loose sole of her shoe slapping against the marble floor, her head held high. She was aware of the damnation in the glare of the parish priest but she didn't care.

Chapter 10

"Granny, it's me, Ivy. Can I come in?" Ivy pushed the door to Granny's basement room open.

"You've been running in and out of this room like it was your own private hideaway since you were knee-high to a grasshopper. Why should today be any different?" Granny's voice was sharp enough to cut glass.

"I got the milk and tea yeh wanted." Ivy ignored the old woman's moan and visually checked that Granny was warmly dressed. The wizened apple face was still gleaming from the quick wash Ivy had given it earlier that morning.

"Maisie Reynolds stopped me." Ivy grinned at Granny, both women knowing that getting away from Maisie Reynolds took skill. The long-time neighbour loved to hear herself talk. "She gave me two crubeens. Her Petey picked up a load from the last hog-butchering. He pickled them up himself. Maisie passed me these two on the sly."

Ivy bustled around the old woman's room, more comfortable here than in her own rooms.

"I know how much you love crubeens." Ivy had been watching Granny suck the toes of pig's feet for years. "I was hoping to have them this evening but they're that salty it would bring tears to your eyes. I'll have to put them to soak. We can have them tomorrow. I'll mention to Alf Connelly to check if a head of cabbage and a few potatoes fall off the back of one of his trains."

Alf Connelly worked at the local train depot. The man seemed to have a genius for ripping small holes in the netting used to transport vegetables. He often had onions, carrots, potatoes and other items for sale. When she could afford it Ivy passed Alf a brown penny for the ingredients for a "blind stew". The meatless dish was filling and nourishing.

Ivy wrapped her shawl around her head, grabbed the galvanised bucket and hurried out of the room to fetch fresh water. She needed to get on with her own chores.

Ivy groaned at the long line of women and children waiting to draw water from the only tap in the yard. She couldn't wait. She had a lot of things to get done yet today. She'd give Granny the water she'd drawn for her own use. She'd been out at the tap this morning before anyone else was awake. Ivy hurried to unlock the back door to her own place. She hurried through her da's room with a grimace. She still hadn't touched the place. She must get it done. Her da had been dead for weeks and she could not continue to ignore that fact.

"Sit yourself down, girl," Granny snapped as soon as Ivy returned. "Yeh've time for a cup of tea." Granny's room had the only free-standing stove in the tenements. It had been a nine days' wonder when the woman had the thing installed. The coalburning cast-iron stove was used to heat the room. The top was ideal for slow cooking. Granny kept an old black kettle on the back of the stove simmering throughout the day.

"I could murder a cup of tea." Ivy cleared off the top of the table that was used for Granny's fine stitching – close work, she called it – and eating. "What time is yer woman coming for the tablecloth?" Ivy had spent ten long, cramped, backbreaking hours the previous day doing invisible mending to a Belgian lace tablecloth.

"She'll be here when she gets here." Granny watched the

younger woman buzz around her room like a blue-arsed fly. There were people who swore Ivy Murphy had been born running. "Are yeh short of a few bob?" Granny knew the bulk of the payment should go to Ivy. The girl did all the fine sewing now. Granny's hands were crippled and her old eyes were giving up the ghost.

"When has anyone around here enough money?" Ivy checked on the ham hock and lima beans she'd put on to cook that morning when she'd knocked to awaken Granny. She'd begun taking her meals with Granny since her da died. It was working out well for both of them.

"Here, girl, sit down." Granny had set the table while Ivy prepared a pot of tea for the two of them. "I made yeh a bite." She pushed a chipped plate covered with bread and drippin' towards Ivy.

"Thanks, Granny." Ivy touched Granny's hand with the tips of her fingers. The old woman's hands were crippled and knotted and her dark-brown eyes were slowly being covered by a film of grey, but the old woman was still fiercely independent.

"I talked to Father Massey this morning about yer da." Granny always attended the first Mass of the day – Ivy made sure she was on hand to awaken the old woman. "I don't understand why his death hasn't been mentioned from the altar. For all his faults yer da was a regular Mass-goer." She glared at Ivy, her avoidance of organised religion an old bone to pick between them.

"I told Father Leary about me da's death." Ivy jumped up to pour the weak tea. She couldn't be bothered waiting for it to brew. "Then I went and saw Father Massey so I'd be sure he entered me da in the altar list of the dead." Ivy had been waiting for the reaction to the news of her da's death but nothing had happened. "I can do no more."

"You should go and see Father Leary again yerself, Ivy!" Granny snapped. "It isn't right, it isn't decent. Yeh never even waked the man."

"Granny –" Ivy bit back the sour words she longed to pour

90

from her lips. She knew her da hadn't meant to die but he'd left her in such a state she was having a hard time forgiving him. Ivy stuffed the drippin'-covered bread Granny had prepared into her mouth and swallowed it with most of the tea in her cup. She couldn't say what she was thinking about Father Leary aloud.

"I know, I know!" Granny waved a hand in dismissal. They'd had the same argument many times over the years.

"Those beans should be ready for you to eat for your dinner," Ivy said, meaning the midday meal.

"The best thing yer ma ever did was teach yeh to cook," Granny grinned.

Violet Murphy had been raised with servants. She'd no more idea how to cook than fly. Granny had taught Ivy everything she knew about cooking. In fact, from the first time Ivy waddled into Granny's room the old woman had been teaching and training her. Ivy didn't know how the Murphy family would have survived without the knowledge Granny Grunt shared with her.

"Sarcasm is the lowest form of wit, Granny." Ivy stood to refill Granny's cup. "I have to get back to me round. I'm losing daylight."

Granny poured the fresh tea into her saucer. She closed her eyes in pleasure as she sucked the cooled liquid into her toothless mouth. "I have to admit," she said, "I thought yer ma was out of her mind when she talked about going begging to the big houses on the square but the woman knew what she was talking about."

"Well, me ma would know all about those houses from the other side." Ivy shrugged. "I better get on." She jumped up to tidy the table.

"I'll see yeh later." Granny knew she hadn't much more time on this earth. She wanted to see Ivy settled before she went. "Pop into yer place first and light yer fire. I'll have a bite to eat ready for yeh when yeh finish yer round."

"Yes, master!" Ivy laughed. Granny liked to give the impression she was still in control. "I'll get on."

Ivy pulled her ratty old coat on and resettled her shawl. She had a few more houses she needed to visit before she could call it a day.

Late that same day Ivy stood in the open doorway of her da's room. She stared around the echoing space, feeling her heart break a little more. It was hard to believe her da was really gone. She was still expecting him to explode through the door demanding a meal, a clean shirt, a few bob for his entrance fee to the pub.

Ivy sighed sadly. She'd promised herself she'd tackle his room today. It was time and past for Ivy to claim this room as her own. Ivy could almost feel her da's eyes on her, daring her to go into his room, daring her to touch his stuff.

Ivy, as was her habit, had been back home several times throughout the day to unload her loot and check on Granny. She preferred to collect little and often. It wouldn't do to allow certain shifty characters to see how much she managed to collect on her rounds. The unemployed men who hung around the streets were always on the lookout for an easy mark. The news that Ivy didn't have her da's protection any more wasn't public knowledge yet but Ivy knew. She had to be doubly careful, now she was on her own.

It never ceased to amaze Ivy, the articles people threw away. Still, it wasn't her place to judge. She'd been making money off other people's discards for years. Ivy knew the servants in each house helped themselves to the best of the discarded stuff. It was only right they should have first pick of the items thrown away.

With her weekly visits to their back door, Ivy had become a trusted go-between for the lower-house servants. They allowed Ivy to sell the buttons, ribbons and pins they managed to score for themselves. Ivy, for a small fee, would pass the items on to her contacts. This service had become very lucrative for Ivy over the years.

The upper servants – butler, cook, housekeeper, nanny – had their own contacts for the stuff they managed to score. Violet

Murphy had been shocked by the amount of pilfering that went on in each house. She'd had no idea that servants had their own small trade going on beneath their employers' noses.

On her way home for the last time that day Ivy had stopped at Smith's the greengrocer's to cadge a couple of orange boxes. The wooden crates used to ship oranges were the furniture of choice for the people in The Lane. The crates were in much demand and hard to come by. Now Ivy, standing in the doorway that separated the two rooms, wished she could huddle by the fire and examine her loot but she knew she needed to do something about the back room. The extra space would be a godsend.

Earlier in the evening Ivy had put a match to the fire in her room before joining Granny. Since her da's death Ivy had been able to spend more time with the old woman. Sharing the cost of food and eating together was working out well – for both of them. They'd finished off the pot of ham hock and beans between them then Ivy had got the old woman ready for bed before she left her. She turned her head, looking back over her shoulder to watch the flames in her own fireplace with a dry mouth. She wanted a cup of tea. Ivy did her best thinking sitting at the table under the window with a cup of tea in her hand.

"Well, Da, your name still hasn't been mentioned on the altar list of the dead," Ivy said aloud to the empty room. She'd fallen into the habit of speaking with her father every time she was alone. The man had never listened to her when he was alive but in death he was proving to be great company. "At least no-one's said a dickie-bird to me about your death. That's not normal around here, Da, as you know. I'm sorry about that. I know how you'd love the fuss. I'll probably be excommunicated after that run-in I had with the parish priest a few weeks ago but I did me best."

Ivy didn't feel comfortable in this room. She needed to make this space her own. She sighed and stepped away from the door post. The longer she put off the work the harder it would be for her to clear away all signs of her da. The two rooms were her home now. She could sleep in the back room and set up a workshop in the front room. The thought of being able to spread her stuff around and leave it out without getting a clip around the ear was exciting. She'd have a better idea of what she had and what needed to be done to it. If, that is, she could ever work up enough courage to walk into this darn room and actually touch the things littered around.

"Well, Da, I'm going to pull away that board now."

Éamonn Murphy had covered the black range that was built into the chimneybreast of the back wall. He'd refused to listen all of the times Ivy had begged to be allowed use the range.

"Here goes!" Ivy was surprised by the ease with which she moved the heavy wood panel. She'd expected to need tools to remove the board but the thing came away in her hand. Ivy carried the panel over to the far wall and propped it upright there. She took a deep breath before turning back around, dreading what she'd see. "Ahh, Jaysus, Da!" Ivy pressed her hand to her mouth, pushing back the tears. She wanted to sit on the dirty floor and sob like a baby.

The bloody range was gleaming, polished to within an inch of its life.

"Did you do it for her, Da, for me ma?" Ivy sobbed. The beautiful range was blackened, the brass fittings polished. It shone, gleaming in pride of place. A huge monster of a thing, that stove had allowed Violet Murphy to lord it over her neighbours, now it would make Ivy's life easier.

Violet had demanded that her husband black-lead-polish the stove daily. Ivy remembered her parents giggling like children whenever Éamonn tried to show Violet how to do the work herself. The brass tap gleamed in the light coming from the other room. Ivy was so surprised she lit the gaslamps in this room for the first time in her life. In the bright light the range was still there, still beautiful.

The black range had been the main reason Éamonn Murphy wanted to rent these two rooms. The top of the range could be used for cooking. Violet Murphy had kept the buckets of stew from the penny dinners hot on the top of that stove. The black kettle had sat proudly on top of that range, steam always coming from the spout, ready to make a pot of tea. One side of the range was an oven. The opposite end was a water-container. The red flames of burning coal would glisten behind the black bars of the fire. You opened the brass tap and had hot water on demand.

"I suppose yeh couldn't be bothered with all the work of hauling in water and lighting the fire in here, Da. Yeh were a lazy bugger. If you'd let me use the stove we'd all have been better off. I can tell yeh, I'm going to have hot water on the go all the time." The luxury of it all! Ivy patted the range lovingly.

For the first time Ivy noticed the large mirror that sat comfortably on top of the range. "You weren't worried about your own vanity, I see, Da. I'll be using that too, Da." She picked up the heavy mirror and carried it over to rest against one wall of the room. She avoided examining her own image, afraid that her father's ghost would rise up and belt her around the ears for her sin of vanity.

Ivy opened the oven door, expecting to see empty shelves. Tins of polish and torn rags were crammed into the space. Ivy hoped the chimney had been kept as clean as the range.

Ivy hurried back into her own room, the front room. She shook her head. She really must remember to call the rooms hers now. She grabbed a supply of loose paper from her stockpile stored in orange boxes. She carried the old newspapers into the back room. With a deep breath and crossed fingers, she opened the front grid of the range and shoved paper into the clean fire pit. She set the paper on fire and stood back. The smoke went up the chimney like the answer to a prayer. She was in business.

For the first time in twelve years a fire was lit in the big black range. The range had been at the very heart of the Murphy family home life. Ivy remembered sitting around the fire with her parents and brothers listening to stories about the old days and the characters her da had met on his travels. She'd forgotten all about those happy family times.

Her mother Violet had told stories too but only when her da was away. Violet's stories had seemed like fairy tales to her wide-eyed children. Violet had told stories of servants, balls, clothes and food beyond belief. A life her children would never experience. Violet had talked about Éamonn Murphy as her prince. The love of her life, the man she'd given up everything for. Violet's children had listened to her words in wondrous delight.

Ivy stood back, staring at the range, remembering. Then she became aware of the tears flowing freely down her face. Shaking her head in disgust at her own stupidity, she grabbed the water bucket. She had no time to wallow in memories. Those times were over and gone, best forgotten. She removed the heavy cast-iron plate cut into the top of the range with the special tool she found hanging in its usual place. She was going to fill the water container, right now.

She wouldn't know herself with the luxury of having constant hot water. She didn't intend to let the fire in the range go out again. She'd have to talk to some of the local lads. She'd need them to start bringing any nuggets of coal they found down the docks to her. She'd have to be careful in her choice of supplier. There were some she didn't want to know she'd the money to pay her way. Ivy sighed. She'd get Conn Connelly to act as go-between. You could trust Conn.

Ivy imagined she could feel the room warming up already. She'd bank the fire with wet nuggets when she was out on her rounds. The cheery glow would always be waiting for her when she came home – cold, wet and footsore.

Ivy ran out into the yard, the water bucket banging against her legs. She almost skipped over to the tap, thinking about the uses she could put the range to. For once no-one stood in line for the water tap, there must be some excitement going on somewhere else. Ivy had the tap all to herself, an appreciated luxury. Her mind buzzed with ideas. She'd leave something, even if it was only a blind stew, simmering on the stove while she was out and about. She'd come home to a hot meal. Ivy's mind was spinning, full of her great plans.

Ivy was vaguely aware of people calling out to her but she hurried on with her chore. She heard the shouts and cursing coming from the neighbour's place but paid it no heed. There was always someone having an argument around the place although there seemed to be more than the usual amount of shouting and colourful abuse being dished out tonight. Normally a right barney was entertainment and Ivy would have joined her neighbours but not tonight. She had too much to do and enough problems of her own to be getting on with. She wanted the water container on the range full to capacity.

She'd be able to make her own bread, Ivy suddenly thought. Granny Grunt had taught her how.

Ivy's ma, Violet, had never prepared a meal or in fact done anything for herself before she'd married Éamonn Murphy. Nor did she learn how to do much afterwards: as a child, Ivy thought every mother bought meals from the Penny Dinners. Ivy smiled sadly, remembering days standing in line with her mother, clutching a big covered tin dish tightly.

The Penny Dinners had been set up to serve the poor of the community. The do-gooders didn't seem to realise that the poor didn't have a penny to spare. Ivy's ma had been one of their best customers.

Ivy stared at the stove, forcing the pain away. She refused to remember how lost she'd been when her ma left her alone to look after four men. Without Granny they'd all have ended up in the poorhouse.

Ivy shook herself. She wouldn't think about that – she'd think about her wonderful stove. Granny Grunt had taught her to make nourishing meals from practically nothing. Making the small quantity of bread she'd need would save her a queer few bob. Maybe she'd even try to bake cakes. Oh, there were so many things she could do with that range at her disposal!

Ivy ran back and forth to the standing tap. She emptied each bucket carefully into the range reservoir. When the water was all the way up to the top of the container Ivy replaced the heavy lid. Then she ran out to fill the bucket once more – she needed clean fresh water on hand.

She fought back the memory of her mother's face. She didn't want to remember. The past was the past.

Chapter 11

With rainwater dripping off the brim of his battered leather hat, down his nose and into his abundant beard, Jem Ryan hunkered down to wait. Staring at the wet cobbled street that sparkled and gleamed under the flickering gas streetlamps, Jem sighed. A month into the new year, and what had he done? He needed to make changes in his life. He'd been drifting, letting life pass.

In this year, 1925, according to the newspapers and those in the know, everything was supposed to be different, better, newer, with more opportunities. Home Rule, no more fighting for Independence. Jem's sigh shook him almost to his boots. Strange how in the new Ireland the same folk were rich and getting richer. The poor, of whom there were so many, kept getting the short end of the stick.

Rosie shook her head, sending rivers of raindrops flying in every direction. A passing paperboy, soaked in the sudden spray, cursed and shook his fist in Jem's direction. Nothing much Jem could do about the situation. The day was cold and wet, miserable in fact. Rosie, the poor old nag, was getting too old for this lark.

With a heavy sigh he decided this would be his last fare of the day. The Galway train was late, again. The long line of waiting hansom cabs snaked around Kingsbridge Station, appearing and disappearing in the grey mist that coated everything. The horses waiting patiently in their harness dropped their heads behind the cab in front, hoping to escape some of the drizzle.

With a screaming roar of steam the Galway train chugged into the station. Dublin, the final stop, for many would be the start of a much longer journey. The long train journey from the West of Ireland brought dreamers and schemers into the city of Dublin. Some of the people getting off the train would be taking ship out of Dublin and on to bigger worlds.

The carriage horses didn't react to the hissing noise. The clouds of white steam, the sudden explosion of noise didn't bother them. The whistles and shrieks, shouts from porters, banging of doors, it was all familiar to them.

Jem counted the cabs in front of him. He was fifth in line. He shouldn't have any problem picking up a fare from the passengers on this train. Rosie danced a little in her traces. She knew what the sudden noise meant. Jem shook the water from the hessian sack that covered his shoulders, protecting his coat against the falling rain. He removed his hat to run his fingers through his explosion of chestnut-brown hair and shook his head, trying to get the water out of his lushly flowing beard. He removed the soaked sacking from his lap, preparing to greet his customers. A friendly word, a helping hand, sometimes meant a bigger tip.

A line of porters pushing heavily laden trolleys began to appear through the mist and rain. In their navy pea jackets, peaked hats pulled down low, the porters blew whistles, shouted and waved their arms around, trying to appear more important than they really were. They too needed their tips. Newspaper boys yelled in a bid to attract the befuddled travellers' attention.

"I hope I don't get that auld besom," Jem muttered as he watched a woman, as round as she was tall, push and prod the child in front of her. There was no need for the poking as far as Jem could see. The little one was moving right along with the crowd. The waterfall of black curls that flowed down the child's back reminded Jem of Ivy Murphy. Ivy had been a joy to watch running wild around the place. That was before her mother took off. Not that Ivy was ever as richly dressed as the young child being battered in front of his eyes.

Jem had enjoyed the chance to spend time with Ivy Murphy. Sharing a pot of tea with her had been the high point of his social life lately. He wanted to have another chance to spend time with her. He doubted it would happen. Éamonn Murphy ran off men who showed any interest in Ivy.

Jem ignored the hustle and bustle all around him. His attention kept returning to the woman and child. He wondered about their relationship. He hoped the woman wasn't the child's mother, not with the pucks and pinches she was giving her. Perhaps she was delivering the child to family in Dublin. Jem made a quick wish for the child, hoping the people she was coming to were kinder than the woman with her now.

The pair were well dressed in rich if plain clothing. The leather boots on their feet were of good quality and showed no sign of wear. The hats on their heads were the work of a skilled milliner. The luggage on the porter's trolley matched and was obviously shop-bought. There was no handmade string parcels in the lot as far as he could see. These two were not short of a bob or two.

Why then, Jem wondered, was the woman so sour-looking? She hadn't stopped poking and pinching the child even when the line of passengers in front of her stopped moving. Jem could see the woman's lips moving. The beady eyes moved all around. He could see her nose wrinkle even from here. He was sure she wouldn't be a big tipper. Jem counted porters' trolleys and by his reckoning the cab in front of him would pick up that pair.

Jem didn't know why he was paying so much attention to the mismatched pair. For years he'd been floating along, moving from day to day without bringing bother to anyone and never being bothered. After the time he'd spent with Ivy Jem saw his life through new eyes. He didn't like what he saw. Perhaps it had more to do with the start of a new year but he didn't think so. He'd never been troubled like this in previous years.

"Oh no," Jem sighed.

The woman was shaking her head and pointing a hand in the direction of Jem's brougham. The brougham was a larger vehicle than most of the other hansom cabs. The heavier vehicle was old-fashioned and it wasn't as fast as the other cabs. Jem knew that but he refused to give in to the current demand for speed. Too many horses were being injured.

"Evening, ladies," Jem called, jumping down from his perch. A fare was a fare after all. He couldn't afford to be fussy. He turned to give the porter a hand with the big trunk and mountain of small leather cases sitting on the trolley.

"Open the carriage door quickly!" Mary Rose Donnelly snapped. "I'll not have my belongings sitting out in this weather. Put it all inside the carriage." She waved her hands around in the fashion of someone accustomed to being obeyed.

"There will be no room for yourself and the little madam inside, Missus," said the porter.

He wanted his dinner and a pint. He wanted to get out of this miserable weather and go home to his wife. Mostly he wanted to throw the luggage off his trolley and get away from the moaning harridan he'd been unfortunate enough to pick up. The porter had seen the wealth displayed by the woman's clothing and her stack of matching luggage. He'd pushed his way to her side, confident of a generous tip. That didn't last long – the woman was a horror. You got them from time to time in his job.

"Would you be wanting two cabs then?" he asked.

He had been forced to listen to this woman complain from the moment he'd picked up her luggage. He needed to get rid of her and her belongings. Then he'd try to pick up another passenger or he'd be returning home without a penny in his pocket.

"Don't be ridiculous!" Mary Rose Donnelly snapped. "Just load the luggage into the cab and go about your business." She longed to box the porter's ears. She would have done if one of her father's servants had been as surly in his manner.

The porter shrugged and exchanged a commiserating glance

with Jem. The two men huffed and struggled to get the large trunk into the carriage. The cab interior hadn't been designed for luggage. It was a comfortable ride for passengers with most of the space being taken up by the long leather seats facing each other. The floor space was designed to accommodate only the passengers' legs and feet.

The two men, swearing under their breath and grunting with the strain, managed to wedge the large trunk between the two seats, taking up all of the available floor space.

"Put the smaller packages on one of the seats," Mary Rose ordered. "We are not travelling far this evening." She shot Jem a look of such disdain he should have frozen in place. "I've made enquiries. I know the address I seek is only moments from this station so do not attempt to take me on a tour of the city. I know how much the fare will be. I will not pay a penny more."

"Yes, Ma'am." Jem picked the child up in his arms. The little one would need help fitting her body into the meagre space left by the luggage stacked on the passenger seat. The child didn't weigh much. One little arm went around his neck and shoulder and Jem found himself looking into the biggest, saddest, greenest eyes he'd ever seen.

"Thank you," Emerald O'Connor whispered. It had been so long since she'd experienced kindness. With a deep sigh she put her head down on the man's damp shoulder. Emerald wanted to go to sleep and wake up somewhere, anywhere away from her aunt. It wasn't to be. The kind man put her carefully into the carriage in the space he'd made for her beside the pile of small cases, and turned his attention to her aunt.

"You may assist me," Mary Rose snapped to the porter.

"You got yourself into this position, Missus," the porter growled, turning away. "Get yourself out of it."

"Allow me." Jem offered his hand to the disagreeable woman. He couldn't believe she was related to the little girl who'd almost stolen his heart out of his chest. The little one was so sad. There seemed to be a world of hurt in her green eyes. Why couldn't this woman be kind to her? Well, he wasn't going to attempt to lift the auld biddy up into the carriage. He'd do himself a mischief. She looked as if she weighed a ton.

"Really, if this is the kind of service on offer in Dublin I'm glad I won't be staying long." With the assistance of Jem she forced her body into the seat, swinging her legs over the trunk and onto the seat across from her. Mary Rose didn't care how inelegant she looked. She refused to spend any of the cash she had secured around her person. She hadn't far to go and then she'd be free. She ignored the child cowering in the corner.

Emerald tried to disappear into the corner of the carriage. She was too close to her aunt's feet. She still had the bruises from the last time her aunt lost her temper and beat her senseless. Emerald knew from the pain in her body that her aunt must have kicked her when she was insensible.

"I wish to go to the Industrial School at Goldenbridge!" Mary Rose snapped, watching her niece cringe with malicious delight. She'd drop the brat off with the nuns. Mary Rose Donnelly had everything planned down to the smallest detail. She was going to follow her own star. She'd take her loot then she'd disappear forever.

"Yes, ma'am." Jem felt the hair rise on his body. He wanted to throw up. What did this woman plan to do at that place? Jem knew more about the goings-on in Goldenbridge than most people. He still had the nightmares to prove it.

"I know it's not far from here, so get along." Mary Rose smirked and nudged her niece with her foot. "The nuns will soon beat you into shape, you little heathen!" She ignored the gaping jarvey. He was a servant after all and not even one in her employ.

Jem closed the carriage door gently. He wanted to slam the thing in the auld biddy's face but the carriage was his livelihood. He needed to take care of it. He walked slowly towards Rosie's head.

"I want you to walk so slow you're almost at a standstill," he whispered into Rosie's ear. He would swear at times the horse understood what he said.

Jem climbed up to the driver's seat and took the reins in his hands.

"Why are we not moving?" Mary Rose Donnelly lowered the window and was leaning her upper body dangerously far out. She was resting the weight of her body on the window rim.

"We're in line, ma'am." Jem hunched his shoulders. Even here in his own little world that woman was ordering him around. "You jumped the line when you picked my cab. I have to wait till the horses in front move off." He didn't think the woman would know he was lying.

"Gives you more time to look forward to your new life at the orphanage."

Mary Rose's voice came quite clearly to Jem. She was making no effort to lower her screech. The malice in the words and tone had him shivering. The woman couldn't possibly mean to leave that little girl in Goldenbridge. It was known to locals as Goldenbridge Girls' Home but, to everyone who knew it, it was Hell.

What could he do? He was just a jarvey, a cab driver. He had no power here, no connections. He couldn't stop this woman doing whatever she wanted.

"The nuns will soon knock all your high and mighty airs out of you! Are you listening to what I'm saying to you, you little horror?"

"Yes, Aunt."

The resigned suffering in that little voice had Jem tightening his hands on the reins. Rosie took that as her signal to move and stepped out of the line, her steel-shod hooves ringing across the cobbles.

"There will be no more 'Emerald' nonsense. The nuns will give you a good Christian name. You won't find anyone to spoil and pet you where you're going. You will soon be down on your knees." Mary Rose laughed aloud. "When you're not on your knees praying for God's mercy you'll be on your knees scrubbing floors. Oh, I wish I could see that. It would do my heart good. Are you listening to me, brat?"

"Yes, Aunt."

Jem wanted to jump down off the box and punch the auld crow. She was torturing the little one. Jem turned Rosie's head. He'd take a diversion, give himself time to think. Was there anything he could do to save the little one from the fate that her aunt seemed to have in store for her? He'd go past Kilmainham Gaol and on towards Islandbridge. They'd reach Goldenbridge eventually.

Jem didn't know what to do. How could he deliver a child into the tender care of the nuns? Jem knew the only way any child escaped the true horror of the nuns' treatment was if she had relations that visited. If a child had someone who checked to see that they were safe, the nuns kept their hands to themselves. Was there some way he could claim to be a relative of the little girl being tormented in his carriage?

Of course, Jem, he jeered himself mentally. The nuns are going to believe a great big hairy galoot like you is related to that dainty little girl. Why not go the whole hog and claim to be her father come to take her home! That'll work a treat. A bitter smile creased the wall of hair that covered Jem's face.

Jem listened to the woman spew her hatred out at the child. He'd never before heard such bitterness. It seemed that everything that went wrong in the woman's life was always someone else's fault. He listened while the vile woman hissed venomous curses on her father's head, her brother, her dead sister – the child's mother apparently – all came in for their share of bitter curses.

Jem took a relieved breath when the bitter diatribe stopped. Too soon. The woman wasn't finished. She began to vilify some cleric, some bishop no less. The bishop must be as demented as the woman calling down curses on his name. Bishop Troy had apparently suggested that the bitter, twisted woman travelling in his cab would make a good nun. As Dubliners would say, sure she'd make a great nun where none are wanted.

"He should have married me!"

Jem jerked at the shouted words.

"He was far too old for my sainted sister! The fool man married her and carried her off. *Why couldn't they have stayed away?*" The last was the scream of an angry cat. "How dare they think I would be happy to look after their child? I was forced to look at his eyes in your face every cursed day!" Mary Rose was finally free to say everything she'd been bottling up inside for so long. "What is that noise?"

Mary Rose Donnelly again opened the carriage window and poked her body out of the carriage. Jem was surprised she'd been able to hear anything over the sound of her own voice.

"You need to be careful, Missus." Jem turned to look over his shoulder and down at the disagreeable face glaring at him. The woman was a great deal younger then he'd originally thought. She dressed like an old woman and her constant bickering stopped anyone from looking closely.

"There is some kind of demonstration going on outside Kilmainham Gaol." Jem turned to examine the crowd pushing and shoving around his carriage. He couldn't make out what they were shouting. He knew he didn't want to be caught up in whatever this was.

"I was not informed our journey would take us past a gaol!" Mary Rose shouted. With her anger riding high, she shoved her body further out of the carriage, shaking her fist up in the jarvey's direction.

"If you'd sit back down, Missus, I'll get us out of here."

Jem didn't like the mood of the crowd. In horrified slow motion he watched a stone shoot out from the crowd. The stone hit his passenger bang in the middle of her forehead. He could actually hear the noise of the impact. The child inside the carriage screamed. Jem watched his passenger slide bonelessly back into the interior of the carriage.

"Gee up, Rosie!" Jem grabbed the whip that sat in the holder at the side of his seat. He cracked the old leather whip over the heads of the crowd. Rosie, unaccustomed to the noise, neighed almost fiercely and shook her head. She danced in the traces, her steel shoes striking sparks from the cobbles that covered the road. He had to get out of here. The shaken sobs coming from the interior of his cab broke his heart.

Jem inched his carriage out from the crowd that backed away from the dancing horse. He needed to get as far away as possible. With his hand shaking violently he returned the whip to its upright holder. He allowed Rosie to take control of the carriage. The horse knew what she was about. Jem was shaking too much to be of any use. The woman must be very badly hurt. He had heard the rock hit her head.

Jem stopped the carriage moments after Rosie turned into Islandbridge. The road passed directly in front of the Goldenbridge building. Jem didn't even want to think about that. When he'd made doubly sure the brake was in place, he jumped down from his seat. He walked back quickly to the carriage and pulled the door open. The child screamed and jumped from the carriage directly into his arms. Her entire body was shaking.

"Ssssh, it will be all right." Jem patted the little back gently. "Let me see here." Jem tried to push the child away from him but she clung like a limpet. "I need to check if you're hurt, petal."

"No!" Emerald shook her head frantically.

Jem put his hand behind the child's head and glanced into the carriage. His heart almost stopped. Unless he was very much mistaken his passenger was dead. She lay where she'd fallen, her mouth open, her eyes glazing over as death took the life from her body.

"Everything will be fine, petal."

Jem needed to think. He could drive the carriage to the nearest police station. He could prove he had nothing to do with the woman's death. But if he did that what would happen to the child? She'd be taken to Goldenbridge and forgotten. He couldn't do that to any child.

"I'm going to let you talk to my horse. Her name is Rosie." Jem put the girl on the ground by the horse's head. He watched carefully, checking the little girl wasn't afraid of the animal that towered over her head. Sensing no problem, he left the child and hurried back to the open door of the carriage.

Jem stood staring, incapable of thought. He didn't feel capable of movement. His heart was beating so hard it almost rattled his ribcage. The woman whose voice had called down curses on the heads of everyone she knew was dead. There was no mistaking that look. Jem had seen it too many times. She was on her way to meet her Maker. Jem blessed himself, his arm like a ton weight as he forced himself to complete the motion.

The sound of an approaching horse and the noise of wheels turning snapped Jem out of his frozen state. He leaned into the carriage and with hurried movements pulled the woman's body straight. With the trunk between the seats he was able to drape the body over the entire space. It was a blessing the woman was so short. Her feet and head reached from one side of the carriage to the other. He pulled her cloak around her body, passed his hand over her face and shut her staring eyes. Jem turned and with a casual wave in the direction of the passing cabby went back to the horse's head.

"Your aunt is sleeping," Jem said to the little girl. "If I help you up into the carriage will you be able to sleep too?"

"Are you going to take me to the place where they lock bold little girls away?" Emerald O'Connor didn't believe her aunt was sleeping. "Did I kill her?"

"No, you most certainly did not!"

"May I stay up there with you?" Emerald didn't want to go back into the carriage with her aunt. She didn't care if she never saw her aunt again.

"You'll get soaking wet." Jem didn't want to put the poor creature in with her aunt's dead body. He needed to get out of here. He had to get away in case any questions were ever asked about him and his vehicle.

"I don't mind," Emerald whispered. She'd far rather stay with this man who had kind eyes and hands.

Jem made a sudden decision. "I'll wrap you in the impermeable I keep for Rosie." He needed to move. He'd think about this situation as he travelled along. What in the name of God was he going to do now?

He wrapped the child, lifted her onto the driver's seat and climbed up beside her.

"This is nice." Emerald liked being so high up. She yawned hugely and with a sigh buried her head under Jem's arm.

"Walk on!" Jem snapped the reins and Rosie began to move slowly down the gaslamp-lit street.

Jem resisted the urge to hide the child as he passed in front of the dark gloomy building of Goldenbridge. He would not be pulling in there this evening.

Jem hoped the clip-clop of Rosie's hooves and the familiar rattle of the wheels over the cobblestones would help him relax. The little girl was fast asleep, her head nestled into his armpit. He checked to see the child could breathe. With his heart in his mouth and a dead body in his carriage Jem drove through the silent Dublin streets, desperately trying to think. He wanted to keep driving around Dublin's streets but knew he couldn't – the little one needed to be somewhere warm and dry – she was beginning to shiver.

"Let's go home, Rosie." Jem snapped the reins to signal the horse.

Jem felt sick, his heart was jumping every time someone passed by. He needed to be somewhere safe, somewhere he could think in peace. His teeth were rattling in his mouth. He wasn't cold, he was terrified. What was he going to do? He knew he should drive to the police station and leave the woman and child in their hands but he couldn't do it. He knew what would happen to the little girl nestled so trustingly against him.

Jem's uncle had driven the "death wagon" for years. When Jem first arrived in Dublin his uncle insisted Jem accompany him on his rounds. The death wagon was a lucrative portion of the cabby business. The sights Jem had seen over those years haunted him. The first thing Jem did upon his uncle's untimely death was cancel the agreement. Jem couldn't bear to continue doing something so soul-destroying every night. But the loss of income meant Jem had to work longer hours.

The death wagon rattled around the Dublin streets in the darkest part of the night. The drivers picked up unclaimed bodies from hospitals, homes and the city morgue. The tiny young battered bodies were the stuff of nightmare. Jem hadn't minded so much picking up dead adults. They'd lived their lives. The children and babies he had seen thrown without care into the back of the open wagon had sickened him.

The number of times the wagon picked up some innocent little white body from Goldenbridge had struck Jem as excessive. He'd shocked his uncle by examining some of the young corpses. The marks of constant physical abuse had horrified Jem. He wouldn't allow a cat of his to be housed in Goldenbridge. There was no way he could deliver the little girl snoring softly by his side to that house.

"What am I going to do with you?" Jem whispered down to the little girl at his side.

Jem tried to think of some family he knew who might take in a lost child. He mentally ran through a list of the couples he knew with young children. They were all having a hard time financially. He couldn't ask them to take in another mouth to feed.

He could offer to pay Ivy Murphy to take care of the child for him but he'd never give another young girl child into Éamonn Murphy's hands. The good Lord alone knew what that man would make the child do to earn her keep. But Ivy might know of a family who could help him out. Ivy travelled the squares and blocks around the lane on foot practically daily. She might know of some woman who could help. Jem would work harder than ever to pay for the child's keep.

He'd been stopping earlier and earlier to protect Rosie. He couldn't continue on like this. He'd been letting the business drop off in the two years since he'd inherited it from his uncle. The livery had been a going concern in his uncle's day – bustling. Jem had neglected everything but Rosie and this carriage. That had to stop.

Jem's mother Mary Ryan would click her tongue in disgust and tell him he was being a hard-headed moron. Mary Ryan would have seen the events of this evening as a sign from above. She'd have clapped her son around the ears and told him to wake up. Jem could almost hear his mother's voice in his ear. "How much more of a sign do you want, you great gobeen? Maybe you'd like an angel with a flaming sword?" With this evening's events it would appear some deity was taking an interest in Jem Ryan's life. He'd better start paying attention to what was going on around him. His sigh shook his body.

"Bide a minute, petal." Jem let the little body drop onto his seat. He jumped down from the high driver's seat and with a slap on Rosie's rump he passed the horse and prepared to pull open the huge double doors leading into his livery.

Jem was sure eyes were watching him but he couldn't think about that right now. He needed to lead Rosie, still in her traces, into the barn-like structure. He'd close and lock the doors at his back. Then he'd be free to think about the nightmare situation he found himself in.

He'd need help. There was no two ways about it – he couldn't handle this on his own. There was only one person Jem could think of who could help him now. Ivy Murphy. The woman was quick at thinking on her feet. Jem needed help now more than he ever had in his life before. He'd ask Ivy Murphy.

Chapter 12

Ivy pulled the tea chests from the side of the fireplace. She'd be able to leave them out. There would be no-one to shout at her about the mess. She put the bed platform on top of the boxes and spread her day's takings on top.

She'd scored two damaged porcelain dolls today. Ivy had a tea chest full of doll parts. She'd see if she could mend these two dolls. She had women at the Haymarket and the Daisy market who bought all the dolls she could score. If she couldn't mend them she'd keep the parts and sell the clothes.

Violet Murphy had started her 'round' out of desperation. She'd gambled on being able to pass the stuff people threw out on to others at a profit. Violet's knowledge of quality goods had been a bonus. She'd taught Ivy to appreciate and recognise quality items. Violet's 'round' became the main income for the Murphy family.

Violet had been able to keep Éamonn in check with a smile and a kiss. But when Ivy took over the business she learned to hide the best of what she scored. The items she'd known would bring in a handsome sum, she'd left with Granny. She'd sold those items only in an emergency. She couldn't do that too often or her da would have caught on. The man seemed to have a nose for the scent of money.

Ivy returned to the back room. She stood making a mental list of things she wanted to do. The bed kept drawing her attention. She didn't remember what it felt like to sleep in an actual bed. The sheets needed to be boiled. The luxury horsehair mattress that repelled all known bugs needed to be turned.

Ivy remembered her ma and da giggling in that big bed. Ivy hadn't understood when things started to go bad. The fights between her ma and da frightened her. The worst fights always came after a visit from Father Leary.

"I can't live this life any more!" Ivy remembered her ma screaming at her da with tears pouring down her face. "I don't want a baby a year! It will kill me! We can't feed and clothe the children we have. Father Leary can talk all he likes about 'increase and multiply'," Violet's voice when she said those words had been ugly, "but that fat lump doesn't have to find the money to run a household."

Ivy understood now. She'd seen the girls she'd grown up with marry young and produce a baby a year. The girl she'd been closest to growing up, Nancy Hackett, was trying to raise six children under five years old and look after a husband, all in one room.

That didn't mean Ivy forgave her mother. If Granny Grunt hadn't helped, what would have happened to the children Violet left to fend for themselves?

A soft sound, like a dog scratching the rear door, had Ivy jumping in fright.

"Ivy, thank God you're home! I was hoping I could attract your attention without alerting The Lane. You know what people are like for talking." Jem Ryan stood outlined in the open doorway.

"What's wrong, Jem?" Ivy had never seen Jem Ryan is such a state. The man was trembling if she wasn't mistaken.

"I can't tell you here." Jem looked over his shoulder. "I need you to come over to my place, please." He shrugged. "If you could turn invisible that would help."

"You're being very mysterious." Ivy grinned. "How the heck

am I supposed to turn invisible? The gas lamps are shining in case you haven't noticed."

"I'll explain everything if you'll step over the way."

"You go back. Leave the people portal open." Ivy was referring to the small human entry way cut into the giant stable doors. "I'll follow in a few minutes."

Jem nodded gratefully and left.

Ivy closed and locked the door.

"How am I supposed to become invisible?" She pushed her fingers through her short hair. With her fingers buried in her hair she froze. She might be able to pass herself off as a young lad.

Ivy dropped her skirt and pulled on a pair of her da's trousers. They were clean. She was planning to sell her da's clothes. Éamonn Murphy's stuff was of the best quality and hardly worn. Ivy thought she'd get a good price for them. It was only fair since it was her earnings that had paid for the clothes.

Ivy pulled a ratty old jumper that dwarfed her, from one of her tea chests. With her da's spare jacket on, and her da's old cap pulled down to her ears, she left by the front door. If someone saw a young lad leaving her place it would give them something to talk about. Ivy locked the door, buried her chin in her chest and hurried across the courtyard. Her hand had only touched the handle of the smaller door of the livery when it was pulled open and she was jerked into the stables.

"In the name of God, Jem!" Ivy felt like kicking the man. He'd frightened the life out of her.

She opened her mouth to blast him but the sight of the little girl huddled against Jem's chest stopped her cold.

"What's going on, Jem?"

"I need help." Jem said simply. "I can't explain right now." Jem's head dipped in the direction of the child in his arms. "Can you put Emerald to bed? I need to put Rosie up for the night." Jem didn't comment on Ivy's outlandish appearance. He'd asked her to become invisible and, God bless her, the woman had done her best.

"No problem." Ivy was mystified. "Do you have a nightdress

or something she can sleep in?" Ivy didn't imagine the little one normally slept in her clothes, the quality of the child's garments screamed money to Ivy.

"There are clean undershirts in the chest of drawers by my bed use one of them until I sort everything out." Jem hadn't thought of something for the child to sleep in. He hadn't been able to think about anything but the dead body in his carriage.

"Right. Emerald, is it?" Ivy waited for the child to nod. "I'll give you a piggyback."

Ivy bent down, expecting Emerald to climb on her back, but the child just stood there, looking mystified.

What kind of child doesn't know how to piggyback, thought Ivy.

"I'll carry the little one up the ladder, Ivy. Then I'll come back and take care of Rosie."

Jem was up the ladder with the child like greased lightning, leaving Ivy to follow. Ivy was pleased with the freedom the trousers gave her.

"I'll leave you to it." Jem disappeared from the room. Jem's living area was a well-built large room with its own walls and entrance, set well back from the lip of the stable loft.

"Let's get you settled." Ivy wanted to take the time to look around the room but first she needed to take care of the little girl sitting so still and silent upon the bed. She did take the time to notice that the place was spotlessly clean and everything was in its proper place. "We'll get you out of these clothes." Ivy dropped to her knees and began to open the laces on the little girl's boots. The child looked sweaty and clammy. Ivy assumed it was the result of travelling. "We'll give you a quick lick and a promise of a wash and get you into bed." She pulled off one boot and then the other. "Oh, sweetie, I'm sorry!"

The little girl's feet were bleeding. The expensive stockings were stuck into the bleeding spots. The boots, a superior quality child's boot, were at least a size too small. Ivy wouldn't question the child but she'd be demanding an explanation from Jem.

"We'll leave your socks alone," Ivy said gently. "I don't know my way around so we'll wait until Jem comes up. We can soak your feet in warm water. The socks will float right off."

Ivy felt she was talking to a ghost. The little girl watched everything with her big sad green eyes. She hadn't even complained at the pain she must have felt when Ivy pulled the boots off her feet.

"We'll get these clothes off you." Ivy had to struggle to get the coat off the child. In spite of the wealth demonstrated by the quality of the cut and fabric, the coat was several sizes too small. Ivy helped the child struggle out of clothes that were meant for a child a lot smaller than this little girl.

When Ivy opened the ties on the cotton slip she bit back a cry. The little one's back was covered in bruises. It was obvious some kind of switch had been used with a great deal of force to beat the dickens out of the child.

"Right, Rosie is in her bed and ready for sleep." Jem forced cheer into his voice when he joined the two females. "How are things in here?"

"We need a bowl of warm water." Ivy gave a jerk of her head towards the child's feet.

The look of horror on Jem's face answered one question at least. He'd had no idea of the state of the child.

"Let me get that organised." Jem kept the fury out of his voice with effort. "Do we need any medicines?"

"No, warm water will soak off these socks."

"The funny lady said my socks would float away," Emerald was bold enough to say. She felt safe now the man with the gentle eyes and hands was here.

"Why am I a funny lady?" That accent isn't from around here, Ivy thought. It's also an upper-crust accent if I'm not mistaken.

"Because you're wearing a gentleman's trousers and hat!" Emerald giggled.

"So I am." Ivy grinned.

Jem and Ivy busied themselves getting the child ready for bed. Jem soaked the little feet then Ivy wrapped her in a soft cotton long-sleeved winter vest belonging to Jem. It covered the child from neck to feet and then some. The sleeves, until Ivy rolled them back, hung down in a way that had little Emerald giggling in delight. Ivy brushed the child's hair with a brush belonging to Rosie. The two adults made every effort to reassure the little one. While they fussed and petted the child both adults wondered about the strange situation they found themselves in.

"She's asleep." Ivy had been sitting on the side of Jem's big bed, gently rubbing the child's back. The deep breathing and gentle snores reassured both adults.

Ivy stood and poked Jem in the chest. "Start talking," she said softly but in deadly earnest.

"Where to start?" Jem's sigh came up from his boots.

"At the beginning is usually the best place." Ivy pulled Jem away from the bed by his elbow. They didn't need to wake the child. "Where in the hell did that child come from?" She pointed across the room at the little figure on the big bed. "She's not from around here, that's for sure, and unless I'm very much mistaken she's a member of the quality. What the hell have you got me into, Jem Ryan?" Ivy's whisper was almost a shout.

"*Shh . . .*" Jem glanced at Emerald. She hadn't moved. "I've got meself into a right pickle. That's the truth."

"That doesn't surprise me." Ivy poked Jem again. "What I want to know is where that child came from. Where's her family?"

"Her aunt's dead body is downstairs in my carriage." Jem began to giggle hysterically. The stresses of the evening were finally getting to him.

"In the name of Jaysus, Jem!" Ivy croaked. "What's going on here?"

"I'll put the kettle on," Jem calmed down enough to say. "It's a long story and I haven't a clue about the ending."

"The ending is usually a dead body."

"That's only the start." Jem sighed and pulled open the door that led from his room out into the stable loft. "I'll fetch water."

"Jem?" Ivy stood in the open doorway and watched Jem's head disappear over the ledge as he used the ladder to slide down to the stable floor. She turned to glance at the sleeping child.

With a bewildered shake of her head she closed and bolted the bottom part of the half door that led into Jem's room. She walked over to the lip of the loft and watched Jem below her fill the kettle. "Jem!"

"What?" Jem looked up.

"Is there really a dead body in there?" Ivy pointed her chin towards the carriage.

"Yes, there is and I don't know what the hell I'm going to do about it."

"You'll be explaining to me how you come to have a dead body on hand, Jem Ryan." Ivy stood with her hands on her hips, practically glaring holes in Jem's shoulders as she gazed down on him.

"Look, there was an accident – she got hit on the head, I'll explain everything to yeh, Ivy, I promise, but can we leave it for the minute . . ." Jem twisted the tap closed with a force that almost snapped the top off, "I'll explain it to you as soon as I figure out how the feck I got meself into this mess."

"I don't claim to know a great deal about dead bodies." Ivy started to climb down the ladder. It would be better to have this conversation out of the child's hearing. "But hadn't we better get it out of your carriage?"

"Jaysus, she could stiffen up!" Jem dropped the kettle in fright.

"I'll give yeh a hand." Ivy walked up behind him. Seeing the worried look Jem sent in the direction of his room, she added, "I left the top half of the door to your place open. If the little one wakes up and tries to open the bottom half of the door we'll hear her."

They hurried over to the carriage standing in the middle of the large open area inside the entrance of the livery building. Jem hurried around to the other side of the vehicle.

"It's all right." His voice came from the interior of the carriage. "She's not stiff yet, praise the good Lord, because she's a woman who liked her food."

Ivy opened the door nearest to her and stared in at the dead woman. Jem had clambered in on top of the large trunk which was wedged in the floor space. "You're not joking'," said Ivy. "She's like a ruddy barrel. Here, give her a shove over here. I'll pull her out by the feet."

"Show a little respect," Jem said, forced to work on his knees as he struggled to push the woman forward.

"Me nerves are shot, Jem Ryan, so don't you be talking to me about respect." Ivy groaned as she tried to pull the dead weight from the carriage. "Hold it, hold it!" she shouted.

"What's wrong?" Jem demanded, straining to move the woman's body.

"Don't talk soft! 'What's wrong?'" Ivy snapped. "We're manhandling a dead body, for Jaysus sake! What's *right* about that?"

"Ivy, me arms feel like I'm swinging a baby elephant around the place!"

They wrestled and pushed until the woman's body was finally half in, half out of the carriage door nearest to Ivy. Jem jumped out and rushed around to give Ivy a hand.

"We need to pull her all the way out. You can hold her up against the cab." Ivy was studying the clothes the woman wore. "We need to get her out of these fancy clothes."

"What? Jaysus, Ivy, you want me to strip the woman naked?"

"Well, you already killed her. How much worse could stripping her be?"

"I did not kill her, Ivy Murphy!" Jem roared. "She got hit in the head by a flying stone! It was an accident. I told yeh."

"Well, the woman's dead and we can't leave her in these fancy clothes."

"What's wrong with her clothes?" Jem gritted his teeth. They needed to get the bloody woman all the way out of the carriage.

"They shout money and lots of it, you fool!" Ivy dropped to her knees. "I'll get her boots off before we pull her all the way out." She opened the laces and pulled the boots from the woman's feet. There was no sign of cuts or bleeding from these boots. Ivy gave the butter-soft leather a look. The boots looked awfully big for the little fat feet they covered.

"Right," Ivy stood up. "We can pull her all the way out now. You hold her up while I get the rest of this off her."

"I can't be stripping a woman naked," Jem objected.

"If it offends your delicate sensibilities, close your feckin' eyes!"

"You don't half know some big words, Ivy Murphy." Jem kept his eyes averted. He obeyed Ivy's barked orders to move, budge, shift, while she ruthlessly stripped every stitch of clothing from the dead woman.

"It comes from listening to the storytellers whenever I got the chance and making me brothers read to me while I sewed of an evening."

It didn't matter what they talked about. It helped to take their minds off what they were doing. With swift skilled fingers Ivy opened what needed to be opened and pushed and shoved at whatever else there was.

"I remember you sitting on the staircase, your eyes as big as saucers." Jem hadn't always been able to attend the frequent story evenings put on in one or other of the tenement buildings. "You were always asking questions, it seemed to me." Jem desperately wanted to be finished with this chore.

"If you don't ask questions how can you learn anything?"

"I suppose."

"I always thought the storytellers were magical."

Finally she straightened up. The woman was naked as the day she was born. Ivy tried not to look at her. The woman deserved some dignity.

"That's it. We need something to wrap the body in."

"Ivy." Jem blushed scarlet under his covering of hair. "The body is going to empty itself." He didn't know how to explain what was about to happen.

"Help me lower her to the floor," Ivy snapped. "You get a stall ready and be quick about it. This woman was obviously a great lover of food."

"What?"

"Jaysus, Jem! The horses don't use a chamber pot!" She

glared at him. If her hands had been free she'd have given him a box around the ears. "Put a load of hay down and we'll lay your one out. If we cover her up with a load of hay we can leave her here while you tell me what the hell you've got me into."

"Oh, right." Jem jumped to obey his instructions. He was glad Ivy was able to think. He was still frozen in horror at the events of this evening.

Between them they wrestled the figure to the stable floor.

"What did your one want with all this luggage, do you know, Jem?" Ivy looked at the bags stacked in the carriage interior. It beat thinking about the naked dead woman at her feet. "Do you know which one belongs to the child?"

"I haven't a clue." Jem shouted from the empty stall he was preparing. He kicked straw into a bed that would cushion the woman's body. "Okay, this is ready."

Between the two of them they dragged and pushed the remains of Mary Rose Donnelly across the floor, into a stall and onto the hay. Panting from the effort of moving the heavy body, Ivy left the stall without a word while Jem covered the body with more hay.

Jem walked out to join Ivy in the aisle outside the stall. He closed both sections of the stall door, top and bottom, and locked it. Not that it was necessary – Mary Rose Donnelly was going nowhere.

"You better bring that kettle up," Ivy reminded. "I don't know about you but I could really use a cup of tea."

Back in the comfortable space Jem called home, he put the kettle on to boil on the stove while Ivy checked on the child. Jem remembered the pretty cups Ivy had served him tea in. He went to the effort of rinsing out a cup and saucer belonging to a tea set that had sat at the back of one of his cupboards for years.

"Tea's served, Ivy."

Jem put a bottle of milk and a package of sugar along with a plate of biscuits onto an occasional table he'd pulled away from the wall. He poured the tea and put the teapot on top of the cast-iron free-standing fireplace that he used to heat his room. Then he collapsed onto one of the two chairs he'd put by the table, put his elbows on the table and buried his head in his hands.

"Take your time." Ivy sipped her tea, delighted by the delicate china cup and saucer. She took a biscuit from the plate. A biscuit was a rare treat. She studied the man across the table and waited for him to speak. When she'd first seen the little girl's green eyes she'd thought the child might be Jem's. That didn't seem to be the case. So, she'd drink her tea, nibble on these delicious biscuits and wait.

"The dead woman." Jem sat back against the wooden back of the chair. "I don't even know her name. I picked her and the little one up from Kingsbridge train station. I don't know how long ago." Jem was rambling but Ivy let him. "I drove around for what seemed like days trying to think what to do."

"Tell me exactly how she got dead?" Ivy asked when it seemed Jem was through talking.

"We were passing Kilmainham Gaol. I was taking the long way around, trying to give myself time to think . . ."

The story began to pour out of Jem. It seemed he'd kept the words blocked up long enough. Ivy gasped and stared but she didn't interrupt. She couldn't believe any woman would willingly put a child into Goldenbridge, but then everyone knew the rich were strange.

"Jem, you have to decide now, tonight, what you're going to do." Ivy stood to refill their tea cups. Jem looked fit to collapse.

"I don't know what to do, Ivy. I don't know why I knocked on your door tonight. Everything just happened."

Ivy was used to taking control. She'd ruled four men in her time. "Well, the way I see it, we need to take care of that body downstairs first. What did you plan to do with it?"

"I haven't a clue!" Jem almost wailed. "It's not something you have to think about every day."

"I'll grant you that." Ivy said. "But nevertheless, you have to think about it now."

"I thought about driving around and just dumping the body somewhere."

"Not smart." Ivy could almost feel her own brain turning over. "I don't think a naked dead woman would go unnoticed anywhere in Dublin. Certainly not one as well fed as that one down there." She pointed her chin in the general direction of the stalls.

"I thought about burying her somewhere."

"You'd be seen and have to explain yourself." She stared at Jem, waiting to hear his next hare-brained scheme.

"There's this wagon . . ." Jem was going to tell Ivy something he'd sworn to keep secret. It wasn't an official secret. He wasn't breaking his sworn word but the men who drove the death wagon agreed to keep the existence of the wagon secret. People would be horrified to think a body could be thrown away. Without any of the signs of respect most hoped and prayed for upon their death. He'd have to approach the subject delicately.

"The death wagon." Ivy watched Jem choke and splutter when the tea he was sipping went down the wrong way.

"How in the name of God do you know about that?" Jem was red to the gills. His feeling of outrage shimmered in his watering green eyes.

"Never you mind how I heard about it." Ivy wasn't about to be intimidated. "I know you and your uncle were out and about at all the hours God sends. Did you two drive these death wagons?" A perfectly straightforward question as far as Ivy was concerned.

"Yes." Jem stared across the small table at Ivy. The woman had practically shot him in the face. The explosion had knocked him back in his seat. Yet she sat there and calmly waited for him to answer a question that should never have been asked.

"Right." Ivy slapped the table, glancing guiltily at the sleeping child. "I presume it's not like the rubbish cart? You can't just throw a body up on it, can you?"

"No, you most certainly can not!" Jem pushed his hands through his hair. His life was going to hell in a hand-basket while he sat sharing a pot of tea and chatting about death. "You can't just murder your granny and throw her on a cart, you know."

"I've no intention of murdering me granny," Ivy said calmly. "You need to calm down. You're getting hysterical."

"You're right." Jem took a deep breath. "I feel like I'm losing my mind."

"We need to get this settled tonight." Ivy was accustomed to being the voice of reason. "We can't leave your one down there stinking up your stalls."

"Jaysus, Ivy, can you be any more hard-hearted?" Jem didn't know what he'd expected when he'd knocked on Ivy's door but her calm, collected manner in the face of this disaster amazed him.

"Have a look at that child's back." Ivy pointed over to the still snoring Emerald. "Have a look at her feet. Think about what her aunt was going to do to her. Does the woman downstairs really deserve any consideration?"

"Truthfully, when I was listening to her pour scorn and abuse on the poor child's head I wanted to kill her myself. But you have to admit, Ivy, this situation is a bit out of the ordinary."

"Yes, it is. But we have to deal with it, Jem, and we have to deal with it now. Tonight."

"The wagons don't go to every hospital every night."

"The porters would know if a wagon was due, wouldn't they?" Ivy had been impressed by the porter she'd met at Kevin's Hospital. She thought briefly of suggesting they ask Ann Marie Gannon for advice but quickly discarded the notion. She couldn't involve the woman in something like this. She and Jem would have to sort it out between them.

"The door porter, yes, yes, they should do." Jem was nodding his head frantically.

"Well, there is part of your answer." Ivy shrugged. "Walk over to Hollis Street Hospital and ask if the wagon is coming tonight."

"Just like that?" Jem was glad Ivy was on his side. The woman hadn't been fazed by anything he'd thrown at her this evening.

"Cry a little," Ivy suggested. "If we're going to dump your one on the death wagon then you could let the porter think she's someone belonging to you."

"How am I going to cry?" Jem thought he was getting past the point where he could be surprised by anything Ivy suggested. The woman was just full of ideas.

"Have yeh an onion?"

"Yes."

"Get it." Ivy watched as Jem went to search in the bottom of a nearby cupboard. "Jem, not to be too delicate about the thing, but what do the people in the death wagon usually wear?"

"*What?*" Jem roared. The speed at which he turned around to stare at Ivy knocked him off his feet and onto his arse.

"Well, I don't know, do I?" Ivy glared at Jem who remained sitting where he fell. "For funerals people are dressed in their best but I don't suppose anyone gets dressed up to go in the death wagon, do they?"

"Ivy Murphy, you've a mind that beggars belief." Jem pushed himself up from the floor. "I don't know if I'm coming or going."

"Well, then, while you're figuring that out answer me question."

"Mostly the people are naked." Jem closed his eyes at the horrific memories his words stirred up. "Now and again people are wrapped in an old sheet."

"It's a hell of a way to go right enough." Ivy shrugged. "We need to get ourselves organised, Jem."

"I know," Jem stood with the onion in his hand, feeling like a right fool. "What do I do with this?"

"Give it here." Ivy stood. "You don't want the smell of it on your hands. That's a dead giveaway." She cut the onion in half, skin and all. Hollis Street Hospital was only a short walk away. Jem's eyes should still be red and watering when he reached the porter's desk. "Here, take a deep sniff. You can take a couple more sniffs and then take yourself over to Hollis Street." Ivy watched the tears flow down Jem's face into his beard. "You can walk over and see what the porter says. I'll wait here for yeh."

Jem shook his head and without a word took his hat and coat off the peg before hurrying away to obey his orders.

"I can't sit here doing nothing," Ivy said into the silence. "I'll go see if your one packed anything for the child." She jumped to her feet, stepped close to the bed and listened to the deep breathing. "I'll leave the top half of the door open again and I'll hear if you call out," she whispered to the child.

She took a large oil lamp from its place on a nearby shelf. She knew to be extra careful – the things were deadly but she needed the light. She took the box of matches that sat beside the lamp and carefully climbed down to the stable floor.

She set the lamp down carefully but didn't light it yet. For the moment she could see well enough by the light coming in from the streetlamps. The carriage was still standing just inside the doorway. Thankfully there was plenty of room in the wide main aisle of the building. Ivy climbed inside and kneeling on top of the trunk, began throwing the cases out into the main aisle of the stables. Soon there was a pile of luggage alongside the clothes she'd removed from the dead woman.

Ivy jumped from the carriage and with a lot of effort and groaning she pulled the giant trunk out onto the floor. Everything was locked. Ivy lit the wick of the oil lamp. In its glow she saw a hook attached to a nearby support beam that was obviously made to hold a lantern. She secured the lamp and turned it up as high as it would go.

Ivy began to search the floor around her feet. She remembered unbuckling a leather holder from around the woman's middle. She hadn't really thought about it then but she kept her own money tied up in socks and secured around her own ribs. Maybe this woman did the same thing.

"Sweet Mary, Mother of Jesus!" Ivy stared at the wad of white five-pound notes in her hand. There were no keys in the money belt but there was more money than most people she knew would ever see in their lives. Ivy was only able to identify the note itself because she'd received one for her hair. She'd never seen a five-pound note before that day.

"In the name of all that's good and holy!"

Ivy spilled a rainbow of precious stones and gold filigree out of one of the small leather pouchs the women had stashed away in the holder with her cash. She might not know what every stone was called but she knew they spelt money, lots of money.

"If you were carrying all this on your person," Ivy said in the direction of the stall that hid the dead woman's body, "what in the name of God do you have under lock and key in all these boxes?"

Ivy began to search through the goods scattered all around her. She was searching for the woman's boots. The boots that were much too big for the dead woman's feet. She wouldn't be the first one to hide things in her boots.

Ivy found the boots. Each toe was stuffed with little purses that would have protected the woman's feet from the cold steel of the keys that were stuffed inside each purse.

Ivy began opening locks. The sheer extravagance of the contents of the cases took her breath away. The wealth of rich fabrics used to construct the woman's clothing tempted her to linger – but she couldn't. The woman had been carrying a fortune about her person and her luggage was stuffed to the gills with silverware. Ivy's heart was in her mouth. She stared at a small mountain of individual, handstitched, blue felt bags. She was almost afraid to touch them.

Taking a deep breath she picked up one of the royal-blue bags. She jerked gently on the drawstring and emptied the contents into her open palm. Ivy saw an exquisite silver snuffbox. If pushed she could probably even put a price to the article. In horrified fascination she opened each small bag to reveal a mouthwatering collection of gold, enamelled, jewelled and silver snuffboxes.

What on earth was the dead woman doing with all of this stuff? What had she been planning? Where in the world had she been going with all of this portable wealth? The woman even had two down-filled pillows and the finest linen sheets Ivy had ever seen, in the big trunk. There was not one single thing that could possibly belong to a child.

A sound at the door frightened Ivy. She jumped to her feet. She doused the lamp and stood staring at the people-portal section of the stall doors. The handle turning almost caused Ivy's heart to stop beating. What was she going to say about the fortune lying around her feet?

"Jem!" Ivy stood with her hand pressed to her chest. "You frightened the life out of me."

"Who else would it be?" Jem stepped through the door with a quick check over his shoulder. The coast was clear. He quickly locked the door at his back.

"Wait until you see what I've found." Ivy lit the oil lamp again and stood waiting. Jem stared open-mouthed at the fortune in jewels, silver, gold and cash lying around his stable floor.

"It looks like the end of the rainbow." Jem couldn't believe his eyes.

"I'm having a hard time believing this meself. Your one even had her own down-filled pillows and bed linens in that great big trunk." Ivy turned to survey the bounty lying around her feet. She jerked her chin in the direction of the trunk sitting open on the floor, a trail of fabric pouring over its edge. "If we clear that out we can shove all the valuables into it and lock it. There's a load of papers as well. We can lock those away too."

"Ivy," Jem was slumped against the door, "what the hell have I got the two of us mixed up in?"

"I don't know, Jem." Ivy shrugged. "All I know is that the stuff here," she pointed her toe at the goods that littered the ground, "this stuff is all that child's inheritance." She pointed towards the loft. "We can't make any decisions about it. It belongs to Emerald as far as I'm concerned."

"You're right." Jem agreed completely with Ivy. He had wanted to rescue the child but he was no thief. "We can't even think about that now anyway." He bent and began to remove the bed linen from the trunk, passing it to Ivy.

She stood looking around for a place to put the armload of material. She didn't want to put it on the floor. She finally decided to dump the stuff back onto the seats of the nearby carriage.

With impatient hands Ivy and Jem dumped the scattered valuables and papers into the now empty large trunk.

"I have a key for this thing," Ivy said, holding up the key.

"Let's lock it all away." Jem suggested. "It's too much for me to think about right now."

"How did you get on over at the hospital?" Ivy asked.

"The death wagon is calling in there tonight." Jem shrugged. "We're in luck."

"If it's agreeable to you . . ." Ivy had been thinking about the bed linen the woman carried. They couldn't use the sheets to wrap her in. The quality of the linen would make the men on the wagon suspicious. If anyone ever asked any questions the men would remember those sheets. "Only if you're willing, mind . . ." Ivy didn't know how to make the suggestion.

"Ivy, I'm tired. I'm confused and more uncertain then I have ever been in my life." He stared at Ivy. "Whatever it is, just spit it out."

"Well, the woman was carrying her own bed linen." Ivy couldn't meet Jem's eyes. "I wondered what you'd think about me taking them sheets and bringing an old sheet I have on hand over to use instead?"

"That's fine with me." Jem didn't care about sheets right now. He'd more to worry about. "What am I going to do with all these women's things?" He pointed at the women's clothing and effects peeking out of his carriage and several of the smaller cases.

"I'll take them over to my place wrapped up in one of the sheets." Ivy had been giving the matter a lot of thought. "There is nothing here for the child, Jem. The woman didn't even put in a change of underwear for the little one."

"She was going to dump Emerald in Goldenbridge, Ivy." Jem shook his head. "I suppose she thought the nuns didn't need any high-quality clothes."

"I think the woman has been planning to do this for a long time, Jem," Ivy said slowly. "The clothes I took off Emerald belong to a much smaller child – perhaps Emerald herself when she was younger. The boots and everything else were much too small for her."

"We'll never know," Jem sighed.

"Give me a hand packing all this stuff into one of these sheets.

I'll carry them across the way and bring back the old sheet to wrap the body in."

"Right, let's do that." Jem began to shake out one of the linen sheets.

"Jem, I've been thinking."

"I've noticed you think a great deal, Ivy." Jem grinned down at the woman kneeling, folding clothes, at his feet.

"I think you should push the body over to Hollis Street Hospital on your wheelbarrow." Ivy watched the white cloud of sheet drift up then float down to the floor. She wanted to cry. It would get so dirty but time was moving on and they needed to get sorted out.

"I thought I'd take Rosie and the small two-seater cab." Jem began to pick up items and hand them to Ivy.

"If you could afford your own cab you could afford a fancy funeral." Ivy took the items and stacked them neatly.

"I suppose," Jem agreed.

"You should push her over in the wheelbarrow. The onion is upstairs. A few sniffs of that and you'll be crying again. Then you can tell the men driving the death wagon that the dead woman is your wife. Say something about her eating herself to death. God knows she weighs enough."

"Nobody is very chatty on the death wagon, Ivy." Jem remembered his trips with his uncle only too well. Something else he knew but wouldn't mention to Ivy: this woman's body would be sold to a teaching hospital. The men would get a good price for an unusual body like this. Jem didn't care. He just wanted the aunt gone from his life.

"I bet you don't normally pick up such heavy bodies though, do you?" Ivy had never seen a body as fat as the aunt's.

"That's true." Jem agreed. "Most people are skin and bone."

"Right, give me a hand knotting this up." Ivy stood and stared around the space. "I think I got everything. Be sure to make a check in the morning. The light will be better. If I've missed anything bring it across. I'm going to use this stuff to make clothes for the child. She'll need something to put on her back."

"Are you coming back?" Jem didn't want Ivy to leave.

"I'll have to." Ivy put her shoulder under the weight of the package. It wasn't really that heavy but it was awkward. "Someone has to stay here with Emerald while you take the body across to Hollis Street."

"Right. Good." Jem opened the door and helped Ivy pass through. "I'll stand here and watch you cross."

"Fair enough."

Ivy wasn't going to take the time to go around the tenement block. Not with this weight slung over her shoulder. Someone was bound to notice the strange goings on and ask questions. She couldn't think about that right now. She'd deal with whatever problems were raised – when she had to. She crossed the cobbled courtyard that separated the area between her tenement block and the livery in minutes and was soon hurrying down her own steps. She unlocked her entry door and without pause opened the inner door to her room and slung the bundle inside.

Then she hurried into the back room. She put more coal on the range. Without stopping to think she stripped the sheet from the big brass bed. In moments she stepped quickly back out of her own home. She locked the door and then was on her way back across to the stables, praying no-one had seen her.

"That was quick!" Jem held the people door open wide and Ivy stepped through into the main livery. He tried desperately to ignore Ivy's men's clothing but it was difficult.

"How long do we have to wait before you leave with the body?" Ivy asked over her shoulder. She was throwing the well-worn, frequently darned sheet on the floor by the locked stable stall that hid the body of the dead woman.

"It will be the wee small hours of the morning."

"Right, we'll have some more tea then."

Ivy led a bewildered Jem up to his own room.

"I know nothing about tending the dead," Ivy admitted as Jem filled the teapot from the kettle of fresh water. "I don't know how long it takes for a body to empty itself." Ivy ignored her own blushes. They needed to talk about this.

"It varies," Jem mumbled, with his back firmly turned to Ivy. He couldn't believe the woman was taking all of this so calmly. He was a nervous wreck.

"Right," Ivy said when Jem put a cup of fresh tea on the small table. She'd been standing looking down at the sleeping child. "I think we should wash the body." She walked over to sit at the table. "It doesn't sit right with me throwing the woman away like a piece of garbage."

"Me neither, though I don't believe we have to have weeping and wailing in the streets at our passing." Jem joined Ivy at the table, his own mug of tea in hand. "The men who drive those wagons have to learn to harden their hearts. I never could."

"I wouldn't wonder, Jem Ryan – you're not a hard man. Well, this won't get the baby a bonnet." Ivy slapped the table then turned to glance in the direction of the bed. The sudden noise had disturbed the sleeping child who mumbled and turned in her sleep. "We'll do the thing as decently as we know how."

"I'd like that." Jem reached behind him for the teapot. He re-filled Ivy's cup. "It would help me sleep easier at night. If she should ever ask I'll be able to tell Emerald that we did all we could for her aunt."

"You're going to keep the child then?" Ivy asked.

"What else can I do, Ivy?" He stared at her, almost waiting to see if she could come up with a solution.

"I think giving Emerald a loving home is important. That's a lot more than her own aunt planned to do. You said the woman was the child's mother's sister?"

"That's what the woman said when she was moaning and complaining in me cab earlier."

"I shouldn't find it so hard to believe." Ivy of all people should know that not all families took care of their own. Ivy had grandparents, aunts and uncles locally. They did not recognise the children of Violet Burton, their blood relative.

"There is another problem."

"What's that?" Ivy wondered. "I thought we'd taken care of everything."

"No, not quite." Jem stared into his tea, waiting for divine intervention. "I wish we had some kind of death certificate, Ivy. I'd only need to flash it around. It's the colour of your money that matters. But a death certificate, that would stop them wondering and maybe asking questions."

"Do you know the men who'll be driving the wagon?" Ivy thought there was a good chance that Jem would know the drivers.

"I should know them – it's a money-making job and I doubt the men I passed the work off to have let it go . . ." Jem had been afraid to ask the porter what he knew about the men who'd be picking up the bodies from the hospital that night.

"Will they recognise you?"

"I doubt it." Jem touched his flame-red beard. "They've never seen me with this."

"You are going to have to shave that thing off when you get back." Ivy had been giving the matter a great deal of thought. "That beard is too noticeable. You could use a haircut as well."

"I don't want to." Jem reared back in his chair, his hand patting the beard.

"You are going to, Jem Ryan," Ivy ordered. "You're a young man and that beard and your wild hair are not attractive." She nodded to give emphasis to her opinion. "I can't even remember what you look like under all that hair."

"All right, all right!" Jem threw up his hands. She was right. The beard had to go. It would be remembered. Not that he thought there would be any questions asked about the dead woman but just in case. It made sense to change his appearance.

"The men on the wagon," Ivy had made a decision, "do they examine this paperwork?"

"I doubt they can read. They were probably pulled out of school as often as I was. Someone has to earn enough to feed the family. They're good men but I doubt they can read more than the cartoons in the paper."

"How do they know what the paper says then?"

"A death certificate," Jem explained, "no matter where the

body is removed from, is an official document and has all kind of seals and markings on it. You know what it is from them more than the words."

"I have a death certificate you can show them," Ivy whispered softly.

"You have what?" Jem stared. "Whose?"

"Me da's," Ivy gulped. "I have me da's death certificate." Her body suddenly shook with the force of her tears.

Jem sat with his mouth open, staring at the crying woman across the table from him. Éamonn Murphy was dead. When? How?

Chapter 13

"Shh, it will be all right." Jem stood and pulled Ivy up from her seat and wrapped her tightly against his body. He rocked slightly, patting her back, making nonsense noises, as he'd done for the child earlier in the evening. Without conscious thought he pressed his lips into the delicate skin of her forehead. "You cry all you like, alanna, get it all out." Jem thought there were probably years of tears locked tight inside Ivy Murphy. She'd been the strong provider when she should have been petted and protected.

Ivy's body shook with the force of sobs that felt as if they were tearing her body apart. For the first time in her memory she was being held tightly in someone's arms. The feel of Jem's big strong body supporting her was an unexpected delight. His arms holding her tightly came as a complete shock to her system. She'd never before realised the comfort you could get from being held tightly in someone's arms. This hug stuff was mighty.

"When did your da die, Ivy? How?" Jem whispered.

"He . . . he drowned . . . drunk as a lord . . . on New Years' Eve," she sobbed.

"I'm sorry for your loss." Serves the feckin' bastard right, thought Jem, and gently kissed the top of her head.

135

Jem would have been content to stand all night holding Ivy Murphy tight in his arms. But they had a dead body to dump. At the thought, his big body began to shake with suppressed laughter. If there really was a God he had to be looking down laughing himself sick.

"What's up?" Ivy pulled free. She stood wiping the tears from her face with the cuff of her jumper. She stared at Jem, bent over laughing like a madman.

"Sorry, I'm sorry." Jem shook his head at his own foolishness. "I was enjoying the feel of you in my arms and then I thought of the situation we're in with your one below."

Ivy glared at him.

"Well, I *was* enjoying it. You, Ivy Murphy, are a delightful armful and you can't shoot a man for thinking that."

"I wasn't going to shoot you!" Ivy snapped, completely confused.

"That's not what your eyes were telling me." Jem grinned.

"You are a daft man, Jem Ryan. I never noticed that before." Ivy sat back down at the table with as much dignity as she could manage.

"I'll make a fresh pot of tea." Jem turned to check the level of water in the kettle. "I'll need to get more water." He grabbed the heavy black kettle as if it weighed no more than a feather. "When I come back, Ivy, we are going to talk." Jem disappeared with the kettle in his hand.

Ivy listened to the sound of Jem's boots going down the ladder and across to the tap. She pushed her chair back and jumped to her feet. She rushed over to the door and went outside.

"If you have a bucket to hand, Jem, fill it up while you're there!" she shouted from the rim of the loft. She looked guiltily over her shoulder – she kept forgetting the sleeping child. "We need hot water to wash your woman."

"No problem." Jem shook his head in wonder. Ivy Murphy, she never seemed to stop thinking, planning.

Back upstairs, Jem filled the metal teapot from the kettle of fresh water he'd carried up and put the teapot on the stove – he'd boil the water for tea in the teapot. He filled the kettle from the bucket and put that on the fire too. They'd need a lot of hot water. The dead woman had a lot of flesh to wash.

"Do you have any holy water about, Jem?" Ivy asked.

"I don't know." Jem looked over his shoulder at Ivy.

"I'd feel better if we blessed the body with holy water and used a bit of oil on her forehead like the priest would do." Ivy shrugged. "It would seem respectful."

"Well, the Church says it's possible to baptise a child in a case of emergency. Maybe we could speak a few words over a drop of water and bless it ourselves?" Jem joined Ivy at the table.

"Why not?" Ivy agreed. "We seem to be taking a whole lot into our hands tonight. What's one more thing?"

"We'll do that then." Jem went to make the tea. "It's early yet – the pubs haven't even let out," he said over his shoulder. "We've time in hand."

"What are you going to do with the little girl, Jem, if you keep her?" Ivy asked when they were both seated and sipping at their fresh cups of tea.

"I have no idea," Jem admitted. "I've been chasing my tail ever since that stone hit the aunt's head to tell you the truth."

"Well, you'll need to think up a story to tell people." Ivy selected a biscuit. "She'll have to go to school." Ivy glared at Jem. "She bloody *is* going to school."

"Of course she'll go to school." Jem had no idea where the heated glare in Ivy's eyes was coming from.

"Her eyes are green." Ivy pointed her chin in the sleeping child's direction. "It's a rare old blessing that she has green eyes like you." She nodded her head. "You can claim a relationship to her. Do you have a sister?" Ivy was surprised by how little she knew about Jem's life.

"I have several." Jem's eyebrows rose over laughing green eyes. He was enjoying himself. He didn't know what was going to come out of Ivy Murphy's mouth next.

"Well, you can't say one of them has died. That would be flying in the face of God. At a pinch you could claim to be her father but unless you invented a dead wife that would only cause the child more problems than it solved."

"Any lie causes headaches, you know that. A lie just keeps on growing. But we need to come up with a believable story before anyone claps eyes on the child."

"What's this *we*, Jem Ryan?" Ivy huffed. "You got yourself into this mess."

"And you're helping me out of it and don't think I don't appreciate that, Ivy Murphy." Jem was feeling better than he had all evening. In fact Jem felt better than he had in a long time. He felt more alive, more vibrant. It was almost a tingling sensation in his blood.

"Right!" Ivy slapped the table then looked guiltily over at the child who had stirred in her sleep. "We better start to get your one downstairs organised. There's steam coming out of the kettle." She pushed away from the table. The thought of what they needed to do was hanging over Ivy's head, turning her stomach.

"Right enough." Jem stood. "Do you want to speak a few words over the water or will I?"

"You better do it, Jem." Ivy grinned. "I think I've been excommunicated."

"What?" Jem stared at Ivy, a look of profound horror on what she could see of his face. Excommunication was no joking matter.

"I'll tell you about it as we go." Ivy let Jem grab the kettle of steaming water. She couldn't see a cloth they could use. She supposed he kept his cleaning rags downstairs in the stables. If the worse came to the worst, she'd tear a bit of the old sheet away and use that.

"Grab the olive oil, Ivy" Jem pointed his chin to a small green bottle standing on a nearby shelf. The practically empty bottle had been standing in the same place for years. "We'll need something to put the water in for blessing."

Ivy grabbed the oil and one of the teacups from the cupboard for the water. They were ready. Ivy took a breath so deep it shook her body. She wasn't looking forward to this.

"It's a shame we don't eat humans," Ivy placed the cup and small bottle of oil on the stall floor well out of the way. Jem had uncovered the dead woman. "This one would keep the entire Lane fed for a month."

"Ivy Murphy, will you show a little respect for the dead?" Jem knew what Ivy was doing. He was feeling a bit like a monster himself. "Besides, this one was so sour if you ate her she'd turn your stomach." He shook his head, amazed now at what was coming out of his own mouth this evening.

"Do we even know her name to say a prayer for her?" Ivy whispered.

"I suppose her name is somewhere in those papers you found." Jem sighed. "I've no intention of searching for it now. I never heard the child refer to her as anything but 'aunt'. It was all 'Yes, Aunt, no, Aunt, three bags full, Aunt'." He wished he could spare Ivy this chore but he was heartily glad of the help.

"Well, if God is all-knowing I'd say he knows who she is." Ivy couldn't believe the wads of fat that covered the body. "We'll just say we are returning his servant to his care."

"That's nice." Jem prepared to turn the rigid body over. "We should take her hair out of that bun thing. We need to brush the straw out of it before we put her in the sheet." Jem grunted and had to use the strength in his legs to shift the body off the soiled straw.

"Jaysus, even her hairpins glitter!" Ivy gasped when she touched the woman's mousey brown hair. "What was she planning, Jem? I noticed she'd jewelled brooches on her hat and coat. Look, she has fancy rings on her fingers. Nobody in their right mind keeps this much wealth out in the open." Ivy shoved the bejewelled hairpins and rings into the deep pockets of the men's trousers she was wearing.

"If I had to guess," Jem continued to wash the body clean, "I'd say she was doing a runner. She had all that silverware and stuff. That belongs in a big house somewhere. I've heard tell rich women travel with silver-topped bottles and silver-backed brushes but this woman had a lot more than personal items packed away in all of those bags she had with her." Jem allowed his thoughts to roam. It was a lot better than thinking about what he was doing. "I'd say she was going to dump the child then do a runner. She had her ill-gotten gains to keep her comfortable for the rest of her days." Jem said. "We'll probably be able to figure out where she was going when we examine the papers she carried. I'm no great shakes at the reading but between the two of us we should be able to work it out."

"You think the stuff is half-inched?" Ivy blushed at the very thought of admitting her stupidity to Jem Ryan. How could she tell him she couldn't read anything, not even comics?

"What's 'half-inched'?" Jem was pulling Ivy's leg. He was from Sligo but he'd been living in Dublin for thirteen years now. He knew the slang terms.

"Pinched, stolen," Ivy explained.

"Without a doubt," Jem nodded his head. "Right, she's clean. Give me a minute to wash out the stall. I'll put more hay down before we bless her and wrap her."

"Fine." Ivy stepped out of the stall.

In a strange way caring for this woman in death was a balm to her spirit. She hadn't been able to do anything for her da in death. She'd add a silent prayer for her da when she sent this woman to her Maker.

Jem sluiced out the stall with buckets of water from the horse trough as Ivy waited, clinging to Rosie's neck. The horse was looking out through the open top half of her stall door and seemed to be giving Ivy some comfort. Jem didn't listen to the words Ivy was whispering in the old horse's ear. Some things were private. He often talked to the horse himself

"Right!" Jem called Ivy back into the stall. "We need to get this done." He'd filled the teacup with water from one of the buckets he'd carried in. He stood holding it in his hand. "I'll bless the water, you bless your woman."

Ivy stood over the naked body Jem had rolled onto the edge of the sheet he'd spread over the straw. She bowed her head waiting.

"Father, you know we have no idea what we are doing here," Jem croaked. "I hope and pray that you understand how we've come to this pass. I know nothing about blessing water," Jem had been an altar boy at one time but this was outside anything he'd ever experienced, "so, I'm going to leave it in your all-knowing hands. Please, bless this water for us." He made the Sign of the Cross over the cup of water. "In the Name of the Father and of the Son and of the Holy Ghost. Amen."

"Amen," Ivy croaked.

"Right, your turn."

Ivy dipped her fingers into the water. She dropped to her knees by the body of the dead woman.

"Come down here." Ivy glared over her shoulder until Jem dropped to his knees in the fresh straw at her side. "Father, we are sending this woman into your care. I hope and pray you will be kinder to her then she was to the people down here." Ivy used her thumb to make the sign of the cross on the woman's forehead and chin. She dipped her fingers into the water Jem held again. She repeated the motion of making the Sign of the Cross down the woman's body.

"Father, we don't know this woman's name and what we know of her character isn't wonderful but we commit her to your care nonetheless."

She touched the shoulders, the chest, the waist and hips. Ivy thought she might as well bless as much as she could with the water they had.

"We are doing the best we can, Father." Ivy used the last of the water on the woman's feet and hands. "Give us a hand wrapping her in the sheet, Jem. We'll use the oil on her forehead and chin. I think that will be enough."

"You're doing fine, Ivy."

They made a pleat pocket over the feet with the sheet before tightly wrapping it around the body. They stopped when they reached her face. Jem took the almost empty bottle of oil. "Do you think we should bless the oil too?"

"Couldn't hurt." Ivy bowed her head while Jem repeated his plea for God's understanding and made a Sign of the Cross over the oil.

"In the Name of the Father and of the Son and of the Holy Ghost, Amen," Jem completed his prayer.

"Amen," Ivy tipped the oil bottle in Jem's hand wetting her fingers. "Father, we are committing your daughter into your care. That's as much as we can do for her now. I hope we haven't displeased you, Father. In the name of the Father," Ivy dragged her oil-soaked fingers over the woman's forehead in the shape of a cross, "and of the Son and of the Holy Ghost, Amen."

"Amen," Jem added.

"That's it then." Jem stood and pulled Ivy to his side. They stared down at the wrapped body. They'd cleaned it, blessed it with water and oil and wrapped the body securely in the old sheet.

"I'm going to get a bit of rope to tie around the body, Ivy. We don't want that sheet peeling off." Jem took Ivy's hand and stepped from the stall, pulling her with him. He left Ivy standing while he grabbed rope from his stable supplies. With a sigh he returned to the stall and used the rope to secure the wrapping. He stood and blessed himself again before walking out and locking the stall door.

The noise of drunken men stumbling down the lane echoed around the stables.

"What exactly happened your da, Ivy?" In the soft dark night Jem thought it might be easier for her to tell him about her father's death.

"He drowned. New Year's Eve or maybe it was New Year's Day." Ivy sighed. "I don't really know." She walked over to run her hands through Rosie's mane.

"That was why Officer Collins came to see you." Jem had

wondered about that. "Jaysus, Ivy, that was ages ago! Why does no-one know?"

"Father Massey wrote me da's name down in the altar list of the dead but it can't have been announced from the pulpit," Ivy felt tears gather in her eyes, "because no-one has said a word to me."

"Why wouldn't the Church pray for your father?" Jem was stunned. Éamonn Murphy had attended church every Sunday, every saint's day and every day of obligation.

"I don't know. I told Father Massey but I had a bit of a run-in with Father Leary, and he must have decided not to allow me da's name be mentioned from the altar." Ivy admitted.

"He's a man of God, Ivy," Jem insisted. "He has a duty to his flock."

"Not that I've ever noticed." Ivy leaned in to the horse's warmth. "But I don't want to get into the whys and wherefores of that right now. I went to the church and told Father Leary me da was dead." Ivy felt tired to her soul. She couldn't force the parish priest to allow prayers be said for her da. The Lord knew she'd sent up enough prayers herself.

"I could take you down to the Franciscan friars. You could have them say a Mass for your father."

"Don't you think we have enough problems on our hands right now?" Ivy turned away from the horse and nudged Jem gently. She was touched by his offer but she knew her da would want any mention of him to be made at his own church. Éamonn Murphy would want to make sure his cronies heard the news. "Anyway, I'm going to walk into the pub and make an announcement one of these days. He was in the pub more often than he was ever in a church."

"All right – we'll leave it at that. Let me know if you change your mind. I'd be happy to take you down to see the friars."

"We'd better check on the child, Jem."

"Right – and while we're about it we'd better try and come up with a story. We need something to explain a strange child's sudden appearance in The Lane." Jem let the matter of Éamonn

Murphy drop. He hadn't been a great admirer of the man when he'd been alive. He wasn't going to turn him into a saint now the man was dead.

Ivy and Jem sat at the small table trying to invent a life history for Emerald. The little girl snored softly several paces away from where they sat. They wanted to keep the story simple. The little girl would have to be told what lies she needed to tell. Neither of them felt comfortable encouraging a young person to lie.

The idea of turning the child in to Goldenbridge made the lie seem the lesser of two evils. Eventually it was decided that they would simply say the child was a relation of Jem's come to live with him because her upper-class family had fallen on hard times. That should be enough. The gossip mongers could make up the rest themselves.

"Do you want to lie down beside the child?" Jem said when Ivy's yawns were so wide they were almost cracking her jaw.

"I'll wait and give you a hand getting the body out of here." Ivy felt she could sleep on broken bottles. "It won't take you long to get across the road to Hollis Street Hospital."

"That would be good, thanks, Ivy." Jem touched Ivy's hand which rested on the table between them. "I appreciate more than I can ever tell you all the help you've given me this evening."

"Well, Jem Ryan, you've certainly added a bit of excitement to my life." Ivy grinned sleepily.

"It's almost time." Jem took a deep breath and prepared to do something he considered a sin. To protect an innocent child, he was willing to sin and sin again, if that's what it took to keep Emerald safe.

After all the soul-searching, worrying and sick apprehension the deed was done without a hitch. The colour of Jem's money along with the very obviously crackling-fresh death certificate he flashed around made the disposal of the body pass without incident.

Long after Ivy had returned to her own home Jem lay in his bed listening to Emerald's gentle breathing, thinking about the events of his day. The most miraculous of all happenings, it seemed to him, had been his inexplicable inclination to turn to Ivy Murphy and ask her for help. He'd no idea what had possessed him to run to Ivy. Thank God he had. The woman had been a tower of strength. Ivy had taken every problem at hand and dealt with it. Jem sighed. She'd had a lot of practice taking hard knocks. Ivy Murphy had learnt at a young age to roll with the punches life handed out.

Jem thought about everything Ivy had done for him that evening. Her ability to lend him a death certificate had been unexpected to say the least. In front of his astonished eyes she'd taken it from somewhere under the heavy jumper she wore. She'd simply fumbled a little, then whipped the thing out. Jem felt as if he were watching a magician produce a rabbit from a hat.

Emerald whimpered in her sleep and almost crawled onto his chest. "Shh," Jem whispered. The poor little mite. What was she going to make of the new world she'd come to? Jem knew he was going to need every bit of Ivy Murphy's help and advice to deal with the situation he found himself in. A big grin split Jem's whisker-laden cheeks. He'd be seeing a lot more of Ivy Murphy. That wasn't such a bad thing as far as he was concerned.

With the down pillow in her hand Ivy fell onto the bare mattress of her da's big brass bed. She was exhausted but knew she'd never sleep. There was so much to think about, so many changes in her life. So much she wanted to do to improve her circumstances. The range she'd banked for the night gave off a soft light. The warmth of the room was an unaccustomed luxury. The feel of a soft pillow under her head thrilled her. Ivy gave a soft sigh, turned once and passed out.

Chapter 14

Ivy felt as if she'd just shut her eyes when the alarm chime sounded from the front room. She sat up on the bed trying to get her bearings. She'd slept in the brass bed for the first time. The events of the previous evening came back to her and she groaned aloud. She'd slept in her da's trousers and the old jumper.

Ivy was glad of the light from the burning embers in the range. She'd forgotten to bring her candle into this room. So early of a winter's morning it was pitch black outside. Ivy was tempted to fall back into bed and allow Granny to miss morning Mass, just this once.

"I need the po and a cup of tea before I'm human."

Ivy felt her way into the front room and lit one of the gas lamps. The glitter from the hairpins and rings she'd dropped on the mantelpiece when she'd returned home last night frightened the life out of her. She jumped before her brain processed what she was seeing. Shaking her head at her own silliness, she silenced the chimes of the clock on the mantelpiece, found the fancy porcelain po she'd scored on one of her rounds and sat to relieve her aching bladder.

Business taken care of, Ivy hurried to make a pot of tea. The hot water from the range cistern made making tea a much quicker chore this morning. Ivy gulped two cups standing up, trying to organise her thoughts for the day ahead. With a shrug she covered her da's trousers with her long black skirt. The wraparound rag she used to hold up the too wide skirt would keep her da's trousers up as well. Ivy tucked the trouser legs into the top of her hand-knit wool socks. The wide trousers gave the long skirt a fullness it had never had before. It almost looked as if Ivy was wearing petticoats.

"The chance of me being able to afford petticoats would be a fine thing." She laughed aloud. "Still, what the eye doesn't see the heart will never grieve over." Ivy grinned. She'd be warm as toast today without a draft up her skirt.

"Granny, are yeh up?" Ivy rapped on Granny's door. She waited till she heard the old woman stirring before she left to return to her own rooms.

She checked the black range carefully – wondering what she needed to do to keep the fire burning steadily throughout the day. She filled her big black cast-iron kettle with cold water from the bucket and put it on the range top before hurrying in to help Granny Grunt get ready for the first Mass of the day.

"Granny, are ye decent?" Ivy didn't want to walk in on the old woman on the po.

"I've been up and around for hours, girl," Granny grunted. "Get yerself in here. The tea's made."

"I brought yeh something." Ivy had a huge pair of flannel drawers stuffed under her jumper. She'd noticed the things among the dead aunt's belongings last night and pulled them out. The knickers would keep Granny warm on these cold winter mornings. Ivy fell into one of the chairs pulled up to the table placed under Granny's only window. "Are yeh not going to look at what I've brought for yeh?" Ivy waved the drawers in the air.

"I don't know who raised yeh!" Granny glared from the chair across the table. She dropped her cup into its saucer and grabbed the thick flannel drawers out of Ivy's hand. "Did yeh get these in yer travels yesterday?"

"I did." Ivy was glad she could answer truthfully. "I thought they'd be grand for keeping your kidneys warm on these bitter cold mornings."

"They'll come to smell, Ivy." Granny hung her head in shame. She tried to keep herself clean. She was getting old. Her body had smells that mortified her.

"They can be washed," Ivy said gently. "Besides, I have more than one pair. I'll sort the others out."

"How much are ye asking for 'em?" Granny filled her saucer with tea, not looking at Ivy.

"When have I ever charged you for anything, Granny?" Ivy knew the old woman was embarrassed.

"Still."

"Listen, Granny, today's me day for the market."

"I'm not doddering, girl!" Granny snapped. "I know that."

"Right – anyway, I won't be around all day. I'm going to ask Conn Connelly to look in on yeh." She waited for the argument.

"Going to lunch with your fancy new friend, are yeh?" Granny had never met Ann Marie Gannon. She didn't approve of Ivy mixing with her betters. Who knew what might come of it?

"Yes, I am. Ann Marie is working out her notice at the hospital. She's training her replacement, as you know." Since her da's death Ivy met with Ann Marie on market days.

"Strange place to be having lunch if yeh ask me! The morgue. I'd be scared stiff." Granny had been shocked to hear Ivy speak so casually about meeting your one from the morgue. Still, it was none of her business.

"The people in there can't do yeh any harm, Granny." Ivy shrugged. "Anyway, is it all right with you if I ask Conn Connelly to look in on yeh?" Ivy worried about Granny when she had to spend the entire day out and about.

"That young man has better things to be doing with his time than visiting an old woman,"

"No, he doesn't, Granny," Ivy sighed. They had the same discussion every time. "Conn is out of work, you know that. He's glad of anything that earns him a few coppers. If yeh give him your tin can he'll fetch the two of ye a meal from the Penny Dinners."

"Waste of good money, that." Granny enjoyed a meal someone else prepared but she had to have a moan. It kept her juices flowing.

"Granny!" Ivy shook her head and gave up. The old woman would do whatever she pleased. "Let's get yeh ready for Mass."

Ivy jumped to her feet. She took a white enamel bowl from a nearby shelf. She filled the bowl with boiling water from the kettle, cooling it with cold water from the bucket before fetching Granny's hand rag and soap.

"Can yeh manage?" Ivy asked the same thing every time. They both knew Granny needed help.

"I'll wash me own private bits." Granny held out her hand for the freshly soaped rag Ivy held. Granny washed her armpits and ran the cloth over her private parts before pulling the flannel drawers over her naked flanks, sighing at the warmth.

"You get about your business now." Granny sat in her soft chair by the fire. "I'll bide here a while. It's a bit early yet to leave for Mass. Biddy Moore will knock for me when she's ready."

"I'll have Conn check on yeh." Ivy tidied the room quickly. "I don't know what time I'll be back."

"Fine, fine, get along with yeh. I want a few minutes to meself to say me prayers." The old woman rested her head back against the chair.

Ivy almost ran from the room. She had so much to do today. She wanted to try and get an outfit for little Emerald to wear. Later she'd make the child some clothes out of the aunt's clothing. It didn't really matter if the child stayed inside today. She'd be better off resting inside Jem's cosy room. Time enough to let her meet the neighbours when she'd recovered from yesterday's happenings.

Ivy grabbed the handle of her pram which was sitting outside her back door. She pulled the empty pram through the back door, grinning at the luxury, and wheeled it into the front room. She'd make a pot of tea and bring it in here to drink while she worked. The freedom to leisurely pick and choose the stock she'd take to market delighted her.

Ivy prepared her tea, lit the two gas lamps in the front room and, teacup in hand, made her selection.

She took everything worn by Emerald. Ivy planned to trade them in to a dealer she knew. Maggie Wilson carried superior children's clothing on her stall. Ivy was hoping she could dress Emerald from Maggie's stall from the skin out. If she was really lucky Bill Burn would have shoes that would fit the child.

Ivy looked at the two porcelain dolls with a sigh. She'd planned to repair them but they'd have to wait until she had the time.

She began to fill her pram. She checked the items she planned to trade to the dealers in the Haymarket this morning. She had a small pile of ribbons and bows that had been passed to her. It would be so much easier if she could just write down who gave her what. Having to remember every little detail sometimes gave her a terrible headache.

Ivy looked at the articles spilling out of the aunt's linen sheet. She'd pulled the flannel drawers out earlier and left a terrible mess behind her. She didn't have time to sort it now. She knotted the sheet back up. She pushed two tea chests apart and with her foot forced the bulky package into the hole she'd made. That would have to do until she returned home.

She remembered to put the good lisle stockings Ann Marie had given to her into the bottom of the pram. The good shoes were added. Ivy would change into them before meeting Ann Marie at the hospital. She'd have to keep an eye out for a decent second-hand coat.

With her pram packed and every item and its position noted in her mental file, Ivy prepared to meet the day. She'd push the pram down to the Haymarket. Ivy checked her pockets, making sure she had a few coppers tucked away. Conn Connelly would be hanging around the streets hoping for a few odd jobs. Ivy would grab him before anyone else did. Conn was a good honest worker and he liked Granny. The two got on like a house on fire.

Ivy looked around the rooms, checking to make sure she'd forgotten nothing. She'd banked the range and sat the kettle in the wide grate. She hadn't anything to leave on the burner. She'd take care of stocking up today. Ivy pulled the back door closed behind her. She turned the key in the lock and with her head held high pushed the big pram through the yard.

Ivy pushed her pram through the back streets of Dublin, her mind in a constant whirl. She had a great deal to get done before she met Ann Marie for lunch today. She was vaguely aware of her own hunger. She hoped Hopalong had set up his tea stall in the market. She could do with a cup of tea and one of his sausage sandwiches.

"Morning, Ivy!" Big Polly, still wiping the sleep out of her eyes, joined Ivy at Hopalong's fire. "Anything for me today?"

"Let her have a cup of tea first, Missus, for God's sake!" Hopalong grinned, showing pink toothless gums.

"I'll be over to see yeh later, Big Polly," Ivy promised. "I want to see Maggie Wilson first."

"What? Yeh're doing business in childer's clothes?" Big Polly almost choked on her tea. Ivy was a well-known character around the marketplaces of Dublin. Big Polly had never seen her with children's clothes.

"I've just a few things I want to trade." Ivy put her tin mug on the makeshift table Hopalong kept by his fire. She didn't usually have children's clothing to trade. The nanny in each house took the best of that stuff. "I'll see yeh later." She pushed her pram away before she could be asked any more questions. It didn't do to tell everyone your business.

With a firm grip on her pram, Ivy set out to begin a day of dealing. She loved haggling, and the laughs and insults flying around the market entertained everyone. What was life if you couldn't have a laugh.

151

Chapter 15

"Ivy, thanks be to Jaysus!" Maggie Wilson was dancing in place while setting up her stall. "Stand here and keep an eye on me stuff, will ye? I'm dying for a widdle." Without waiting for a reply Maggie waddled away, almost cross-legged.

Ivy pushed her pram behind the homemade stall. The long sturdy board supported by old table legs was covered in children's clothing. Ivy began to eye up the merchandise on open display, trying to find something that might fit Emerald.

She saw that there were parcels wrapped in white paper on a shelf under the stall. The shelf was formed of a board and attached to the table legs. Ivy was curious – the shelf was hidden from passing traffic. She opened the parcels to reveal gorgeous, delicate baby wear – not something she was interested in but she could admire the workmanship. She fingered the handknit garments in admiration. It was very fine work.

"I know some of the other women widdle where they stand." Maggie Wilson returned from the side lane she'd used to relieve herself. "But I couldn't bear to stand in me own piddle all day." Maggie shrugged. "Not having a baby, are ye, Ivy?" Maggie's eyes tried to check out Ivy's figure under all her layers of clothing.

"I'd have to be the next Virgin Mary in that case, Maggie."

152

Ivy grinned. She knew the women of the market gossiped constantly. "If the Angel Gabriel comes to visit I'll be sure to let yeh know."

"You do that, flower!" Maggie laughed. "It'll give us something to talk about." She wrapped a leather apron she used for change around her bulky coat. "What can I do yeh for, this fine brisk day?"

"I'm going to have a look through your stuff as yeh put it out, Maggie." Ivy was hoping to find enough to keep Emerald going for a while. She wanted to get an idea of how much Maggie charged for her stuff before entering into negotiations. It never did to jump into a deal without all the information you needed.

"Yeh planning to dress every kid yeh know, Ivy?" Maggie commented half an hour later. She was surprised at how much time Ivy was willing to spend at her stall and had been amazed to see her laying claim to the best of her stock.

"I want to do a trade." Ivy knew the coat and dress she'd taken from Emerald would cover the cost of most of the things she'd taken from the stall.

"Yeh must be pretty sure of what yeh've got." Maggie didn't only sell from her stall. She had private customers who paid over the odds for some of her stuff.

"Come over here and have a look." Ivy pulled the cover off her pram. She'd arranged Emerald's outfit on top. Out of the corner of her eye she saw Maggie's mouth almost drop open at the quality of the outfit she was offering. The two women began bartering, both determined to get the best deal.

"Are yeh going to trade in them boots?" Maggie wanted to rub her hands together. Her family would eat well for a week with what she'd make off the outfit she'd just bargained for. Ivy Murphy might have been trading for years but she didn't know what some people would pay to make their kids look good. This little lot would see her laughing. Maggie wanted the boots but it wouldn't do to cut into another stallholder's trade.

"Yeah, I'm going to see Bill Burn next," Ivy said. The shoe trader, whose true name nobody knew, had been badly burned as a baby. His nickname of Bill Burn was typical Dublin humour.

Ivy knew Maggie would be across the market like a shot. The woman wanted the boots but the two traders could sort it out amongst themselves.

Ivy left the market fighting to keep the wide satisfied grin off her face. She'd traded Emerald's outfit and boots for three complete changes of clothes that would fit the young girl. She'd managed to get slippers and sturdy shoes in trade for the boots that had cut Emerald's feet so badly. Ivy knew the two traders thought they'd put one over on her but she was thrilled with her finds. Emerald would have something to wear until Ivy could make her more clothes.

Ivy's pram wasn't empty. She'd done a brisk trade in the used clothing she'd brought with her today. She'd stocked up on dried foodstuffs. She'd managed to find barely used sheets to cover the brass bed. There was no way she was using the aunt's sheets for her bed. The quality of them sheets was too fine for the likes of her. Ivy sighed in contentment. All in all a good morning's work.

She walked through the back streets of Dublin, an invisible figure, one of many women pushing prams and plying trade. She exchanged a grin and a shouted remark with the street traders. She passed women pushing prams piled with fruit, vegetables, fish, flowers and penny tin toys – in some cases with a couple of children pushed into the prams with the offerings. Ivy knew these women and they knew her. The street traders were a tough bunch. If they thought Ivy was muscling in on their territory they'd scratch her baldheaded.

Ivy was worried. She had money stashed all over the place. The money she'd made from the sale of her hair was a fortune to Ivy – add in the money she got for her da's corpse and she was really loaded. She was running out of safe places to stash her loot. The difference in her takings in the weeks since her da had been gone frightened her. She didn't know what to do with her cash.

At Kevin's Hospital Ivy parked her oversized pram alongside the other ones tied up in the cement shed used for bikes and prams. She changed her shoes and stockings in the shed. She couldn't do anything about the state of her coat. Ivy sighed. Ann Marie would just have to take her as she found her.

She'd made a bundle of her purchases and paid one of the stallholders to tie everything up in a brown-paper-and-string parcel. She removed this from the pram and with the bundle in hand began to stroll towards the morgue.

"Ivy, can we go for a stroll around the hospital grounds?" Ann Marie wanted to spend more time with Ivy. Today was the last day they would be able to share lunch here in her office. Ann Marie didn't want to lose touch with Ivy but where on earth could they meet in the future? Ivy refused to allow her to step into what she called 'The Lane'.

"Sure yeh want to be seen in public with me?" Ivy didn't know what Ann Marie wanted with her but an unusual friendship was developing between them and she'd hate to lose that now. The meals they'd shared here in the morgue office had been richer than anything she'd ever tasted before in her life. The talks the two women had, entertained her and made her think. "I'm not leaving off me coat and freezing me parts off for yeh."

"Don't be silly!" Ann Marie stood and stepped away from her desk. She'd tidy up later. Ivy didn't know it but all the cheeses, roast meats and tarts they ate came from the kitchen of Ann Marie's aunt's house. Ann Marie would pack the dishes and cutlery back into the wicker basket when she returned from their walk. There was no food left over. There never was, no matter how much food Ann Marie brought with her.

"I need to stretch my legs, that's all." Ann Marie was unaware of Ivy minutely examining the hip-length coat she pulled over her long tweed work skirt.

"Fine with me." Ivy shrugged and they left the office.

Ivy was astonished when the glamorous woman linked her arm through hers. "Ann Marie? What are you going to do with yourself when you finish up here?" Ivy jerked her chin back towards the hospital.

"I'm not really sure."

Ann Marie wasn't being completely truthful. Ivy Murphy was introducing her to a world she had never known existed and she desperately wanted to be a part of that life. She knew she had things she could offer – not only money, though she certainly had that – but knowledge of the wider world. She didn't want to lose contact with Ivy. Ann Marie needed a purpose in her life, needed to feel she was making a difference.

"I'd go out of my mind sitting sewing a fine seam, Ivy." Ann Marie sighed. "I can't imagine spending my days gossiping, shopping and making the occasional social visit. It's not the life for me."

They walked on in silence for a while, each lost in their own thoughts. Ivy turned towards the canal and Ann Marie followed along. Ivy watched the graceful white swans glide along the canal, her thoughts in a muddle. She needed advice but didn't know how to ask for it. Jem was going to need to do something about the fortune of metal and jewels he had hidden away in his stables but how was Ivy supposed to ask someone like Ann Marie about those things? It wasn't her place to talk about Jem's problems and, besides, it would involve Ann Marie in a very shady affair.

"Ivy . . ." Ann Marie pulled on Ivy's arm and stopped walking. "I don't want to lose touch. I want you to agree to come visit me at my aunt's house." She was holding her breath. It wasn't an ideal solution but for the moment it was all she had.

"Yeh think yer aunt would let me past the door?" Ivy stared down at Ann Marie. "Auld Foster would lay a duck egg if I tried to knock on the front door of Number 8. Yeh have to face facts, Ann Marie. We live in two different worlds. There's nowhere we can meet as equals."

How she wished Ivy would allow her to purchase a decent walking outfit for her but Ann Marie knew just suggesting such a thing would be the end of this unusual friendship. Ivy Murphy wore her pride like a badge of courage. It was the only thing she had that was truly her own and Ivy guarded it zealously.

"I don't want to lose touch, Ivy." Ann Marie was frustrated

by her inability to come up with a solution to this problem. "Can we meet when you come to the back door of Number 8?"

"I'm not going to ask your aunts' servants to pass on messages, Ann Marie," Ivy stated. "They'd get into trouble with Foster which is not something I would ask any of them to do. They have to live with the man."

"Sunday. Let's meet on Sunday." Ann Marie was becoming desperate. This was ridiculous. Ivy lived alone but refused to invite her to visit. Ann Marie wasn't happy living with her aunt. It was time and past she did something about that situation but all of that would take time and Ivy would slip out of her life.

"Don't yeh go to Mass on Sunday? What about yer Sunday lunch?"

"Ivy, I'm not letting you go until we make arrangements to meet up again." Ann Marie was frantically trying to think of a meeting place. The private park close to Merrion Square would have to do – it would be freezing cold but she'd have more time to plan. She checked her watch. "I have to get back," she said, pulling on Ivy's arm.

Ivy had left her package in Ann Marie's office so turned to go with her.

"I finish work today, Ivy. Let's make plans to meet up in Herbert Park this Sunday, please," Ann Marie insisted. She would ignore Ivy's wishes and go into The Lane if she had to but she'd prefer not to upset Ivy by poking her nose into her affairs without invitation.

"All right – Sunday," Ivy agreed. She was, in fact, anxious to meet with Ann Marie – she wanted to speak to her about a lot of things. But first she had to sort out her own thoughts and wishes. She needed time to take stock of her circumstances.

Ivy collected her brown-paper parcel from the morgue office, put it back in her pram and turned for home. She decided to walk along the canal. She'd visit the shop Jem had taken her to and go in alone to buy fresh milk. She wanted to test herself in this lonely world she found herself in.

Chapter 16

"Ivy Murphy!"

Ivy suddenly became aware of someone shouting her name. How long had someone been trying to catch her attention? Ivy didn't really give a hoot. She was on her own now and answerable to no-one. "Ivy Murphy, in the name of God, woman, will you answer me?"

"Maisie Reynolds, what are you making all that noise about?" Ivy grinned at the woman who rented the rooms over her head. She'd wanted to bring the clothes she'd found over to the livery but that would have to wait until Maisie had told all she knew. The woman had a heart of gold but she did love to gossip.

"I was watching for you coming home." Maisie, a slim woman in her forties, stood waiting at the gates that barred the top of the steps leading into Ivy's place. Maisie's dishwater blonde head was covered by her shawl – underneath it her pale blue eyes sparkled with anticipation. "I didn't know if you'd heard the latest. Although you'd have to be deaf to miss the goings-on yesterday. I saw you out filling your buckets when all the fun was going on. I was going to come out and talk to you but I was too busy listening to the roula-boula coming from next door. You must have heard it, girl." Maisie couldn't wait to tell all she knew.

"I heard it." Ivy had heard the shouting when she was fetching the water to fill the water container on her range but she'd ignored it. "Grab a hold, will ye, Maisie?"

She waited while Maisie took hold of the pram handle, then with Ivy going down the steps backwards the two women went down into the basement. It would have been simpler for Ivy to walk around the tenement block but Maisie would never have stood for that.

"I'll wait while yeh get the fire going, will I?" Maisie had no intention of leaving without having a good old chinwag. She spent all day on her own taking care of her two rooms and her men. A bit of woman's company was a blessing.

"What have you done to your hair, girl?" Maisie got a clear look at Ivy when the shawl covering her head fell back. The crown of tumbled coal-black curls on Ivy's head came as a shock to Maisie. The girl looked beautiful. The style suited her delicate features. Her blue eyes looked enormous.

"I had a haircut." Ivy opened her front door, touching her head self-consciously. Only Granny and Jem had seen her with her hair cut short. Ivy had no intention of telling anyone she'd sold her hair. Who'd believe her?

"Well, it suits you, flower." Maisie smiled, worry showing clearly in her pale blue eyes. Éamonn Murphy was a hard man. He wouldn't be happy about this. Ivy looked beautiful even in the rags she wore. There'd be wigs on the green when the bold Éamonn got a look at this. She sighed, deciding to keep her opinion to herself. Ivy knew what her da was.

"So, yeh heard the commotion?" Maisie couldn't wait to tell Ivy what she'd missed.

"It's not unusual to hear shouting around here Maisie. I paid it no mind." Ivy glanced over her shoulder at the woman who'd lived upstairs from her all her life. Telling Maisie about her da's death would be like taking an advertisement out in the papers. People would have to know sometime. She couldn't hide her da's absence for much longer. She wouldn't take Maisie into the back room just yet but she'd have to tell the woman something.

"Do you fancy a cup of tea?" Ivy asked.

"Go on then." Maisie took a seat at the table. "I've time and it's lovely and warm in here. It must be because of the lower ceilings." Maisie looked around surprised at the state of the place. Éamonn Murphy would do his nut when he saw this mess. "There are days I have to practically crawl into my fireplace for a bit of a heat."

"The fire will only take a minute to get going." Ivy didn't want to just blurt out the news about her da's death. Her stomach clenched at the thought of putting it into words. "What was all the noise about anyway?" Ivy was buying time. She put her precious cups and saucers on the table, thanking God she'd left the tea makings in this room.

"You'll never guess!" Maisie was practically bouncing in her seat. Imagine Ivy not knowing what was going on! "You won't guess, Ivy, not in a million years."

"I don't have to guess," Ivy laughed, "because you're going to tell me."

"Well . . ." Maisie's mouth was open to spill all.

"Wait until we have a cup of tea in front of us." Ivy grinned at the look of surprise on Maisie's face. "I think better with a cup of tea in me hand." She began to unload her pram. "You're in luck – I bought a bottle of milk on me way home." Ivy grinned, delighted with her own bravery. She'd entered that shop Jem had shown her as if she owned the place. "Look at that! The water gets hot enough in no time at all." Ivy grabbed the loose material of her skirt to remove the bubbling teapot from the fire. She'd used extra sticks to get the fire burning fast. She quickly spooned tea leaves into the pot and returned it to the fire.

"You're a funny cow, Ivy Murphy," Maisie said.

"Right!" Ivy said, plonking the milk on the table. "I'm sorry I can't offer you a biscuit to go with your tea." She carried the teapot from the fire and poured two cups of tea before returning the teapot to the grate. "So, go on, tell me everything."

"Liam Connolly has come home for good." Maisie grinned so hard her face wrinkled like a dried apple.

"What, from the seminary?" Ivy was suitably shocked.

"Yes!" Maisie's head almost shook off her shoulders she wagged it with such force. "Liam walked home, from Maynooth, all that way! Can you imagine it?"

"No wonder the Connellys were roaring." Ivy and everyone in The Lane knew the pride the Connelly family felt because one of theirs was going to be a priest.

"It was better then the fillums around here last night!" Maisie clapped her hands in delight. "Liam Connelly walked through the tunnel into The Lane bold as brass."

"Why shouldn't he? This is his home after all." Ivy hadn't much time for Liam Connelly. He'd been a sanctimonious little article from the time he could talk.

"Not to hear his da tell it." Maisie sipped her tea and stared at Ivy with innocent delight in her faded blue eyes. "He near to killed the lad. Honest to God, Ivy, the shouts and yells were something to hear. I don't know how you paid it no mind."

"So the bold Liam doesn't want to be a priest." Ivy wasn't terribly surprised. As far as Ivy could ever make out Liam just liked to hear himself talk. The lad had never struck her as priest material – not that she knew what priest material was, but still.

"He wants to go on the stage!" Maisie clapped her hands to her mouth while her shoulders shook with almost hysterical laughter. "Can you imagine what his da said? 'He wants to go from a priest to a clown!' – that's what his da shouted all around The Lane. The windows fair rattled, I can tell yeh."

"Well, he comes by it honestly, I suppose." Ivy shrugged. "Alf and Lily Connelly have often made a few extra bob singing and winning those talent competitions at the Royal. Liam would think it was easy money." Ivy stared at Maisie. "Does he want to be an actor now, like that lot at the Tivoli?"

"No, it's better than that!" Maisie snorted tea out of her nose she laughed so hard. "I heard it all. Well, everyone in the place and down the town must have heard Alf Connelly roaring. Liam brought this bitch home with him!"

"Maisie, that's not a bit nice!" Ivy interrupted.

"A dog, Ivy, I'm talking about a dog!"

"Oh, all right!" Ivy started laughing like a fool. "This story just keeps getting better and better." She stood to fetch the teapot. She'd freshen the tea cups before the next episode.

"It's some kind of a collie dog." Maisie sipped at the fresh cup of tea, trying to calm herself.

"What, one of those things that run the cattle and sheep into the market?"

The running of stock into the cattle market on the north side of the city was a huge attraction to the people of Dublin. At some time or another all of the local children dreamed of owning one of the dogs that ran and nipped after the herds being pushed through Dublin.

"Yes, it's one of them. I've seen it." Maisie nodded her head frantically. "The kids went wild when they saw Liam walk through the tunnel followed by the little creature."

"I can imagine." Ivy knew most families had a hard time feeding their children. A dog, any kind of pet, something that needed to be fed was a burden not a pleasure to the families living in The Lane.

"Anyway, I heard Liam telling his da. Really, I heard him screaming at his da." Maisie was trying to be honest. "It seems Liam had taken to visiting a farmer and his family. The man delivers milk or something to the seminary." Maisie shrugged. That wasn't an important part of the story as far as she was concerned. She waited to see if Ivy wanted to question her about the farmer.

"So, what happened?" Ivy prompted.

"The farmer wanted to get rid of this bitch." Maisie waited while Ivy refilled their cups. "It seems the dog likes people more than cattle or sheep or whatever." Maisie waved her hand around to dismiss all interest in livestock. "So Liam took her. But of course he couldn't keep her in the seminary."

Ivy stared at Maisie. "Are you telling me Liam Connelly gave up his chance at the priesthood for a dog?"

"Yes, that's what he said. He told his da he's going to train the dog's pups when she has them. Liam claims this dog is the smartest animal in the world."

"The dog is about to whelp?" Ivy laughed. "This just keeps getting better and better. How long has Liam been away from here anyway?"

"It must be five years or more since Liam went to the seminary." Maisie tried to remember the exact time Liam had gone away. Time was marked by the passage of events of importance. "Wasn't it about the same time as your Eamo left?" Maisie named Ivy's eldest brother.

"It must be all of that," Ivy agreed. "Liam was only eleven." Ivy kept her opinion of the tradition of sending boys of eleven away to be priests to herself. "That would make him sixteen now."

"Something like that although he's a well set-up lad."

"He'd have been well fed at the seminary."

"Well fed and well educated. You should have heard his da going on about the education the lad had and now he wants to be a clown on the stage. I can tell you Alf Connelly had a lot to say."

"How does Liam plan to feed the poor dog and her pups when they come?" Ivy wondered aloud. The thought of all the education Liam had received fascinated Ivy.

"Oh, Liam told his father the Lord would provide!" Maisie buried her face in her hands and giggled until tears poured between her fingers. "Honest to God, Ivy, it was better than the fillums!"

"Father Leary won't just let Liam leave the seminary." Ivy hadn't meant to say that aloud.

"That's what Alf Connelly said." Maisie used her skirt to wipe away her tears. "Alf said he wasn't going to have Father Leary knocking on his door morning, noon and night."

"So what's Liam going to do? Do you know?"

"I heard him tell his da that he'd sleep on the stairs." Maisie was delighted to be able to supply all the information Ivy needed.

"He's going to sleep alongside the homeless men?" Ivy couldn't imagine the proud Liam Connelly doing any such thing.

The women of the tenements allowed homeless men to sleep on the four extra-wide, extra-long steps that graced the foyer of the tenement houses. The stairs formed the base of the staircase that led to every floor of the tenement building. The men slept wrapped in newspapers. Most of the unfortunates wrapped newspaper under their clothes and in their shoes. The newspaper acted as insulation against the bitter cold. Old newspapers served a great many purposes other than reading material.

The homeless men knew they had to leave the stairs clean or they wouldn't be allowed back. There could be no drink spilled and no bodily fluids left behind. The women of each house took turns scrubbing the stairs down every morning. A spotlessly clean entryway was a matter of community pride.

"That's what Liam said. I heard him. Loud as you please he told his da he'd sleep in the entryway." Maisie shook her head. "I heard Lily Connelly cry out at that but Alf is not going to let Liam stop under his roof."

"Well, it's between themselves." Ivy shrugged. "There's not much we can do about the situation."

"That's the God's honest truth." Maisie had said everything she came to say and now she wanted to get back and see if there had been any new developments while she'd been out and about. "Thanks for the tea." She stood up. "Your hair really does suit you, you know. You look a picture. You better get this place cleaned up." Maisie waved a hand at the tea chests all over the floor. "You know yer da will pitch a fit if he sees the place like this."

"Me da isn't coming home, Maisie." Ivy took a deep breath. This was it. "Me da is dead. He drowned on New Year's Day."

"Sweet Divine Jesus!" Maisie blessed herself frantically. She fell back down into her seat, staring in shock at Ivy. "You let me sit here and blather on about bloody Liam Connelly when your da is dead and no-one knows? In the name of Jesus, Ivy, what were yeh thinking of?"

"I told Father Leary me da was dead," Ivy whispered. "I had Father Massey note it down to have it read from the altar." She shrugged. "I thought everyone knew me da was gone." Ivy was lying but she wasn't willing to tell Maisie about her problems with the parish priest.

"Jesus," Maisie counted the days on her fingers, "that's more than a month now, Ivy. What about a funeral?"

"Me da drowned, Maisie," Ivy repeated. "There was no body for a funeral."

"In the name of Divine Jesus," Maisie prayed as she blessed herself again. "What about yer ma, yer brothers, do they know?" She was shaking at the shock of the thing. Éamonn Murphy hale and hearty one minute and gone the next. She didn't like to ask Ivy whether it was in the canal or the Liffey her da drowned. It was likely the canal while he was stumbling drunk – that's how she'd tell it anyway. "What will yeh do now, Ivy? Yeh can't stay here all on yer own. Where will yeh go?"

"I don't know how to get in touch with me ma and brothers, Maisie," Ivy hated to admit that. "I don't know where they are."

"Sweet merciful heavens!" Maisie touched Ivy gently on the arm. "Do you mean to tell me, after all yeh did for those three brothers of yours, they took themselves off and never looked back? That can't be right, Ivy."

"I don't know if me brothers kept in touch with anyone here, Maisie." Ivy didn't want to admit her brothers knew she couldn't read any letters they might want to send her. "I only know me ma and brothers took the mail boat to England and disappeared. I don't know where they are to tell them about me da's death."

"One of them needs to come home and look after yeh, Ivy," Maisie stated with conviction.

"I can look after meself, Maisie." Ivy smiled sadly. "I've been doing it for years."

"Of course yeh have, pet." Maisie patted Ivy's arm. "Still, a woman on her own, it's not right, not decent."

"It's the way it is, Maisie." Ivy said.

"It's your da's fault. I don't mean to speak ill of the dead, Ivy, but yeh should have been allowed to walk out with a young man like any girl of yer age. Yeh'd have been married with yer own childer by now but yer da wanted to keep yeh tied to him. He was always that fond of his little girl." Maisie was putting a good face on the fact that Éamonn Murphy didn't want to give up his cushy way of life. A way of life that Ivy's trading paid for.

"I need to be getting on, Maisie." Ivy stood. Maisie was free to spread the news of her da's death now. Then they'd see what they'd see. "I have to go and take care of Granny."

"Does that old woman know about yer da?" Maisie wanted to spit feathers at the thought of Granny Grunt keeping this news from her.

"Granny knows, Maisie," Ivy said tiredly, having a good idea what Maisie was thinking. "Who would Granny tell? She only sees old Biddy when the two women go to Mass. Otherwise Granny spends the day all on her own." Conn didn't matter. Granny would never discuss anything of importance with a young man.

"Well, I suppose." Maisie wrapped her shawl around her shoulders, already thinking about who should be the first person she'd tell this bit of shocking news. "I'll check in with yeh again later, Ivy, but I need to get home and get the dinner started for me men coming in from work." She was lucky enough to have three men employed. A minor miracle in that day and age.

"I'll see yeh later, Maisie." Ivy stood in her open doorway, watching while Maisie practically ran up the steps. She sighed, closing the door, dreading what would happen now.

Chapter 17

"Granny," Ivy pushed through Granny's door after a short sharp rap on the door. "the news is out about me da."

"About time." Granny was sitting knitting, her feet held out towards the grate. The delicate lace knitting was something she could still do.

"I'm going to put those crubeens I've had soaking on to cook." Ivy hurried to suit word to action. "You'll have to have them with a chunk of bread this once."

"I don't suppose yeh could have asked Alf Connelly for the vegetables under the circumstances. I've heard about the Connelly lad from Conn." Granny continued to knit. "It's a right old state of affairs."

"I'll be back later to check on yeh, Granny." Ivy was ready to run again. "I'm going over to the livery."

Ivy ran back to her own rooms. She'd rearranged the parcel of clothing for Emerald, including the underwear she'd picked up from Guineys bargain basement on her way home. With her fingers crossed and holding her breath, Ivy prepared to leave her home by the front door. Aware of the many eyes digging into her back she prayed she could get across the cobbled courtyard without anyone stopping her.

Jem Ryan was standing in his livery doorway, the small door open at his back. He watched Ivy almost fly across the cobbles. He'd heard the wave of shocked whispers about Éamonn Murphy and guessed Ivy wouldn't want to stay in her own home.

"Come on in, Ivy," Jem said with a smile. He stepped back and as she flew in he closed the door behind them.

"I've clothes and things for the little one." Ivy shook the package she held in her hand.

"Come on up!" Jem led the way. "Miss Emmy Ryan has been sitting around for most of the day doing nothing."

"I heard that, Uncle," a little voice echoed through the stables.

"You were meant to, Nosy! Come meet the lady you were asking about." Jem laughed. "Ivy, I want you to meet Miss Emerald O'Connor as she tells me, now Emmy Ryan." The little girl had been telling Jem about herself and asking what seemed to Jem to be a million questions about everything.

"If you'd let me up, Jem," Ivy called from below him on the ladder. "You can get lost while we ladies see to things."

Ivy was soon standing in Jem's room. A smiling little girl, still wearing Jem's vest, greeted her. Ivy saw no sign of the anxiety she'd been expecting. It seemed the newly named Miss Emmy Ryan was taking her new circumstances well in hand.

"I'll need a bowl of hot water and a washcloth, Jem." Ivy threw the package on the bed.

Emmy was washed and dressed in no time at all. Ivy had chosen Maggie Wilson's stall because the woman was known for washing and ironing all of the clothes before she put them on her stall. Maggie loudly proclaimed this increased the value of her goods. The clothes were nowhere near the quality of Emmy's old outfit but they fit.

"Uncle Jem!" The little girl flew across the room and out the door to stand shouting down into the stable. "Come look, Uncle Jem! Look at my new clothes!" Emmy did a twirl, holding out the skirt of her Kelly-green dress. The little handknitted emerald-green cardigan was almost the colour of the child's eyes. With her freshly brushed hair falling down her back and tied back by a white ribbon, Miss Emmy Ryan was a vision.

"Well, begod, you're a little beauty, Miss Emmy Ryan!" Jem was standing in the aisle, a pitchfork of soiled hay in his hand, grinning up at the little girl. "I'll be up in a sec. Tell yer Auntie Ivy to put the kettle on, there's a good girl." Jem could hear the commotion out in The Lane. Ivy wouldn't be able to hide out here for very much longer. Someone would come knocking, demanding explanations.

"Aunty Ivy bought me a new brush and comb as well as lots of clothes, Uncle Jem," Emmy giggled. "I won't have to use Rosie's brush any more."

"I'll tell Rosie, she'll be that pleased." Jem grinned behind his beard.

"Well, ladybird," Ivy grinned down at the child when she dashed back to her side, "what did your uncle think?"

"I'm not ladybird!" Emmy grinned. She didn't know where her Aunt Mary Rose had gone and she didn't care. She'd enjoyed today with this new uncle. She hadn't been pinched or slapped once. Emerald, now called Emmy, sighed. It felt so good to be able to run and laugh again. "My Uncle Jem calls me 'petal'. I'm petal."

"Very smart of you, petal!" Ivy laughed. "A ladybird sits on a petal though."

"Ladybirds eat petals!" Emmy giggled.

"Is that a fact?" Ivy enjoyed the sound of the child's delighted laughter.

Jem arrived in the loft. "Well, would you look at that!" He smiled at the madly grinning child. "My petal has turned into a princess! And she's forgotten all about her Uncle Jem's cup of tea." Jem looked around the room with a sad expression on his face. "No-one's put the kettle on."

"Time enough for your tea, Jem Ryan. A princess needs a prince." Ivy grinned. "Sit down. I have me sharp scissors with me. I'm going to start on that growth on your face."

"Ahh, Ivy!"

"Don't you 'ahh Ivy' me, Jem Ryan!" Ivy stood with her hands on her hips, glaring at the laughing male. She hated that beard and wanted it gone. Jem used it to hide behind. That had to stop. "The beard is going, Jem, and I'm cutting that haystack you laughingly call a head of hair."

"I don't know where me razor is." Jem tried to delay his shearing. He had his uncle's open razor stored in the kitchen cupboard with his own towel and soap.

"That's not a problem. I'll run over to my place and get me da's." Ivy wasn't to be put off.

"I give up!" Jem threw his hands up in the air and collapsed into the chair Ivy held.

Ivy set to with a vengeance. Using her well-sharpened scissors she cut the beard as close to Jem's face as she could. She took great pleasure throwing the fiery red bristles onto the floor. She stepped back to look at Jem – even that much made a difference. Ivy attacked the hair on Jem's head next. She had plenty of experience in cutting men's hair.

"Emmy – here, petal, you take this." Ivy gave the little girl the brush and shovel from the fire set. "You get ready to brush up your uncle's hair and we'll throw it into the fire together – all right, petal?"

"All right, Aunt Ivy!" Emmy's bright giggle echoed around the room, bringing smiles to the two adults. "I'm ready."

"I'm being attacked by two dangerous women!" Jem groaned.

"Poor, poor you!" Ivy took the rag she'd wrapped around Jem's shoulders and shook it into the coal bucket.

Jem, resigned, stood by the basin of hot water Ivy had prepared and with the open razor in hand tried to remember how to shave

Emmy awkwardly swept the floor. It was obvious the child wasn't accustomed to domestic chores.

"I'll put your kettle on, Jem," Ivy said after she and Emmy had thrown the hair into the fire.

Emmy sat at the table watching Jem scrape his face clean.

"My, my, Mr Ryan!" Ivy said when Jem came to join them

around the table. "You are a very handsome man! Who knew?" Ivy might have been speaking lightly for the sake of her audience but Jem Ryan was what her friend Nancy would call a fine figure of a man. The beard had concealed a very handsome face. Jem's newly naked cheekbones were high, his jaw determined, his nose patrician and his mouth . . . Ivy had to look away and catch her breath. The man was gorgeous.

"Let me make the tea." Jem blushed at the attention. He set to, using his everyday dishes to serve the tea. He had plans for the fancy set in the cupboard.

"Jem," Ivy had been staring around his room, fascinated by the bright white walls, "would it cost a fortune to buy whitewash for my two rooms?"

"You want to decorate?" Jem glanced over his shoulder.

"I want to brighten up my two rooms. I don't know how much something like that would cost me." Ivy didn't want to admit that the rooms had been untouched for twelve years. Her da had refused to spend money on what he called "woman rubbish".

"I have all the whitewash you could need downstairs, Ivy." Jem served tea and to Ivy's delight again gave her a selection of biscuits to choose from.

"I couldn't take your stuff, Jem!" Ivy objected.

"Ivy," Jem stared into Ivy's serious eyes, "I like to keep the place downstairs nice and white. I always have whitewash on hand. The whitewash comes in a big bag – it's powder. I'll use your water to mix it if you insist."

"I thought I'd ask the Connelly boys, Conn and Liam, to do the work." Ivy had an ulterior motive. She wanted to see Liam Connelly, see the kind of man he'd become.

"How does tomorrow suit you to start the work?" Jem grinned at Ivy's shock. "I'm taking a few days off to take care of things." He shrugged, not willing to go into any more detail with the child listening to every word.

"I normally visit the backstreet shops on Saturday." Ivy sat back in her chair to think about the situation. She had regular customers. But she supposed the world wouldn't come to an end if she missed one day.

"We could make a day of it." Jem suggested. "I'll head up the work detail and, with Conn and Liam both helping, we could have the place finished in one day."

"What about me?" Emmy asked. "What will I do?"

"I have a job for you," Ivy said slowly.

Her mind was in a whirl. For the first time ever she realised she'd structured her life around her da's comings and goings. Her mornings and early afternoon were taken up with dealing in her second-hand goods. She always ran back to have the place warm for her da and a meal on the go. She didn't have to stick to that routine any more. She was free to make her own hours. Ivy felt cast adrift at the loss of her purpose.

"I think you, Miss Emmy, will be in charge of Liam's dog." Ivy hid her sorrow behind a smile. "How does that sound to you?"

"Yes, I can do that!" Emmy clapped her hands in delight.

Ivy shook off her sad mood. Time enough for brooding when she was on her own.

The mood in Jem's room over the stable stalls was light and full of laughter. Jem couldn't remember the last time he'd enjoyed himself so much. He'd taken a day off to stay with Emmy. He couldn't afford to do that often. He was glad he had. It had given him a new lease of life. He looked down at the head of dark curls collapsed against his chest. Emmy had taken a couple of sips from her cup and with a big yawn curled up to sleep. The sound of her little snores was becoming familiar to him now.

"Should she be doing that, Ivy?" Jem was concerned. "The little one seems to fall asleep at the drop of a hat."

"I'm not certain, Jem, but it seems to be that Miss Emmy Ryan has been through a great deal of change and strangeness. Maybe this is her little body's way of dealing with things."

"I don't know much about childer," Jem admitted.

"Put Emmy down on the bed for a short nap, Jem. She won't

sleep long but the poor little thing has to be all out of sorts." Ivy stood to fetch more tea. She watched Jem put the little girl on the big bed. He took such tender care of the child it almost broke Ivy's heart.

"Jem, I've been giving things a great deal of thought." Ivy grinned at Jem's protracted groan of despair. "Seriously, Jem, we have to think and plan for the things that have fallen into our grasp. Not least of which is the very precious Miss Emerald O'Connor."

"I agree but I'd hoped to put off thinking about it for a while." Jem shrugged. He was still reeling from the changes that had taken place in his life.

"You can't take time to think about all of this, Jem." Ivy shook her head. "You have to do something with all that money."

"I'm not spending the child's inheritance!" Jem used a pulley to get the trunk up into the loft. He was fair sick to his stomach at the thought of all that wealth sitting in his hayloft. "I've been sitting here worrying and wondering." Jem pushed his fingers through his freshly shorn hair.

"I'm not suggesting you should spend the child's money in a wild spree, Jem. However, it's paper money and paper rots. It would be the height of stupidity to allow the small fortune in cash that woman was carrying to rot. I've a suspicion the money was actually left with the aunt for Emerald's care."

"I don't know what to do, Ivy." Jem dropped his head into his hands. "How can I go about me daily business and leave all them sparkles sitting around? I'd never get a tap done with the worry and that's the God's honest truth."

"I've met someone."

Ivy's soft whisper sliced through Jem to the bone. He should have known. A woman as fascinating, kind and downright beautiful as Ivy Murphy wouldn't be without admirers. He schooled his features to acceptance as he removed his hands from in front of his face. He wished he still had his beard.

"Her name is Ann Marie Gannon. I met her in the morgue of all places. She lives in the square."

173

Jem began to breathe again.

"I've been spending time with her. Jem, the world she lives in is a different place to the one you and I live in. She has her own automobile!" Ivy waited to meet his astonished eyes. It was a rare person who owned an automobile. "Ann Marie drives it herself. Honest she does! Anyway, what I wanted to say, I'm meeting Ann Marie in Herbert Park on Sunday. I'm going to ask her to take me to the bank one day next week. I'm going to open an account in my name. I'm going to ask Ann Marie to explain to me what a bank does. She's really smart, Jem. I don't know anything, I'm stupid."

"Ivy Murphy, you most certainly are not stupid!" Jem barked. He knew where Ivy had heard those words spoken about herself. "I never want to hear you say anything like that again."

"Do you have a bank account, Jem?" Ivy ignored Jem's words. She knew she wasn't smart.

"No. My uncle had an account but I closed it when he died. I've never had enough money to open a bank account in my own name." Jem shrugged. That was just the way it was. That was something the toffs did, not the likes of him.

"Miss Emerald O'Connor has more than enough cash to open an account," Ivy said softly, her head nodding in agreement with her statement. "I heard tell that you can rent a box, Jem. The bank keeps all kinds of things in these boxes. They keep them safe under lock and key inside the bank."

Ivy didn't mention it was her da she'd heard mention these boxes. Éamonn Murphy, when well away with the drink, had often spoken aloud about the kind of wealth sitting in these boxes in the bank. Boxes just waiting for anyone brave enough to walk in and take them.

"You need to get one of those boxes, Jem." Ivy touched his hand resting on the table with the tip of her fingers. "You can't keep all of the sparkles lying around."

"I wouldn't know how to go about these things, Ivy." Jem was completely out of his depth – but he agreed – he needed to put the wealth he had stashed away somewhere safe.

"We can ask Ann Marie to help both of us," Ivy said simply. "The woman has been rich all of her life. She knows stuff that you and I never learned. She'll help us figure something out. We won't tell her anything about Emerald O'Connor of course. We don't need to involve any more people in this little drama." She looked towards the peacefully sleeping child. "Jem, I think you should write down everything you did, everything you heard last night. We can lock it away with the sparkles."

"Why?" Jem couldn't believe Ivy thought she was stupid. She was one of the smartest people he'd ever met. The woman never stopped thinking.

"A feeling I have," Ivy shrugged. "I can't believe that someone won't come looking for that little girl." Ivy jerked her chin in Emerald's direction. "It might not be today or tomorrow but someday someone is going to come asking questions and we better have the answers."

"I had time today to look through the papers the aunt had with her, Ivy," Jem admitted with a shrug. He'd had little enough to do with his day. He couldn't leave the stables with all that liquid wealth lying around and in any case he had to stay with Emmy. While he waited for Ivy to fetch something for the child to wear he'd sat and thought about his options.

"What did the papers say?" Ivy asked softly. Imagine being able to pick up a paper and read it!

"The woman's name was Mary Rose Donnelly." Jem had felt soiled after reading the journal the woman carried. He could hear the woman's voice in his head as he read through the poison written down in her personal journal. "She was from County Cavan if that's any help to us."

"Did yeh get any clue as to where she was coming from or going to?" Ivy leaned forward eagerly.

"The woman had Emerald's, I mean Emmy's papers, her birth certificate, her parents' marriage license, her mother's death certificate and so on. In her journal she talks about burning the papers."

"The devil's warming a seat for that auld besom!" Ivy almost

175

spat. "Those papers need to be locked away in the bank too, Jem."

"The woman thought making little Emerald O'Connor disappear would be a great joke. The idea delighted the auld besom. She planned to dump the child with the nuns at Goldenbridge. She wasn't even going to take the child inside. She was going to dump her as a little nobody, a nameless little orphan child. She was going to just dump the little girl out of my carriage." Jem took a deep breath through his nose at the thought of the little girl softly snoring nearby being put in that place.

"And?" Ivy prompted.

"Miss Mary Rose Donnelly had tickets for a luxury cabin aboard one of the boats leaving Dublin today."

"Do you think she was going to meet someone on board ship?" Ivy was trying to think of the problems in front of them. "Will someone be looking for her? Jaysus, Jem, what if someone has raised the alarm already?"

"I don't think so," Jem sighed. "The auld besom hadn't a good word to say about anyone when she was in my cab. Her little book is much of a muchness. She talks a lot about disappearing. She writes about starting a new life far away from anyone who knows her. I don't think there is a soul on this earth that will miss that woman." Jem thought that was the saddest thing he'd ever said. What an epitaph!

"Thank God." Ivy closed her eyes in relief. "I've been thinking about those new Garda detectives and soldiers searching the city for her."

"Ivy, every time you get to thinking it makes my head ache." Jem rubbed his face. "But you're right and I know better than to ignore your advice. I'm not a scholar but I can manage to put my thoughts down on paper. I'll use the blank pages in the aunt's journal. It will all be in one place." Jem sighed. "Do you really think someone will come searching for the child?"

"How could they not, Jem?" Ivy stared at the sleeping child. "Someone has loved and cared for that child very well, if I was to judge from her clothes only. I think the aunt hasn't had her hands on the child for all that long – though long enough for her to grow out of those clothes."

"I want to believe yeh, Ivy." Jem hated to think of any child subjected to the kind of treatment the aunt was dealing out to Emerald yesterday.

"Anyway, even if someone doesn't come looking," Ivy groaned at the thought, "one day Emerald O'Connor will go looking for answers herself. We need to help prepare her for whatever she finds."

"You've given me a lot to think about." Jem stood and stared down at Ivy.

"I'll talk to Ann Marie." Ivy stood too. "I'll make arrangements for you to meet her. You need to get that money and those sparkles out of your place." Ivy put her hand on Jem's arm. "You need to take a look at the sparkles. We just shoved them any-old-how into that trunk but I had a chance to look at them while I was waiting for you to come back from Hollis Street. It seemed to me that they were made for a much slimmer neck than the aunt's."

"Ivy, do me a favour and shut up." Jem dared to brush his lips over Ivy's. "You're giving me a headache."

A rapid bang of knuckles on the livery door broke the tender moment.

Emmy woke from her brief nap with a start.

Ivy stared at Jem. She thought she knew what was going on. She'd been trying to ignore the noise from the street below but it had carried easily up to this room. It was time for her to face the music.

"Ivy Murphy!"

Ivy groaned. She recognised that voice – Nelly Kelly.

"Ivy Murphy, get yer skinny arse out here now! I want to talk to yeh." The stable door rattled. Nelly must have started kicking.

"I'll come with yeh – give me a minute," Jem said.

"I'll wait for yeh below," Ivy wasn't going to refuse the offer of a big strong man at her back. She ran from the room and down the ladder. She had to open that door before the crowd kicked the feckin' thing down.

"Ivy Murphy!" Nelly Kelly screamed when Ivy opened the small door cut into the stable door. "You get out here and tell this lying cow that Éamonn Murphy isn't dead!" Nelly was holding a terrified Maisie Reynolds by the elbow and shaking the woman with every word.

"In the name of God, Nelly, let the poor woman go!" Ivy stepped forward and pulled Maisie from Nelly's grip.

"Tell her," Nelly stabbed Ivy's chest with her finger. "The gossiping cow is telling everyone that Éamonn Murphy is dead. That he's been dead for weeks." Nelly's face was streaked with tears as she fought to deny the truth.

Ivy stepped back, rubbing her chest. Nelly's finger had hurt. She looked around the large crowd of women and young men.

Taking a deep breath, she opened her mouth and said: "Me da is dead, Nelly." Ivy ignored the mutters from the crowd. "He drowned the first day of the year. Officer Collins came to tell me."

"*Yeh unnatural bitch!*" Nelly pulled back her arm to knock Ivy into next week. A strong hand wrapped around Ivy's elbow from behind and jerked her back.

"In the name of God, is this any way to behave?" said Jem. "The woman lost her father – the only relative she has here in Dublin – and all you lot can think about is yourselves. Yeh should be ashamed."

"Father Leary never told me!" Sheila Purcell pushed herself to the front of the crowd. "I do for the priest as you all know!" Sheila practically glowed as she announced her own importance. "I'd have been the first to hear the news of something like this. Father Leary would want me to know."

"I told Father Leary of me da's death as soon as I heard." Ivy held her head high and stared down her old neighbours. She noticed Conn Connelly standing to the side of the crowd. The young man with him must be his brother Liam. The dog at his feet was a dead giveaway.

"Father Leary wouldn't pass the time of day with yeh!" Sheila

Purcell practically spat the words out of her mouth. "Many a time that sainted man has said to me, 'Sheila,' he says, 'Sheila, that Ivy Rose Murphy is damned to the eternal fires of hell!'"

The crowd muttered and moved at these words.

Jem felt the hair rise on the back of his neck. Ivy had said something about the parish priest to him before but he'd let the matter pass. Having the parish priest spread rumours about you was bloody serious. The man could be dangerous, a threat, to a woman living alone. The parish priest carried a great deal of real power. Ivy needed to be very careful.

"What a very Christian way for a man of God to speak about someone, don't you think?" Ivy had no respect for Father Leary but she wasn't fool enough to state her feelings aloud before this crowd. They'd lynch her.

"Sheila Purcell, will yeh sell your stamps somewhere else!" Nelly Kelly shouted. "I want to know about my –"

"Yer what, yeh slut, yer fancy man do yeh mean to say?" Sheila Purcell didn't want to lose the spotlight. It wasn't often the neighbours listened to what she had to say.

"Ladies!" Jem shouted. "This is neither the time nor the place!" Jem tightened his grip on Ivy's arm. He'd left Emmy alone, he needed to get back to her.

"Mr Éamonn Murphy drowned on New Year's Day. Officer Collins of the Dublin Garda came to tell Ivy Murphy of that sad fact. She knows no more than that." Jem held Ivy in place. He jerked his head towards the two Connelly boys, indicating he wanted to talk to them.

A scream like that of a banshee came from the crowd. Nelly Kelly had fallen to the cobbles and was tearing her hair out. The women gathered around her, not wanting to miss a minute of this little drama.

"Uncle Jem!" a little voice carried over the screams. "Uncle Jem, I don't want to stay up here all alone."

"Oh Lord!" Ivy closed her eyes – what more could happen this day? "You need to see to the child Jem."

"Wait for me." Jem was torn. He needed to see to Emmy but

he could not allow Ivy to face that crowd alone. He pulled Ivy back into the stable and shut the door. "I'll get Emmy and we'll walk you over to your place."

"I bought a hat and coat for Emmy while I was out." Ivy wasn't going to refuse his offer. "Be sure and wrap the child up warmly." She waited, leaning against the stable door, listening to the continuing drama outside while Jem ran up the ladder to attend to Emmy.

"Right, let's be on our way," Jem was back with a big-eyed Emmy bundled up against the cold on his hip.

"Wait a minute." Jem passed Emmy to Ivy. "I'll get the Connelly lads to help us. We don't want anyone in that crowd to stop us."

"They're all too busy enjoying Nelly's commotion," Ivy said tiredly.

"Well, that was pleasant!" Ivy sighed and passed Emmy back to Jem when the door to her own place closed at her back. She stared at the three tall men who'd practically frog-marched her across the courtyard.

"Liam Connelly as I live and breath!" Ivy stared.

Liam was growing into a handsome man, no doubt about it. The plentiful nourishment he'd received at the seminary had filled his young body out. His skin glowed with health. His black hair was thick and shining with life. Conn, his brother, standing by his side had the same potential for looks. Ivy liked that young man. He always had a smile and a helping hand to offer. To her eyes he was the more attractive even if the lack of life's bounty showed on his face and body clearly.

"Miss Murphy," Liam shrugged. What was he supposed to say? He was sure everyone in The Lane had heard everything about him by now. His da hadn't been exactly whispering when he'd cursed Liam up one side and down the other.

"I'm sorry about yer da, Ivy," Conn Connelly said softly. "I'm very sorry for your loss."

"You're one of the few to say that to me, Conn." Ivy could feel her eyes well up. She wanted to be alone. "I thank you."

"Thanks for the help, lads." Jem cuddled Emmy close. The little one was taking everything in. "Ivy wants some work done in here – are you two available?" He knew they were but it was polite to ask. They couldn't continue to stand here like tailors' dummies.

"What do yeh need?" Conn stared at Ivy. He'd do anything for the woman. Ivy took such good care of old Granny. Granny was a woman with a tongue that would slice you in half, a tongue that drove most of the neighbours away from her door. Besides that, Ivy made sure that if there was a job going that would earn a few bob she gave it to Conn.

"Come across the way, lads." Jem could sense Ivy was at the end of her tether. He'd get this lot out of her way. "I'll explain to you what's needed."

"Before we go," Liam blushed slightly, "I could make a sign to put on the top gate. It would save you from having to answer any more questions tonight."

"That's a good idea, lad." Jem opened the door. "Come across the way and we'll discuss it." Jem, with Emmy still on his hip, practically pushed the two young men out the door in front of him.

"Thanks, Jem," Ivy said softly, "for everything."

"We'll see yeh tomorrow, Ivy." The three men and the young girl called goodbyes softly. There was still a crowd gathered and gossiping in the open area by the livery.

Ivy sighed deeply and shut the door. She wanted time alone. She needed to think. She went to put the kettle on. The worst had been taken care of for the moment. She'd told everyone of her father's death. She could only wait to see what happened now.

Chapter 18

"I can't believe the change a couple of coats of whitewash have made to these rooms." Ivy stood gazing around the changed rooms in sheer delight. The three men had worked like Trojans. Ivy had left the back and front doors standing wide open during the day which had refreshed the rooms further.

Even with both fires lighting it was cold in the rooms. A lot of the neighbours had seen the open door as an invitation to stop by. They demanded details of her da's death from Ivy. She'd poured an ocean of tea and told the same story over and over again. Her da drowned – there was no body for burial. Ivy had been polite to everyone who stopped by. Fortunately, the men working to paint the rooms meant the curious neighbours didn't stay long.

Ivy closed both doors now and stood admiring the sparkling white walls. The improvement opened up a house-proud side of Ivy she hadn't known existed. With her hands clasped to her chest she walked slowly around her rooms, examining every angle. She took a minute to admire the shelves Jem was putting up in the nooks that framed either side of the chimneybreast in the front room. She grinned to see Conn giving the place a good going-over. He was applying a lot of elbow grease to remove all trace of paint droppings.

"I was hoping to find a chance to talk to you, Liam. Would you step down and tell your ma that you and Conn are eating here this evening?" Ivy didn't want to cause any problems with her neighbours. "It's only fair since Conn tells me your dog caught the rabbits we're going to eat. Yeh might ask yer ma to give yeh a couple of plates and spoons. I don't know where anything is."

Ivy looked around at her belongings pushed into the centre of the room and covered with newspaper. She didn't have enough plates but the mess gave her a good excuse for having to borrow the dishes she'd need.

"It sounds like you have your orders, Liam." Jem grinned across at the young man.

Liam and Conn had worked really hard helping Jem get the ceiling and walls of the dark, grimy rooms sparkling white. The workers had stopped only for the many cups of tea and bread with bacon drippin' Ivy prepared.

Emmy had been responsible for the care and watering of the dog, much to her delight. The little girl had met a large number of the local children – they'd all been fascinated by the strange girl and her dog. The ice was well and truly broken.

The smell of the rabbit stew Ivy kept simmering on the stove all day had stomachs rumbling as the light disappeared from the sky.

"I'll just nip up and report in," Liam sighed. His father would be home from work. Hopefully the silent treatment was still in effect. Liam much preferred it to the yells and slaps.

"I'll go with him." Conn glanced around to check he'd left nothing left to be done. "I'll get cleaned up."

The two young men left.

"All this talk about the stage takes a bit of getting used to, doesn't it?" said Jem. While the two young men painted walls and ceiling, and pushed furniture around the room, Liam had filled Jem in on all of his plans. "Do you really think he has a chance of making a living on the stage with this dog act of his?"

"Thankfully, Jem, that's not our problem." Ivy sighed. "Liam is sixteen – at that age anything is possible. He has a lot to learn.

Give us a hand bringing the table and chairs into the back room, will yeh? With the door shut the stove will soon warm that room up." Ivy didn't know how she was going to arrange her rooms but she'd figure it out when she was alone. "I only have the two chairs so you men will have to sit on upturned orange boxes."

"We could shove your two fireside chairs in the back room as well," Jem suggested, moving the table from under the window. Ivy carried the two chairs. "That would leave this room as your work area."

"I need to tidy all of this up." Ivy looked around at her rooms. She'd a lot of work in front of her. "Get the door, petal!" she called at the first knock on the back door.

"Come on in, lads," Ivy called to the two brothers. "I'm afraid it will be rough and ready. I'm not organised yet but there is plenty of stew and I made dumplings so there should be full and plenty." It thrilled Ivy to be able to say that.

"Right, everyone, let's get organised!" Ivy clapped her hands. "Conn, if you'd be good enough to carry a bowl in for Granny I'd appreciate it. Tell her I'll be in to see her later."

Ivy filled Granny's tin can full of the rich broth, setting three dumplings on top before replacing the lid.

"We'll have everything ready by the time yeh get back." Ivy watched Conn leave with a feeling of deep satisfaction. She might have had to run back and forth to Granny's to prepare the stew out of the men's way and borrow ingredients but by God she'd cooked it in her own home!

"I'll serve up and leave the pot on the stove," she said as soon as Conn returned. "There's plenty for everyone so speak up if you want more."

With enormous satisfaction she served the people sitting around her table. She might not have a dining room and fancy silver but the food was as good as you would get anywhere. Ivy knew she was a good cook and was enjoying this chance to show off.

"This is yummy, Auntie Ivy." Emmy was almost ramming the spoon into her mouth. She'd never tasted anything like this stew.

"Thank you, petal." Ivy smiled.

The men were silent but then everyone knew silence is the best compliment to a cook.

"It really is delicious." Liam had almost cleared his plate. The dog was sitting under the table lapping up the old bread and stew Ivy put down for her.

Ivy waited until the men had finished their first bowls, then, without asking, she stood and refilled the bowls. Emmy was still working on hers.

"When I saw yeh last night, Liam, I was hoping to get a chance to talk to yeh." Ivy put the refilled bowl on the table in front of Liam. She hated to have this conversation in front of others but she couldn't afford to be embarrassed.

Liam slowly spooned the rich broth into his mouth. "About what?"

"I know your plans for the future, Liam." Ivy wouldn't be put off. She was determined to improve her lot in life.

"You've been listening to me blether on all day and I'm sure everyone in The Lane heard my father screaming my intentions to the world," Liam shrugged.

"What do you plan to do while you wait for the dog to whelp?" Ivy looked down at the dog on the bare floor. It was a sweet-natured animal. "Conn will tell you there's not that much work around. It will take time and money to train up the pups. You'll need to feed them and take care of them."

"I know and I know I've been foolish just jumping into this. But I really believe this is something I want to do." Liam didn't know how to explain his need to change his life. He wanted something he could do that would allow him to travel and earn while he did. He'd come home hoping to have somewhere safe where he could plan his next move. His father's attitude shouldn't have come as a surprise to him but it had. Having to avoid Father Leary as well was a nightmare.

"I have a job for you," Ivy said slowly.

"I don't know how to sew or knit." Liam grinned then glared at his brother when Conn poked him in the ribs.

"I want you to teach me to read, write and do arithmetic," Ivy said with a blush. She hated to admit her shame to the world but she refused to keep hiding her head in the sand. She needed to learn and this was her chance.

"If you want to improve your skills, Ivy, I don't know how much use I can be to you." Liam knew he'd had a better education then most of the people around the lane but he was sixteen years old not a college professor or anything like that.

"You misunderstood me, Liam." Ivy took a deep breath. She had to say this. She'd never get a chance like this again. "I don't know how to read."

"Oh! What did the teachers at school say was wrong with you?" Liam asked with not a great deal of tact.

"In the name of God, Liam," Conn wanted to punch his brother. "You didn't become a priest, yeh know. People are not going to let yeh get away with that kind of rudeness. Will yeh for Christ's sake think before yeh open that big mouth of yours!"

"I've never been to school." Ivy was aware of Jem's spoon pausing on the way to his mouth. She ignored the argument between the two brothers. "I need someone to teach me. I need to start at the baby level." Ivy was mortified but determined.

"I can teach you, Auntie Ivy." Emmy suddenly joined the conversation. "Bishop Troy says I'm a changeling child because I know too much." The child looked under her eyelashes to see if she'd shocked her new family. "Bishop Troy says I'm the devil's child because I learn too fast."

"Bishop Troy –" Ivy bit back the words she wanted to say, "doesn't know what he's talking about." She leaned over and kissed Emmy on her little nose.

"I don't understand, Ivy." Liam didn't know what to do. He knew Father Leary said Ivy Murphy was damned. Now he heard a bishop had said the child was a changeling. Was he keeping company with the devil?

Conn opened his mouth to say something. He could almost see the thoughts in his kid brother's head. Jem beat him to it.

"You need to start thinking, Liam." Jem wanted to knock

some sense into the lad. "Isn't that why you say you left the seminary? You want to learn to think for yourself. Make something different of your own life. Well, that new life starts now." Jem glared at Liam.

"I'm sorry." Liam blushed scarlet. "That was a knee-jerk reaction and I apologise heartily. You've been nothing but kindness itself to me." Liam stared at Ivy with apology written across his young face.

"To return to the question you asked me . . ." Ivy wanted to let Liam off the hook. She didn't care what he thought of her. She needed his help. "I've never been to school. Father Leary and me da decided that a girl child didn't need to be taught such nonsense." Ivy allowed her bitter feelings to show. Liam needed to realise that Ivy didn't have a good word to say about Father Leary.

"That wasn't very bright of either of them," Jem remarked softly. "Especially since that particular girl child has been the family's main provider for most of her life. And it should be noted that the same girl child has provided the meal for not just the humans here but for your dog as well, Liam." Jem wanted to kick something, hard.

"I'd be happy to help you learn," Liam said, abashed. He was eating the woman's food, sitting by her fire and he'd been prepared to look down on her.

"I'll help too, Auntie Ivy," Emmy promised.

"Thank you, petal." Ivy smiled at the little girl who'd wormed her way into her heart. "I'll take all the help I can get."

"We'll need supplies. I'll think about it and make a list." Liam wanted time alone. He wanted to pray. Ask the Lord for advice. "I need to take my dog for a run now."

"Where are you going to sleep tonight?" Jem asked before Liam could escape.

"On the stairs again, I suppose." Liam shrugged.

"It would be more comfortable for you and the dog to sleep in the hayloft." Jem offered. "Go for your walk now and call in to see me when you get back."

"Thanks, both of you. Thanks very much."

Liam almost ran out of Ivy's home. These two people, virtual strangers to him had offered to share everything they had with him. He'd been prepared to pass judgement on them, find them lacking. He wasn't proud of himself.

"Yeh can tell me brother isn't used to taking care of himself." Conn stood with a sigh. "I thank yeh kindly for the food, Ivy. It was wonderful, the best stew I've ever eaten. Please don't tell me ma that." Conn grinned and picked up the plates and utensils he'd carried into Ivy's.

"Don't worry – I won't!" Ivy laughed.

Conn had his hand on the doorknob when he remembered the information his mother had asked him to pass on to Ivy and anyone else he met. "Willie McConnell is having a story night tonight, Ivy."

"Really, Conn, what time?" Ivy loved story nights and tried never to miss one.

Story night was an old tradition in the tenements. People would meet up, adults would congregate in the rooms leading off the main hallway, children were usually arranged sitting on the staircase while the storyteller sat inside the closed front door of whichever building was hosting the event. If someone was in the money a few bottles of stout might be available.

'Willie McConnell?" Jem said. "Him that plays his fiddle on Grafton Street?"

"He tells the best stories, Jem!" Ivy was giddy at the prospect. "Willie McConnell has travelled the world. He tells stories from around the world and he uses foreign words and plays music he learned in the places he visited. It will be a great night, Jem – you and Emmy have to come."

"So I'll see you later at McConnell's place," Conn said.

"Thanks for all your help, Conn," Ivy said.

Jem was going to pay the two lads out of money Ivy would pass to him.

"I'll give you a hand tidying this lot up." Jem stood and began to help clear the table while Emmy ran over to sit in one of the comfortable chairs in front of the range.

Ivy made a mental note to herself to make a rag doll for the little girl. She'd do it when she was repairing those two porcelain dolls for sale. The child needed something to play with.

"Ivy, it seems to me Father Leary has it in for you," Jem murmured while taking dishes off the table. "Are yeh sure you should be asking Liam to help yeh? You're just giving the man more ammunition to use against yeh." Jem wasn't a deeply religious man. He went to Mass on a Sunday and when he remembered he said his prayers, but he was not devout. He lowered his voice further: "I didn't like what the little one said about that bishop either."

"She's a grand little girl, Jem." Ivy deliberately ignored Jem's mention of Father Leary. There was nothing she could do about the parish priest and his attitude towards her. She didn't want to talk about that man. She continued to fill the old basin with hot water. "I don't think she could have been with the aunt or the bishop for long." Ivy started laughing. "'The Aunt and the Bishop' sounds like a music-hall turn!"

"Liam would enjoy that." Jem let the subject of the parish priest drop, for now. He took a cloth and began to dry the dishes as Ivy washed them.

"I'll put the kettle on and we'll have a cup of tea before we get ready to go out."

"You do that." Jem grinned. "You all right there with Ivy for a minute, Emmy?"

"Where you going?" Emmy glared at her new uncle. She didn't want him to leave her. Everyone went away and left her.

"I'm running across to our place to fetch something." Jem squatted down beside the chair and pulled one of Emmy's curls. "I'll be back lickety-split. All right?"

Emmy stared into Jem's eyes for a long time. "All right," she finally agreed.

"I'm borrowing one of your orange boxes, Ivy." Jem grabbed the empty box he'd sat on. "You listen for my knock, Emmy, and let me back in!" he called back over his shoulder as he hurried from the room.

"He's a nice man, your new uncle," Ivy remarked, completing her chores.

"Shh!" Ivy turned to see Emmy with her finger to her lips. "I'm not supposed to say he's my *new* uncle," she whispered, big green eyes wide in her pale face.

"I'm sorry, petal." Ivy joined the child, sitting carefully on the arm of the chair. "I know better. I won't make that mistake again."

Emmy nodded and whispered, "I like my new life. I love my new uncle. I love my new auntie. I love Rosie the horse. I love the dog and I like Conn and the sad boy."

"You love lots, don't you, petal?" Ivy had never heard anyone express love aloud like that before.

"My papa says love makes the world go around. I miss my papa." Suddenly there were tears in the big green eyes.

"Do you know where your papa is?" Ivy whispered.

"Papa went to sea to mend his broken heart." Emmy sighed. "I heard them talk. His heart is broken because Mama broke when the new baby was coming. Papa is going all the way to China to see if he can mend his heart." Emmy offered this information with a big innocent smile.

Ivy almost fell off the chair.

"That's my uncle!" Emmy screamed with delight at the sound of fingers rapping against the front door, all sadness gone. "I have to answer the door. That's my uncle!" Emmy charged through the rooms, eager to keep her promise to open the door.

"Here you go, Ivy." Jem placed the straw-filled orange box on the cleared table top.

"A box of straw." Ivy smiled. "How will I ever be able to thank you!"

"I'm surrounded by smart alecs." Jem shook his head sadly. He couldn't wait to see Ivy's face when she saw what he'd brought over. "I have a tall smart alec and a small smart alec. What is a man supposed to do?"

Emmy threw herself at Jem, grabbing him around his knees. He pulled her up into his arms and buried his chin in her little neck. Emmy screamed with delight.

"Well, go on, have a look." Jem settled Emmy on his hip and

stood watching Ivy. He pointed his chin towards the box. "Go on, see what's in there. It won't bite."

Ivy had never in her life received a gift. She didn't know what to do. The curiosity was killing her though. She had to know what was in the box. She poked at the straw, prolonging the moment.

Ivy dipped a finger into the straw and froze. She gaped at Jem. She moved more straw around. She stood staring into the orange box, her hands pressed to her mouth.

"I thought you'd like something pretty to put on your new shelves."

"Let me see!" Emmy threw herself towards the floor. "Let me see!" Jem lowered the child to the bare floor.

"Careful." Ivy held Emmy away from her gift. She removed a delicate china cup and saw a matching saucer sticking out of the straw. "I thought this was one of the most beautiful cups I'd ever seen when you served me a cup of tea in it," she whispered as she held aloft her prize. She held the cup and saucer down to Emmy's level for her to examine.

"What's that?" Emmy pointed. "I know that's lavender."

"That's dragonflies flitting through a field of wild lavender," Ivy told the child without removing her eyes from Jem's face. "It's the most beautiful cup and saucer I've ever seen." Ivy smiled with such delight and gratitude at Jem he felt twenty feet tall.

"Take out the rest," he said.

"There's more!" Ivy screamed like a girl and began to throw the straw all around her clean room.

"Looks like we need a brush and shovel again, petal." Jem grinned down at Emmy. The little girl ignored him. She was too busy watching Ivy uncover her treasure. "I guess I'll have to take care of it myself." Jem shook his head. The two females were ignoring him completely.

"Look at this!" Ivy held up a matching china teapot. "Just look at all these wonderful things." Ivy uncovered a milk jug, a sugar bowl with two handles and a lid, something she'd never seen before. "Jem, you couldn't have given me something which would give me more pleasure if you searched the length and breadth of Ireland!"

"Want to put it on one of your shelves." Jem grinned, delighted with his surprise. The tea set had sat at the back of his cupboard for years gathering dust.

"I have to properly prepare the shelf for the honour it's about to receive." Ivy giggled. "Something this beautiful can't be put on a plain shelf. I have to think about the proper placement."

"Well, excuse me!" Jem grinned.

"I've the tea made." Ivy turned suddenly and almost walked into Jem. "We're not drinking out of these cups though. Not until I can serve a tea the likes of which this tea service deserves."

Ivy picked Emmy up from the floor and spun around with the laughing child in her arms until they were both dizzy. Ivy stopped her spin in front of Jem and, standing on her toes, pressed a kiss against his jaw.

"I don't know how to thank you, Jem Ryan. I'm over the moon with my gift." Ivy kissed his other cheek. "You and Miss Emmy here will be my first guests for high tea served with my new, beautiful, exquisite tea set."

"We'll take you up on that offer." Jem was thrilled he'd thought of it. It was so little and had given Ivy so much pleasure. "But please," he made a big production of looking miserable, "can I have a spot of tea now. I'll take it in a jamjar. I don't mind. Just, please, something wet!"

"Oh sit down, you daft man!" Ivy shoved Jem into one of the chairs by the table. "I'll serve you a big mug of tea. A man's mug."

"I've never had tea in a jamjar," a little voice interrupted the tender moment.

"Haven't you, Emmy?" Ivy picked the little girl up and put her on Jem's knee. They only had two chairs and she wasn't sitting on an orange box. "You've been deprived. I'll correct that oversight straight away."

"Ivy, if you don't mind me asking?" Jem didn't want to break the mood of the moment but he was curious.

"After giving me that fabulous tea service you can ask me

anything." Ivy smiled across the table at the man and child. They looked so natural together.

"I heard what you said to Liam." Jem shrugged. "How do you know so much if you've never been to school?"

"The school of life, Jem. Besides I've been listening to stories and tall tales all of my life. The storytellers love to hear the sound of their own voice. They don't make concessions for children. There is always someone to explain what you don't understand. On top of that I imagine the people of the tenement know more about the world around them than most people. We live right by a sea port, for goodness sake, Jem."

"Still and all, Ivy Murphy, you don't half say a mouthful sometimes."

"I suppose it helped that my mother had a dictionary." Ivy's eyes lit at the memory. "I thought it was the most wonderful thing ever. I longed to be able to read it." She sighed. "At night when I was busy sewing or knitting the lads would read to me and sometimes we played a game." Ivy grinned at the memory. "I'd stick a finger between the pages of the dictionary and the boys would read out the words on that page. Did you know a dictionary actually tells you how to pronounce the words as well as what they mean? I thought it was magical." Ivy grinned.

Éamonn Murphy had put an end to his children's enjoyment. He delighted in using the pages he tore from the dictionary to wipe his arse. As far as Éamonn was concerned he'd lost his wife because of the education she'd received. He wasn't about to lose his children to the same thing.

"I want to talk to you about Emerald O'Connor." Ivy didn't want Jem questioning her further about the dictionary. She deliberately used Emerald's full name. She repeated what Emerald had told her about her papa.

"The poor man!" Jem looked down at the child listening to every word they said. "Do you think she got it right?"

"I think children know and understand a great deal more than we credit them with." Ivy stood up. "Now, Mr Ryan, I'm going to throw you and yours out of my place. I have a great deal yet to do before I can go to story time. I'll see you both there . . .."

"Did yeh enjoy your meal, Granny?" Ivy filled the enamel basin as she asked.

"I did that," Granny smacked her lips. "Yeh can't beat a rabbit stew and your dumplings, girl, were a credit to me."

The two women laughed and set about the business of getting Granny ready for bed. Ivy had asked the old woman to accompany her to story time but Granny couldn't be bothered. The old woman would sit up and knit for a while.

"I want to have you come for an official visit when I get me rooms ready, Granny." Ivy grinned.

"I'd be delighted." Granny was thrilled to see Ivy act like a happy young woman. The girl had carried too much on her shoulders for too long. "Get yerself away, go listen to that Willie McConnell's tall tales," Granny grunted. "I'm fine."

Ivy ran back into her own place. She'd wash her face and comb her hair before joining her neighbours for a night of great entertainment.

Ivy leaned against her closed door with a contented sigh. What a great evening, people had asked questions about her da at first but they'd soon lost interest in death, having come prepared to be entertained. Willie McConnell had been in fine voice. The never-empty pint glass of stout at the side of his chair guaranteed a fund of stories and music. Ivy knew she'd never sleep now, her blood was fizzing. She was going to do something she'd been longing to do. She carried a brace of candles over to place it on the top of the broad plank covering her tea chests.

She'd drawn the curtains tight in the front room and left the door between the two rooms open. Holding her breath she pulled the sheet-wrapped goods out from their hiding place. She put the orange box holding her tools onto the plank.

"Do yeh see this, Da?" she whispered while she opened up the aunt's coat. "The woman must have been toasty warm in this. Imagine having a coat with a cloak attached!" Ivy spread the garment out. "Did yeh ever see such beautiful material in your life, Da? What do you think this is called? Is it a special tweed, do you think?" Ivy wasn't expecting an answer. "Yeh know, it's funny, Da. All them years of sitting here on me own. First when the boys would be asleep in bed and I'd be up working and waiting for you to come home. I never thought of talking to you as if you were here. Now that you're dead, Da, I've got to say –" Ivy giggled, "you're great company." The fabric of the coat had fascinated Ivy from the first time she'd seen it. She'd never in her life seen such fine tweed. The mixing of deep heather colours with dark green was truly beautiful to her eyes.

"I'm going to ask Mr Solomon to make me a suit out of this material, Da." Ivy wanted to have something she could wear when in company with Ann Marie. She wanted to be able to hold her head up high and go where she pleased. "You always said Mr Solomon is a master tailor, Da. You told me he worked in that fancy gentlemen's shop on Grafton Street."

Ivy started to unpick the seams of the garment. The handwork on the coat was impressive. She'd supply Mr Solomon with loose pieces of fabric and pray the man could make a suit for her out of all the material. Mr Solomon and his family had the entire top floor of one of the tenement buildings in The Lane. All of that space for one family was a constant wonder to the rest of the inhabitants of The Lane.

"You remember how great the suits he made for the lads turned out. I was so proud of them on their Communion and Confirmation days. Me ma and Mr Solomon certainly knew what they were about."

Violet Murphy had been the brains behind turning discarded male suits she collected from the Merrion Houses into Communion and Confirmation attire for young boys. With Mr Solomon's superior skills and Violet's determination the scheme had been a great success and Ivy had continued the practice.

"Merciful Jesus!" Ivy prayed as she unpicked the seams to

reveal more large white five-pound notes stitched into the space between the outer layer of material and the lining of the coat. "How much feckin money did yeh think yeh'd need?" Ivy picked the hems of the garment to reveal a silver flow of half-crown coins. "Yeh weren't going to leave yerself short, were yeh, yeh auld besom!"

Ivy stared at the money in stunned amazement. She couldn't keep this amount of money about her person. She'd hand it all over to Jem in the morning. Seeing the money piled up on the table reminded Ivy of her own money concerns. She needed to rethink her way of doing things.

Ivy continued to carefully unpick the coat. She found ten-bob notes stitched into the sleeve cuffs, easy to get at and a small enough note that no-one would notice it.

"I need a pot of tea."

Ivy stood up. Using a piece of the lining to fashion a small purse for the money, she scooped the coins from the makeshift table and put them into it with the folded notes. Then carefully she sewed it into her skirt pocket. It would be safe enough there till the morning.

Ivy sat at her table, staring around at her freshly whitewashed back room. The fire in the range burned brightly. The big black kettle had steam puffing out of its spout. The big brass bed was pushed back against the wall separating the two rooms. Ivy had taken the time to make the bed up with the new sheet she'd bought. She planned to put the aunt's sheets in the tin tub to soak. They were far too fine for bed linen. She planned to buy actual pillowcases and blankets sometime in the near future. In the meantime her brother's old coat served as a covering.

"Begob, I won't know meself."

Ivy sipped tea from a cup from the china set Jem had given her. She felt tears pour down her face. She didn't know what she was feeling. So much had happened in such a short space of time. Her da's death had totally rocked her world on its foundations. She was going to have to work hard to find her feet again.

"I guess you'd say me ship came in, Da." Ivy raised her arm and wiped her tears on the sleeves of her blouse. "The thing is, Da, I don't know what to do with the feckin' thing."

Ivy stood – the smell of fresh paint in the room wasn't unpleasant. She'd lie in her big bed and think.

"I'm going to have that bath I promised myself tomorrow," Ivy grinned. "See if I don't."

Chapter 19

"Da, it's me, Ivy." Ivy knelt before the statue of Saint Francis. The church in what Dubliners called John's Lane, actually Harry Street, off Grafton Street, was empty this early in the morning, the only candles flaming the three Ivy had lit for her father.

Ivy stared at the flickering flames trying to gather her thoughts. So much had happened in the three months since his death.

"You've heard all this before, Da, but I'm not sure if talking to you in me rooms is the same as Church so you'll have to forgive me if I repeat meself. Yeh got yer Requiem Mass. Wherever yeh are, did yeh hear the Mass?" Ivy tried to keep a pious expression on her face but she failed. A huge grin split her features. "Nelly Kelly wouldn't shut up about it." Ivy looked around to check she still had the church to herself. At five o'clock in the morning who else would be fool enough to be up and about? Still, it was better to be safe than sorry. "I think she shamed Father Leary into it, if such a thing is possible. Yeh had a great turnout, Da. The place was packed. I was sitting front row centre, did ye see me, Da?"

Ivy remembered that day with mixed emotions. Jem Ryan and Emmy had been sitting alongside her. They'd been like a little family that day.

"I wore the suit Mr Solomon made for me, Da. I looked a picture, if I do say so meself."

Ivy shivered, remembering the look in Father Leary's eyes that morning. She'd have dropped dead on the spot if that man had his way.

"I know yeh always told me 'self praise is half scandal', Da, but I wanted yeh to be proud of me."

The suit Mr Solomon had fashioned from the remnants Ivy gave him, copying the jacket she'd borrowed from Ann Marie for the purpose, was a work of art. The man was a genius. The look on auld Leary's face had been a picture no artist could paint.

"I think Father Leary would have had me thrown out of the church if he could have, Da."

Ivy shivered again, remembering the sheer hatred in the glares the parish priest had sent her way.

"I don't know what I ever did to make that man hate me, Da. It would make a cat laugh." Ivy's smile was bittersweet. "Yer friend Nelly is only a step away from a streetwalker, not that I'm judging the woman. She has to make a living like the rest of us. Still, Father Leary welcomed her into his church."

Ivy didn't understand the priest's attitude towards her. She tried not to think about it because it hurt to be hated for a reason she couldn't understand.

"After the Mass I treated yer cronies and the neighbours to a right bash at the pub. Free drink and sandwiches – it was standing room only, Da."

Jem had insisted Ivy use one of the five-pound notes she'd found in the aunt's coat to give her da a right royal send-off. Ivy had begrudged every penny of it. But afterwards she'd noticed a definite improvement in the way people treated her. She supposed that made everything worth it.

"I have to tell yeh, Da. I went into a bank."

Ivy held her breath. Ann Marie had taken both Jem and Ivy to open accounts at the Bank of Ireland. The thought of entering the beautiful building across from Trinity College had almost crippled Ivy with nerves. "I nearly ran away but I didn't, Da. You should have seen the state of me. I wore me good suit, held me head high and walked into that place as if I owned the gaff. I opened an account in me own name, Da. I'm going to have me own cheque book. Imagine, giving out bits of paper instead of money! I bet yer sitting up there on your cloud laughing like a drain, Da. Can yeh believe it? Me, I ask yer sacred pardon!"

Ivy cringed as the sound of her own laughter echoed through the church.

"I'm worried about Granny, Da." Ivy sighed. "I don't think the old woman has long for this life. She's ready to go, yeh can tell it from her."

Ivy bowed her head. She said a prayer for the woman who'd taken her in hand as a little girl. The Murphy family owed that woman a debt of gratitude.

"Me two rooms are looking a treat, Da." Ivy didn't want to think about Granny right now or she'd cry. The old woman hadn't been able to get out of bed to go to her morning Mass lately. A young priest, Father Coyle, came by every morning to give her the sacraments. "Granny gave me her big dresser for me rooms." Granny decided that, since Ivy was doing all the cooking for both of them, she needed the huge cabinet to store her foodstuffs and utensils. Conn and Jem had moved it into Ivy's back room.

"I'm learning to read, Da." Ivy's grin could have lit up the dark church. The wonder of being able to make out words in the newspaper would never fail to delight her. "I do me homework every day with Emmy. I know yeh won't be happy with me decision to send Emmy to the school Ann Marie recommended, Da, it not being Catholic and all – I had to fight Jem on that one. I have to tell yeh, Da, everything Ann Marie tells me about the Quakers makes a lot more sense to me than the laws of the Catholic Church." Ivy hunched her shoulders, half expecting the roof to fall in on top of her. "I never knew that the Jacob's biscuit factory and Bewley's cafe was run by Quakers, did you, Da?"

Ivy, wearing her new suit, had been to take morning coffee at Bewley's café on Grafton Street. She'd felt a proper swell. What with wearing her fancy new suit with the hand-knit purple lace sweater that Granny had made for her, Ivy felt like the bee's knees. She'd been waited on by a woman wearing a black dress and white apron, for heaven's sake! All of it had been a wonder to her. The price they'd paid for two cups of coffee and a couple of scones had nearly made her faint but the experience had been priceless.

"Anyway, Da, the education that child is getting at the Quaker school the Jacob's factory runs, is second to none." Ivy grinned proudly. "She's helping me with me learning. Da, I'm really smart. Did ye know that, Da?" Ivy had been astonished by the ease and speed of her learning. The world was opening up to her and she was hungry for knowledge. "Anyway, Da, Liam says me mental arithmetic is a wonder to behold." Ivy smiled. Liam had her perform like a trained pet for the enjoyment of Jem and Conn. "I won't go on about it, Da – yeh'll say I'm being vain but it's a wonder to me that I have a brain."

Ivy again hunched her shoulders.

"I did something I'm not sure about, Da. I went down to the Franciscan friars. I did it for Liam." Ivy knew her father wouldn't approve of her going outside Westland Row for help. "The lad is failing, Da. He's skin and bone and his skin is grey. It doesn't have anything to do with hunger, Da. It's in his head. He needs help. I had to do something. Anyway, nothing has come of it but I thought I'd better let yeh know."

Ivy pushed herself to her feet.

"I have to get on. I have things I need to get done today." The candles were still burning brightly. She stepped out of the pew and genuflected in the aisle. "I enjoyed our little visit, Da. I'll come again."

Ivy pushed her well-laden pram through the streets Dubliners called The Warren. The streets were narrow, the houses built so close together they seemed to lean towards each other. No sunlight would dare to shine on the dark narrow lanes and alleys. It was ironic that the streets carried names like Queen Street and such. The area was called The Warren because of the hundreds of bare-arsed children who ran wild around the place.

Ivy had business to conduct down these dark alleys. Dotted around these streets men and women ran second-hand shops from the front room of their two-up, two-down houses. Ivy was happy to think she'd had no need of the backstreet pawnshops in years. Her pram was heavy with items she was sure she could shift at a handsome profit.

She'd been spending her evenings delving into her tea chests. She was clearing out years of accumulated items she'd had stashed away. Ivy had found little treasures, like the silk underwear she'd put aside until she had the time to mend it. A selection of old-fashioned long skirts had been at the bottom of one chest. Ivy had pulled these apart and refashioned them. The sheer amount of knitwear she'd kept had astonished her. The freedom to empty the chests out completely and leave the items out until she'd made a decision about their disposal was increasing Ivy's business. Her new-found ability to make notes and write signs never failed to delight her.

Ivy wasn't quite sure of her direction today. She was looking for someone. With the increased income from her round, plus the time to stop and think, she had been making plans. She'd come to the conclusion she needed more hands. She couldn't do everything she wanted to get done herself. Just the thought of paying someone to do work for her had Ivy sick to her stomach. At the same time she was that proud of herself she could strut. Her world was certainly changing.

Chapter 20

"Mrs Reilly, thank you for joining me."

Brian Sarsfield nearly dropped the silver salver he was placing on the dining-room sideboard. That was a turn-up for the books. The gentry thanking a housekeeper, what was the world coming to?

Brian had been deputised to serve Miss Gannon whenever she met with the housekeeper. Foster considered the serving of a housekeeper beneath his dignity. That didn't stop the man from demanding Brian repeat everything he heard.

"Not at all, Miss Gannon." Agnes Reilly bowed her head elegantly and waited for the footman to pull out her chair. She intended to get every bit of pleasure out of these occasions. Iris Jones, the cook, would be hanging on her every word when she told her about this.

"If you don't mind, Mrs Reilly, we'll serve ourselves." Ann Marie wanted to scream. Was there no way to simply hold a conversation in this house? Why had she never noticed the servants before?

"Shall I place the salver on the table, Miss Gannon?" Brian Sarsfield wasn't going to pretend he was deaf.

"That would be ideal . . ." Ann Marie raised her eyebrows at Mrs Reilly, hoping she'd remind her of the man's name.

"Brian," Mrs Reilly offered in a whisper, "Brian Sarsfield."

"Thank you, Mr Sarsfield," Ann Marie said as the tray was moved from the sideboard to the end of the long highly polished table nearest to the two women.

Brian Sarsfield almost fainted. She'd called him 'Mr Sarsfield' as if he was important. He'd be telling everyone about that. "If you need anything else, Miss Gannon?"

"That will be all." Ann Marie glanced at the tray. They could hold out for a week on the amount of food on it. Ann Marie stood to serve the housekeeper herself as Brian withdrew. "I hope you don't mind, Mrs Reilly." The family were out for the day on one of their many social visits. Ann Marie had the run of the house. This was the first time the two women had actually met in the dining room. Ann Marie had been having meetings with the housekeeper in her own suite of rooms. "I want to talk to you privately."

"Not at all, Miss Gannon." Agnes Reilly prepared to be served.

"I want to thank you for all of your help over the last weeks." Ann Marie placed the china plates covered in lace doilies, with attractively arranged finger sandwiches, on the table between them. "I can't thank you enough for all the times you acted as go-between for Miss Murphy and myself."

Agnes waited, knowing by now Miss Gannon would get to the point when she was ready.

"Just a little cream in your coffee, isn't it, Mrs Reilly?" Ann Marie asked, holding aloft the ornate silver coffee pot.

"Yes, thank you." Agnes Reilly imagined herself quite the lady of the house. It was a delightful little fantasy.

"Miss Murphy has asked a favour of me," Ann Marie said as she sat down with her own coffee.

"Indeed, Miss Gannon." Agnes Reilly didn't know what else to say. The thought of little Ivy Murphy asking the gentry to help her out should have shocked Agnes Reilly rigid but Agnes was proud of her ability to handle the new way of doing things she was learning with Miss Gannon.

"Ivy wants me to visit The Lane." Ann Marie was delighted, at this final sign of acceptance. She couldn't wait to see where

Ivy and Jem lived. After all the stories Ivy had told her Ann Marie couldn't wait to see the place for herself. She felt as if she'd been invited to visit another planet not simply a nearby area. "Are you all right, Mrs Reilly?" Ann Marie jumped up to pat Mrs Reilly on the back.

The woman had choked on the sip of coffee she'd been about to swallow.

"Miss Gannon," Mrs Reilly signalled she was okay, "Ivy Murphy asked you to visit her in The Lane?" She stared at the woman taking her chair again across the wide table. "Is she out of her mind?" The words escaped before she could censor them.

"I'm really looking forward to the experience." Ann Marie grinned widely with delight.

"Rather you than me." Agnes Reilly had said it before and she'd say it again: the quality were funny in the head.

"Ivy is to purchase an outfit for me to wear." Ann Marie looked at the polished satin skirt of her day dress. "She informs me that I can't walk into The Lane wearing my normal attire."

"I should think not." Agnes Reilly said simply. She'd been serving as go-between, passing on messages and intriguing parcels at the back door of Number 8. Agnes Reilly was enjoying the change in routine but sometimes in her private heart she wondered what planet the rich lived on.

"I wanted to have an outfit made for me but Ivy vetoed that idea." Ann Marie didn't see the problem. "I don't know why – after all, I will wear it more than once."

"How would you make the thing look old and worn?" Agnes Reilly wanted to sigh. "The material will need to have the shine that only much wear brings to a garment."

"I see." Ann Marie shrugged. "Well, I don't really, but Ivy has already told me I'm blind as a bat to the world around me." Ann Marie didn't know Agnes Reilly almost needed the smelling salts at this point.

"A visit to The Lane." Mrs Reilly said. This woman in the Lane, it didn't bear thinking about. She'd be lucky to get out with all her skin intact.

"Ivy is deeply concerned about a neighbour of hers." Ann Marie refilled the housekeeper's coffee cup, unaware of the havoc she was causing in the smooth running of Foster's household. "An old woman who is very feeble."

"What does she think you can do?" Agnes Reilly had heard it all now. They were never going to believe this below stairs.

"I won't know until I've seen the woman." Ann Marie knew Ivy was hoping she would use her connections at Kevin's Hospital to get the old woman a bed. Ivy had told Ann Marie so much about Granny Grunt she almost felt she knew the woman.

"Well, I'm glad you've got something to look forward to." Agnes Reilly didn't know what else to say. The world was going to hell in a hand-basket as far as she was concerned. She settled back to see what else would come up in this conversation. No-one could say Agnes Reilly wasn't ready to move with the times.

The two women settled into a gossip session with Ann Marie picking Mrs Reilly's brain for ideas on how she should behave on her very first visit to The Lane.

"I won't come in, Patsy, thanks."

Ivy stood in the tenement hallway staring at the woman in front of her. She wanted to swear. She knew Patsy O'Malley and would never have willingly knocked on the woman's door. She must have taken a wrong turn somewhere. She'd asked directions around the Daisy Market and was sure she was at the right address.

Ivy knew Patsy O'Malley wasn't much older than her own age of twenty-one but the woman in front of her looked old and tired. Her body was swollen with what Patsy sourly told her was the sixth O'Malley "babby".

"What do ye want with our Sadie, Ivy Murphy? What did she do?" Patsy O'Malley was a woman who always looked for the worst to happen. Her sour attitude to life was carved into her face. Her life wasn't that different to the lives of everyone else around her. The difference was Patsy's attitude.

"I just want to chat a while with Sadie – pass the time of day."

Ivy thought she'd walked every street in Dublin but following the directions she'd received from one of the women selling fruit from her pram had led her through a world even more downtrodden than anything she'd seen before. The walls seemed to lean in towards each other, making sure bright light wouldn't dare to enter the miserable streets.

The houses were packed so tightly together women living across the street from each other held conversations without stepping away from their own front door. The wet laundry strung on ropes between the buildings cast an unpleasant haze over everything.

"What would our Sadie have to say to the likes of you?" The cheek of this one coming around here, coming to visit if yeh didn't mind, as if she was someone!

"Everything all right, Patsy?" The door directly opposite opened and a short, blonde woman stood in the opening.

"Sadie, have yeh got a minute?" Ivy grinned with relief.

"Will you step in?" Sadie Lawless opened her door wider and stepped back. "Yeh can bring yer pram in. I'll put the kettle on."

"Thanks, Sadie," Ivy hadn't planned to bring her pram into Sadie's room but she didn't trust Patsy as far as she could throw her.

"Oh, yeh keep yer place lovely!"

The room Ivy stepped into was spotless. Everything, including the two girls playing on the mat in front of the empty fire grate, was ruthlessly organised.

"Howaye, girls?" Ivy smiled at Sadie's daughters.

"Sit yerself down Ivy. I'll make a pot of tea and you can tell me what's brought you down here." Sadie turned to put water to boil on a small Primus stove.

Ivy searched her pockets and found two brown pennies. She held a penny in each hand towards the girls. "Girls, why don't ye go to the shop while I talk to yer ma?" Ivy had been surprised to see the two girls at home.

"Don't let your Aunty Patsy see that money, girls," Sadie warned, knowing Patsy could almost smell coppers.

"Thank you." The tallest girl held the coin out on her palm, her eyes wide in astonishment.

"Go out for a while, girls." Sadie hated knowing her girls wouldn't spend the money. They knew she needed every brown penny right now.

"Sit down for goodness sake Ivy you're making the place look untidy." Sadie pulled a chair out from the big table pushed under the window overlooking the street. "You've never come to my door before, Ivy Murphy."

"Sadie, yeh can tell me to sod off if yeh want but something isn't right." Ivy kept her eyes firmly away from the empty grate. It was freezing in this room. "Yeh're not yer usual smiling self."

"Then yeh haven't heard." Sadie turned to check the water. "I thought maybe yeh had and that's why you'd come."

"What's going on, Sadie?" Ivy watched Sadie make a pot of tea.

"It's me fella." Sadie's breath hitched. "He had an accident at work." Tears began to flow down Sadie's face. "Twenty years he's worked every day God sends at the Haymarket and in minutes it's all taken away from him. A bale of fecking hay broke his back. Hay, the like of which he threw over his head morning, noon and half the feckin' night."

"What!" Ivy was shocked. This was desperate news. Without a man's income coming in Sadie and her girls would be in dire straits. No wonder there was no fire in the grate. It was miracle Sadie had been able to offer Ivy a cup of tea. Ivy thought of Sadie's big laughing husband with sadness.

"My John's in Kevin's Hospital. He's been there the last two weeks. The doctors don't know if he'll be able to walk again." Sadie buried her face in her hands and sobbed.

Ivy sat silently and waited. Sometimes you needed a good cry.

"Sadie, I'm that sorry for your troubles." Ivy didn't know where to go from here.

"If yeh knew nothing about my John, why on earth have yeh come visiting, Ivy Murphy?" Sadie had known Ivy from a distance for years. However, they'd never been friends, just exchanged a casual greeting from time to time.

"I had things I wanted to talk to you about, Sadie." Ivy had thought long and hard about the people she knew before deciding to approach Sadie Lawless.

"What kind of things, Ivy?" Sadie stood to fetch the tea. She hoped Ivy liked weak tea because her supply of tea leaves was running low. She looked over her shoulder at the woman who was carefully looking down at the table. Sadie appreciated the fact that Ivy wasn't gawping at everything. "I don't mean to be awkward but I've enough on me plate at the minute."

"Sadie, I know we've never been what yeh could call close," Ivy stared into Sadie's eyes wanting the woman to see her sincerity, "but I have to ask yeh – how are yeh for money?"

"The people at the Haymarket had a whip around for me fella." Sadie referred to the habit of asking people to contribute whatever they could afford to help someone out. "It was good of them of course but none of them are exactly loaded."

"Doesn't answer me question, Sadie," Ivy shifted on her seat. "I've a reason for asking, Sadie. How are yeh fixed?"

"I'm sick with fear, Ivy Murphy, if yeh must know the truth!" Sadie put a cup of pale weak tea in front of Ivy. "I don't know which way to turn."

"Did the hospital give yeh any idea how long John would be in there?" Ivy had come to Sadie's with a plan in mind but this changed everything.

"Yeh know what they're like, Ivy," Sadie sighed. "They talk as if they have a plum in their mouth and you are so far beneath their notice it offends them to look at yeh. They haven't told me nothing."

"I'm sorry, Sadie." Ivy touched the other woman's hand gently. She took a small sip of tea, managing not to grimace.

"What did yeh want to talk to me about, Ivy?" Sadie gave a ghost of her usual smile. "Before I dumped the woes of the world on your shoulders, that is.

"I've seen the knitted stuff you've done for Maggie Wilson, Sadie." Ivy had thought long and hard about this but now she was unsure of herself. "Are yeh still doing it?"

"Naw, I couldn't make it pay." Sadie shook her head. "By the time I'd bought the wool and such there was no money in it for me."

"That's a shame, Sadie – it was lovely stuff." Ivy had an idea that Maggie Wilson had taken advantage of Sadie's soft nature. The knitted garments she'd seen under the stall were top quality.

"What are yeh going to do now, Sadie?" Ivy didn't know how to talk about what she wanted. Not with things so changed in Sadie's life.

"Oh Ivy!" Sadie held her tea cup in two hands staring down at the table. "Me girls are going to have to go into service. I never wanted that for them." She hiccupped "It's the only way I can be sure of a roof over their heads and food in their bellies."

"What about yourself, Sadie?" Ivy asked softly.

"Me brother said I could move over the hall and live with them." Sadie groaned.

"You and Patsy!" Ivy gasped.

"It's not what I want, Ivy, but 'needs must when the devil drives'," Sadie said pathetically.

"Sadie, can your girls knit? As good as you, I mean?"

"They can – my John and all. He'd kill me for telling yeh but it was my John who taught me to do all the fancy stitches." Sadie felt her spirits lift at the memory. "Ivy, will yeh just spit out whatever yeh want to say for Christ's sake?"

"How much do yeh need to live on a week, Sadie?" Ivy knew she was stepping over the line but she needed to know.

"Ivy Murphy, that's none of your bee's wax," Sadie snapped, using the Dublin expression to tell someone to mind their own business.

"I have a job in mind for you and the two girls, Sadie, but I need to know how much money it will take to keep yeh going every week."

Ivy couldn't support Sadie and her kids. She didn't know if the amount she was thinking of would be enough to at least keep the roof over their heads. That was the most important thing at the moment.

"What kind of job?" Sadie stared at Ivy.

"I have a small mountain of old jumpers and things I need taken to pieces." Ivy didn't want to spend her time doing the painstaking work. "I want the wool washed, brushed soft and ready to be reused."

"I'll be honest with yeh, Ivy. I'll take anything I can get and glad of it but picking jumpers apart won't take long and it won't keep us going for weeks," Sadie sighed.

"There's more to me idea than that, Sadie, but if you'd be willing to pick the jumpers apart and wash,stretch and brush the wool, that would be a start." Ivy needed to know what the situation was with John Lawless. If John's injuries were so bad that Sadie was forced to break up her family and move into Patsy's overcrowded rooms, Ivy's idea would never work. Patsy would turn Sadie into her personal slave.

"Look, I came down here for two reasons." Ivy didn't want to give Sadie false hope and she needed to move – she was freezing into place. "I wanted to talk to you about those jumpers and I need to go see a man called Pa Landers. Do you know where his place is? I want to look through what he has on hand. I've heard that the old man's stuff is of the best quality."

"He's not too far from here." Sadie stood and began picking up the teacups. "I'll just grab me shawl and show yeh. The walk will do me good." Sadie needed something to heat her up. The room was freezing. Sadie knew if she didn't knock in for Patsy she'd have hell to pay from her sister-in-law later. She couldn't care less. Let that one sit in her own home and stew in her own bitterness. She wasn't going to knock on her door and tell that woman her business.

"Sadie, do ye have a pram, something to haul stuff around in?" Ivy said just before Sadie opened her front door.

"No," Sadie said sadly. She'd been told she'd never have more children after the birth of her youngest, Dora. It had fair to broken her heart but the way things were perhaps it was for the best. Her sister-in-law Patsy across the hall seemed to get pregnant at the drop of a hat.

"That's a shame." Ivy shrugged. "I don't suppose yeh could borrow one from Patsy?"

"Patsy's pram is always in use," Sadie said softly.

The two women, with a gang of youngsters following in their footsteps, made their way to Pa Landers. The old man ran his business from the front room of his house. A table with cheap offerings was guarded by a youngster out front of the house. Pa Landers greeted them himself with charm and manners. Ivy explained her needs with a great deal of imaginative lying. Within minutes the two women were examining a black suit, skirt and jacket that were worn but obviously of good quality.

"Perfect!" Ivy declared after she'd used the tape measure she'd borrowed from around Pa Landers neck. "The skirt is a little long but that can be altered."

"Maybe you shouldn't bother," Sadie offered. Ivy had told her a little about her friend Ann Marie on the walk over. "The extra length might come in useful."

"You're probably right – we'll see." Ivy tried to imagine Ann Marie wearing the suit and had to bite back a grin.

"Shoes?" Pa Landers asked.

"Better to be sure than sorry," said Sadie. "You'll need a shawl as well."

"Certainly, ladies." Pa Landers hunted through his supplies. He didn't often sell so much at one time. He'd have to give Sadie Lawless a little something for bringing this customer to his door.

"Will that be all, ladies?" Pa Landers, looking at the selected items on the table he used as a shop counter was almost rubbing his hand in glee.

"How much?" Ivy grinned, getting ready to bargain. You never paid the asking price.

"Let me see." Pa Landers rubbed his bristled chin, preparing to enjoy himself.

Sadie stepped to one side. She watched and listened with delight as the two people entered into a round of abuse and complaint. Both of them shouted and shook their fists, all the while with huge grins on their faces.

"Right, I'll just pay this auld robber off," Ivy said at last. She was delighted with the deal she'd struck.

"Don't come around any more with this one, Sadie!" Pa

Landers took the money Ivy held out. "She'll have me in the poorhouse." He wrapped the suit, shoes and shawl in brown paper. An unusual courtesy – newspaper was the more usual wrapping but the woman had spent quite a bit of money with him. He could afford a bit of brown paper and perhaps the woman would come again.

"Before we leave, I just want to have a look around." Ivy wanted to have a look through the old man's stock for something for Emmy. The clothes on offer were of good quality, clean and in most cases flawless.

"Right." Pa Landers was delighted and stood to one side.

Ivy pulled a selection of young girls' winter wear from a pile.

"I'm looking for a fancy coat for meself, Mr Landers," Ivy remarked as she pounced on a child's wool dress that looked like it had never been worn The rich red colour would suit Emmy a treat. "I don't see any coats I like right now but if you'd let Sadie know if you get more coats in I'd appreciate it."

"I'll do that." Pa Landers ran a mental checklist through his contacts, wondering who could supply him with an upmarket coat.

"I'm going to call me girls." Sadie stood in the open doorway and yelled, "Clare, Dora, I want yiz!" The cry went up, repeated over and over again as the children playing in the street outside passed the message along. Sadie waited, sure the message would eventually reach her two girls, where ever they were playing. It was an efficient message system used by every mother around the place.

"I'll wrap these items." Pa Landers grinned as he took the young girls' clothes from Ivy's hands.

Sadie's two girls arrived panting and flushed with healthy colour. She took them by the hands and, with Ivy pushing her pram and leading the way, they set off to walk through Dublin. Sadie didn't want to go back to that freezing cold room just yet.

The women walked along, chatting away, until they reached O'Connell Street and there they stopped. Sadie didn't want to go any further. They still had the walk back home.

"Thanks for your help, Sadie." Ivy pressed a silver half crown into Sadie's hand.

"I'm not taking charity from yeh, Ivy Murphy!" Sadie tried to return the coin. "I might have agreed to do a bit of work for yeh but I haven't started yet." They'd agreed that Sadie and her girls would be home tomorrow, Saturday, when Ivy would deliver the old jumpers.

"It's not charity, Sadie," Ivy said and pressed the money, more than most men earned in a week, into Sadie's hand. "Besides, it's not my money."

"All right then." Sadie couldn't afford pride. "We'll see yeh tomorrow bright and early."

"See yiz!" Ivy grabbed the handle of her pram and headed for home.

Chapter 21

"Is that yerself, Ivy?"

Ivy pushed open the heavy wooden door set in the granite wall of the alley running behind the houses of Merrion Square. She pushed her pram in first, heartily glad her day outdoors was almost over. It had been a busy Monday so far and it wasn't over yet.

"Lovely weather for ducks!" ten-year-old Davy O'Malley, the bootblack at Number 8, grinned from his position crouched in the stone portico that framed the back door.

"How's it going then, Davy?" Ivy shouted pushing her heavy pram across the wet cobbles leading to the back door of Number 8. "What are yeh doing out here?"

"Keeping an eye out for yeh and cleaning the muck off his Lordship's boots." Davy held up the befouled soft leather boot he held. "Better let them know yeh're here." Davy stood, opened the door at his back and in his bare feet hurried down the long dark hallway to let the staff in the kitchen know that Ivy had arrived. He didn't linger, that would get him either a thick ear or another job to do.

"Do yeh ever feel like telling them they're big enough and bold enough to clean their own boots?" Ivy stood under the

215

protection of the stone portico now and called out to the skinny lad hurrying down the hallway towards her.

"I never see them to tell them anything Ivy." Davy, his dishwater blond hair standing up all over his head, grinned. "The likes of me only gets to see their dirt."

"Well," Ivy wanted to kick herself. It wasn't for her to make the lad uphappy with his lot in life, "is Miss Ann Marie ready for her outing, do you know?"

Davy O'Malley, eldest son of the sour-faced Patsy, was happy as a clam at Number 8. He slept in the inglenook and was first up every morning to blacklead the grate and build the fire in the range back up ready for Iris Jones the cook. He hauled buckets of coal from the shed at the end of the garden for the maids and carried away the ash. Any and all dirty work was left for Davy the bootblack.

"I don't know nothing about the goin's-on upstairs." Davy took up his crouched position again, reaching for the boot he'd dropped. "I saw me da yesterday when he come to collect me wages."

"Did you?" Ivy didn't know what else to say. She stood with Davy at the back door while the rain pelted down, enclosing them in a little bubble of greyness.

"Me da said yeh'd been down to see me Auntie Sadie," Davy used the back of the shoe brush he held in one hand to knock the mud off the boot he held in the other.

"So I was." Ivy knew Davy wanted something and was working up to it slowly. She leaned against the wall and waited.

"Them's a grand pair of boots you've got on today, Ivy." Davy looked longingly at the boys steel-capped work boots Ivy was wearing.

"I got them down the market." Ivy pushed out one foot to admire the boots. She'd been lucky, Bill Burn told her – boots like these were usually passed down through the family. The pair Ivy had bought off him had practically no wear on them. Ann Marie had balked at wearing someone else's shoes so on Saturday Ivy had stopped at Bill Burn's stall to buy a pair of new boots for Ann Marie. When Bill held up a pair of practically new boots Ivy had dived on them for her own use.

"Me da lets me keep a penny from me week's wages," Davy said shyly.

"Does he?"

"How long do you reckon it would take for me to save enough for a pair of boots like those?" Davy's dirty, cold blue toes clenched.

"How much have yeh got?" Ivy knew what it was like to long for something warm and dry to cover your feet.

"I had a shilling," Davy said proudly. Twelve pence was a lot of money. "But I had to lend it to me da."

"I'll keep me eye open for yeh and let yeh know," Ivy promised.

While Ivy and Davy waited in the cold and rain Ann Marie Gannon was dancing in front of her bedroom mirror. She was delighted with the way her second-hand suit changed her into someone she didn't recognise. She held up the long skirt to admire her workmen's boots. Ann Marie spun in place, delighted with the world in general.

"Come in," she called when someone knocked on her bedroom door.

"Ivy Murphy is downstairs waiting for you, Miss Ann Marie," Mary Coates said, coming into the room. She began to pick up the garments scattered around the room. She picked up the pale-peach silk gown Ann Marie had dropped carelessly to the floor. Out of the corner of her eye she watched Ann Marie dance around, admiring her image with more delight than she'd ever shown for the expensive designer clothes Mary so admired.

"Where's my shawl, Mary? What did you do with it?" Ann Marie stood away from the mirror and looked around the room as if expecting the shawl to rise up at her words.

"It's here, Miss," Mary went to the free-standing dresser of drawers and, kneeling, removed the black knit shawl from the bottom drawer. She stood, closing the drawer with the side of her foot.

"You will need something to hold the shawl in place, Miss." Mary turned to the hat pin stand on top of the dresser, searching for the plainest hat pin she could find.

"Thank you, Mary." Ann Marie stood waiting. "Whatever would I do without you?"

"Yes, Miss." Mary offered the standard servant response to all comments. She draped the shawl over Ann Marie's head, pulling the long ends of it over her back and shoulders. When the shawl was settled to her satisfaction Mary shoved three solid-silver hat pins with enamel heads into the shawl and through Ann Marie's hair. "That should hold, Miss." Mary stood back to admire her work. The pins were well hidden.

"Oh Mary!" Ann Marie hurried back to the mirror. She stood gazing at her own image a delighted grin almost splitting her face. "My own mother wouldn't recognise me." Ann Marie almost giggled.

"Yes, Miss."

"Is Ivy having a cup of tea in the kitchen?" Ann Marie continued to admire the stranger in the glass.

"Not as far as I know, Miss," Mary offered.

'But it's raining so hard," Ann Marie looked over her shoulder with a frown. "Surely Ivy isn't standing out in the rain?" Ann Marie turned and stood with her hands out in front of her – waiting for Mary to pass her gloves. When nothing happened she frowned. "My gloves, Mary."

"You have no gloves suitable for that outfit, Miss," Mary said.

"I should go out with bare hands?" Ann Marie asked.

"Yes, Miss."

"Oh, very well." Ann Marie wanted to get on her way. She couldn't wait to see this Lane she'd heard so much about. "I mustn't keep Miss Murphy waiting." Delighted with the world at large she turned to hurry from the room.

Ann Marie stopped before actually opening the door and turned to Mary standing at her back. "Mary, could you please check the way is clear for me?" She didn't want to bump into any of her relatives and have to explain her strange clothing.

"Yes, Miss." Mary opened the door and stepped into the hallway. "There is no-one about, Miss."

"Wonderful!" Ann Marie stepped outside and waited while Mary closed the door. "I'll use the back stairs, Mary."

"Yes, Miss." Mary mentally shook her head and led the way down the servant's stairway to the kitchen. If there were any servants lingering in the kitchen they were about to get the shock of their lives at one of the family entering their domain.

"Miss!" Iris Jones pushed to her feet. She'd been sitting at the well-scrubbed kitchen table enjoying a well-deserved cup of tea.

"Don't mind me!" Ann Marie called gaily hurrying to follow Mary into the back hallway. At any other time she would have enjoyed stopping to examine her surroundings but today she had places to go, people to see.

"Ivy!" Ann Marie shouted when she saw her friend standing outside the open back door. "I'm ready."

"So I see," Ivy sighed. Ann Marie looked like a child who was being taken to see the circus.

"Do we not need an umbrella?" Ann Marie looked out at the rain sheeting down. She didn't notice the young boy pushing himself back into the corner of the portico.

"Come on, Ann Marie," Ivy shook her head. "the day will be over before we get started." She took her pram by the handles and turned away from the door. Ann Marie could follow as she would.

"I'm so excited, Ivy." Ann Marie hurried to follow Ivy out through the slowly closing back door.

"I can tell."

"I've never come out this way before."

"Now there's a surprise."

"Where do those doors lead?" Ann Marie pointed at the long grey granite wall broken by doorways that formed the opposite side of the long back alley.

"Buck Lane," Ivy supplied. "That's a row of townhouses now but it used to be the carriage houses to places like yours." Ivy didn't bother looking around. She knew this area like the back of her hand.

Ann Marie said no more but hurried to keep up with Ivy's pace. Her head was constantly turning to catch a glimpse of the world around her. It was fascinating. At the end of the Lane Ivy turned right towards the main road. Ann Marie could see horse-drawn carriages and the occasional motor vehicle pass. She felt almost faint with excitement. At the main road Ivy turned left in the direction of the Grand Canal. Ann Marie had thought she knew this area extremely well but she had no idea where Ivy was heading.

"Almost there," Ivy offered.

"Really," Ann Marie looked back over her shoulder. They were mere minutes away from her uncle's home.

"Hey, young ones!" A drunken wag stumbling out of the pub attached to the tunnel leading into the Lane shouted. "Here's young fellas!"

Ivy ignored him, well aware of Ann Marie's big-eyed wonder. "Don't let any part of yeh touch these walls," she warned, turning into the tunnel, "and watch yer step."

Ann Marie walked silently through the tall, wide tunnel trying desperately not to breathe. The stench of urine was overpowering. She gasped with relief when the tunnel was cleared. With her mouth still open Ann Marie stood staring at a place she'd never known existed. She'd expected a long dark alley because Ivy always referred to this place as The Lane. The reality was very different.

"Ivy, wait!" Ann Marie almost tripped on the cobbles. She hurried to catch up with Ivy who was hurrying over to two young men standing outside what she thought was a long, high barn. She desperately wanted to just stand still and take everything in.

"Conn, Liam!" Ivy called to the two Connellys standing outside the main stable doors to the livery. "What are the two of you doing standing outside in this lovely weather?"

"Howayeh, Ivy!" Conn and Liam touched fingers to the brims of their soft caps.

"Jem asked us to keep an eye on the place," Conn offered.

"This is me friend, Ann Marie," Ivy said when Ann Marie arrived at her side. The lads touched their caps again but said nothing. "I'm going to take her over to visit Granny. Can I leave me pram here with you two?"

"We'll put it inside out of the rain," Liam said. His faithful dog, looking as if she was about to burst, sat at his feet.

"Grand, I'll be a while." Ivy grabbed Ann Marie by the elbow and practically towed her along at her side. "If Emmy gets home from school before I'm finished keep her with yiz, will yiz?"

"Ivy, for goodness sake will you let me take a breath!" Ann Marie pulled her elbow free and stood looking around her.

"I'm in a bit of a hurry, Ann Marie." Ivy wanted to get Ann Marie stashed away with Granny before The Lane was invaded by swarms of children shouting and screaming with delight at the end of the school day. And before the men kneeling and standing around the nearest lamppost, decided to take a minute away from the toss school to ask questions.

"What is that?" Ann Marie nodded towards the long building the two young men stood before.

"That's Jem's livery."

Ann Marie tried to make sense of what she was seeing. She wondered if the livery had once upon a time been a way station for travellers. With the public house backing onto one wall and the sheer size of the extra long barn-like structure it would have been an ideal location for travellers. Its placement was ideal, minutes away from the city centre and the Grand Canal.

"What are those?" Ann Marie pointed to the long low buildings that covered the end-space between the row of tenements and the livery. She thought perhaps at one time the space might have been dormitories for travellers.

"Double-front houses." Ivy took Ann Marie's elbow again. "Come on."

"I'm coming." Ann Marie stared at the row of tenement houses that Ivy was towing her towards. Each house had a main door that stood open to the elements. In some doorways women stood staring out, each with a shawl wrapped around her shoulders and head.

"How's yerself, Ivy?" one woman shouted.

"Can't complain. Ethel."

"Lovely day for ducks, Ivy!" another woman offered.

"I'm glad it's good for something, Ruby." Ivy didn't stop pulling Ann Marie towards one of the open doors.

"What's going on, Ivy?" Maisie Reynolds shouted from her doorway.

"I'm on me way to see Granny." Ivy wanted to get Ann Marie inside before they felt brave enough to walk over and demand answers. The women of The Lane liked to know what was going on.

Ivy towed Ann Marie up the well-scrubbed steps of the third house from the tunnel. The long, broad, stone steps led up to a wide doorway. Tall, wide windows on both sides of the doorway sported spotlessly clean white net curtains. Ann Marie only had time to catch her breath before Ivy pulled her through the open doorway.

"What's going on, Ivy Murphy," A tall thin workworn woman stood in the open doorway on one side of the main hallway.

"I'm taking me friend Ann Marie down to see Granny," Ivy groaned silently. She hadn't wanted to drag Ann Marie around the tenement block to Granny's back basement room. She'd hoped she could get through the house without being noticed but another door was opening across the hallway.

"What's going on out here?" A woman, slightly younger but as worn as the first, stood in the open doorway, four small grubby children clinging to her skirts.

"Dolly, Gertie, this is me friend Ann Marie. I'm taking her down to see Granny," Ivy offered. "You'll be seeing her from time to time. She's going to check on Granny sometimes when I'm not here."

"Good afternoon," Ann Marie said softly.

The hallway they stood in was in size and shape almost a carbon copy of the house her uncle lived in.

The hemp rope hanging from the highest banister would not have been tolerated in her uncle's home, nor would the tow-haired youngster with a runny nose be allowed swing from that rope.The young girl sitting halfway up the broad staircase with an open book on her lap, surrounded by a gaggle of small children would never have been tolerated either.

"Hope that's not another one of them do-gooders, Ivy Murphy," Gertie said.

"I knocked on Granny's winder when I was out getting water," Dolly sniffed. "I asked if there was anything I could get her. She gave me the sour edge of her tongue for me trouble."

"You know Granny, Dolly." Ivy understood Granny's attitude – wherever Dolly went her brood of runny-nosed, nimble-fingered toddlers went with her. You'd need eyes in the back of your head when that lot were around.

"She's me friend, Gertie." Ivy grabbed at Ann Marie and towed her towards the back of the hall. A heavy door blocked the entrance to the basement stairs. Ivy wanted to get through that door and away. "I'll see yeez later."

"Quick!" Ivy slammed the door at her back, pushing Ann Marie onto a small landing before her. "Let me go in front. It's pitch black on these stairs. Put your hand on my shoulder."

Ann Marie, feeling like she'd fallen down the rabbit hole, followed along.

"So, I finally get to meet your fancy friend." Granny was propped up against the two down-filled pillows Ivy had taken from the belongings of a dead woman. The old woman's grey hair hung down on either side of her face, in well-maintained plaits.

"Good afternoon." Ann Marie stood just inside the open door of the basement room. The place was cluttered to put it kindly.

"You're letting the hot air out. Come in and stop standing there like a statue!" Granny snapped. "Girl, move the kettle over to boil!"

Ivy hurried to do her bidding.

"Come in," Granny snapped again when Ann Marie made no effort to move.

"Here!" Ivy pulled one of the wooden chairs from the side of

223

the table under the window. "Sit here." She put the chair by the side of Granny's bed. She'd re-arranged the room so Granny's bed was closer to the fire. Granny's belongings had been pushed in a heap at one end of the room.

"Girl, get that," Granny waved vaguely at the ground.

Ivy understood – she'd got the whiff when she first came in. Granny's po needed emptying.

"Have yeh fresh water?" Ivy fell to her knees to search out the po which was stashed away under the bed.

"Young Conn got me some." Granny leaned back on the pillows. Her old eyes had never left Ann Marie's face.

Ivy stood up with the po in her hand. She didn't stop but hurried from the room. "I won't be long."

"I haven't time for niceties," Granny said as soon as the door closed at Ivy's back. "Ivy calls you her friend – are you?"

"I want to be." Ann Marie was conscious of the intent scrutiny Granny was subjecting her to.

"I'm going to get rid of Ivy." Granny could hear the girl coming back. Ivy never walked when she could run. "I want to talk to you. We'll have to be quick about it."

"Did yeh rinse your hands?" Granny snapped as soon as Ivy stepped over the threshold. "Use the water from the kettle to wash them," the old woman ordered. "There's a new bar of Sunlight soap beside the basin. I'll visit with your friend while you make us all a cup of tea."

"Yes, Granny," Ivy, her back turned to Granny, grinned. The old woman was making sure they knew who was boss.

"This coverlet is beautiful," Ann Marie said, admiring the cover on the woman's bed.

"Ivy's blood, sweat and tears!" Ivy and Granny said in almost one voice.

"We made this coverlet out of all the pieces of needlework the girl put together," Granny added.

"That cover is the history of my years under Granny's thumb," Ivy offered.

"It's wonderful," Ann Marie said.

"Girl, did yeh think to bring in any milk?" Granny snapped.

"Oh, I forgot! It's in me pram." Ivy took her hands out of the enamel bowl of warm water she'd filled. "I'll run over and get it – won't be a minute."

"Take your time!" Granny shouted at Ivy's disappearing back. "That girl will break her neck one of these days."

"I've been looking forward to meeting you." Ann Marie didn't know how to address the woman.

Granny tried to push herself into an upright position. "We won't have much time before she's back again."

Ann Marie jumped to her feet. She helped Granny to get into a sitting position. "Is that better?"

"Sit down," Granny said. "I know I'm being impolite. I know me manners but I'm old and don't have much time left to me. Listen, Ivy tells me you're not short of a few bob, is that right?"

Ann Marie felt her back stiffen. "I'm comfortably situated."

"I'm not after yer money." Granny liked the look of this woman. She might be good for her girl. "Well, I am, but not in the way you think. Do you see that sewing machine over there?" She pointed towards a heavy black wrought-iron item with a wooden top.

"I don't see a sewing machine." Ann Marie didn't know what she'd expected from this meeting but this was not it.

"It folds down into the base." Granny waved a hand. "I want you to buy that machine off me for Ivy. No!" Granny held up her hand when Ann Marie looked as if she was going to say something. "I'd give Ivy the machine and gladly but I need to be able to pay my way. I've been taking jobs I'm not fit to do. Ivy does them and gives me the money. I don't want that to go on. If you buy that machine off me – and we'd keep that fact between us – well, I'll give Ivy the machine. It will make her life a great deal easier."

"I can do that."

"I know you've offered to buy Ivy a coat. She'll never agree. All that girl's got that's her own is her pride but pride doesn't put food on the table." Granny began to cough violently. "She can't

225

keep going like she has," she said when she could. "She is running herself ragged looking after me. I won't have it."

"Ivy is very fond of you . . ."

"Call me 'Granny', everyone else does."

"Very well, Granny."

"Now, the money from the sewing machine will let me pay me rent for the rest of me days. I haven't long. I've been waiting for the good Lord to take me but he's taking his time. I never thought I'd live to this age." The old face on the pillows was wrinkled like an apple left out in the sun too long. "Ivy's paying young Conn Connelly to look in on me – out of her own pocket. I know she's not taking any money from me jar for the vittles."

"That sounds like the Ivy I've come to know." Ann Marie waited. She was sure there was more.

"I'm happy for you to visit me here." Granny said. "Ivy is out and about every day. We'll have time for me to tell you what you can do to make Ivy's life a little bit easier. What do you think?"

"I think you are a very crafty old woman!" Ann Marie said. "I'll buy the sewing machine from you, willingly. I'll listen to your advice but in return I want you to tell me everything you know about Miss Ivy Rose Murphy."

"It's a deal," Granny only had time to say before Ivy exploded into the room.

"Sorry it took me so long." Ivy held the can filled with fresh milk in her hand. "Conn was telling me he's got a few days' work at the butcher's. He'll be able to get his hands on a bit of tripe and some gooseneck giblets for us. We'll be eating high off the hog, Granny!"

"You're going to have to give this one lessons in making tea, girl," Granny grunted. "She's sat in that chair with her hands folded in her lap the whole time you were gone."

"What . . . ?" Ivy held the steaming kettle in her hand.

"Never mind, I'll do it meself," Granny said. "I'll soon have your woman beat into shape. You can't go visiting the sick if you don't know how to make a cup of tea."

"Is Ann Marie going to be calling on you, Granny?" Ivy kept her back turned while she made a pot of tea.

"Yes, she is, girl," Granny agreed. "We're going to get to know each other."

Chapter 22

"Auntie Ivy, Auntie Ivy, come quick!"

"Miss Emmy," Ivy pulled open her front door and grinned down at the little girl practically dancing in place. "What's the matter?"

"I opened the stall door, Auntie Ivy. Uncle Jem said no but I opened the door. The pups are out, Auntie Ivy!" Emmy tried to pull Ivy out of her doorway. "You have to come. Uncle Jem will be so angry with me. Uncle Jem said to be careful but I let the pups out." Emmy was talking so fast and wailing so much her words tumbled over each other.

"We'll get the pups back in their stall, Emmy. Uncle Jem won't be mad at yeh." Ivy turned into her front room to fetch her keys and a shawl. The longer days and brighter evenings led local kids into all kinds of mischief. Why should Emmy be any different? "How was school today?" Ivy asked.

Emmy insisted on sharing her schoolwork with Ivy. Each evening Emmy and Ivy sat at Ivy's table and worked at their lessons. Emmy was endlessly patient, taking her teaching duties very seriously.

"School is easy. I love my reading, writing and arithmetic," Emmy said, skipping along backwards without looking where she was going. "I don't like the sewing things!" Emmy tittered at her oft-repeated refrain.

"That's okay for you to say!" Ivy moaned for Emmy's sake. In fact, Ivy was enchanted by everything she was learning. Liam Connelly was a strict taskmaster. Ivy sometimes felt like the village idiot but she was learning and loving every minute of it.

"I heard the sad boy say you are sucking him dry of all knowledge." Emmy shared this bit of news with great solemnity, her big green eyes shining with respect and awe.

"Come on, you little baggage!" Ivy pulled Emmy with her as they ran towards the livery. The little girl was precocious to say the least. She refused to call Liam by name, always referring to him as "the sad boy". She picked up information at a frightening speed and seemed capable of repeating everything she heard or saw.

"*Harlot!*" a voice rang out across the cobbles. "Father Leary has you in his sights. You are doomed to eternal damnation, Ivy Murphy. Father Leary knows what you are. He's right about you. I've seen you myself consorting with young boys, leading them into sin. You're a harlot, Ivy Murphy!"

"Sheila Purcell, have you nothing better to do with your time?" Ivy looked at the woman charging towards them. Sheila was carrying a large cross and waving a bottle of clear liquid around the place. Ivy presumed it was a bottle of holy water the woman was shaking frantically in her direction.

"I know all about you." Sheila Purcell was aware of the eyes and ears that watched her. She was determined to expose this sinner, this harlot, for what she really was. Ivy Murphy should be ashamed to show her face amongst God-fearing people.

"Everyone knows you murdered your own father!" Sheila Purcell screamed her accusation. "Everyone knows you did it, Ivy Murphy, but no-one will say it to your face. Éamonn Murphy, that poor sainted man, killed dead before his time! Everyone knows he was killed by his own daughter. You had to be shamed into having a Requiem Mass said for the repose of his soul. Shame on you, I say, shame on you, Ivy Murphy! You should hang your head!"

"Go peddle your holy water somewhere else, Sheila," Ivy sighed tiredly

"That woman speaks the truth! You are a sinner, Ivy Rose Murphy!" A male voice echoed down the tunnel. The echo lent an impressive depth to the statement.

"Another country heard from." Yes, the longer evenings brought out the headbangers, Ivy thought.

"Run and ask Liam to give you a hand putting those puppies back in their stall, Emmy." Ivy wanted the child out of the way of the train wreck she could see coming. "I'll be along in a minute."

"I want to stay with you." Emmy tried to hang on to Ivy's hand. She didn't like these people. Why was that woman screaming at Ivy?

"Run along, Emmy." Ivy pushed the child gently. "I'll be all right." She wasn't actually sure of that but she wouldn't allow anyone to terrify Emmy. "Look, there's Liam now – he'll help you with the puppies. Go on, now!"

Emmy reluctantly went.

"There you are, Ivy Rose Murphy," Father Leary said as he exited the tunnel. The priest always gave Ivy her full title. He'd told her she was named for a plant that strangled and a flower that slashed and tore at everything around it. The priest's words had bothered Ivy as a child. "I was coming to see you."

"Were you indeed?" Ivy wasn't impressed. She was, however, cautious. Father Leary carried a walking stick. It wouldn't do to let him near enough to her to use the thing as a weapon. Father Leary was overly fond of lashing out at people who annoyed him.

"It has been reported to me that you are consorting with Liam Connelly." Father Leary was enjoying himself. The man loved an audience. "You are leading that young man astray. It will not be allowed. The lad belongs to God."

"Father Leary," Sheila Purcell was almost faint at the honour of being in the presence of the parish priest, "are you going to beat the devil out of her?" She offered her bottle of holy water. "I've holy water from Lourdes if you need it to cast the devil out."

Ivy was aware of people trying desperately to disappear into their own homes. Everyone might pay homage to Father Leary but they preferred not to have to face the man.

"I have matters to discuss with you, Ivy Rose Murphy. Serious matters. You have been seen consorting with a young man destined for the priesthood. Giving him succour." Father Leary loved how that word sounded. It sounded sinful, immoral. He spat the word out, convinced he was the only one there who would know the actual meaning of the word. "By your actions you have encouraged and permitted the boy to go against the will of his parents and the Holy Church. You meddle in things you can't understand, Ivy Rose Murphy."

Father Leary was red in the face and had to stop to catch his breath. Ivy waited for him to continue his diatribe.

"You didn't come to me when your sainted father went missing. Éamonn Murphy was a God-fearing man. He would have wanted my prayers in his hour of need. You denied that good man his final sacrament, Ivy Rose Murphy." Father Leary wished he was still in the tunnel. He'd enjoyed the gravitas the echo had lent to his words.

"My father was never missing, he died." Ivy deliberately used her 'posh' voice. She knew it annoyed the priest. The man was constantly annoyed at her for some reason or another. Ivy preferred to be hung for a sheep as a lamb. "My father died suddenly in an accident. I told you that when I came to see you almost four months ago." Ivy was aware the people of The Lane were hiding behind their windows, listening to everything being said.

"You haven't darkened my doorstep since that day." Father Leary raised his walking stick. Ivy stepped back smartly out of range. "I want to talk to you, Ivy Rose Murphy – come along!"

"Where?" Ivy wasn't willing to go anywhere with this man.

"I'll talk to you in your father's house."

"No, you won't." Ivy was sick with fear but she would not allow this bully into her home.

"What did you say?" Father Leary could not believe his ears. The hussy had refused him.

231

"My father is dead as you know perfectly well." Ivy kept well out of the way of the waving stick. She positioned herself so she could keep an eye on Sheila Purcell. Ivy wouldn't put it past the woman to hit her over the head with the large cross she held. Sheila would delight in dragging Ivy, like a human sacrifice, over to the furious priest.

"My father is dead," Ivy repeated. "He has no home here. Everyone knows he never paid the rent on the home he did have. I'm the official tenant."

"You slander the good name of your dead father. You show me no respect. I can have you evicted!" Father Leary shouted. "Have you no shame, Ivy Rose Murphy?"

"You need to calm down." Ivy refused to give the man the title he used so shamelessly. "You're getting overexcited."

Ivy was genuinely concerned. The priest was red in the face, perspiration pouring off him. That couldn't be healthy, not in this cool weather.

"Sheila Purcell, you're so concerned for the good of the Church," Ivy didn't dare take her eyes off the priest, "you should take this man into your place and make him a cup of tea."

"*How dare you!*" Father Leary didn't feel well. It was all the fault of the disgraceful female standing before him, defying him. Him, the Parish Priest. Well, he'd soon take care of her. He'd make her miserable life a hell on earth. He had that power and he'd use it.

"Oh, I couldn't – I'm not worthy," Sheila Purcell said. She might be a God-fearing woman but she couldn't entertain the parish priest in her own home. It wouldn't be right.

"I have things to do." Ivy didn't turn her back on the pair as she moved away in the direction of the livery. "I'll be getting about them."

"Ivy Rose Murphy, you stop right there!" Father Leary waved his stick in the air, unable to believe the impudence of this woman. "I've said I came to speak to you. We will go to your father's home. You can serve me tea while we discuss the error of your ways."

"Thanks all the same." Ivy was almost at the door of the

livery. She hoped Liam was standing inside, ready to let her in. "But I have things to do. Maybe you should dwell on your own sins a while. Correct me if I'm wrong but isn't gluttony one of the Seven Deadly Sins?"

For this man, this priest, to come among starving children and flaunt his obvious opulence outraged Ivy. The priest, on his very rare visits, never left The Lane without demanding money from the people there. He took what little they had and left them to struggle on.

"*How dare you!*" Father Leary was so incensed he actually threw his silverheaded walking stick with a great deal of force at Ivy's head.

She ducked and the thing glanced off the door by her head. She jumped out of its way when it bounced back off the livery door.

"What in the name of Heaven is going on here?"

Ivy turned her head to look in the direction of the voice. Just what she needed! A Franciscan friar, if she wasn't mistaken. The man was wearing a long brown hooded robe. His feet were naked inside strapped sandals. The friar was standing in the mouth of the tunnel staring at the scene before him. A gaping Officer Barney Collins stood at his side.

"I repeat," the friar said in a voice with the power of his beliefs behind it, "what is going on here?"

"It is no concern of yours." Without looking away from the Franciscan, Father Leary accepted the walking stick Sheila Purcell picked up and held out to him. "I came to offer this woman, this Ivy Rose Murphy, the ungrateful heathen, my counsel." Father Leary wanted to use his stick to wallop the ungrateful trollop but he stayed his hand.

"Indeed." Brother Theo, a Franciscan theologian, wondered if the priest often descended into violence with his parishioners. He would not call the man to account in front of a crowd of interested strangers but he was not prepared to let the matter drop either.

"This woman came to me to report her father's death."

Father Leary could feel a trickle of cold sweat down the back of his shirt. "I have reason to believe she may have done damage to the sainted man. A man strong in his beliefs and faithful to the Church. I simply wanted to confirm the matter. I see you brought a policeman with you. He can get to the bottom of this matter. Perhaps you too have heard of something unsavoury happening to one of my flock?"

"The policeman is here as my guide. I'm afraid I got lost on several occasions trying to find this place."

Barney Collins didn't know what to do. If he'd seen any other man try to inflict bodily harm on a woman he'd have arrested the bugger. He couldn't arrest a priest. But he could tell the truth.

"Ah, I can confirm the demise of Mr Éamonn Murphy," he said. "The man drowned. I myself was a witness to the event. I was the officer who informed his family of his sad passing." Barney Collins didn't know what had happened to Éamonn Murphy's body but he'd heard of the drunken wake in the man's name so he said no more.

"If you gentlemen will excuse me I have things I need to do." Ivy wanted to get away from this lot.

"If you could hold on just a moment, young lady." Brother Theo indicated that Ivy should stay where she was. "Officer, let me thank you for leading me here. I am very grateful." Brother Theo grinned and offered his hand to the visibly uncomfortable police officer. "I wasn't looking forward to returning to the friary to report my failure to find my way, yet again."

"You are very welcome, Brother Theo. I'll be on my beat around the neighbourhood if you should need me." Barney hoped to God he wouldn't be needed in here again this evening.

"Thank you again." Brother Theo watched the policeman hurry from the place. He didn't blame him.

Theo sighed and turned to deal with the overweight bombastic priest. He'd have something to say to the man at a later date. Right now he just wanted him to leave this place.

"I don't know your name or parish, Father." Theo waited for

the priest to introduce himself. He was genuinely horrified when the man told him he was the Parish Priest. How had such a man come to lead a parish?

"I have to be on my way." Father Leary knew he was in trouble and laid the blame at Ivy Rose Murphy's door. The woman was evil. He'd always known it. Today everyone had seen her evil.

Theo waited until the parish priest had disappeared into the tunnel, then turned to Ivy. "Miss Murphy, it's yourself I've come to see."

"Father, in the name of God, protect yourself!" Sheila Purcell almost fell to her knees. It was a well-known fact that monks were the holiest of the holy. "You heard Father Leary. The woman is a known sinner, spawn of the devil. You are in danger of losing your immortal soul!" Sheila Purcell was shaking at her own daring.

"Sheila, for the love of Jaysus, will you go home!" Ivy shook her head. Sheila was more to be pitied than laughed at. "Go say a decade of the Rosary or take a bath in holy water or something."

"Are you all right, Ivy?" Liam Connelly finally found the courage to open the small door and look out. He knew Father Leary was gone – he'd heard him take his leave. Liam nearly passed out when he saw who was standing outside with Ivy.

"I'm fine, thanks, Liam." Ivy rolled her eyes. "Did you get the pups back in the stall?"

"They're all accounted for." Liam almost stuttered in fright. What was a Franciscan friar doing here?

"Could you keep an eye on Emmy until Jem comes home?" Ivy knew Liam had little to do with looking after Emmy. It was more the other way around. Emmy had an old head on her shoulders.

"Yes, I'll do that." Liam disappeared without another word.

"Is that the lad you want to talk about?" Brother Theo whispered.

"That's him," Ivy replied. "Follow me." Then she stopped

and turned. "I'm sorry. I don't know how to address you. Do I call you Father or Brother?"

"I'm Brother Theo." Theo held out his hand to the young woman who was examining him quite closely.

"Would you care for a cup of tea, Brother Theo?"

"That would be much appreciated, Miss Murphy."

"Call me Ivy."

Ivy reached into her skirt pocket for the key to her door. She led the friar towards her basement entry, aware of every eye in the place on her.

"This is my work area," Ivy said of the area she'd set out to serve as her base of operations. She led the way into her new parlour. "Sit down, please." Ivy pointed to one of the chairs tucked under her table. "I'll have the tea going in no time."

"You are the young woman who left a message at the friary?" Theo looked around. The room was sparsely furnished with no sign of wealth, but it was clean and comfortable with charming touches of whimsy around the place.

"I am." Ivy glanced over her shoulder while she filled the teapot. "I'm worried about Liam Connelly, the young man you just saw cowering behind the stable doorway." Ivy delighted in laying out her tea set.

She'd covered her worn table with a tablecloth made of oddments she'd fashioned herself. To her eyes it looked beautiful. Ivy had made scones she'd intended to share with Liam and Emmy. She displayed these on a large plate and put them on the table.

"Tell me about him." Father Theo was studying the woman who'd been at the centre of that storm he'd interrupted. What was it about her that caused a man of God to behave like an unmannered hooligan?

"Liam Connelly is sixteen years old." Ivy joined the man at the table. "He went away at age eleven to a seminary." Ivy filled in the little she knew of Liam's history.

"He is no relation of yours?" Theo took a scone and bit into it. He didn't make the mistake of looking around for butter or jam.

236

"No, he's not." Ivy shrugged. "To be honest, Brother, I never had a great deal of time to spend studying the young people of The Lane. I have three younger brothers. I raised them myself. That kept me running around tending to my own business. I knew Liam only as an obnoxious young lad that hung around the place."

"Ivy, you went out of your way to call in at the friary." Theo said. "What do you think we can do that his own advisor can't?"

"You just met his advisor." Ivy refused to say more than that.

"Ahh, that could be a problem." Theo wanted to bang his head off the table. This situation was farcical but according to this young woman it could easily become a tragedy.

"You think?" Ivy snapped. "I'm sorry. I shouldn't be so rude but Father Leary and I have a long history of trouble."

"Tell me why you chose the friary." Theo sipped his tea and waited. "The friar you spoke to, Brother Roderick, is very concerned by the situation." Theo would make a point of thanking Roderick for bringing this matter to his attention. He had come only to keep his promise to Roderick. Obviously the situation was as dire as his fellow-friar had made it out to be.

"Liam is floundering." Ivy sipped her tea and tried to gather her arguments. Liam needed help and she'd a feeling only a man of God would be acceptable to him.

"In what way?" Theo waited.

"I've said he went away to be a priest. He came home in a fashion almost guaranteed to show him up as a fool." Ivy shook her head and, with laughter glittering in her big blue eyes, explained what Liam had done since he left the seminary.

"The young can be delightful surprises." Theo smiled.

"I agree." Ivy stood to serve fresh tea. "Liam was full of his plans when he first arrived home. Since then he's been subjected to vicious abuse from his father and his priest. I've watched him almost fall apart. He isn't eating. He isn't sleeping. He's stopped planning for the future." Ivy stopped when her voice began to break.

"You see a great deal of the lad?" Theo had heard enough of the slander being poured on this woman's head. He wouldn't make any judgements until he'd heard her out.

"He's teaching me." Ivy's smile was bright and full of the joys of learning.

"I beg your pardon?"

"Liam – I asked him to teach me to read." Ivy was almost bouncing in place as she tried to explain.

"The nuns failed to educate you?" Theo was surprised. The nuns had a certain reputation.

"Father Leary allowed my father to convince him I needed no schooling."

Ivy explained what had happened. She didn't try to hide her bitter resentment of the two men involved. She had loved her da but she wasn't blind to his faults. She wouldn't badmouth the priest to his fellow cleric.

"Unfortunate." Theo didn't want to say more but he was furious. The abuse of power involved would have to be investigated.

"Right." Ivy grinned across the table at him. "Anyway, when Liam came home I wanted to help him stay alive." She shrugged. "We all have to have a roof over our heads and food in our mouth."

"Indeed." Theo smiled and held out his cup for more tea.

"I didn't want to offer Liam charity." Ivy waved her arms around her living area. "I can't afford to offer charity anyway."

"He spends his nights here?" Theo still didn't understand the venom he'd heard in the Parish Priest's voice and was looking for a reason.

"Of course not." Ivy snapped. "He sleeps in the hayloft of the livery across the way. He spends time here eating and teaching."

"How is he as a teacher?"

"To be perfectly honest," Ivy grinned, "Emmy is a better teacher. She has more patience."

"Emmy?"

"Jem Ryan is the man who lives at the livery. He has a six-year-old niece, Emmy. She comes to me after school. I prepare a meal for the three of us to have together – Liam, Emmy and I. Emmy will show me what she learned in school. She loves turning into a teacher. She has endless patience with my fumbling."

"Fascinating." Theo didn't know what else to say. "Does Liam interact with anyone else?"

"No." Ivy sighed. "His father is frightened of the consequences of Liam's actions. Liam doesn't want to involve his mother and brothers and sisters in a family feud. He's been keeping away from the very people who might help him. He's deeply unhappy. I sincerely fear for him. He believes he failed God. The burden is crippling him. He needs guidance desperately. Someone he can respect who will listen to him and advise him." Ivy bit her lip.

"So you came to the friary." Theo didn't wonder any more about the effect this young woman had on Brother Roderick.

"I thought a friar might impress the bejabers out of Liam!" Ivy laughed at the look on Brother Theo's face. "Well, when you go looking for help you might as well go for the big guns."

"You, young lady, are an imp." Theo enjoyed a mind that seemed to see the world so clearly. What a tragedy that this woman had been denied a basic education! He would take his time but he would not allow this woman to rely on a young boy and a girl child for her education. He'd delight in teaching her himself. He'd find some way of arranging it, but not yet.

"I've been called worse." Ivy laughed.

"So I heard." Theo left it at that. "I need to spend time with Liam."

"Saint Francis was a great one for the animals, was he not?" Ivy had a fondness for the stories of Francis of Assisi.

"Truly, a very cheeky imp!" Theo laughed. "Would you be suggesting I sit in the hay with this young man and his dog?"

"The dog is nursing four young pups." Ivy shrugged. "Liam will be tied to her side for a while. I'll bring Emmy over here for something to eat. You and Liam will have the livery to yourself. Saint Francis sat in the hay with the animals. Will you?"

"A challenge, by heaven!" Theo laughed with true delight. It had been a long time since anyone challenged him. He was so tired of the unhealthy awe he was held in. "I'll go talk to your confused young man." He stood away from the table. "Will you permit me to call on you again?" Theo found he was almost holding his breath.

"You'll be welcome here any time." Ivy promised. "As long as you agree to converse, not lecture me."

"I can do that."

"Good," Ivy smiled in relief. "I'll take you across and introduce you to Liam. I'll take Emmy out of your way."

She led the way from her home.

"The young man's lucky to have a friend like you." Theo was aware of the women standing in open doorways and neighbours staring from behind their curtains. He deliberately walked slowly with his head bent towards Ivy. He needed to show his approval of the woman openly. She didn't deserve the notoriety he'd witnessed when he first arrived. One of the first things Theo intended to do when he returned to the friary was begin an investigation of the local Parish Priest. Theo would not allow such bully-boy tactics to flourish under his nose.

"Liam!" Ivy knocked on the people portal. "Liam, open up!"

"He's hiding." Emmy opened the door. "The sad boy is crying," she whispered, rolling her eyes. "Again."

"Liam, I've brought someone to meet you." Ivy set her shoulders, determined to force Liam out in the open.

"Let me handle this." Theo put his hand on her shoulder, stopping her stepping through the door.

"If he needs someone to sit with the pups," Ivy took Emmy by the hand, "we are available." Ivy fervently hoped Liam could be helped before he lost his mind completely. "Come on, Miss Emmy." Ivy smiled down at the serious little girl. "We have a dinner to prepare."

"Can we do our lessons on the floor again?" Emmy skipped along beside Ivy.

"I don't see why not," Ivy agreed.

Emmy used the black stones of Ivy's floor as a blackboard. The little girl set out homework for Ivy on them. The two of them enjoyed scrambling around the floor, learning as they went.

"Will the man in the dress help the sad boy?" Emmy asked as soon as Ivy had closed the door at their backs.

"I hope so." Ivy shrugged. "It's not a dress he's wearing – it's a robe."

"It looks like a dress."

"So it does."

"What are we making for dinner?" Emmy wanted to know. "Is my uncle eating with us?"

"I think so." Ivy was worried about Jem. He was coming back to the livery earlier each day. Then as soon as Emmy was in bed, and with Liam as a baby-sitter, Jem left again to spend most of the night trawling for business. He couldn't be earning enough to support three people and all those dogs. Jem insisted on supplying most of the ingredients for the meals they all ate together. Things had to change.

While Emmy and Ivy prepared a meal, Brother Theo was trying to deal with a young man who was being eaten alive from inside. The best solution as far as Theo could see would be to take the young man away with him.

Liam Connelly was falling apart at the seams. He needed to be surrounded by people who would understand his moral dilemma. People whose opinion the lad would respect. The situation was indeed as dire as Ivy had indicated to Brother Roderick. The poor lad couldn't take care of himself, let alone five dogs.

"I think you should come with me," Theo suggested tentatively.

"I can't be a priest!" Liam sobbed. "I really can't!"

"I'm not suggesting you take up your studies again." Theo wanted to punch something. How had this lad been allowed get to this point of despair? There were safeguards in place that obviously had not even been attempted. "I just want you to come with me for a period of respite. You can sit and read. Talk with the brothers who will be happy to listen to your concerns. You can work at restoring your health both mentally and physically."

"I can't leave here." Liam buried his hands in his dog's coat. "I have responsibilities."

"Do you think Ivy Murphy would agree to take care of the dog and pups until you return?" Theo wanted to get this young man into care.

"Poor Ivy, everyone dumps their responsibilities on her!" Liam groaned, coming up onto his knees and staring into Theo's eyes for the first time. "Do you know that she was the sole financial provider for her family since before her ninth birthday?" Liam hadn't known that. His mother had told him recently.

"Really?" Everything Theo heard about Ivy Murphy deepened his fascination with the woman. She was a case he would delight in studying.

"Ivy Murphy and her friends are the most Christian people I've ever met." Liam wanted to have someone in power on Ivy's side.

"Is that so?" Theo waited.

"Father Leary tried to ban the people in The Lane from any dealings with Ivy." Liam glared at Theo. "The woman goes out of her way to help." Liam buried his fists in his hair. "I hate to ask her to take on more responsibilities. It will mean a financial outlay for her as well. It's not cheap to feed a load of dogs." Liam almost wailed.

"I'll talk to Ivy," Theo said. "Do you want or need to say goodbye to anyone?"

"No." Liam refused to face his family.

"Do you have anything to pack?"

"Only the clothes on my back! Which I have courtesy of Ivy Murphy."

"She is an exceptional human being." Theo smiled softly. "I'd already figured that out for myself."

"Her lessons!" Liam yelled. "I forgot all about her lessons!"

"I'll take care of that too," Theo promised. He intended to see that Ivy Murphy received the best education he could provide. A mind so bright, a true seeker of knowledge, was a gift to a teacher. She'd been brought to his attention now. He wouldn't fail her.

Chapter 23

"Morning, Davy," Ivy greeted the young bootblack when his dirty face appeared in the slowly opening back door of Number 8. "Is she up yet?"

"Mary took Miss Gannon's breakfast tray up some time ago!" Iris Jones shouted from the kitchen before Davy could open his mouth. Iris didn't want to be left out of the strange comings and goings around Number 8. "Come away in, Ivy."

"I'm here, I'm here!" Ann Marie, suitably dressed in her second-hand suit, shouted as she almost ran into the kitchen.

"Let me see yeh," Ivy said. The brightly lit room had her squinting her eyes in reaction. "Where's yer shawl?" Ivy rolled her eyes towards the ceiling. "And yeh can't wear them gloves, Ann Marie." Ivy pointed at the cream calfskin gloves in her friend's hand. "Where's the gloves Granny gave yeh?"

"I'm afraid of ruining them." Ann Marie admitted. "I've never been given a hand-knitted gift before."

Granny had knit a matching hat and gloves for Ann Marie. After meeting Ann Marie for the first time the old woman had been completely won over, to Ivy's profound relief. Granny wanted to be involved in Ann Marie's 'disguise'. Ann Marie's frequent visits to the old woman seemed to have lifted Granny's spirits.

"I'll get your shawl, hat and gloves, Miss." Mary Coates almost pulled the gloves out of Ann Marie's hand and hurried from the kitchen.

"Ivy, I asked Cook to bake bread for us to take with us." Ann Marie accepted the cup of tea Cook put into her hand without even noticing. "I don't like to go visiting empty-handed."

"Have yeh yer money safe?" Ivy stared at Ann Marie. She'd taken the time to slit the seams of the suit skirt-pocket and sew a button-down purse inside the material.

"I do." Ann Marie patted her skirt with a grin, delighted with everything.

"Cook, yer blood should be bottled!" Ivy watched Iris Jones wrap two loaves of bread in greaseproof paper. A circular fruit cake was next to be wrapped.

"It was the Miss that gave me the nod to bake extra." But Iris beamed at the implied compliment.

"Ann Marie might have given you the go-ahead, Cook, but you did all the hard work. The blessings of God on yeh." Ivy had finally given in to Ann Marie's constant begging to be allowed to accompany her on her travels around Dublin. This Tuesday morning Ivy planned to visit Sadie and her girls after a morning spent at the Haymarket. The bread and cake would be a welcome addition to Sadie's household.

"Yeh need to bring extra shoes with yeh, Ann Marie." Ivy examined Ann Marie's feet, comfortably shod in her work boots "Them boots will eat the feet off yeh until yer skin hardens."

"I've two pair of thick socks on, Ivy." Ann Marie noticed Ivy's accent thickened whenever her aunt's servants were about.

"I made the Miss a bag," Davy said from his place by the fire. He raised his eyes from the shoes he was polishing, a grin splitting his face. The servants in Number 8 were enjoying a type of notoriety and not one of them wanted to be left out. The entire army of servants that worked in the square's households wanted to be kept up to date on the latest chapter in the Ivy and Ann Marie saga.

"Davy, how kind of you!" Ann Marie watched as Davy, a

young boy she'd been unaware existed until recently, pulled a hessian string sack he'd fashioned into an over-the-shoulder bag from its hiding place under his skinny rear end. "Thank you so much."

"I figured yeh'd need it." Davy was looking at Ann Marie's boots with longing. In his heart of hearts he prayed the Miss would pass the boots on to him when she got sick of this malarkey. They'd be a bit big like but he could stuff them with newspaper until he grew into them.

"I'll pack the bag for you, Miss." Mary Coates hurried around, preparing the bag.

Ivy watched, wondering if Ann Marie was even aware that her every need was catered for before she was even aware of it.

"I made a bite to eat for you to take along, Miss." Iris Jones put a packed lunch on the kitchen table before putting it alongside the bread and cake in the bag Davy had made.

"Everyone is being so kind," Ann Marie grinned. "Thank you all."

"Are yeh about ready, Ann Marie, or should I call one of the men to carry yeh in case yeh're feeling tired after all you've done this morning?" Ivy intended to stop and have a cup of tea and a sausage sandwich at Hopalong's stall. It was part of her routine. It gave her time to look around, see who was about, who had what on offer and what she might be able to add to their stalls.

"Are you sure you'll be warm enough, Miss?" Mary Coates arranged the knit hat on Ann Marie's head and pulled the shawl up over it and around her lady's shoulders. She shoved the hat pins she held into the shawl and hat.

"Ann Marie, if ye don't get yer skinny arse out of here right now, I'm leaving yeh here!" Ivy turned and made her way outside. She could hear the frantic mumbling and stumbling coming from the kitchen but she didn't care. If Ann Marie wanted to come with Ivy she needed to get a move on. This was not a pleasure trip.

"This is so exciting, Ivy." Ann Marie attempted to pass the heavy hessian sack to Ivy.

"Ann Marie, I've got news for you." Ivy's accent was once

again refined. "That," she pointed at the sack hanging from the tips of Ann Marie's wool-encased fingers, "is your bag. You brought it along. You carry it."

"Can't you put it in your pram?" Ann Marie didn't see the problem.

"No!" Ivy snapped, gripping the handle of her pram tightly. "I don't know what's in that thing. Suppose cook put something that might spill in there. I can't afford to have my goods damaged."

"Oh, of course, I didn't think." Ann Marie held the sack out from her body and waited.

"Ann Marie, you're a useless article!" Ivy sighed. She took the sack and passed the long strap over Ann Marie's head. "Wear it like that." Ivy pulled Ann Marie's arm out through the opening. "It's easier to carry that way. Now for God's sake, will you get a move-on? I'll be late."

"It's so early, Ivy." Ann Marie was looking all around her with wide eyes. This was a different world to the one she knew. "The Corporation water carts aren't even out yet." She was speaking of the horse-drawn water wagons that washed the Dublin streets.

Ivy ignored Ann Marie's ramblings. She turned into Holles Street, turned down Denzille Lane and into Fenian Street. She needed to get on. She hadn't time for Ann Marie to stop and admire everything.

"Morning Ivy, is that yerself?" a voice called out of the darkness.

Ann Marie jumped. She hadn't seen anyone.

"Morning, Betty, what are yeh after today?"

"Tomatas."

"Keep us a few, will yeh?" Ivy shouted to the figure appearing from the early-morning haze. The figure was pushing a heavy pram at speed along the street. "I'll see yeh down there." Ivy had to grab Ann Marie by the elbow and pull her out of the way.

"Ivy, is that yerself?" another voice called when Ivy turned onto Westland Row, heading towards Pearse Street.

"It is, Lissy." Ivy didn't stop. She didn't even slow down.

"If yeh get to Donnelly's before us," Lissy's voice echoed through the gaslamp-lit street, "get's a pound of his sausages, will yeh? I'll see yeh right."

"Will do!" Ivy shouted over her shoulder.

"Ivy," Ann Marie was breathless at the speed Ivy travelled, "who are those people?" She hadn't been able to see much as the women were well wrapped in dark clothing.

"Dealers," Ivy answered. "They have to get to the market early and pick up their goods."

Ann Marie didn't answer. She needed all of her breath to keep up the killing pace Ivy set. She passed through streets she didn't know existed, following after Ivy's dark, silent figure. She almost wept with relief when they finally came in sight of the well-lit market square.

"Watch where yeh're going!" Ivy pulled Ann Marie to a halt to allow a heavily laden farm cart to trundle past them. The horses' heads were hanging but they were picking up speed. Farmers and their horses had been making this trip twice a week for centuries. These horses knew they were almost there and wanted a nosebag of oats and a drink of water.

Ann Marie gasped as a crowd of youths suddenly appeared and began to pull hay by the handful from the wagon. The farmer shouted and cursed at them but everyone else ignored them. It was a common sight. The stolen hay was used for the tiny backyard 'farms' dotted through the Dublin lanes.

"Morning, Ivy!" Hopalong gave Ivy a gummy grin. "Yer usual?"

"Twice please, Hopalong." Ivy scanned the gathering dealers. The stalls were up and stuff was being put out. She was late. She was aware of Ann Marie collapsing onto a nearby bale of hay. She'd be safe there for the minute.

"Here's trouble!" Hopalong grinned, taking Ivy's money.

"Big Polly!" Ivy called out to the tall full-figured woman powering her way towards the tea stall. "I want to see yeh!" Ivy began to pull the cover back from her pram.

"Maggie Wilson is looking for yeh, Ivy." Big Polly stood tall, spread her legs and urinated where she stood. With a relieved sigh she then stepped over the puddle she'd made and walked over to Ivy's side. A quickly suppressed squeak was all the reaction Ann Marie allowed herself.

Big Polly was one of Ivy's best customers. The woman was built along the same lines as the Morgan twins. Big Polly was taller but it was all leg. Ivy had simply to use the material from one twin's discarded skirt to lengthen the other and she had a high-class outfit to offer Big Polly.

"Yeh said yer eldest was getting married." Ivy held the pram cover away from the suit she was hoping to sell. "That suit will make yeh the talk of the town." Big Polly, like the Morgan twins, loved frills and fancies. Ivy normally removed all of the ribbon, braiding and beads the Morgan twins insisted upon and made money off it. For Big Polly, however, she left everything in place.

"Gi's a look." Big Polly wanted something that would show up that snobby cow her son was marrying. "Hopalong, pour us a cup of tea for feck's sake! I feel like one of them fellas that walks across deserts. I'm bloody parched."

Ann Marie sat on her hay bale, drinking tea from a chipped cup and clutching a sausage sandwich. She watched Ivy's world unfold before her. She watched Ivy and Big Polly shout and poke at each other, all the while eating and drinking the food they held. The price Ivy mentioned for the suit seemed ridiculously cheap to Ann Marie but it obviously horrified Big Polly. The two women were shouting abuse that had Ann Marie's ears blushing.

"Ivy Murphy!" Maggie Wilson had walked up unnoticed by the squabbling women. She had waited until the deal was struck before speaking – it didn't do to interrupt trade. "I've a bone to pick with yeh."

"Oh yes? Hang on." Ivy grinned at Big Polly. Ivy had made a handsome profit on the suit and Big Polly knew she'd got a bargain. "I'll have Bill Burn wrap this in brown paper for yeh, Big Polly. Yeh won't know yerself."

"Thanks, Ivy." Big Polly returned her cup to the stall. "I'll see yeh later over at my place." She was referring to her own stall. "I'll fix yeh up then." Big Polly walked away, delighted with herself. She'd show that stuck-up young madam what's what. That a son of hers could pick such a woman! Still, on his own head be it.

"Ivy, what do ye mean getting Sadie Lawless to knit for yeh?" Maggie Wilson pushed her nose up to Ivy's face. "The woman is one of me best workers."

"How is Sadie?" Big Polly stopped halfway down the aisle separating the stalls. Everyone in the market knew what had happened to Big John Lawless.

"She's in a bad way," Ivy said sadly.

"Hey, answer me question!" Maggie Wilson wasn't willing to be ignored. Ivy Murphy was hurting her trade.

"Sadie isn't knitting for me Maggie," Ivy could say truthfully, "but I do have her and her girls doing a few little jobs for me." Ivy's woollens were being turned into usable wool at a great rate.

"What's the news about John?" Hopalong leaned over his stall to refill the cups.

"He's still in Kevin's, still crippled," Ivy informed the gathering crowd of listeners. "His family are struggling."

"That's only to be expected." Frank Jameson shook his head sadly. "Twenty years he worked, never missing a day in all that time. One little accident and a good man and his family are destroyed. It ain't right."

The crowd mumbled in agreement. They all feared something of the sort happening to them.

"Maggie Wilson," Ivy said, "I know Sadie was a good little earner for yeh." And she knew Maggie charged a lot for the little outfits Sadie knit. "It wouldn't do yeh any harm to have Golly Black deliver a bag of coal to them, Maggie. The three of them are sitting in front of an empty grate."

"I'll do that, Ivy," Maggie Wilson was shamed into promising.

"Ann Marie, come on," Ivy said when she'd conducted all the business she could around Hopalong's stall.

Ivy didn't hold a street trader's license. She couldn't sell to the public. She needed to make her money selling to the people who did hold a trader's license.

"Yeh can put yer bag in here now." Ivy held open the cover of her pram. She'd sold everything she'd brought to the market. She'd also bought supplies for her own needs that now lined the bottom of the pram.

"Thanks." Ann Marie put the sack, which had grown heavier through the morning, in the pram with a sigh of relief. Her head was spinning with everything she'd seen and heard. She had a million questions she wanted to ask Ivy.

"Ivy, don't forget yer tomatas!" a woman standing by her pram on a street corner shouted. The pram was almost buried under a tower of big red tomatoes.

"Thanks, Betty." Ivy stopped. "I want two bags of yer best." She waited while she was served, glancing around at the other prams to see if they had anything else she wanted. "Where's Lissy parked?"

"She's down the block." Betty pointed with her chin.

"Thanks, Betty," Ivy put the tomatoes in her pram and continued on her way down the block. She could hear Lissy shouting out her sales pitch and prices now. "Toys, Lissy?" Ivy stared at the woman's pram in surprise. "That's not yer usual."

"Me fella got them off a Russian straight off the boat and needing a few bob." Lissy's face was lined with sadness. "He got them cheap but they're not moving, Ivy."

"They won't down here, Lissy." Ivy knew Lissy's husband was unemployed like so many but he tried to bring in a few bob for his family. "Lissy, yeh know no-one down here has a spare penny. Yeh need to go somewhere like Henry Street or Earl Street."

"This is me spot, Ivy." Lissy knew Ivy was right but a dealer's spot was sacred. You couldn't just barge in anywhere you liked.

"I'll settle up with yeh for the sausages."

While the two women were conducting business Ann Marie was examining the clever little wooden toy. Two wooden sticks held a monkey on a string. When you pressed the sticks the monkey gyrated.

"Ivy, I'm no trader," Ann Marie was loath to make trouble for Ivy by interfering in something she knew nothing about, "but these little toys are wonderful."

"Who's your one?" Lissy glared.

"Ann Marie, Lissy – she's keeping me company today." Ivy turned to Ann Marie with raised eyebrows. Ann Marie saw things the rest of them didn't.

"I don't understand why you can't go to Henry Street, Lissy." Ann Marie offered shyly. "But in any case you are not charging enough for these little toys." She'd heard the price being shouted.

"If she went onto someone else's patch she'd be in big trouble, Ann Marie," Ivy said simply. In fact the woman would be in actual physical danger from the other dealers. A patch was sacred and handed down through a family for generations.

"Yeh really think I should charge more for these things?" Lissy played with one of the toys. They were wonderful but she'd be putting them on the back of the fire if she couldn't sell them.

"Yeh could take yer fella with yeh to Henry Street, Lissy." Ivy shrugged. Lissy needed to make a living like the rest of them. "See how it goes."

"You should double the price at least." Ann Marie was still playing with the monkey on a string.

"Yeh're nuts, Missus." Lissy stared at Ivy's friend in astonishment. The woman wanted her bumps feelin' – she was obviously a brick short of a load.

"In fact," Ann Marie hoped she wasn't stepping out of line, "I'll take a dozen at double the price."

The two dealers turned to stare at her. You never offered someone twice the price they were asking.

Lissy looked like her Christmas was coming early. She didn't question the madwoman but quickly started counting the toys into a bag.

"Who are ye buying these things for, Ann Marie?" Ivy didn't think Ann Marie knew a dozen childer.

"Davy would love one of these, Ivy." Ann Marie was delighted at the opportunity to use her hidden purse. Ivy had insisted Ann Marie bring coins and ten-shilling notes. The notes had to be pinned to her skirt for safe keeping. She'd been warned not to pull out notes. "I thought Emmy and perhaps Sadie's two girls would enjoy a toy."

"On yer own head be it." Ivy wouldn't deny a child a toy and Ann Marie could afford the gesture.

"Thanks, Missus." Lissy took the money with a glad heart. Her kids would eat tonight. "Here," she passed an extra monkey over, "have one on me! I'm going home to get me fella and then by God I'm going to Henry Street." Lissy started packing up.

"Good luck!" Ivy shouted, "Come on, Ann Marie, before yeh offer to go with her!"

"Dear Lord, Ivy," Ann Marie couldn't keep her mouth shut any longer. "Does the water wagon never come down these streets?" The dark streets smelled of human waste and disease. The barefoot, half-clothed children broke Ann Marie's heart. She'd never seen such poverty.

"It's a long way from Merrion Square, Ann Marie," Ivy said simply. "We're almost at Sadie's. Yeh need to wipe the shock off yer face or yeh'll insult the woman."

"Ivy, I've been keeping watch for yeh!" Sadie shouted from her steps. "I'll give yeh a hand with yer pram." Sadie ran down the steps leading up to the tenement house.

"Put the kettle on, will yeh, Sadie?" Ivy said, accepting the help.

The three women climbed the steps together, Ann Marie trying to take everything in at once.

"I'm that hungry, Sadie, I could eat the north end of a southbound mule." They were hardly in the door when Ivy began to pull foodstuffs out of her pram. "I hope yeh don't mind if me and Ann Marie grab something to eat while we talk." She lied to spare Sadie's feelings.

Ann Marie opened her mouth to object – it was obvious from

the cold hungry look of the children that this woman had nothing to spare. Ivy kicked her.

"I bought a load of Donnelly's sausages, Sadie, and Ann Marie has a packed lunch she didn't get a chance to eat." Ivy put the paper-wrapped parcel of sausages and the packed lunch onto the table. "Will ye join us in a sandwich?"

Sadie wanted to object but the hungry look on her daughters' faces kept her mouth firmly shut.

The two girls watched food appear from the pram and onto their bare table as if by magic.

"Girls, will yeez get the wool we have ready, please." Sadie felt almost faint just at the mention of the sausages. She watched her daughters run into the other room to collect the work that was the only thing keeping the roof over their heads.

"Ann Marie didn't want to come empty-handed, Sadie," Ivy continued to pull items from her pram. "She brought some of her morning bake with her. I hope yeh don't mind." Ivy put Mrs Jones' bread and cake on the table.

"I'm sure we'll enjoy your baking," Sadie said over her shoulder. She had the sausages already in a pan she held over the little primus stove. She wouldn't be able to afford gas for it when the cylinder was finished. "Thank you."

"Just put the wool on the floor, girls, thanks," Ivy said when the two girls returned with bags of the high-quality refashioned wool. The jumpers Ivy was paying them to take apart were of the finest wool available. "Clare, if you'll cut the bread, and Dora, you cut the tomatoes, we'll soon be ready to eat."

In no time at all Sadie was bringing the sizzling sausages to the table and they all sat down.

"Ivy, are yeh really sure about what yeh're doing with all that wool?" Sadie was fighting to keep the tears from her eyes. Her daughters were doing her proud. The girls had cut one loaf into neat thin slices. The tomatoes gleamed red and moist. She knew the girls wanted to fall on the food but they were politely waiting.

"I'm taking a gamble, Sadie, the first in me life." Ivy was slowly chewing the food, watching as Sadie and her girls dug in. Ann Marie was nibbling politely on the thinnest slice of bread she could find.

"Well, the girls and me are about ready to get stuck into your latest bright idea. You can't blame us if it doesn't work. We'll do the work and gladly." Sadie savoured her tea with the milk Ivy had brought. She tried to slowly chew and swallow every delicious mouthful of her sausage-and-tomato sandwich. As she did, she watched her girls enjoy the food. She didn't take a second sandwich herself, wanting to leave the food for the girls but she kept the tea coming. Ivy was a terror for her tea.

"By the way, Pa Landers told me he has a couple of coats in." Sadie looked at the food still remaining on her table. She'd be able to fry the bread in the grease in the sausage pan for later. Her girls would go to bed with a full stomach tonight. "He doesn't know if they'll suit but he wanted me to tell yeh."

"I want something that will give a good impression, Sadie. I know that thing," Ivy pointed to her old coat hanging half off her pram, "is ugly but it keeps me warm."

"I'll come with yeh to see Pa Landers," said Sadie. The other two women seemed to be finished with their food. She stood away from the table. If she got the other two out of here, her girls could stuff their faces without minding their manners.

Ivy and Ann Marie pushed their teacups away from them and stood.

"Can I leave me pram here?" said Ivy

"Grand. I'll get me shawl." Sadie smiled at her two girls. "Lock the door behind me, girls. We don't want yer Auntie Patsy sticking her nose into Ivy's business." Sadie didn't want the other woman helping herself to whatever was on offer.

The three women walked to Pa Landers with the usual escort of ragged children. Ann Marie felt her stomach heave at the blue tinge to the skin on the little boys' and girls' arms and legs. Most of the children were barefoot.

"Sadie, you've brought me customers." Pa Landers recognised the suit Ann Marie was wearing.

"I told Ivy you got some coats in."

Sadie watched Ivy examine the coats Pa Landers offered. Her posh friend just stood inside the door staring around. She was a queer one all right.

"There's nothing here I want." Ivy turned away.

"There is another coat but I doubt it would suit," Pa Landers said. "I know someone wishing to sell a very expensive coat." Pa wished he could sell the coat. His commission would keep him going through the winter. "I don't know anyone who could afford a coat the like of which this woman wishes to sell."

"The dancer from the Gaiety!" Sadie gasped. "The one renting yer upstairs room? Her that's out to here?" Sadie pushed her arms away from herself, making the understood sign for a pregnant woman.

"The very one," Pa Landers said.

"You two know someone who works in the theatre?" Ivy couldn't believe her ears.

"We don't really know her." Sadie said honestly. "She's been staying here but she doesn't exactly talk to people."

"Could I speak to her, please?" Ivy said, thinking of Liam. The woman might have information she could use. It didn't do any harm to ask.

"I suppose I could ask." Pa Landers didn't give much for their chances. "She calls herself Desiree. It would be good for the young woman to talk to someone, I think." Pa Landers wasn't a hardhearted man. The young woman renting his upstairs room was in trouble.

"I'll take them up," Sadie offered and Pa Landers opened the door separating his home from his business.

Upstairs, Sadie knocked on the door Pa usually rented.

"What do you want?"

The young woman standing in the partly open doorway was not the picture Ivy had formed of a glamorous dancer. She was tall and, except for the swollen stomach, was painfully thin. Her hair hung in knotted tangles around her sallow face.

"This is Ivy and this is Ann Marie," Sadie said before the girl could slam the door shut.

"What's it to me?" Molly Riordan, otherwise known as Desiree, wanted to die. She'd got herself into the oldest mess in the world.

"I believe you have a coat you want to sell?" Ivy said quickly.

"You couldn't afford one of the feckin' buttons!" The girl looked at Ivy from head to toe and sneered.

"You never know." Ivy grinned. "Appearances can be deceiving."

"Ain't that the truth? You better come in, I don't know if all of yeez will fit."

"I want to see the coat," Ivy said. The room, with its scattered clothing, looked more like a market stall than the one downstairs. "I'd also like to ask a few questions about going on the stage."

"You!" Molly looked Ivy over. "You might be able to make it as a dancer but I'd need to see you without that God-awful coat."

"No, not me!" Ivy laughed. "A friend of mine dreams of going on stage with his dog act." Ivy shrugged. "He hasn't a clue what's involved. I thought you might know of someone he could talk to."

"You've got a bloody cheek, I'll say that for you!" Molly collapsed into a chair. "The coat's in that box." She pointed.

Ann Marie, following the pointing finger, wanted to faint. She recognised the bespoke gilded lettering on that box. What in the name of goodness was it doing here?

"Sweet Jaysus!" Sadie opened the big white cardboard box sitting on the floor. "This isn't a coat – it's a bleedin' bank statement."

"Here, try it on, Ivy." Sadie shook out the thick white fur coat. "Come on, try it on. I dare yeh!"

Ivy was staring at the coat with her mouth open. Ann Marie was leaning faintly against the door, incapable of movement.

"Jaysus, I couldn't put something like that on me." Ivy stepped back as far as she could in the cluttered space.

"You"ll never get another chance." Sadie held the coat open and waited.

"Oh my God!" Ivy dropped her coat to the floor and stepped into a slice of feminine heaven. The collar of the coat was cloak-like and was meant to be lifted around the face. Ivy buried her face in the rich fur and almost purred.

"It was made to go with the shorter skirts that are in fashion now." Molly Riordan was remembering her own reaction to the coat.

"It was made to say 'This woman is for sale', you young twit!" Sadie snapped. The pregnant girl didn't look much older than her own daughters. "I'll bet this coat got you in that state, didn't it?" Sadie was standing hands on her hips, glaring at the pregnant woman.

"Not on its own, it didn't!" Molly hit back.

"You need to take a good long look in the mirror!" Sadie roared. "What yeh got up to to earn this feckin' coat is going to be the death of yeh!" Sadie didn't like the look of the girl. "You haven't been taking care of yourself, have yeh?"

"There's no point." Molly pointed at her expanded stomach with dislike. "After this thing is out of me I'll get me figure and me life back."

"What are yeh goin' to do with the baby when it gets here?" Sadie snapped.

"Put it on the steps of the poorhouse." Molly shrugged. "They find homes for the babies. They get put in good homes with wealthy couples that want a baby."

"What fairy tales have you been reading?" Sadie wanted to kick something. She'd spent hours on her knees praying for a miracle. She'd cried bitter tears because she wanted more children and here was this young girl pregnant with a child she didn't want. Still, who said life was fair?

"Everyone knows the only thing those babbies get is an early grave, yeh young twit! Yeh need to think about now, start using the help available. You can get free oranges and milk from the Saint Vincent de Paul and the Penny Dinners are free for a pregnant woman. If you don't start taking care of yourself the only home you and that baby will get is a pauper's grave." Sadie knew she was wasting her breath but she had to try.

"Sadie?" Ivy had been lost in the feel of the silken fur gliding through her fingers. She'd never felt anything so luxurious in her life and never would again.

"Did you look at the label on that thing?" Sadie pointed to the coat with hatred. "It's made of winter wolf fur. My John has a book all about artic wolves and the hard life they live. He read it to us, every evening – me and the girls. They mate for life you know, wolves. They take care of their young as a family. Those animals died so this young fool could strut her stuff."

"Keep your hair on, Missus." Molly snapped. "I didn't shoot the bleedin' things."

"Where's the old fool that bought that thing?" Sadie wanted to shake someone.

Ann Marie, still incapable of speech, desperately wanted to hear the answer to that question.

"Charlie isn't old." Molly stuck her tongue out at Sadie. "So there, yeh interfering auld hag!"

"Sadie!" Ivy had to actually clap her hands to stop the two women staring daggers at each other.

"Desiree, it's a coat I'm looking for, something to wear daily. This thing," Ivy couldn't resist giving the coat another stroke, "while the most beautiful thing I've ever seen in me life, is white. White is for the very rich, Desiree. This coat would be more expensive to keep than a family of four."

"Are ye listening, ye twit!" Sadie couldn't keep her opinion of that to herself. "The feckin' coat costs money to keep, for Jaysus' sake!"

"Amn't I trying to get rid of the bloody thing, Missus? Where do you get off coming in here and insulting me?" Molly

Riordan knew she'd been a fool. She didn't need these women to tell her.

"We don't know yeh from Adam," Sadie shrugged, "but we won't stand by and see yeh kill yerself."

"I'm not going to kill meself. Jaysus, Missus, you're crazy!" Wasn't she trying to sell the feckin' coat, trying to make enough money to keep herself going?

"You *are* killing yourself." Sadie would have sold the clothes spilled around this room to feed herself and her family. This girl could have done the same thing. The girl didn't seem to realise the danger she was in. "Look at yourself, go on, take a good look!"

Sadie pulled a struggling Molly out of the chair and over to a nearby mirror.

"Look at the colour of your skin, is that normal?" Sadie was practically holding the girl up. "You're skin and bone! The babbie is taking what it needs whether you give it to it or not. You are killing yourself and that babbie too, you twit!"

"Stop calling me a twit!" Molly shrugged off Sadie's hands and turned to Ivy. "Yeh may as well have a look at yerself in that coat, Missus. It doesn't half suit yeh."

"I give up!" Sadie threw her hands in the air.

"I know I'm a twit, all right?" Molly watched Ivy admire herself. The coat made the woman look stunningly beautiful.

"Yeh don't wear this coat," Ivy whispered. "The coat wears you." She slipped her arms out of the coat and passed it to the fuming Sadie.

"Yeh need to get out in the fresh air." Sadie wasn't giving up. "This room stinks, open a bloody window. You could sell some of these clothes to buy food, and the odd bottle of milk, have a bottle of Guinness now and again."

"You won't find anyone in this neck of the woods to buy that coat. It's a work of art meant to be worn by a very rich woman." Ivy had been looking and listening. She didn't know anything about having babies but the girl did look sickly to her.

"I'll need me clothes for after, " Molly whispered.

"When did you last eat?" Sadie knew nothing about work-of-art coats but she knew about pregnant women. There was food at her place she could share.

"I couldn't tell yeh." Molly was in a bad way and she knew it.

"I might know of someone who'd want the coat." Ann Marie was green to the gills. "How much are you asking?"

Chapter 24

"This is nice, Ivy." Jem settled his aching bones into one of the easy chairs in front of the range.

"You're working too hard, Jem." Ivy tidied the table. She and Emmy had been playing 'school' and the table was covered in their 'schoolwork'. "You look like a man who needs a week of good nights' sleep."

"I'm fine, Ivy." Jem felt like he was running in place, chasing his tail. He didn't want to burden Ivy with his problems. He wanted to enjoy this time with her. "Tell me the latest on Vera Connolly and the pups."

Liam's brother Conn and his sister Vera had taken the dog and her pups into their care. They'd built a kennel of sorts in the backyard of the tenement block. Vera was taking the training of the pups very seriously.

"You should see it, Jem!" Ivy laughed. "Those dogs will have no problem performing in public. They get more attention for their every little move than any other dog before in the world. Every child in the lane acts as an audience. If a pup sits down by mistake the kids roar in appreciation! Emmy found this book at school, didn't you, Emmy?"

"It's a book about training dogs, Uncle Jem!"

"Emmy sits on that hay bale you put out by the dog's kennel in the yard," said Ivy, "and gives directions. Today Vera had the dog jumping through the iron rims the lads play with. The noise, you'd have thought the circus had come to town!"

Emmy bustled around importantly – putting the art supplies and books away in the orange crates Ivy kept for them. The little girl loved doing little domestic chores.

"Have the family had any more trouble with Father Leary?" Since Liam Connelly left The Lane Jem had been hearing whispers that frightened him. Father Leary posed a real danger to Ivy.

"You know Father Leary thinks visits to The Lane beneath him. If it wasn't for Liam Connelly he wouldn't darken our doorstep." Ivy didn't want to talk about the parish priest.

"Father Leary could cause you a great deal of trouble, Ivy." Jem worried that idiots like Tim Johnson and his cronies would take the priest's loudly voiced disapproval as permission to torment Ivy. The man could claim the Church's approval of any action he cared to take. Jem couldn't stay around The Lane and protect Ivy.

"Jem, I don't want to talk about that man," Ivy sighed.

"I just want you to be careful, Ivy." He could see he was upsetting her. "We won't talk about him any more tonight. Tell me what you and your sidekick got up to today."

"I took Ann Marie back to the Warren again this afternoon. I told you about the pregnant dancer, didn't I?"

"I have to say, Ivy, it seems a bit peculiar to me that Ann Marie would get so involved in a stranger's life." Jem shrugged. "It all seems a bit fishy to me."

"You should have seen Ann Marie today, Jem." Ivy shook her head in silent admiration. "The woman's a force of nature when she gets going. I've never seen the like in my life. I could tell she had the bit between her teeth when I went to pick her up. It was just as well we'd arranged everything in advance. Nobody could have refused Ann Marie today, the mood she was in. She had that box with the fur coat under her arm and Desiree, the dancer, packing before ye could say Jack Robbins. I can't believe it myself and I was there."

"Still, to move that pregnant woman bag and baggage into Sadie's place!" Jem shook his head. "That seems a bit extreme to me. I know you've told me Sadie and her girls can really use the extra money Ann Marie is going to pay them for the woman's care, but still, Ivy, something isn't right."

"Ann Marie is a woman who needs to feel she can help the less fortunate, Jem. Look at the way she is with Granny. She picked Granny up earlier this evening and took her for a drive if you can believe it! They're not back yet as far as I know." Ivy's smile almost split her face. "She drove her car through the tunnel and into The Lane. Jaysus, Jem, the place exploded! I don't think there was a person left inside a building. Granny walked out on Conn's arm like the Queen of the May. She was waving and grinning to the crowd. It did me heart good to see her enjoy herself like that."

"The automobile was beautiful." Emmy stopped sweeping the floor for a moment.

"I can't wait to hear what Granny thinks of her first trip in an automobile." Jem laughed. "You have to give the old girl credit. There's not many women her age would be willing to get into an automobile!" Jem sighed. "I'm sorry, Ivy. I'm not trying to say there is anything wrong with your friend. I like Ann Marie – I just worry that she is moving people around like pieces on a chessboard."

"Ann Marie could see Sadie and her girls were struggling to survive, Jem. If the empty grate hadn't been enough. Sadie and her two girls looked like miserable wrecks that day we went to their place." Ivy thought Ann Marie's solution to the problem brilliant.

Three days ago they'd left the pregnant woman, promising to return with the money to buy the coat. As soon as they'd got back to Sadie's rooms Ann Marie had sent the girls out to play with the toys she gave them. Then the three women had sat at Sadie's table and talked. Ann Marie had waved her magic wand

– money – and by the time they'd finished they'd rearranged a shellshocked Sadie's world.

"Still and all, Ivy, for Ann Marie to make herself responsible for paying Sadie to look after a pregnant stranger – it seems a touch off, if yeh get me drift."

"Ann Marie can afford it, Jem! To you or me the amount of money involved seems a lot. Honest, the money Ann Marie offered Sadie a week to look after Desiree is less than she spends on cream teas at Bewley's Café."

"I suppose but it still all seems strange to me." Jem sat back in his chair, patting his knees for Emmy to sit up – the little girl had finished her chores. He'd enough problems of his own to be getting on with.

"Jem, I've been thinking . . ." Ivy dropped into the chair opposite Jem's at the range. She hoped Jem didn't think she was butting in to his private affairs but she really wanted to help him.

"Oh, no, please, not that!" Jem grabbed Emmy onto his knees and hid his face in her neck. The little girl giggled in sheer delight. She loved coming to her Aunt Ivy's house.

"Jem Ryan," Ivy leaned forward and slapped Jem's knee. "I'm trying to have a serious conversation."

"Ouch!" Jem looked pitifully towards Emmy, looking for sympathy, grinning.

"I want to talk about the livery." Ivy wished Liam was over at the livery. He could have watched Emmy while they talked privately. "I'm sorry if you think I'm poking my nose in where it's not wanted or needed but I'm concerned, Jem."

"What about the livery?" Jem asked.

"Jem, you can't go on like this," Ivy began. Emmy had her head buried in Jem's neck but Ivy knew she was listening to every word. Ivy met Jem's eyes, struggling to find the words she wanted to say.

"Ivy, what are you trying to say?"

"Being around Ann Marie has got me thinking, Jem." Ivy desperately wanted to explain what she was feeling. "My eyes have been opened to a lot of things. It's the way Ann Marie behaves. She expects people to jump when she's around. She knows who to go to for information. She has – I suppose you could call them connections. Something you and me have never had."

"That's the way of the world, Ivy." Jem rubbed Emmy's back gently.

"No!" Ivy almost shouted. "It's the way of *our* world, Jem, and I'm not willing to put up with it any more. You and me have a chance to change things and I think we should take it."

"Ivy," Jem sighed, staring at the woman who meant so much to him. He couldn't ask her to share his life. He couldn't afford to support a wife. "We were both born poor and we'll die the same way. That's just the way things are."

"*It's bloody not!*" Ivy did shout now. "That is defeatist thinking, Jem Ryan, and you're the one told me about that." Ivy nodded to underline her opinion.

"We can't wave a magic wand and make ourselves rich, Ivy." Jem looked down at the little person he'd promised to protect.

"You don't have to." Ivy pointed her chin at Emmy. "You have money."

"I'm not touching that." Jem glared.

Ivy sighed. The man was pigheaded. "I'm not suggesting you take the child's money and flitter it away. The money is sitting in the bank doing nothing. You and I, Jem, can't walk into the bank and ask for a loan. The bank manager would laugh himself sick before having us thrown out. That, yes, is a fact of our life. But you have a chance now, Jem. It fell into your lap. I think you should use the money. Think of it as an investment in the livery. Use the money but treat it as a loan and pay it back over time."

"Jesus, Ivy!" Jem stared open-mouthed.

"Think about it, Jem. You can't continue on like this. I've seen you dragging yourself home every night. The frown lines on your face are getting deeper. I know you're worried but you never mention anything." Ivy couldn't sit still. She stood to prepare a pot of tea.

"You must be behind in the rent on the livery building. That place is huge and must cost a fortune to rent." Ivy couldn't help Jem out financially. She kept Emmy with her when Jem went out at all the hours of the night but it couldn't continue. The man was killing himself.

"I own the livery building."

"Yeh what?"

"I own the livery building." Jem grinned at the look on Ivy's face. "I inherited the business from my uncle. You know that. Well, he owned the building and now so do I."

"Yeh jammy bastard!" Ivy punched Jem on the shoulder. "Yeh never said!"

"Didn't think it was important." Jem grinned. "What does that have to do with the price of eggs?"

"I was sick with worry about you making the rent on that place!"

"I own the building, Ivy, but that doesn't mean I haven't got money worries."

"Everyone has money worries, Jem." Ivy carried a small table over to the range. "But knowing the roof over your head is yours – in my eyes that makes you rich."

"I suppose." Jem shrugged.

"Right!" Ivy placed her tea service carefully on the table. "That gets rid of one of my worries but it doesn't take care of the rest."

"Ivy, I don't want you worrying about me. I'll be all right." Jem smiled. "You don't need to concern yourself with my problems. You need to think about yourself."

"You said it yourself, Jem, Rosie is getting old." Ivy groaned when she heard the rapping of knuckles at her front door. "I don't know who the heck that is but I'll soon get rid of them." She jumped up and hurried from the room. She hit the door between the rooms so hard it slammed shut at her back.

"It's Ann Marie!" Ivy shouted from the front room as she looked through the window to check who was at her door before opening it. She pulled her front door open.

"I hope it's not too late for visitors." Ann Marie was glad of the opportunity to see where Ivy lived. Up to now she had timed her visits to Granny for the hours Ivy worked – at Ivy's request. This was the first time she'd been here in the evening. "I have something to confess."

"Come on in, I'm glad you're here." Ivy stepped back. "Jem, open the through door. Ann Marie needs a little light to see her way." The front room was almost black. Ivy could walk it in her sleep.

"Jem is here?" Ann Marie was frantically trying to take everything in.

"Hello, Ann Marie." Jem stood holding the door open, Emmy in his arms.

"Jem, nice to see you. I won't stay long." Ann Marie stood in the back room, trying not to stare. "I have something to tell Ivy and I didn't think it should wait."

"So how did Granny enjoy her trip?" Ivy got out an extra cup and began moving the tea service over to the big table.

"Granny is in Kevin's Hospital, Ivy," Ann Marie said. "I took her in myself this evening. She didn't want me to tell you. The old lady wanted to walk out of here with her head held high."

"I've been expecting this," Ivy whispered to herself.

This was the reason she'd asked Ann Marie to start calling on Granny. Ann Marie had those connections Ivy had been speaking about. She could get someone a hospital bed with one phone call.

"Sit down both of you, for goodness sake!" Ivy snapped. "You're making the place look untidy. Ann Marie, take the weight off your feet. Jem, sit back down. Emmy, you need to put your baby to bed." Ivy had made Emmy a black-haired rag doll the child loved. They'd used an orange crate and an old baby blanket to fashion a bed for the doll.

"She's good at giving orders." Jem waited for Ann Marie to sit down first.

"So I've noticed." Ann Marie sat at the table with her back to the wall. She had full view of the room. Ann Marie had to bite back a gasp when she recognised Ivy's grotty old coat on the bed, obviously being used as a bed cover. Had Ivy no blankets? Surely she made enough from her round to purchase a couple of blankets? The brass bed was a monstrosity.

Despite the obvious poverty the room was warm and clean. The touches of feminine whimsy were delightful. Ann Marie wanted to stand and touch the little bits of artistic handwork that dotted the room. The lace work that drifted down the shelves of the huge wood dresser was particularly attractive.

"How long has Granny got?" Ivy asked as soon as Jem and Ann Marie were seated around the table. She busied herself moving the tea fixings over to the table.

"She's been ready to go for a long time, Ivy." Ann Marie picked up one of the teacups to admire the design. "She had a turn for the worse today. When I described Granny's symptoms to a doctor friend of mine he ordered me to take the woman to Kevin's, immediately."

"I'm surprised you got her to agree to go with you," Jem said.

"It wasn't easy, Jem, but she's frightened. I hope you don't mind my taking charge, Ivy?" Ann Marie didn't want to overstep herself. "Granny insisted I pick her up and take her myself. She didn't want you to worry. I'm sorry, Ivy. It was the only way I could get Granny to agree to go into hospital."

"I'm glad, Ann Marie." Ivy sighed. "I've been worried sick about Granny for some time." Ivy knew her friend was dying. Every time she went into Granny's room she'd been afraid of finding the old woman dead in the bed. "I'll go in and see her tomorrow."

"I'll take you, Ivy." Jem said. "I wouldn't mind saying me goodbyes to the old woman." Jem wanted to prepare Ivy for what was coming.

"Thanks, Jem." Ivy slapped the table. Granny was ready to go. The old woman had lost the will to live. Ivy could do nothing about that. "Now, since you're here, Ann Marie, Jem and me were having a talk. We could use your advice."

"Ivy, what are you doing?" Jem liked Ann Marie but he didn't want her sticking her nose into his business.

"Think about it, Jem." Ivy put her hand on Jem's arm and shook it slightly. "Ann Marie sees our world through different eyes. We should ask her opinion."

"I don't see how she could help." Jem glared. "No offense to you, Ann Marie."

"You won't know till you ask!" Ivy snapped.

"I don't want to cause trouble between you two." Ann Marie was dying of curiosity. "If I can help in any way I'd be more than willing."

"Right," Jem pushed his fingers through his hair. He looked at the little girl kneeling with her doll on the bed, pretending not to listen. "I'm surrounded by bossy women all of a sudden."

"Jem, just lay the matter out." Ivy poured the tea nobody but herself seemed to want. "All you're doing is asking advice. It won't kill you."

"It's like this, Ann Marie . . ."

Jem explained the situation he found himself in. He had to retire Rosie. He didn't know if he wanted to continue being a jarvey but he didn't know what else he could do.

Ann Marie sipped her tea and listened without speaking while Jem talked. The man really opened his heart to the two women. Jem freely admitted he'd let the business fail through lack of interest after his uncle's death. Ann Marie was impressed by his honesty.

"Jem, there is no delicate way to ask. How are you fixed for capital – money?" Ann Marie almost blushed to ask.

"I have some money." Jem glared at Ivy.

"Right, well, I'm really glad you asked me about this because I've already been giving your livery some thought." Ann Marie pushed up the sleeves of her second-hand jacket and leaned forward. "I want you to bear with me. I have some ideas but I have no idea how feasible they are."

"Talk away." Jem was prepared to listen.

"I've noticed a lot of young men hanging around this area." Ann Marie had become a frequent visitor to The Lane in the short time she'd been visiting Granny. She'd made an effort to pay attention to everything she saw.

"It's hard for lads from The Lane to get work," Ivy said, nodding.

"I've been paying more attention to my surroundings lately." Ann Marie grinned and pointed to Ivy. "That one told me I went around the place with my eyes closed and she was right."

"I've never seen anyone so unaware," Ivy grinned behind her teacup.

"It seems to me that there is a lot of work for jarveys," Ann Marie said. "I've noticed so many people in the street whistling and shouting to attract their attention. Of course we have two automobiles available to us at Number 8 but I've seen the footmen of other households on the square trying to attract the attention of passing jarveys." Ann Marie waited.

"That's nothing out of the ordinary." Jem shrugged.

"Not if you had a telephone service." Ann Marie grinned when Ivy clapped her hands in delight.

"No jarvey could afford to put in a telephone," Jem stated.

"Think about it, Jem!" Ivy said. "You wouldn't have to be out in all weathers waiting. You could take a phone call and know when you got the horse out you were guaranteed a fare."

"I was actually thinking bigger than that, Ivy." Ann Marie grinned.

"What do you mean?" Jem was intrigued.

"Well, it seems to me a man with a telephone, for a fee of course, could offer his services to the many jarveys around the city." Ann Marie couldn't believe she was involved in a business discussion sipping lukewarm tea across the table from a man sitting on what looked like an old wooden box.

"That's a shocker." Jem gulped his teacup dry.

"You could give the lads that hang about The Lane jobs. Perhaps train them to work for you. Pay the lads to drive for you eventually, if you want to run a city-wide service. As soon as the phone line is installed you would be able to offer a service to the other jarveys. You take orders by telephone. Use the lads to take the request to the nearest jarvey on the list you'll keep. For every call you take and pass along you take a small percentage of the fare for your service."

"My God," Jem saw where she was going. "You don't think small, Missus, do you?"

"Is it possible?" Ann Marie asked.

"It would take a great deal of planning." Jem was excited by the challenge. "I'd have to buy a lot of equipment. I'd be able to retire Rosie. I've spare carriages but I'd have to buy younger horses. The horses could be trained up along with the lads I'd hire to drive them. I'd have to learn a lot of new things meself." Jem grinned.

"Would it be possible to provide an automobile service alongside the traditional pony and trap?" Ann Marie suggested."I could approach my aunt's chauffeur about giving you driving lessons in his own time, Jem. You would be welcome to use my vehicle."

"By God, Missus," Jem was stunned by the idea, "you've taken me breath away."

"Normally I would suggest we consult someone with experience at this point," Ann Marie said slowly, "but I don't think anyone is offering the kind of service we're talking about."

"I'd be the first." Jem swallowed at the size of the risk he would be taking. But the rewards, Mother of God, the rewards!

"I would like to be a part of this, Jem," Ann Marie suggested. The business would give her an interest and a reason to hang around with the people who were coming to mean so much to her.

"You want to be a jarvey?" Jem laughed. "I know you love your automobile, Ann Marie, but I can't see you hiring yourself out!"

"No, that's not what I meant." Ann Marie laughed, her eyes sparkling behind her glasses. "Although the idea is fascinating." She imagined herself driving around Dublin picking up strangers. The idea tickled her fancy. "I was thinking more in terms of financial investment. I'd be able to give some assistance setting up the office you'd need, too, now that I come to think about it."

"Honest to God, Ann Marie, I can't believe it!" Jem grinned in delight.

"I've been thinking." Ivy had been listening without saying a word – she'd had nothing to contribute.

"Oh God!" Jem groaned. "Not that!" He laughed at the look of disgust on Ivy's face.

"Eejit!" Ivy slapped Jem without malice. "I was thinking about the lads Ann Marie mentioned. We know them all, Jem. Have watched most of them grow up."

"So?"

"We'd know who was trustworthy," Ivy said slowly. She was working out the idea in her head as she spoke. "You could use them now."

"What are you thinking, Ivy?" Ann Marie asked.

"The woman's a marvel when she starts thinking," Jem said to Ann Marie.

"You could give them a few pennies for doing jobs for you, now." Ivy said slowly. "The lads we know did well in school. You could give them notebooks and send them out."

"To do what?" Ann Marie asked.

"To take notes." Ivy grinned.

"Notes about what, Ivy?" Jem wondered.

"The lads are used to hanging around corners." Ivy laughed. "They could make notes about the places the most people stand shouting for jarveys. They should make notes about anything they see that might be of interest. I don't know!" Ivy shrugged.

"People hire horse and carts for all kinds of things – moving furniture, delivering supplies, things like that," said Ann Marie. "The lads have eyes and ears. They could use them and give you more of an idea of what's needed."

"It would get them off the street and give them a few pennies in their pockets," Jem agreed. "It's a great idea but it'll cost money."

"It would be a worthwhile business expenditure." Ann Marie could feel her blood fizzing – her fingertips were tingling. "There is an opportunity here, Jem. An opportunity for a farseeing man."

"I've been dragging my bones around this city," Jem sighed.

"I've been thinking about my problems and trying to find a solution. I see now I've been thinking too small. You two have taken me breath away with this plan."

"If you wouldn't mind, Jem," Ann Marie said, "I'd like to be shown around the livery. Get an idea of the space available."

"I'll take Ivy by the hospital in the morning. I could show you around when I get back, if you're free," Jem agreed.

"That would suit me fine," Ann Marie said.

"What about you, Ivy?" Jem asked now. "Do you see yourself helping out at the livery?" He wanted Ivy close to him.

"No, Jem, that's your business." Ivy smiled. "I've spent a lot of years setting up me own little business. Thanks to Ann Marie I realise I have a lot of contacts. I've always had them." Ivy laughed. "I just didn't know what they were called. I have plans for expansion. I'm working on something . . ."

"*Ivy!*" A great banging exploded from the back door. The thing moved in its frame. "Ivy Murphy, for the love of God, open the door, Ivy!"

"What the –" Ivy opened the door.

Conn Connelly fell into the room. The young man was shaking, his face pasty white.

"Conn! Sit down!" said Ivy.

"No time," Conn panted. "Tim Johnson is rounding up a lynch mob and they're coming here, Ivy. Tim Johnson and his cronies spent the afternoon in the pub getting legless. Then the lot of them went round the rent office. They dragged the rent man and the housing agent out and are bringing them here, by force. He has me da with him."

"Is Father Leary with them?" Ivy closed her eyes and sagged visibly where she stood.

"I don't think so," Conn panted. "I ran around to warn you. I sent our Vera to get the police."

"Right." Ivy pushed up the sleeves of her old jumper. "You go out the way you came, Conn. You don't want to get mixed up in this."

"Good lad." Jem had been afraid of something like this

happening. "You did well." He looked down at a big-eyed Emmy. "Would you take Emmy with you, Conn? The little one doesn't need to be here. And Ann Marie, you should leave with Conn."

"I most certainly will *not*!" Ann Marie stood and prepared to face whatever was coming.

"It could get nasty, Ann Marie." Ivy sighed.

"I will not scurry away to safety!" Ann Marie snapped.

"I need to lock the gate at the top of the steps." Ivy locked the door behind Conn with a frowning Emmy in his arms.

"That won't stop them," Jem said.

"It'll make them think!" Ivy snapped. "I don't want a crowd blocking my stairway."

Ivy grabbed her hockey stick and charged up the steps to lock the gate at the entrance to her stairwell. She stood with the stick over her shoulder, waiting. She could hear the noise of the crowd in the tunnel. She was sick with nerves but she wouldn't back down. This was her place and no drunken gang would drive her out.

"Ivy, you should come back down." Jem stood at her side, trying to move her out of the way. "I'll stand here."

"You will not, Jem Ryan. I've put up with enough from these drunken bullies over the years. Well, no more. It ends now."

"Ivy, they might become violent." Ann Marie couldn't believe this was happening. This was Dublin not the Wild West.

"Ivy Murphy!" Tim Johnson was feeling big and brave at the front of the crowd. He stalked into The Lane like the cock o' the walk. "We're coming for you!" Tim wasn't quite drunk – he just had a happy buzz on.

Ivy stood with the hockey stick over her shoulder and waited. She wanted to see who had joined Tim Johnson in this madness. It was good to know your enemies.

"What the hell is going on out here?" Maisie Reynolds stood in the open doorway at the top of the tenement steps, glaring down at the approaching crowd.

"You'd better go inside, Maisie," Ivy shouted.

"I will in me eye!" Maisie Reynolds stepped out of the

doorway. "I'd like me job letting the likes of Tim Johnson get the better of me!"

"Ivy, I'm that sorry." Lily Connelly stood on the steps of her tenement building with her children around her.

"Woman, get back inside!" Alf Connelly shouted from the crowd. "Don't you talk to this harlot!"

"You're wrong, Alf!" Lily Connelly shouted.

"See what you started, Ivy Murphy!" Tim Johnson was enjoying seeing the uppity bitch get hers. "You are a troublemaker, a harlot! We don't want your kind here. This is a decent place. We'll have none of your type around our families." He grabbed Greg Norton and pushed him to the front of the crowd. The man stumbled and almost fell. "Do your job!"

"That's right!" Alf Connelly shouted, red in the face with fury. "She led my lad astray and everyone knows it! He was going to be a priest, my Liam. That bitch took him away from God!"

"You're a rotten liar, Alf Connelly!" Maisie Reynolds shoved up her sleeves and yelled. She had been joined by her husband and two adult sons. "Liam left the priesthood for a bitch all right. Everyone knows that, but the bitch had four legs!" The crowd tittered at that.

"This could get very ugly," Jem said over his shoulder to Ann Marie.

"Keep them talking, Ivy," Ann Marie whispered. She'd seen a lad standing by the tunnel give a signal and was praying it meant the police were nearby.

"Mr Norton, what are you doing here?" Ivy asked the man she paid her rent to every Monday morning.

"He's here to give you notice to quit, Ivy Murphy!" Tim Johnson shouted.

"I am here against my wishes, Miss Murphy," Greg Norton felt brave enough to say.

"Where's Billie Powell?" Tim Johnson shouted. "Send him up. Billie Powell is the man for the job, not this limp wrist!"

The crowd shifted and pushed a reluctant man towards the front.

"Well, well," Ivy tapped the foot of her hockey stick against her hand. "Billie Powell, it's long and many a day since you were brave enough to face me. Did he ever tell you where he got that scar, Mr Norton?" Ivy pointed the stick at Billie Powell's forehead.

"She's lying." Billie Powell was sweating.

"She hasn't said anything yet, Powell." Greg Norton had never liked the rent collector.

"I gave him that scar when I was eleven years old." Ivy was fed up keeping secrets. "He tried to put his hands all over me. Offered to give me something off the rent if I'd let him touch me." Ivy smiled coldly at the shaking man. "You and Tim Johnson are two of a kind if you only knew it, Billie Powell. Tim Johnson tried to force himself on me and all. I didn't get the chance to scar him but me da sure did, didn't he, Tim? You're feeling real brave with a crowd at your back now you know me da's dead, aren't yeh, Tim?"

"Don't they say the dead can haunt yeh?" Maisie Reynolds shouted with glee.

"What the hell is going on here?"

The police had arrived. Four big men in police uniform stood glaring at the crowd. The men at the back tried to disappear but, without them noticing, they'd been surrounded by a crowd of women. The women wouldn't budge.

"Officer," Greg Norton pointed at Tim Johnson, "I want you to arrest that man for kidnapping!"

"What?" Tim Johnson tried to disappear into the crowd he'd brought to give him courage.

"Is that a fact?" Officer Barney Collins was thrilled. He'd wanted a reason to lock that one away for years. He gave the nod to his men and they grabbed a struggling Tim. "I'll need details." He was trying not to grin as he removed his notebook from his pocket. "Do we have witnesses?" He looked at the men trying to disappear into the cobblestones.

"I was locking up my office when these men broke in. They forcibly removed me from my business premises." Greg Norton looked at the crowd of men with disgust. "There were many witnesses to that event, Officer. I'm sure they'd be happy to speak with you. My office clerk will be happy to supply you with a list of names."

"Right, what else is going on here?" Officer Barney Collins looked around. "Miss Murphy, I'm sorry for the trouble being brought to your door. I'd appreciate it if you'd come down to the station and file a complaint."

"You've been very helpful to me in the past, Officer Collins – I appreciate it." Ivy smiled. She took a deep breath, aware she was about to step 'out of her station'. "I'd be happy to file a complaint against Tim Johnson." Ivy was aware of the shock running around the crowd but she'd had enough of being meek and mild. The people of The Lane didn't hold with talking to the police. She knew that. "If you give me a time, Officer Collins, I'll be there."

"What are the rest of you men doing here?" Barney Collins was enjoying the sight of a still-struggling Tim Johnson being forced through the tunnel opening. The man was making a show of himself with his weeping and begging.

Ivy was ashamed of the delight she felt hearing Tim Johnson's cries of shock. The man was a bully and a coward. Seeing Tim Johnson being marched off made her day. She could rest easy in her own home now. She wouldn't have to look over her shoulder whenever she went down the yard. For the moment, anyway, she was safe from his attentions.

"We want that woman gone from here!" Alf Connelly wasn't willing to let the matter drop. "This man –" he pointed to Greg Norton, "is the landlord's agent. We want him to evict Ivy Murphy, throw the bitch out in the street where she belongs!"

"Miss Ivy Murphy pays her rent every week," Greg Norton protested. "I have no reason to remove a valuable tenant."

"You are?" Officer Collins licked his pencil and stared at Alf Connelly. He'd get the names right. There were a lot in this crowd he'd be happy to see bound over to keep the peace. Then they'd only have to step out of line once and he'd have them.

"An auld eejit!" Lily Connelly stepped forward and belted her husband around the head. "Two pints and he doesn't know his own name." Lily pushed the sputtering Alf towards his own home.

"Mr Norton, I'll ask you to come down to the station and fill out a complaint." Officer Collins directed the men with him to take names. It amused him to note that the women at the back of the crowd were making sure the men gave the right name. The men were drunks and not from The Lane so the women were shouting out corrections with glee.

"I'll come down to the station with pleasure," Greg Norton said. "I'm terribly sorry, Miss Murphy." Greg went to tip his hat before remembering the men hadn't allowed him to grab his overcoat and hat.

"I suppose you want a cup of tea now," Jem said softly in Ivy's ear. He was grinning openly. Tim Johnson was under arrest. Ivy was safe from the man.

"Jem," Ivy watched the women, shouting and waving bunched fists in the air, herd the crowd of men from the lane. She sagged against Jem's body, the strength going from her legs. "I want a pot of the bloody stuff."

Chapter 25

"Uncle Charles, a moment of your time, please." Ann Marie wanted to press her hands to her stomach to suppress the sickness that roiled there. She took a deep breath. She had to do this. This meeting was long overdue.

"Ann Marie, I want a brandy before I change for dinner." Charles Gannon allowed Foster to assist with the removal of his overcoat. He'd already passed his hat, gloves and walking cane to the butler to be passed along to the footman.

"I'll join you." Ann Marie had agonised over the words she needed to say to her relative, without success. She'd have to play it by ear.

Without a word being spoken the footman opened the study door. Foster stood back to allow Ann Marie and her uncle to enter the private room. Foster followed and immediately began to assemble the needed drink. Ann Marie sighed. They were perfectly capable of pouring a drink themselves.

"Sherry, Ann Marie?" Charles Gannon liked his niece, enjoyed her company, but he resented her presence in his study. This was the only room in the house he could call his own.

"I'll have a brandy, Foster." Ann Marie signalled her uncle with her eyes. She wanted Foster to leave.

"That will be all, Foster." Charles Gannon relaxed into the comfortable chair behind his desk. He accepted the balloon glass of the finest cognac from the silver salver his butler held in his white-gloved hand. The butler made no attempt to serve cognac to a lady. It simply wasn't done. "We'll ring if we need you."

"You're behaving very strangely, Ann Marie." Charles watched his niece pour a healthy measure of brandy for herself.

"I feel feckin' weird, as my new friends would say." Ann Marie threw herself into a leather-backed chair facing her uncle's desk.

"Ah yes, your new-found friends and your participation in their little lives appears to be doing you a world of good." Charles stared into the amber liquid he swirled in his hand. "In fact, my dear, your looks and health have improved enormously. It's done my heart good to see it." He smiled across the desk.

"I have been having a truly marvellous time," Ann Marie admitted. "I feel as if my life has a purpose. That's something that has been lacking for a long time. I've also come to a greater appreciation of my own privileged lifestyle. However, Uncle . . ." Ann Marie paused.

"Ah, we come to the reason for the barely suppressed fury." Charles Gannon wondered what had put the fire in his niece's cheeks and the steel in her spine.

"Uncle Charles, where is that obscenely expensive fur coat you bought Aunt Beatrice?" Ann Marie felt sick to her stomach but she had to do this.

"Charles Junior took it to Graham's the furriers. He expressed some concern about the care the coat was receiving. You know furs must be stored in a climate-controlled environment." Charles sat back, wondering what that blasted fur had to do with anything.

"Would it interest you to know I purchased that very fur for the princely sum of three guineas?" Ann Marie didn't know how she had contained the horror she'd felt when she'd seen that darn coat in the grotty room in the Warren.

"I beg your pardon." Charles choked on his brandy. "That's impossible. The wretched thing cost a king's ransom and well

281

you know it. My ears are still ringing from the lecture you delivered to me on the subject."

"Oh, Uncle Charles, I really don't know what to do." She swigged the brandy. She needed the warmth. "What should I do for the best?" She stared at her uncle as if he had the answers she needed.

"My dear, I don't like to see you like this." Charles Gannon had never seen his niece in such a state. "Can't you tell me what the matter is?"

"Uncle Charles, brace yourself." Ann Marie finished the brandy in her glass and barely prevented herself from slamming the delicate crystal balloon glass down onto her uncle's desk. "Uncle Charles, I recently discovered, much to my horror that you are about to become a grandfather." Ann Marie giggled hysterically, her breath hitching in and out as she fought for control.

"My dear, I'm afraid the brandy has affected your senses." Charles Gannon stared. Neither of his children had married – indeed to his knowledge they showed no inclination to enter into any romantic liaisons.

"Uncle Charles, I met a young, a very young girl, in possession of my aunt's fur coat."

"Ann Marie, my dear, you need to calm down." Charles Gannon stared. "I've already explained that the coat in question has been placed in the vault of the furrier. I fear that you are very mistaken."

"Uncle, that coat is one of a kind. I've seen it, touched it when my aunt wore the thing. I could not be mistaken in the matter. I bought that coat, Uncle, from a young woman in desperate straits. I was horrified, Uncle, shocked that a member of my family could act in the manner the woman described. To my shame at first I thought you were the man who had impregnated the girl then deserted her."

"For heavens sake, Ann Marie, what are you talking about?" Charles Gannon did not believe this was the kind of conversation one held with one's spinster niece. "Who are you accusing?"

"Charles Junior, your son and heir, gifted the coat to a dancer he was seducing. The girl calls herself Desiree. To hear the girl tell her story she and Charles Junior had a romance to defy the stars. I believe they were quite the glamorous couple around town for a while." Ann Marie buried her face in her hands. Listening to that painfully thin, obviously unhealthy young woman telling her tale of romance had saddened her to her very soul.

"Ann Marie, I can't approve of you mixing with that class of person." Charles didn't know what to do, what to say. This was a matter to be handled among gentlemen. His son should have brought the matter directly to his father.

"When Desiree told Charles Junior of her condition, he threw a pound note at her feet and demanded the return of the coat. When Desiree refused he hit her in the face with enough force to blacken both eyes. This is not the action of a gentleman, Uncle Charles." Ann Marie wanted to take a switch to her cousin.

"It is not the kind of story a lady of quality should be told either." Charles Gannon stared at his niece.

"It was completely by chance that I heard the story, Uncle. The young girl lost her job. There is not much call for pregnant dancers. She lost her home, unable to pay her rent. She's been living hand to mouth and I worry that both she and the baby will die in childbirth." Ann Marie intended to do everything she could to secure the life of the unborn child.

"How did this *dancer*," Charles almost spat the word dancer, "contrive to contact you, Ann Marie?"

"She didn't. It was pure happenstance, Uncle." Ann Marie didn't want to go into the details of the situation she'd found herself in.

"I wonder," Charles Gannon said.

"I was in the company of two women who were worried about the girl, a complete stranger to them. These two women, Uncle, have so little it's unbelievable that they manage to survive from one day to the next. They have so little, Uncle, yet give so much. We have so much and give so little." Ann Marie was close to tears.

"My dear," Charles Gannon was at a loss, "are you sure of your facts?"

"I have Aunt Beatrice's coat upstairs in my room." Ann Marie said. "Still in the original box, a box with your name embossed on the lid."

"What do you expect of me, Ann Marie?" Charles Gannon stood and refreshed their drinks. "I admit to being at a complete loss."

"Uncle, the child will be your grandchild," Ann Marie insisted.

"A bastard child!" Charles snapped.

"That is not the child's fault!" Ann Marie almost shouted. "The innocent in all of this, Uncle, is the unborn child. A child, Uncle, who will have your blood flowing in its veins!"

"The child's misfortune is the fault of its parents, both of them." Charles gulped his brandy. "You hardly expect me to demand my son marry a dancer."

"No, not at all, I'm not that foolish, Uncle, or indeed that innocent." Ann Marie sighed. "Not because I think Charles too good to marry the girl but because I wouldn't wish your son on any woman, Uncle. I'm sorry to speak ill of my cousin but Charles is spoilt to the point of uselessness. He stole that coat. If it had been one of the servants you would have called the police. It is not a small matter, Uncle."

"I agree, Ann Marie." Charles wasn't proud of his son but he'd never been ashamed of him before.

"Uncle, it is not my place –" Ann Marie held up her hand when her uncle started to speak. "I know I'm speaking out of turn. Please believe me when I tell you I'm sorry for speaking to you like this but it is out of genuine concern for my family, my blood family." Ann Marie had taken the responsibility for the unborn child into her own hands but her cousin could not be allowed to escape the consequences of his actions.

"I suspect I need to hear what you're going to say." Charles Gannon felt tired. He'd worked at the hospital and his practice today. He'd wanted to come home to a peaceful meal and a restful evening. Was that too much to expect?

"Charles Junior needs to grow up, Uncle. He is no longer a young boy in leading reins. It is time and past it that my cousin became a man."

"I have been remiss in my duties."

"No, Uncle." Ann Marie hated to bring this sadness to her uncle but someone had to be responsible for kicking Charles Junior. Ann Marie knew Charles Junior would smile and ignore anything the females of the house might say to him. "I know the work you do. I know you give so much of yourself to your patients, the people who need you but, Uncle, your children need your attention too." Ann Marie had sense enough not to share her complete disgust for her cousin, indeed for both of her cousins, with their parent.

"Not everyone can have your social conscience, my dear." Charles Gannon was very much aware of his children's lack of purpose in life. His brother's wife had been raised in the Quaker faith. She'd insisted Ann Marie too would be raised Quaker. Charles was beginning to think there might be something in the tenets of "the Friends" as his sister-in-law had referred to them.

"We can't all be alike, Uncle, I appreciate that, but I worry about my cousins. The life they lead can surely not be a fulfilled one." Ann Marie shrugged. "Perhaps I am completely mistaken."

"I will give the matter serious attention, that I promise you." Charles Gannon would speak with his wife. Beatrice would surely know the best way to proceed. "That does not help the young girl, though."

"One of the women I spoke of is tending the pregnant girl. This woman will have no money for special foodstuffs and certainly couldn't afford the cost of a doctor. What she can offer is practical advice and the kind of attention that will insure the baby is born healthy. The mother is in a bad way. She is so young, Uncle. I don't think she realises what is happening to her." Ann Marie made no mention of her own financial contribution to Sadie's household.

"What a bloody mess!" Charles Gannon cursed.

"I will leave it to you, Uncle, to deal with my cousin. And I'm afraid after this conversation I can't sit down to dine in his presence. I would be sure to do or say something that would cause Aunt Beatrice distress and the good lady doesn't deserve that."

Ann Marie stood up and faced her uncle.

"One thing you should know, Uncle. The woman tending to the dancer has offered to take the child and raise it as her own." Sadie had wept bitter tears at her own inability to bear another child. She'd stated clearly that she would have been happy with half a dozen little ones. "The woman's husband was crippled in an accident at work recently so money will be a problem. I see no reason Charles Junior should not be made to pay a small weekly stipend for his child's raising."

Without waiting for an answer, Ann Marie turned and left the room. She returned to her rooms.

The horror she'd felt when she'd seen the coat the young girl wanted to sell was still with her. She'd believed the child to be her uncle's until the girl talked about how young and attractive "Charlie" was.

Ann Marie dropped into a fireside chair, her mind in a whirl. She needed to make changes in her own life. She couldn't continue to live in her uncle's home. She was honest enough with herself to know that she was completely unsuited to living a life without servants. It had been brought home to her, forcefully, that she was incapable of doing the work needed to run a house. Ivy Murphy delighted in telling Ann Marie that she couldn't even boil water. A sad fact of life.

Chapter 26

"Yeh can't be coming in to see me every day, girl," Granny Grunt's yellow crinkled face looked ancient on the starched white hospital pillow.

"Don't be talking rubbish!" Ivy put the grapes she'd brought on top of the bedside locker. "I'm enjoying having a reason to get dressed in me best and go visiting."

"Old Man Solomon did yeh proud with that suit, Ivy." Granny pushed her head back into the pillow. "Yeh look like a fillum star, Ivy, honest yeh do. Yeh're giving the doctors in here whiplash trying to get a good look at yeh!" Granny smirked a little. "Jem didn't come with yeh today?"

"Now, Granny," Ivy grinned, "Jem and me are just friends."

"Yeh could do a lot worse then Jem Ryan, me girl. He's a fine figure of a man. He'd be good to yeh."

"Granny!" Ivy blushed.

"Listen to me, girl!" Granny poked Ivy's shoulder. "I haven't long for this life but I've been around a bloody long time. I know a thing or two more than you." Granny had to pause to catch her breath. "That father of yours chained you to his side. You were a feckin' slave to him and your brothers. The best thing Éamonn Murphy ever did for you was die before his time."

Granny held up a hand when Ivy looked like interrupting. "*I'm* speaking here, girl. I don't have a lot of time to spare. I'll be having a word with your da when I see him, I can tell yeh. I'll be able to say all the things I wanted to over the years."

"What things?" Ivy had never heard a cross word pass between her da and Granny Grunt.

"The things I should have said but I was afraid he'd stop yeh coming to see me." The old woman wished she hadn't started this. She had a lot more important things to talk about than that waste-of-space Éamonn Murphy. "Never mind that!" Granny tried to hitch herself up in the bed. "Give us a hand, will yeh, girl?"

"Yeh need to rest." Ivy jumped to her feet. A passing nurse hurried to help.

"I'll get rest enough where I'm going!" Granny snapped when she was settled comfortably. "I'm old, Ivy. I never thought I'd live this long. I had to see you grow, didn't I? Couldn't leave you to struggle on alone – you needed me."

"I did an' all." Ivy didn't know what she'd have done without the old woman's knowledge and advice.

"Open that drawer." Granny pointed to the bedside cabinet. "The key to me room is there. Take it. I want yeh to clear out the place."

"Granny!" Ivy protested.

"I'll not be returning there. I knew that when I left." Granny was a realist. "I've made me arrangements. I'm donating me body to science." The old woman almost choked laughing at that. "It'll save the cost of a funeral. The doctors here can't wait for me to die. I've lived that long and in such good health they can't wait to take me apart and figure it all out, the fools. I'll have more attention from men dead than I ever had alive." Granny chuckled.

"Granny, I'll be lost without yeh!" Ivy sobbed.

"No, you won't, girl!" Granny snapped. "I'll be one less burden for you to carry. Now, girl, sit up straight and listen to what I tell yeh." She waited until Ivy calmed down. "I want yeh to take everything out of my place – that's important, girl. *Everything*. I've hid the odd half crown and florin around the place. The God's honest truth, I don't know where I put the half of them so check everything. I was saving for me old age." Granny had been terrified of starving to death, lying for days in her own waste while the rats ate her alive. The young woman sitting sobbing by her bed had saved her. "Yeh kept me young, Ivy. And you got me into this clean room with people to wait on me hand and foot. The food's nothing special but it beats what I thought was facing me."

"Granny, I didn't do nothin'!" Ivy protested.

"Your one Ann Marie might have arranged it but it's all thanks to you I'm here and I don't mistake it." Granny was ready to meet her Maker. "Me kidneys are packing it in. That's what's going to kill me. I'll be watching over yeh from heaven if I've any say in the matter. Take whatever you can use from my place and sell the rest on. Go along now, Ivy, go home, I'm tired."

"I'll come again, Granny," Ivy stood and for the first time in her life pressed a kiss into the wrinkled cheek. "God be with you."

"Thanks, girl, thanks for everything."

Granny watched Ivy leave with tears in her eyes. She watched her girl walk down the ward and out through the door. She could die in peace now knowing Ivy was being looked after. That Ann Marie was nobody's fool and Jem Ryan was one of the best. Her girl would be all right now. Granny took a shivering breath, closed her tired eyes and died.

"Miss Ivy Murphy, aren't you a little out of your way?" Brother Theo stood in the aisle beside the pew Ivy knelt in.

"Hello, Brother Theo." Ivy sat back in the pew. She moved along the seat, leaving a place for the friar to join her if he so desired. "I came in to light a few candles."

"Did you?" Theo sat on the bench of the pew, keeping a wide space between himself and the young woman who fascinated him.

"A good friend of mine is in the hospital," Ivy offered with a shrug. "I like empty churches. In fact, I prefer the echoing space around me. It fulfils something inside me."

"Yes," Theo looked around the church, "I suppose it must." He didn't know what to say to this young woman which was unusual for him. He wanted to ask her if she'd had any more trouble from the Parish Priest. Theo had started an investigation into the man but these things moved slowly.

"How is Liam Connelly getting along, Brother?"

"Liam Connelly is a very confused young man." Theo sighed. "The time he is spending in retreat is helping him."

"That's all very well for him, Brother Theo, and I don't mean to sound like a hard-hearted so-and-so but the lad left other people with five dogs to take care of. The animals are Liam's responsibility, Brother Theo." Ivy hadn't expected Liam to just up and leave.

"I think the young man is ready to return home," Theo said. "Liam discovered a book in our library that deals with the training of animals. He's studying it with a great deal of dedication."

"A library – a place full of books! Imagine!" Ivy couldn't imagine a place closer to heaven. Think of all the books you could read!

Theo smiled, having no understanding of the wonder he was instilling in Ivy. To Theo's mind, everyone had a library available to them.

"How are your studies continuing without your teacher?" Theo wanted to know the answer. He planned to work with Ivy himself when she was further along in her studies.

"Emmy has been keeping my nose to the grindstone. She takes her responsibility to teach me very seriously."

"The young girl is not at school with the good nuns?" Theo had checked into the matter personally.

"No." Ivy turned on the bench to face the friar. "Emmy is a very bright little girl, Brother Theo. She is in a Quaker school for the moment. There she is allowed to go ahead at her own pace. The Friends' teachers guide her in her studies. She is far ahead of the other girls of her age."

"You don't have a great deal of admiration for Holy Orders,

do you, Ivy?" Brother Theo was not offended. He'd seen the treatment Father Leary handed out to Ivy. He'd heard a great deal about what he could only term persecution from Liam Connelly. The young man admired and respected Ivy Murphy, not in a romantic fashion. Liam spoke freely about the help Ivy and other women like her offered to any who needed it. It was admirable.

"I object to men and women telling me how to live my life." Ivy took a deep breath. She was in a church speaking to a friar, for goodness sake, but she was entitled to her own opinion.

"The priest and nuns are there to guide people in the Christian way of life," Theo offered.

"Brother Theo, with all the respect in the world," Ivy said, her awareness of the silence of the church keeping her voice down, "how in the name of God can men and women who have completely withdrawn from life know or understand how someone should live their life?"

"You think we withdraw from life by entering Holy Orders?" Theo asked, fascinated by this way of looking at the life he led.

"You don't have to worry about a roof over your head. That is provided for you. You don't worry about where the food in your mouth comes from or who pays for it. You don't even have to worry about clothes to cover your back, yet you feel at liberty to tell those of us struggling simply to exist, how to live our lives."

"You feel strongly about this, don't you, Ivy?" Brother Theo wanted to clap his hands in delight. Here was someone who was thinking, questioning. What a rare prize Ivy Murphy was!

"I resent the heck out of it, Brother Theo, if you want to know the truth."

"The truth is always best, Ivy." Theo grinned.

"You don't want to kick me out of your church? You have no inclination to drag me into the street and call down the wrath of God on my head?" Ivy couldn't believe she was having this conversation with a friar.

"Far from it. I've enjoyed our conversation, Ivy." Theo checked his pocket watch and grimaced. "However, I am late to table and will be lectured for my lack of manners." He shrugged, grinning.

"Have a nice meal, Brother." Ivy shook her head and turned away. The man had no idea.

"What?" Theo turned Ivy back to face him. "I saw that look. What have I done wrong?"

"You need to walk a mile in my shoes, Brother Theo," Ivy said simply.

"I don't understand."

"I know and I don't have time to tell you." Ivy shrugged. "You need to get away. If you're interested come and visit me sometime. I'll explain the difference in our way of living." Ivy slid back down to kneel. She hadn't completed her prayers for her da and Granny Grunt.

Brother Theo stood looking down at the young woman kneeling at his feet. She'd turned away from him. He was more fascinated every time he encountered her.

Theo hurried away. He didn't enjoy the lectures he received from Brother Bernard, their cook, when he was late to table. He would take Liam Connelly home personally. He wanted to spend time around Ivy Murphy and her friends. There was a lot he could learn there.

"Ann Marie I didn't expect to see you here." Ivy was tired. She'd had an emotionally exhausting day. "Shouldn't you be dining in fine style?"

"Don't be bitchy, Ivy Murphy." Ann Marie watched Emmy run to Ivy, confident of her reception.

"What are you doing here?" Ivy swung Emmy up in her arms. She pressed a swift kiss onto Emmy's upheld cheek before settling the young girl on her hip.

"I came to examine the work on the livery." Ann Marie saw the exhaustion on Ivy's face. She hated to be the bearer of bad news.

"How's it going, Ivy?" Conn Connelly came out of the open livery doors, grinning. "Have you come to add your tuppence worth?" Conn was employed full-time by Jem Ryan. He was rapidly becoming Jem's right-hand man.

"I haven't got tuppence." Ivy grinned. She was very fond of Conn. He had a good head on his shoulders and was willing to turn his hand to anything asked of him. "I saw Brother Theo, Conn." Ivy was speaking but at the back of her mind she was wondering what she was going to eat. She was hungry.

"What did he have to say?" Conn was enjoying his new life. He'd spent his life in Liam's shadow. The Connelly parents had made a great fuss of the lad who would be a priest. Conn and his siblings had been largely ignored.

"Liam is about ready to come home," Ivy said simply.

"Is that a fact?" Conn wondered how his sister Vera would react to the news. She'd been looking after the dogs and Conn didn't think she'd willingly give them over to Liam. Vera was the eldest Connelly at eighteen.

"Conn, if I give you the money could you run and get fish and chips for all of us?" Ann Marie knew there was a chip shop on the other side of the canal. It wouldn't take Conn long to cross the lock gate and get there and back.

"That's a lot of people, Ann Marie," said Ivy. She wanted Conn to understand he was included in the invitation. Ivy didn't mind spending Ann Marie's money, within reason. She would not see her friend being taken for a ride but Ann Marie had a lot more of the readies than anyone else she knew.

"I'm all for that." Jem Ryan stepped from the interior of the livery. He and Conn had been taking care of Rosie and planning for the additional horses they were going to buy. "In fact," Jem offered with a grin, "I'll make the tea and we'll have a picnic in the hay."

"Yes, that's a great idea, Uncle Jem." Emmy clapped her hands with glee.

"Emmy, you run tell Vera what we're doing." Ivy suggested, dropping the little girl to her feet.

Ann Marie watched Emmy run around the tenement buildings screaming a greeting to the children she passed. She turned to Ivy.

"I have some bad news, I'm afraid," she said.

"Granny! She's gone!" Ivy sobbed before Ann Marie could say another word.

"She was ready to go, Ivy." Jem put his arm around Ivy's shoulders. "She had good innings. I'll buy a few bottles – looks like we're going to have a wake with our fish and chips." Jem went to put his hand in his pocket for money but Ann Marie waved him away.

"I'm doing this, Jem." Ann Marie struggled to remove the money from her concealed skirt pocket. Most women kept their money in their knickers but Ann Marie changed her clothes from the skin out several times a day so Ivy attached her purse to her skirt.

"Here you go, Conn. That should be enough for everything." Ann Marie almost gave Conn a heart attack by handing him a crisp pound note. More money than the lad had ever seen in his life.

"I think that young man could do with a bicycle, Jem," Ann Marie remarked as Conn dashed away.

"I was thinking that very thing meself." Jem watched Conn run at speed towards the tunnel. "In fact I think a lot of the young lads working for me could use bikes. It would speed things up and I've a few ideas I want to try out – if I can get a good deal on bikes, that is." Jem sat up nights making plans for his new business. The possibilities made him dizzy but he was determined to make a success of the business and pay back every penny he'd "borrowed" from Emmy's funds.

"It looks like we'll be having a wake and a business meeting in the hay," Ivy said. "I'm going to go over to my place and make sure the range hasn't gone out." She wanted to change her clothes and have a little cry in private for Granny.

"Has Ivy told you Father Leary's latest?" Jem whispered to Ann Marie with a quick look around The Lane. He didn't want anyone to hear him.

"No," Ann Marie said softly. "Ivy hasn't said a word."

"The man has visited the houses on the square." Jem had

heard the news from Albert, the Gannon chauffeur, on one of the nights the man was giving him a driving lesson.

"Why would he do that?"

"Father Leary has declared that anyone found helping Ivy Murphy will suffer the displeasure of the Church," Jem said through his teeth. It seemed to Jem that Father Leary was on a personal vendetta against Ivy.

"What has Ivy ever done to the man?" Ann Marie gasped.

"I don't know but the man's dangerous and Ivy won't see that." Jem was scared.

"Can he really stop people giving their discards to Ivy?" Ann Marie wondered aloud. "That would seriously affect her ability to support herself. I have to admit, Jem, I'm lost in admiration at Ivy's ability to turn one person's trash into treasure." Ann Marie laughed. "I've also got the idea that the new business Ivy won't speak about depends a great deal on the items she gets on her 'round'." Ann Marie couldn't bear to see anyone abuse Ivy. It simply wasn't fair.

"The man made a big mistake." Jem grinned. It was typical of the priest but it was in Ivy's favour. "He approached the owners of the houses. It was to them he made his feelings known." Jem laughed. "They never even see the likes of Ivy Murphy!"

"I suppose not but, Jem, I can't help feeling concern." Ann Marie didn't think she could help Ivy in this situation. She wasn't a member of the Catholic Church. She had no power with the Parish Priest.

"Father Leary worries me too, Ann Marie." Jem admitted. "This country fought for its freedom from oppression but it seems to me we are handing over all our freedom to the Catholic Church. These men and women have too much power over us, Ann Marie. To be very honest with you, I fear them. I fear the power we are giving to them."

"I'm not a Catholic, Jem, so I don't feel free to voice an opinion," Ann Marie said carefully. "I don't like what this Father Leary is doing to Ivy. In fact as an outsider looking in it seems to me that Ivy Murphy and people like her are living a life that should be a matter of pride to the Catholic Church." Ann Marie shrugged.

"I think so too." Jem was sick with fear for Ivy. She went along living her life but the Church could squash her like a bug and she refused to see that.

"Here's Emmy with Vera now." Jem said as the laughing little girl approached, pulling Vera along by the hand. "I'll keep a close eye on Ivy, Ann Marie. It's all I can do."

"So shall I, Jem," Ann Marie vowed.

Chapter 27

Ivy enjoyed the sound of her beige leather boots hitting the highly polished hospital floor. The butter-soft leather boots she'd removed from Emmy's aunt fit Ivy as if crafted for her. The early May sunlight gave her an excuse to wear her new ankle-length white linen skirt and fitted jacket. The style accentuated her tall slim figure. Her flattering mop of inky black curls sported a white fedora she'd trimmed with handmade lace.

Ivy acknowledged the greeting of a passing group of doctors, completely unaware of the masculine appreciation gleaming in each man's eyes. She bowed her head graciously as she'd seen Ann Marie do, biting her lip to suppress her grin. They'd greeted her as if she was a real person. Ivy wondered what they'd think if they knew the suit she was wearing so proudly had been made from a dead woman's bed-sheets? The flattering hat sitting tilted on her head had been her da's pride and joy. The boots on her feet had been made to hide a dead woman's keys. The foundation garment she wore was still an old vest. Ivy's body shook with suppressed giggles. Her da would say she was "aping her betters", stepping above her station, but Ivy didn't care.

"John Lawless?" Ivy stopped by the bed of the man she'd come to see.

"What's it to you?" The man in the bed didn't bother to turn his head in Ivy's direction. He'd had just about enough of do-gooders and bleeding hearts. He wanted to be left alone. Was that too much to ask?

"We've met before." Ivy took a seat in the chair pulled up by the hospital bed. She wasn't put off by his attitude. She'd expected it. "My name is Ivy Murphy." She took a brown-paper bag from the depths of her lace-covered handbag. She put the paper bag on the locker by the side of the bed. "Sadie said you liked grapes."

"Ivy Murphy!" John Lawless turned his head to stare at the vision of feminine beauty sitting by his bed. The woman didn't look anything like the ragbag he remembered seeing scurrying around the market places. She was all in white for Christ's sake – only the rich could afford to dress in something so impractical.

"Jaysus, Ivy, you've come up in the world." He didn't want to be interested but he couldn't help himself. It was like something from one of the books he'd read, a body switch or something. "My Sadie thinks you're an angel." He had to admit, dressed all in white as she was she could have been an angel. "Have you come to wave your magic wand around and make me walk?"

"I don't know why I'm here." Ivy smiled at Sadie's husband.

"Look, Ivy, no offense but I've enough problems without people coming in here to take a look at the freak." John Lawless was tired of being poked and prodded.

"Sadie is worried sick about you," Ivy said simply. "I can see why, John. You should be out in this gorgeous sunshine, not lying here brooding."

"Sadie shouldn't worry about me." John turned his head back to staring at the wall. "I hear you've given her and my girls jobs. They're doing all right without me."

"John, your wife and daughter's need you." Ivy wished she was wiser, had more words to convince this man.

"*They don't need me!*" John shouted. "I'm a bloody cripple, useless!"

"John, Sadie told me you are highly intelligent – those are her very words –'highly intelligent'. Was she lying?" Ivy had listened to Sadie singing this man's praises for months.

"My Sadie thinks because I always have my head buried in a book that means I'm intelligent." John shrugged. What did he know about intelligent? He'd left school at eleven.

"Sadie says you read aloud to her and the girls every evening." Ivy smiled. "She says you like knowing how things work."

"What has that got to do with the price of eggs?" John Lawless waited.

"I'm not really sure," Ivy admitted. "I only know that your wife and daughters need you desperately."

"Are you blind?" John pushed himself up in the bed, using his elbows, and glared into Ivy's eyes.

"John, your legs don't work!" Ivy snapped. "Big feckin' deal! The doctors told you they don't know if that's permanent or not, haven't they? The rest of you works, doesn't it?"

"What are yeh doing here, Ivy?" John refused to be a burden on his family.

"Your wife and daughters need you, need to feel your arms around them. That's something they've all missed, John." Ivy didn't know that for a fact but she remembered the warm glow she'd felt whenever Jem Ryan held her tight in his arms. The worries of the world disappeared.

"Lord save me from do-gooders!" John groaned.

"Has Sadie told you much about what's going on?" Ivy needed to find something that would give John Lawless a reason for living. The man had to get out of this bed and rejoin the land of the living. He should be outside taking advantage of the fresh air and sunshine.

"Sadie and the girls are washing wool for you. Turning used wool into big balls of wool to knit toys or some such. Yeh even moved a lodger into my place, big feckin' deal!"

"It's a lot more than that, John," Ivy said. "Jem Ryan, a friend of mine, has this livery business he's trying to turn into something important. He's put in a telephone line, John. We're all learning to answer the telephone. It has to be done in a businesslike manner. We're learning to take messages correctly too."

"What has that to do with me?" John wished the woman would leave him alone.

"You don't need legs to answer the telephone and take messages, John." Ivy had given this a lot of thought. She and Jem had discussed the subject. She wasn't giving the man false hope.

"I thought my eldest, my Clare, was going to train to work in the office." John had heard all about Clare's plans for night school.

"Clare can't work twenty-four hours a day. Jem needs someone to cover the phone day and night. Someone he can rely on to take the messages right, note the details and think in a crisis. You don't need legs for any of that, John." Ivy knew Sadie had tried to get her husband to listen to her but the man was determined to lie here and die.

"I can't get around." He was listening though.

"You won't get anywhere lying here feeling sorry for yourself!" Ivy snapped. "You need to get out of that bed, John, and figure out how you can get around. It won't be easy but Jaysus, John, when was anything easy for the likes of us?" She glared at him.

"Give us one of them grapes." John felt the almost forgotten sensation of a grin on his face. "Sadie said you didn't mince words."

"Life is too short, John." Ivy passed the brown-paper bag over. She accepted one of the big purple grapes and chewed with relish.

"Sadie's been telling me about all of the crazy things you and your friends are getting up to."

"John, you have a wife and two wonderful daughters who think the world of you." Ivy took another grape. "I'm sick listening to them sing your praises morning, noon and night. I've a pain in me head listening to what a great man you are, to be honest."

"I love my girls." John looked away as he admitted to that soft emotion.

"They love you too. You have a wonderful family, John.

You're a good man. I know you've agreed to take in a baby that's not yours. What you have is rare and wonderful, John. Don't let this," Ivy pointed at his legs, "take it away from you."

"What can I give them, Ivy?" John slapped his legs.

"Get out of that bed and see what you can achieve." Ivy wanted to shake the man. "Do you know how many candles your family lights for you, John? It's a bloody wonder the church hasn't burned down. God must be sick listening to the sound of your name they send up so many prayers for you."

"There's a lot going on, John. The world around us is changing. Jem and me, we're determined to be part of that change." Ivy stood. "Get out of that bed and become a part of things, John Lawless. We need all the help we can get."

"Did Sadie ask you to come?"

"Sadie doesn't know I'm here." Ivy waved and turned to walk away. "She'd scratch me bald-headed if she knew I'd interfered in her private business."

John Lawless watched Ivy Murphy walk along the ward towards the door with renewed hope in his heart. If the ragged urchin he knew could turn herself into that fashionable woman, attracting a great deal of male attention, what could he do?

Ivy walked slowly along the hospital corridors lost in thought. She had another reason for dressing up today. She was going to ask someone for a favour. The thought made her sick to her stomach but she didn't know what else to do.

Ivy walked along the city streets, thinking about asking one of the lads to teach her to ride a bike. The walk from Thomas Street to her destination was a long one. She could have been there in half the time if she had one of the bikes Jem's lads rode around the city like demons.

Ivy walked through Dublin's streets, unaware of the admiring glances she attracted from the passing population. Ivy was accustomed to people staring at her. She didn't see the difference between the looks of disdain she normally received and the looks of interest that were coming her way today.

Ivy hoped her visit with John Lawless had done some good. Sadie was desperately afraid her husband would never leave that hospital ward. The woman needed something to hang on to.

"Ivy Murphy, I almost didn't recognise you, can I help you?" Brother Roderick had been passing the vestibule when the doorbell rang. He stood now in the open door of the friary and stared. He remembered this woman very well.

"Is Brother Theo in, please?" Ivy didn't know the correct protocol involved in calling to see a friar. She needed advice and Brother Theo seemed a fountain of knowledge to Ivy.

"Brother Theo is away from home at the moment visiting with his family." Brother Roderick explained. "Perhaps someone else could be of assistance?"

"I don't think so, thank you." Ivy turned away. She'd had a wasted trip. The walk had been a long one in this heat.

"I'd be happy to offer my help," Brother Roderick said. Theo had talked a great deal about Ivy Murphy. He spoke often of the changes Ivy Murphy appeared to bring to the lives of everyone she met. Theo was fascinated by this phenomenon and visited with Liam Connelly and Ivy Murphy frequently.

"I don't know if Brother Theo can help to be honest." Ivy shrugged.

"Won't you tell me what the matter is?" Brother Roderick knew Theo would want him to help.

Ivy figured it couldn't hurt to seek advice. "I applied for a street trader's licence. My application has been refused."

"Did they give you a reason?" Brother Roderick would have thought Ivy an excellent candidate for a street trader's license.

"They didn't bother." Ivy held out the rejection letter.

"Hmm, it doesn't say much, does it?" Brother Roderick thought the letter was derogatory. The tone was most insulting.

"I wondered if Brother Theo knew anyone he could ask for an explanation." Ivy didn't want to accuse Father Leary of stopping her application but she strongly suspected the old priest.

"If you would allow me to take notes," Brother Roderick offered, "I can see what I can find out."

"If you would, Brother," Ivy allowed him to remove the letter from her hand, "I'd be most grateful."

"Just a moment." Brother Roderick closed the friary door in Ivy's face. He hurried into the vestibule and began searching a nearby desk for pencil and paper. Brother Theo had been in discussion with several brothers and church officials about Ivy's problems with her Parish Priest. Roderick suspected the involvement of the man. Hurrying to open the door to Ivy again Roderick prayed he was wrong.

"I'll look into the matter." Brother Roderick returned the letter to Ivy. "How shall I let you know my findings?"

"I'll give you a telephone number." Ivy grinned at the surprised look on Brother Roderick's face. It seemed giving a telephone number was a step up in the world.

Ivy left her contact details with Brother Roderick and with a smile of thanks walked away. She desperately needed something to drink. The sunlight seemed attracted to her white clothes. She was being slowly baked walking along the city streets. Ivy searched her memory for the nearest water pump. She couldn't put her head under the tap as the kids did but she'd made a delicate handkerchief to carry with her. She'd wet that and try to cool herself down.

"Allow me."

Ivy jumped in surprise. She turned to look at the man smiling at her. The man was dressed in summer whites and carrying a tennis racket. Wasn't it a bit early in the year for tennis? Ivy grinned mentally: now she thought she knew something about tennis! She was losing the run of herself. She'd never seen this man before in her life. What was she supposed to do? She'd never had anyone offer to work the handle of a pump for her.

"Thank you." Ivy stepped away from the pump and watched with hidden amusement as the gallant wet his handkerchief for her.

"I've never seen you around here before." Burton Moriarty

knew he'd remember seeing this vision. He couldn't believe his luck – first in. She must be new in town. He enjoyed success with the fair sex. He knew all of the noted beauties. "Are you visiting our fair city?" Burton offered his water-soaked handkerchief.

"No," Ivy took the wet cloth, not sure how to behave. She imagined Ann Marie in the same situation and almost laughed aloud. Ann Marie would never walk miles around the city. "Dublin is my home." Ivy held the cloth over the fountain and removed the excess liquid.

"You must know the ice-cream parlour on O'Connell Street." Burton gave her the grin that had captured female hearts for years. "Would you allow me to accompany you there?"

"Thank you for the offer." Ivy almost groaned in relief as she ran the cold damp cloth over her burning skin. "But we haven't been introduced." Ivy demurred to the manner born.

"Burton Moriarty at your service." Burton grinned and with a practised move removed the cloth from Ivy's fingers. He positioned himself to show off his athletic body and enjoy the feel of feminine admiration as he worked the pump handle again.

"Burton – how unusual!" Ivy had to bite her lips to hide the grin that wanted to spread across her face. The man's posturing was ridiculous to someone who watched men throw ricks of hay over their heads every Tuesday and Friday at the Hay Market.

"It's a family name on my mother's side." Burton shrugged casually. "Burtons have been a leading force in Dublin society for generations," he admitted coyly. "Mother wanted to pay homage to her ancestors." He shrugged, spreading his hands in a 'what can you do?' attitude.

"How nice." Ivy was cool now. In fact, she was practically shivering. This attractive, confident, wealthy man was a relation of hers. The son of one of her mother's sisters – he had to be. The first relation she'd ever seen. What was he, some kind of cousin?

"How about that ice?" Burton grinned, confident of success.

"Thank you but no." Ivy smiled coolly and turned to walk away. She wanted to demand the man tell her everything he knew about her mother's family – but what was the point? They didn't want to know her. She wouldn't allow herself to question this smug, self-satisfied man.

"You can't just walk out of my life." Burton walked along beside Ivy, his racket under his arm. He attempted to take her elbow but Ivy sidestepped his touch adroitly. She didn't allow strange men to touch her. The icy glare she sent Burton told him to keep his distance.

"Let me buy you an ice-cream," Burton persisted, unable to believe this beauty was going to refuse his advances. "We would sit outside in full view of the passing traffic."

"Thank you for your assistance." Ivy did her Ann Marie impression again and bowed her head graciously. "I have matters to attend to." She needed to get away from this stranger who happened to have the same blood as herself running in his veins.

"You haven't told me your name." Burton knew when to back off. He'd bump into her again – bound to – Dublin wasn't that big.

"No," Ivy agreed. "I haven't." She walked away without a backward glance.

Burton Moriarty stood staring after Ivy with an expression of complete bemusement on his face. The woman had given him the cut direct. It was a delightful surprise to Burton. The next time he met that woman he'd be ready. She wouldn't be able to ignore him, he'd see to that.

Ivy walked down O'Connell Street heading in the direction of Grafton Street. She couldn't believe she'd bumped into one of her mother's relations. She was shaking with delayed shock. She turned into the gates of Trinity College. She needed to sit down. She'd sit on one of the benches she knew were dotted around the grounds of Trinity.

Ivy tried to remember the man's features. Had there been a family resemblance? She didn't know. She'd been so surprised when he offered to work the water pump for her. A first for Ivy – she'd never been the subject of male gallantry before. She'd been willing to enjoy the experience. The shock of hearing the man's name had frozen all of her senses.

Her brothers had been boys when they left home for England. Would they be as tall as Burton Moriarty? Bound to be, Ivy told herself – her da had been a very tall man. Her brothers had inherited his looks. They must have inherited his height as well. Ivy was said to resemble her mother uncannily. Was her mother tall? Ivy couldn't remember.

"Would you care for a glass of water, Miss?" Ivy opened her eyes to see one of the university guards smiling down at her. "You appear to be affected by the heat."

"Thank you. That would be very welcome." Ivy allowed her head to fall back against the bench. Was this all it took? She'd been working so hard to make something of herself. Every night her head ached from the hours she spent studying the papers Brother Theo set her when she should have been sleeping.

Ivy had consciously copied Ann Marie Gannon's way of walking, talking and even sitting. She hadn't been trying to become a copy of Ann Marie – simply grooming herself, trying to make something of herself, make herself acceptable.

"Here yeh are, Miss." The guard passed a glass brimming with cool water to Ivy.

"Thank you." Ivy accepted the glass with a cool smile. "This is extremely kind of you." Then she almost froze in terror. Was she supposed to tip the man?

"You need to get out of this heat, Miss." The guard accepted the empty glass and smiled kindly down at Ivy. "Hope you don't mind me saying, Miss." The guard walked away, returning to his duties.

Ivy closed her eyes. The same man, if she'd been wearing her old coat and shawl, would have run her off with curses and even rocks. Was all she needed to be accepted a suit of fashionable clothes? Was that all it took? It didn't matter who or what she was. It didn't matter what kind of human being she was. A suit fashioned from a dead woman's bed-sheets was all she needed to be accepted in polite society.

Ivy fought to regain her composure. She'd dressed like this today because she'd things she needed to get done. She'd hoped

Brother Theo could help with her application for a street trader's licence. She'd half thought she might have to accompany the friar to the law courts or something and hadn't wanted to make a holy show of herself.

Ivy took deep calming breaths and forced herself to think. She'd been denied a street trader's licence. That was a stumbling block. But she could apply for a market trader's licence. Jem had offered his name if she needed it. That wasn't what Ivy wanted. She wanted to be able to walk around the city and offer her goods in areas where she could demand a higher price than from a market stall.

Ivy pushed herself to her feet. She examined her outfit, checking for stains. White was a bloody impractical colour. Ivy normally avoided Grafton Street on her way home, moving through the city using the backstreets and alleys. Ivy knew her kind were not welcome in the richer areas of town – that's just how things were done. Not today. Today she could stroll along, confident she looked as if she belonged.

Ivy stood before a Grafton Street toy store and examined the goods in the window. She smiled at the abundance of toys available to the wealthy. Did rich kids get the same pleasure from their toys as poor kids got from their home-made toys? Must do, Ivy told herself.

Ivy took a deep breath and prepared to do something she'd never done in her life before. She was going to open the shop door and walk in as if she belonged in a place like that. She could do anything today.

"Can I help you, madam?" the plum-in-the mouth female assistant enquired.

"I'm looking for a train set for my nephew," Ivy answered in her best posh voice. She felt faint. She'd done it and the sky hadn't fallen in.

"What age group, madam?" The assistant prepared to offer every help.

"Adam is two," Ivy invented without a hitch. Did it matter what age you were to play with a toy train? She'd never known that.

"This way, madam." The assistant prepared to point out the available stock. Then the bell over the door jangled and a man entered. "The train sets suitable for your nephew's age group are here." She waved her hand at a wall practically crumbling under the weight of train sets. "Please excuse me. Let me know if I can assist you further." She hurried away before Ivy needed to say anything else.

Ivy stood admiring the train sets. She'd always wanted one. The shop was stocked with so many toys Ivy had never seen before. She could spend hours here looking around the place.

Without being aware of it Ivy was listening to the man and the sales assistant. He was trying to sell her something as far as Ivy could make out. There was a great deal of flirting going on but underneath it all they were talking business.

Ivy had to stiffen her knees when she heard the amount of money being mentioned. They were talking about toys, for God's sake! Who would pay that kind of price for a toy? Ivy hadn't been paying attention to the price of the items she was admiring. She looked now. Mother of Jaysus! Ivy almost passed out. They cost a bloody fortune.

Ivy strolled casually in the direction of the two people, who were enjoying themselves too much to notice her. The man was a salesman and obviously well known to the woman. Ivy had assumed the smiling woman was a sales assistant. It began to appear that the woman was either the owner of the shop or the manager. She was talking as if the decision to buy goods was hers to make.

Ivy picked up a porcelain doll and absently examined the clothes the doll was wearing. She'd picked up the doll on impulse, trying to blend in, but the price tag on the doll was truly shocking to Ivy. Did people have this kind of money to spend on toys from a fancy shop?

"Thank you for your help," Ivy smiled sweetly at the flirting couple as she passed them on her way to the door. "I'll be back." She pulled open the door and escaped into the bustling crowds that strolled along Grafton Street.

"Carry your bags, Missus?"

Ivy jumped at the cheerful voice almost in her ear. She turned to glare only to break into a wide grin.

"What bags, you silly sod?" Ivy smiled into Conn Connelly's grinning face. The lad began wheeling his bike around Ivy laughing in sheer delight.

"It was worth a try." Conn grinned. "Jaysus, Ivy, you don't half look a swank in that rig-out. I almost didn't recognise yeh."

"If I wasn't dressed in all me finery, Conn, I'd beg a jaunt on your crossbar."

"I could throw me shirt across," Conn suggested.

"We'd be arrested." Ivy laughed at the mental image of the two of them riding around Stephen's Green.

"Where are yeh going all dressed up like a dog's dinner anyway?" Conn was sitting on the bike's saddle, his feet on either side of the bicycle pedals, walking along at Ivy's side.

"I'm heading for home."

"You should stop off at Stephen's Green," Conn mentioned the leafy green park at the head of Grafton Street. "Take time out to enjoy the day. You work all the hours God sends, Ivy."

"I have a lot of thinking to do, Conn." Ivy was still reeling from everything that had happened to her that day. It had been a day out of time for her.

"I know a leafy glade inside the park that has a view of the water but is well concealed." Conn didn't think Ivy would be left alone by the passing gents if she just sat on the grass in the park. The men who strolled the city streets looking for diversion would think all their birthdays had come together.

"That sounds heavenly." Ivy sighed. "What are you doing around here anyway?"

"I was checking out the Tivoli Billboard for Vera and Liam." Conn shrugged. "That dancer that's helping them put their act together says there's a fella playing at the Tivoli they need to see."

"What kind of fella?" Ivy didn't want Desiree, or Molly as she was now called, leading Vera astray.

"The fella has a dog act that's attracting a great deal of attention." Conn said. "Your one told Vera she heard on the grapevine that this fella won't be in Dublin long. She heard the big guys in London and even Paris have been checking out the act." Conn didn't understand the world his brother and sister wanted to enter but he'd give them all the help he could.

"We really need to see a dog act, Conn," said Ivy. Some people from The Lane were regular theatre-goers. Her ma and da had spent a lot of time at the theatre. Ivy loved her infrequent visits to the cinema but she'd never been to a theatre.

"Have you seen the price of tickets?" Conn shrugged.

"No," Ivy admitted. "I have no idea how much a seat in a theatre costs."

"We could all afford, just about, to sit in the gods as the seats high up on a kind of balcony are called but we wouldn't be able to see much." Conn had talked to a man he'd met sweeping the theatre entry way. The old guy had taken Conn inside and showed him around the place. It was amazing what you could find out from someone most people ignored.

"Let's go home, Conn! The sun's shining, God's in his heaven, what more do yeh want?" Ivy skipped like a child.

"You seem full of beans today, Miss Ivy Murphy." Conn grinned.

"Give us a jaunt, Mister." Ivy didn't care who was looking. She grinned down at her outfit. White was washable.

"You want to get on me crossbar?" Conn laughed aloud. "Hop up, Missus." Conn leaned back to allow Ivy to perch her glamorously attired body on the crossbar of his bike. Then whooping and grinning like a bandit Conn pedalled for home.

Chapter 28

"Ivy Murphy, you don't usually lurk down this aisle." Harry Green hurried down one of the toy aisles of his giant barn which was stuffed to the rafters with every imaginable item.

"Morning, Harry, how are yeh?" Ivy didn't want to share her thoughts with this man. Harry was a lovely human being but he was a shark in business, sharp as a tack.

"Can't complain," Harry grinned. "Well, I could, but who'd listen?" He shrugged his shoulders. His plump body lifted with the movement. "You thinking of branching out?" He nodded at the naked baby doll Ivy was examining with great interest. The doll was bald with a rag body, porcelain arms, legs and head, and its eyes opened and shut. Harry found the thing creepy but he'd thought he'd be able to shift them. He'd put a few of them in his shop in Capel Street but they weren't moving. He'd have to put them on special offer. He hated doing that, his prices were rock bottom and depended on quantity of sales. Any further reductions he made would mean a loss for him. Harry Green didn't like to lose.

"I wasn't really." Ivy hoped she sounded disinterested. "I've an adopted niece, though."

"The little one who came in here with you a few times?"

Harry missed no detail of his customers' lives. Ivy Murphy had been buying sewing supplies and trimmings from him for years. Ivy had been looking a picture lately and Harry was man enough to notice. It looked like the girl was finally coming out of her shell. Not before time.

"Hmm, I was thinking Emmy might enjoy a toy." Ivy let the doll dangle from her fingers. She cast an eye over the rest of the dolls stacked in boxes that reached to the roof. Her heart was beating so hard it was a wonder it didn't show. "What are those things for?" She pointed at several dust-covered boxes jammed into place by the boxes overhead. A thin rubber blonde doll was taped to the outside of each box. The doll looked a miserable specimen with nothing to recommend it, covered in dust with dings in the skinny rubber body – though the ones in the boxes would presumably be in better condition than the samples on view. Ivy wanted those dolls desperately.

"Those ruddy things!" Harry made mistakes, everyone did, but those mangy dolls had been holding up his stock for years. "I've a thousand of them." Harry shook his head in disgust at his own error. He could speak freely with Ivy – she didn't touch toys.

"Tell me about these things?" Ivy held the baby doll she'd every intention of buying by the ankle. "What's the story with this?"

"I bought a load of those too." Harry shook his head. "They take up more space than they're worth to me at the minute." He gave another of his body-shaking shrugs. "May into June – no-one buys dolls. Come December and I won't be able to keep them on the shelves."

"Let's talk turkey." Ivy had bought two of these dolls from one of Harry's shops. Sadie was dressing them for Ivy. She wanted all the baby dolls he had.

"You really thinking of branching out?" Harry liked to see his customers make a few shillings. It helped everyone's business when money was made. Ivy had been a favourite of Harry's from the first moment she came through his doors.

"I want to try something." Ivy smiled shyly. "But I don't want to lose too much hard-earned cash, Harry, so everything depends on how much you're asking for these things." Ivy swung the baby doll up. "How many have yeh got anyway?"

"I've quite a few, Ivy." Harry stared at the young woman, wondering if she had the money to buy his stock of baby dolls. He didn't want to waste his time – time was money. Ivy Murphy might be looking better these days but that didn't mean she'd come into money. Course he'd heard her da was dead. Éamonn Murphy would have been an expensive man to keep and word on the street was that this girl had been keeping her da since the time she could walk.

"Right, let's get down to it, Harry." Ivy hoped her sick dread didn't show on her face. "I need to know what I'm talking about money-wise."

"How're yeh going to get the dolls back to your place, Ivy?" Harry didn't see her pram with her. "I don't do deliveries any more. I've been let down by jarveys too many times. When the jarveys let me down I have to let me customers down. That's bad for business."

"I thought you kept your own horse and driver?" Ivy didn't want to appear too eager to seal the deal. Working with Harry over the years, she'd learned a great deal from watching him run his business. Harry might not look it but the man wasn't hurting for a few pennies.

"Too expensive." Harry shrugged. "That feckin' horse was eating me profits."

"Have yeh a telephone, Harry?" Ivy knew darn well he did. Harry had been the talk of the market when he had the telephone line put in.

"Yeh want to use me telephone?" Harry stared. Ivy Murphy was becoming one to watch.

"I want to call a delivery firm I know." Ivy grinned. "They're very reliable. I have the information in me bag." Ivy pulled out Jem's business card.

"Right yeh are, Missus." Harry grinned. He'd stopped to talk to her simply to pass the time of day. Ivy didn't usually buy enough to interest him personally. "Let's get down to business. I'll have one of me lads count these baby dolls, while we talk money."

Ivy and Harry entered into a very enjoyable argument. While they waited for the lad to count the baby dolls Ivy fought tooth and nail to get the lowest price she could. She needed to keep back the cash she'd need to buy the skinny rubber dolls, all of them.

"Ivy Murphy, you've robbed me." Harry shook hands on the deal.

"I'll telephone for a jarvey now, Harry." Ivy had got the baby dolls for a lot less than she'd expected to pay. Now for the big gamble.

She made the call and then turned to Harry.

"Harry, while I'm waiting . . . what do you know about getting a street trader's licence?" Ivy wanted Harry to think she was going to sell dolls from a moving stall.

"Is that what you're thinking of getting into now?" Harry was surprised. Ivy had a good little business going. Still it made sense to branch out.

"I'm investigating possibilities."

"Street sellers make up a great deal of me business as you know, Ivy." Harry took a sharper look at the woman standing before him. She was up to something but that was okay with him. There was room for all. As long as Ivy didn't cut into his business it was no skin off his nose.

"Do you know anything about getting a licence?"

"I'm afraid to say I don't." Harry shrugged. "I leave that to those who deal with that kind of thing. I couldn't even give you a name to ask for if you went in person to ask for the licence. Sorry."

"Not to worry." Ivy heard the sound she'd been waiting for, the clap of a horse's hooves. The system Jem had put in place – taking the call, sending out lads on bikes to notify the jarveys – was speeding up service. Jem's lads and the young horses he'd bought weren't trained up enough yet to deal with all of his business. She hoped it wasn't Jem himself. The man was too honest.

"That's my jarvey now, Harry. Can your lad lend a hand getting the boxes out?"

"Not a problem."

"Harry," Ivy turned with a frown on her face, "those rubber doll things,"

"What about them?" Harry was directing two lads and the jarvey who'd answered the call.

"How much are yeh asking for them?"

"Ivy!"

Ivy turned at the sound of her name.

"Hey, Ivy!" Conn Connelly strolled into the warehouse. He'd been in the livery when Ivy's call came in. He'd passed the message along to the nearest taxi rank than raced the jarvey on his bike through Dublin's back streets. "Do you need a hand with something?"

"I don't think so, Conn, thanks." Ivy almost grinned. Conn was a good sidekick for someone trying to pull a fast one.

"I'll wait anyway – I'm just doing my rounds." Conn was learning the streets and alleys of the city. He wanted to be able to give directions to the jarveys.

"Ivy, about those rubber dolls?" Harry didn't want to lose the chance of shifting those things.

"What dolls?" Ivy couldn't believe her luck. She didn't have to mention the dolls again – Harry had been the one to bring it up. "Oh, the skinny blonde dolls!" She shrugged. "I thought I might find a use for them. It depends how much you want for them."

"How many were yeh thinking of?" Harry didn't think she could sell the things on but that wasn't his problem.

Ivy took a deep breath. "All of them."

"The full thousand?" Harry had to fight to keep the surprise out of his voice. The customer was always right. That was his motto. It would be an expensive lesson for Ivy but better she learn it early.

"Well, you can't be asking much for them." She pointed at the pathetic rubber dolls hanging outside the boxes.

"You're thinking of buying them ugly things?" Conn had

315

followed Ivy. "Ivy Murphy, you'll be making a donation to Harry's bank account. I didn't know you had money to spare." Conn laughed and shared a man-to-man look with Harry. "You"ll never shift something that ugly, Ivy."

"Mind your own business, Conn!" Ivy snapped though she wanted to kiss him. He was playing it exactly right. "Harry, ignore me young friend." She turned her back on the grinning Conn. "How much are yeh asking for all of them dolls?"

"They cost me four quid." Harry said, doubling the figure.

"They've been sitting there for an awful long time, Ivy." Conn put in before Ivy could speak. "Look at the dust on them things! Ivy, nobody wants them. You've bought something already. You haven't even got your licence yet." Conn hoped he'd read the situation properly.

"Hold your whist, young man!" Harry didn't want to lose the chance of shifting the bloody dolls. "Two squid." He spat in his hand. He would only make his money back.

"Done." Ivy spat in her hand and returned the firm handshake. It was a firm contract between businessmen.

"Ivy Murphy!" Conn yelped. "You're nuts!"

"Help the lads get the boxes out, Conn," Ivy ordered. "Load the things in the carriage and no more back talk." She walked away with Harry, ready to settle her account. She'd made the deal of the century on those rubber dolls. Now she had to prove her big idea was sound.

"That lad of yours plays a good game." Harry knew he'd been played.

"He's learning." Ivy could grin openly now the deal had been struck.

"I know I've been stitched up, Ivy Murphy, but hell if I can figure out how." Harry Green grinned. A good business deal was one where both sides won.

"I'm taking the kind of risk, Harry, that keeps me awake at night."

"Those are the kind of risks that can make yeh rich when they come off, Ivy. I'll wish yeh the best of luck."

Harry watched Ivy and her young assistant leave his warehouse. He'd be keeping an eye on that young woman.

"Conn, you are a star!" Ivy whispered out of the side of her mouth.

"I did good? Thank God. I wasn't sure."

"I got what I wanted at a much better price than I expected. Now I just have to turn the things into something everyone wants."

"That's all?" Conn laughed.

"You've filled me cab up, Missus," the jarvey said to Ivy.

"I'll give yeh a lift home on me crossbar again." Conn offered.

"Get away with yeh, Conn!" Ivy laughed. "I'm going to pay the jarvey to deliver my stuff but I've things to do yet in town."

"See you later, Ivy." Conn rode his bike away whistling. He couldn't wait to see what Ivy did with those ugly little dolls.

Ivy turned to the jarvey. "Hello, me name's Ivy Murphy. Do you know where I want these things delivered?"

"The name's Billy White – back to the livery is what I was told." Billy didn't need to know her name.

"You can leave my stuff with Jem for the moment, Mr White," Ivy said as the man climbed up to the driver's seat. "You know the way?"

"I do now." Billy White grinned. "That tunnel is something. I didn't even know there were houses back there before I signed on with Jem."

"That's cause none of us could afford a cab." Ivy grinned. "It's always been Shank's pony for us. How much do I owe you?" Ivy opened her purse and prepared to spend more of her precious money.

"Miss Murphy, if I could have a moment of your time?"

"Mr Norton." Ivy turned away from the clerk and put her signed rent book back in her handbag. She preferred to pay her rent into the Earl Street office rather than have the rent man call.

"If I could have a private moment, Miss Murphy . . ." Greg Norton invited Ivy further down the tall counter from his listening clerk. It wouldn't do for him to invite a single female into his office. The front wall of this office opening onto Earl Street was glass, ensuring no impropriety.

"Of course," Ivy agreed.

"I'm afraid I've bad news for you, Miss Murphy." Greg Norton's words sent ice down Ivy's spine. "Someone – and, believe me, dear lady, when I say I have no idea who – but someone is causing problems for you with this office." He thought the persecution of this young woman a disgrace.

"What kind of problems, Mr Norton?" Ivy shook visibly.

"Someone is trying very hard to have you evicted." He hated to see the distress in Ivy's big blue eyes.

"Can they do that, Mr Norton?" Ivy had to force the words past what felt like a ball of cotton wool. "I pay my rent on time. I've never missed a payment, Mr Norton, you know that – never." Ivy and her brothers had gone hungry more than once in order to pay the rent.

"You pay your rent weekly. But nevertheless the landlord can ask you to vacate the premises with a week's notice, I'm afraid."

"I can be turned out in the streets with only a week's notice?" Ivy thought she could actually feel her blood turn to ice. "That's not enough time to find somewhere else to live. It's inhuman, Mr Norton."

"I agree, Miss Murphy." Greg Norton sighed. "I haven't been given the order to evict you but someone powerful is behind the rumours I've heard. I thought you might be able to look into the problem – quietly, please." Greg Norton dealt with a great many problem tenants. Miss Ivy Murphy was not one of them.

"Can you tell me who owns the building I live in, Mr Norton." Ivy asked. Father Leary was behind this latest problem, it could be no-one else.

"I really shouldn't but I don't agree with what is being done. I'll look up those details for you, Miss Murphy." Greg Norton needed to think about the step he was planning to take. The slum landlords of Dublin were rich powerful men. It didn't do to make enemies of them.

"Thanks, Mr Norton. That's very kind. I don't want to get you into trouble." Ivy watched Greg Norton disappear into his office.

She waited, trying to control her tremors.

"That block of tenements is owned by MacMore," Greg Norton was saying as he came out of his office reading from an open file. "I believe the reason you haven't been troubled, up to this point, is the sheer size of the company. The rent earned from your rooms is just a drop in the ocean to these people." Greg Norton slapped the file closed. "If someone insists on bringing you to their attention, demanding action, things could turn out very badly for you, You need to take measures to protect yourself, Miss Murphy."

"Thank you so much, Mr Norton." Ivy felt sick to her stomach.

"I hope you can sort something out, Miss Murphy. I'd hate to lose such a good tenant." Greg Norton watched Ivy leave his premises, feeling helpless.

Out in the street Ivy fought the urge to scream aloud. It seemed every time she took one step forward someone was trying to beat her back.

"Brother Theo, was I expecting a visit from your good self?" Father Leary snapped when Theo was shown into his office by his housekeeper. Leary didn't appreciate this friar interfering in his affairs. It would not be allowed to continue.

"I was passing." Theo, back from a week's holiday in his home town had heard from Roderick about this man's latest attempt to cause Ivy Murphy and her friends trouble. He'd decided to pay a social visit and feel out the situation for himself. Theo sighed. He would have to pray extra hard for forgiveness – he simply couldn't like this man.

"I'd heard you make a habit of visiting that harlot, Ivy Rose Murphy." Father Leary's many chins wobbled alarmingly. His gaze would have frozen a lesser man. "You need to be careful, people are talking."

"Yes, indeed," Theo agreed. He hadn't been offered a chair

but he sat regardless. "People are talking but not about my innocent visits to a group of people I find fascinating. What people are truly wondering is why you, a supposed man of God, are involving yourself in Ivy Murphy's personal life?"

"How dare you come in here and question me?" Father Leary slapped his open hand on his desk top. The noise echoed around the room like an explosion. The fury being expressed frightened Theo. The man was on the edge. This attitude was worrying and not acceptable.

"You need help, Father Leary." Theo wished he'd asked someone to accompany him.

"*I am a man of God!*" Leary screamed. "You have no right to question me! I speak with the voice of God." Leary shoved back his chair and leaned over his desk threateningly.

"You need to calm down." Theo was horrified to notice the man was dribbling.

"I need no advice from the likes of you!" Leary shouted. "I am a man of God!"

"We are all God's creatures." Theo was making a mental list of the priests he knew who policed the behaviour of the clergy. He needed someone besides himself to witness this complete loss of control in a Parish Priest.

"That's what that whore Ivy Rose Murphy said!" Leary screamed. "That worthless female dared to stand in my church," he beat his chest with his closed fist, "before my altar!"

"The altar of God," Theo put in quietly. Had no-one noticed this man's complete mental breakdown? How had he been allowed to continue in his position?

"That whore dared to question my right to eject her from my church!" Leary shouted. "Ivy Rose Murphy stood before my altar in my house and defied me. That harlot, I will destroy her, cast her out of my kingdom just as I did with her whore of a mother!"

"What happened to Ivy's mother?" Theo needed to bring in another priest. This was far out of his area of expertise. This man had to be removed from his position.

"*She tempted me!*" Leary screamed. "It was all her fault, my purple-eyed Violet Burton!" The man visibly shook much to Theo's horror. "She looked so innocent, so beautiful, but she tempted me. It was the devil inside her. I saw that, I tried to beat it out of her. The devil inside her forced me to touch her. It was all her fault. She was the devil's instrument. I know that now. Everything was the fault of Violet Burton. Now Ivy Rose Murphy – she's the devil come back to tempt me! I am a man of God!"

"I need to be on my way." Theo wanted to get away from this man. He needed backup. If he didn't know better he'd say the man was possessed. "I'll return another day when you are more yourself." I'll return with men in white coats, Theo mentally added.

"Ivy Murphy, since when did I turn into your messenger boy?" Jem stood grinning in Ivy's open doorway.

"Thanks for putting all this stuff in here for me." Ivy had left her key with Jem. She'd been hoping she'd find what she wanted at Harry Green's. Jem had had his lads dump the boxes of dolls into Ivy's workroom.

"What's wrong?" Jem could see the upset on Ivy's face.

"Someone is trying to have me evicted," Ivy said simply. "Mr Norton just told me on the quiet."

"Ah Ivy!" Jem stepped inside and pulled Ivy into his arms.

"Don't be too nice to me, Jem Ryan." Ivy's voice was muffled by his broad chest. "We both know whose fault this is. I'll be damned if that man will make me cry."

"How can I help?" Jem rocked back and forth, giving comfort to both of them.

"Come through, Jem." Ivy pulled out of his arms. It was getting harder to resist the man's charms. "I'll put the kettle on."

"Of course you will." Jem laughed and dropped into a chair by the kitchen table. "The solution to all your problems, a cup of your life's blood."

"It helps." Ivy busied herself with the familiar routine. "I need to borrow Conn for a while, Jem."

"What do you need him for?" That was Ivy – give her a problem and she came out fighting.

"I want him to investigate a company for me." Ivy looked over her shoulder. "They own this house and who knows how many others in The Lane. Mr Norton said it's a big company. I'll have Ann Marie look into it as well. The woman seems to know everyone who is anyone. But I want Conn – I don't know how he'd go about this business but I trust him to figure something out. I need to know who owns the company and who runs it."

"Give me the details and I'll put him on it." Jem made a note of the details and grinned. "Once Conn knows it's for you the lad will kill himself trying."

"What?"

"You made him a hero when you rode on his crossbar, Ivy." Jem roared with laughter at the shocked look on Ivy's face. "The other lads almost bowed down to him."

"Rubbish!" Ivy brought the tea to the table. It thrilled her to be able to add a plate of shop-bought biscuits to the things on the table.

"All of the lads are a little in love with you, Ivy." Jem shrugged. They weren't the only ones. "It's innocent."

Ivy sat down and poured the tea.

"Tell us why you bought all those dolls today," Jem asked.

"I will, Jem, I promise – just not yet. Oh, before I forget!" Ivy filled Jem in on Harry Green's problem with deliveries. "It should be a good contact for you."

"You spend a lot of time helping with my business, Ivy." Jem appreciated all of her help. Without her none of this would be happening. "The business cards you gave out to all of them butlers you know helped a lot."

"I never told yeh, Jem." Ivy sipped her tea with appreciation. "I sold my hair. I got more than a year's rent money for the hair off me head." She smiled at the shock on Jem's face. "Yes, I nearly passed out too."

"That takes some believing, Ivy." Jem shook his head. "Jaysus, it just goes to show yeh some people have more money than sense."

"It's true nonetheless." Ivy smiled. "I thought having that money behind me would keep me safe. I had one year rent free as it were. I looked at this as a chance to take a year to risk everything. I was paying Sadie and her daughters out of my earnings from my rounds. I make a tidy amount from the stuff I collect on my rounds. I get a lot of things I can sell straight on at a profit. Then there's the money I make from the stuff I alter or mend. I was doing okay."

Ivy didn't mention the difference it made to her not having her da dip his hand into her earnings. She'd been astonished at how much money she took in every week. She'd never before stopped to count her earnings. She never had the time, never had the money in her hand for long. She'd been kept too busy trying to keep a roof over her head and food on the table.

"The news Mr Norton gave me today knocked the stuffing out of me, Jem." Ivy was still slightly in shock. "I didn't know you could be evicted for no good reason. I thought as long as you paid your rent on time and gave no problems you were safe. Seems it doesn't work like that. The power is all the landlords. There's a surprise for yeh, Jem. The one with the money has the power."

"You know you never have to worry about ending up on the street, Ivy." Jem touched Ivy's hand gently. He still wasn't in a position to make her an offer. He was in debt to Emerald O'Connor up to his ears.

Emmy Ryan wasn't keeping track of money she knew nothing about but Jem was. He'd pay back every penny he used from her funds. He was confident of his ability to make his business work. He needed to concentrate all of his time and effort there right now. The time he and Ivy managed to spend together was precious to Jem. Ivy had worked too hard for too long. He wouldn't ask her to take a risk with him. Jem wanted to be able to offer Ivy a life of plenty. She deserved it.

"I know you'd look out for me, Jem. I appreciate knowing that more then I can say." Ivy removed her hand. She wanted a chance to make something of herself before she became involved with a man. Jem Ryan was a big temptation. He could ruin her plans. She wanted to walk her own path for a while. "These two rooms have always been my home. I've worked me guts out to keep them. I'll be damned if I'll let Father Leary or anyone else run me out of here on a whim." Ivy's voice was fierce.

Jem decided it was best to change the subject. "What are yeh going to do with all the dolls, Ivy?"

"I thought about having Sadie and the girls knit jumpers I could sell from a moving stall. You know how that turned out." Ivy put two fresh cups of tea on the table and sat back down.

"Father Leary put a halt to your gallop." Jem accepted the tea.

"In one way, in one way only, Jem." Ivy laughed with genuine delight. "He'd hate to know it but the man did me an enormous favour."

"Has it anything to do with the load of dolls the lads dumped in your work area?" He couldn't imagine what she was going to do with them but he trusted Ivy.

"It has everything to do with those dolls!" Ivy laughed in delight. "Did yeh ever think, Jem, nearly six short months ago now, at the beginning of the year, that we'd be sitting here talking about business?"

"Ivy, if anyone had told me of the things I'd be getting up to this year I'd have told him to get his bumps felt." Jem grinned. "I can't believe the changes taking place across in me livery. I have to stop and look around every morning to check I'm in the right place. Yeh have to hand it to Ann Marie, she has a cock-eyed way of looking at our world but it was just what we needed."

Chapter 29

"This is the life." John Lawless was stripped to the waist, his trouser legs rolled up. He was stretched out on the sand of the secluded Sandymount Strand which the people of The Lane used all summer.

"This kind of day out is the best medicine you could get, John." Ann Marie Gannon grinned. She'd picked John up from the hospital in her automobile and delivered him to this little oasis. She had driven along the road, past this oasis frequently and hadn't known it existed, tucked away as it was behind a railway crossing.

"It's great to have you out of that place, Da." Clare Lawless, looking pretty as a picture in her bright summer dress, giggled with the joy of living. Her da was with his family and her ma was beaming. Everything was right in Clare's world.

"I'm glad you're pleased, love." John couldn't believe he was here stretched out on white sand while his family tended to his every need.

"I'm along as the entertainment advisor." Molly Riordan attempted to settle her uncomfortable body on the sand. Only two more weeks of this torture before she could get rid of this bump and return to her own world.

When Jem heard Ivy's idea for a day out he'd offered to take everyone to the strand on his hay wagon. It was a long walk from The Lane to this hidden oasis and he'd needed time away from the livery. He was enjoying this brief moment away from all of his responsibilities.

"Poor old Rosie doesn't know what's happening to her." Jem looked towards his now retired horse as she walked through the surf. Conn was at the horse's head, while Emmy clung to Rosie's back. The little girl, her curly mop of black hair blowing in the breeze, was wearing a white lace dress Ivy had made for her. Emmy's cries of delight carried on the breeze.

"Do us all good to let the air at our bodies." Ivy was wearing her white skirt hiked up, revealing slim legs and bare feet. She had dared to make herself a white lace camisole that revealed her arms and shoulders. For the very first time in her life, that she could remember anyway, her limbs were out in the air and it felt wonderful.

"It's a nice break." Liam watched his dog and her pups chase the waves and bark frantically at the approaching tide.

It did Liam's heart good to see them. He'd been forced to work the dog really hard to bring her up to performance level. The time he spent training the dog and her pups had helped him too. Liam didn't know what Brother Theo had said to his da but, whatever it was, it worked. His da was letting him live at home now. He and Vera were doing amateur spots with the dog around Dublin. When the pups were a bit older he'd bring them into the act. Dublin theatres offered cash prizes for amateur performers. Liam badly needed to win prize money. He had to buy food for his dog and her pups. He, Vera and the dog were beginning to win first-place prizes now, slowly making their way into the world of theatre.

"I'm so glad you thought of this, Ivy." Ann Marie was barefoot, her shoulders gleaming and sun-kissed. She'd hiked her skirt up and removed her shoes and silk stockings.

"I'm trying to organise tea and sandwiches for twelve here! I need help!" Sadie Lawless grinned. Her John was at her side. It might only be for one day but he was here, large as life and smiling. "I could use a hand from you lazy lot."

"Some people are always moaning." Ivy laughed and stood to lend a hand. Sandymount Strand was only a tiny part of an area that followed the East Coast of Ireland, not all areas were tide free and people-friendly but the coastline was dotted with long areas of silver sand. This little stretch of sand was a comfortable walk away from The Lane. There were other people here but the area was large and each party had the sensation of privacy. The area had a standing tap which was one of its main attractions. A nearby fire made from driftwood and surrounded by rocks was heating the water in Ivy's big black kettle.

"Dora, love – you too, Clare – give your ma and Ivy a hand." John Lawless watched his girls jump to obey him. It wouldn't last but it was nice. "I hope we have enough cups because I'm gumming for a cup of tea."

"Enough?" Jem grabbed his head dramatically. "The women have half the lane here with them! The bloody wagon has so much stuff on it we could stop here for a week. We could set up camp under the flatbed of the wagon and live here happily. God knows we've everything we need."

"Stop your moaning, Jem Ryan." Ivy tapped the back of his head with her hand. "You'll be glad of a cup of tea and something to eat too, admit it."

"I tell you what, Jem," John Lawless sighed, "we are two lucky fellows. We're surrounded by beautiful women waiting on us hand and foot. What more could a man ask for?" John's eyes admired his wife and daughters. The three Lawless women were wearing summer dresses Sadie had run up on the sewing machine Granny left to Ivy. The material was from curtains Ivy picked up cheap at a market stall.

"Liam, we're almost ready here. Where did you stash the milk?" Ivy asked.

"In a rock pond." Liam jumped up to retrieve the galvanised can of milk he'd stored in a nearby pool of cold water. "Do you want me to shout for Conn and Emmy?"

"No, leave them." Ivy grinned. "They'll come when they're hungry."

"This is the gear." Vera Connelly was sitting slightly apart from the group with Molly Riordan, taking everything in. It was great being with a group of people like this. They were all so full of life and fun. "It beats the hell out of gutting fish I can tell yeh!"

Vera worked early mornings in the city fish market gutting and filleting fish. She hated the work, hated how it made her and everything belonging to her stink. It didn't matter how much she washed herself, she stank of fish. She kept doing it because her family needed the money. Liam's mad dream had become Vera's. If she could make a living without having to skin fish she'd do it and grin.

"Yes, it's okay." Molly didn't want to spoil the fun but she'd be glad when she had this bloody thing out of her body and got her life back. She enjoyed a more refined social life. Cute little parties on the sand weren't her style. She had bigger plans for herself.

"I've been thinking . . ." Ivy started to say when everyone had a cup of tea and a sandwich in hand.

"*Nooooooo!*" Jem fell back in the sand groaning. "Not that, please!"

"You, Jem Ryan, are an eejit." Ivy grinned, not in the least insulted.

"When are yeh going to leave that hospital, John? Jem could really use someone like you to help with his business." Ivy knew John had finally agreed to swallow his pride enough to allow Ann Marie to buy him a wheelchair.

"I could really use the help, John," Jem said. "They do say two heads are better than one."

"You need to get out of that hospital, love." Sadie wanted to kiss Jem. He was making John feel important and a part of something.

"Like I said already, John Lawless," Ivy wriggled her toes in the sand, "we have big plans we could use your help with."

"That's the truth, John," Jem admitted readily. "I'm starting something that scares me stiff but I'd never forgive meself if I didn't try."

"The doctors at the hospital see no reason you couldn't be an out-patient, John." Ann Marie added.

"You're ganging up on me." John dropped his body back in the warm sand. "Someone give me another cup of tea."

Dora jumped to her feet. "Who else wants a fresh sup?"

"It's a shame yer ma wouldn't come with us Vera." Ivy was standing to one side of the wagon, using the wagon bed to butter the bread needed for another batch of sandwiches.

"She doesn't want to upset me da," Vera Connelly said softly. The fights were continuing in the Connelly household – worse if anything since Vera began to devote herself to the dogs' training. It saddened her and the rest of the kids but she was desperate. She couldn't fillet fish for the rest of her days.

"How are your appearances at those amateur nights going, Vera?" Ann Marie asked to lighten the conversation.

"Molly helped me and Liam put together something she calls a 'spot'," Vera said. "We can only use the one dog, the pups are too young. We both sing a bit and Molly said it was important to tell a story with our act."

"They've worked really hard," Molly said.

"I thought I'd die of fright the first time I had to stand up on stage and sing," Vera admitted. Thinking about leaving fish guts behind had helped her over that early stage fright. "Me and Liam have begun to come in the money." She knew they had a lot more work to do on the act but the florins they won now paid to feed the dogs and Liam.

"I wish yeh could see our act." Vera grinned. "Ivy and Sadie helped dress the two of us. We look proper toffs in our fancy gear if I do say so meself. Even if he is me brother I have to say Liam looks dead handsome on stage."

"Rosie doesn't want to walk any more," said Emmy as she returned. The group hadn't even noticed the horse making its slow way back to them. "I think she's tired." Emmy yawned and while Conn held the horse she slipped into Jem's waiting arms.

"Are you hungry Conn, Emmy?" Ivy finished putting the next batch of sandwiches together and turned to take the little girl from Jem's arms.

"Yes, and I'm tired too," Emmy said.

"Have something to eat, petal." Jem put one of the sandwiches Ivy just prepared onto a plate. He prepared a jamjar of milky tea for her to wash the sandwich down. Conn served himself from the food on offer.

"When you finish that lot you have a nap in the sand, petal." Jem held Rosie's bridle. "I'm going to tie Rosie up on that bit of grass over there." He pointed at a nearby piece of land.

"All right." Emmy pushed the sandwich into her mouth, smiling happily around it. Ivy watched the little one eat and drink. When Emmy began to rub her eyes tiredly Ivy stood and arranged a small space in the sand for the little girl to lie down. In minutes the sound of Emmy's soft snores could be heard. Ivy remained seated nearby, rubbing Emmy's back from time to time. She didn't want anyone stepping on the sleeping child.

"We men should start gathering shellfish," Jem said when he returned. "I'm sorry you can't join us, John, but perhaps another time."

"From your lips to God's ears!" John grinned. "I'll let you lot do the work and I'll wait here to enjoy a big pot of cockles later. It's been many a long year since I hunted and cooked cockles on the strand."

Ivy kept her lips firmly closed. Picking cockles was about the only bleedin' thing Irish men seemed to do on their own. Some wise woman in the past must have decided to let the men at it and keep her own feet, if not her head, buried in the sand. Good luck to her whoever she was, Ivy thought.

"Ivy, you haven't mentioned your street trader licence in a while." Ann Marie watched Jem, Liam and Conn roll up their trouser legs. The three males picked up buckets and shovels and began to walk slowly along the wet sand.

"Well, I think Father Leary did me a great favour." Ivy laughed. "I was thinking too small."

"From the little I know of yeh that's hard to believe, Ivy," John quipped.

"You need to get out of that hospital and make yourself a part of this motley crew, John." Ann Marie wondered if she should bring up her own concerns here or wait till she had Ivy alone.

"What's wrong, Ann Marie?" Ivy asked, noticing her friend's hesitation.

"Well, it seems so silly to talk about my own problems. Here I am, sitting with a group of people who are trying to improve their lives, people with real problems." She looked at John, a man crippled and struggling to find a way to live his life – Sadie and her daughters doing everything in their collective power to survive without a working man's wage coming into the home – Molly Riordan pregnant and deserted by the man she thought loved her. Ann Marie's own problems seemed so petty in comparison.

"Ann Marie, the blessing of this group is the fact that we all have something different to offer," said Ivy, "something that makes each member of the group stronger."

"Jaysus, Ivy Murphy, and you claim you need my help!" John quipped.

"Come on, Ann Marie! Tell us what's bothering you. Maybe we can help." Ivy said.

"All right." Ann Marie pushed her hands through her hair. "I don't know if everyone here knows I live with my uncle and his family?" She waited for nods before continuing. "I've been unhappy with the situation for a long time. It wasn't until I met a certain Miss Murphy that I realised just how unhappy I'd allowed myself to become."

"Ivy seems to have that affect on everyone she meets," John said.

"I want a place to call my own." Ann Marie didn't mention the estate she owned in Dalkey. Ivy was the only one here who knew just how wealthy she actually was. "Ivy has pointed out, correctly, that I am incapable of actually running a home. I know how to give orders to servants but I can't do any of the chores needed myself. In an ideal world I'd like to live comfortably with the fewest servants possible."

"Must be tough," Sadie said without an ounce of malice in her voice.

"Do you want to lease or buy?" Molly Riordan hadn't been saying much – she was just killing time with these people. But now she had something to contribute.

"Why, do you know of something?" Ann Marie waited.

"I do as a matter of fact." Molly grinned with delight. She'd be able to offer something back if this came off.

"Where and what is this place and how many servants would it need to run it?" Ann Marie wondered if Molly would even know the answers to any question regarding servants.

"The house itself is just across the Grand Canal from where Ivy and Jem live." Molly closed her eyes, trying to remember the details. She tried to remember the exact location of the canal lock in front of the house. "I think, but I'm not certain, that the house I'm talking about is directly across the lock that the people in The Lane use to cross the canal."

"That would be ideal but how do you know the house is up for lease or sale?" Ann Marie was breathless at the possibility of finding a house within walking distance of The Lane.

"The fellow who owns it inherited it from his grandmother," Molly said, searching her memory. "He spent a lot of money on the house. He turned it into a sort of boarding house for actors. The fellow dreamed of making it big in the theatre."

"Can you give me his details?" Ann Marie wanted to jump up and look at the house now.

"Give me a minute," Molly begged. "I'm trying to remember things. Just let me think."

She was actually considering whether she should bother getting involved in the matter. She looked around at the group who'd taken her in hand when she'd been at her lowest. Sadie and her daughters had taken her into their home. They'd looked after her, made sure she ate and exercised. Ann Marie had paid for the food in her mouth and the roof over her head. They were even providing a home for her unborn child. She owed them.

"Right," Molly took a deep breath, ignoring the sharp pang in her back and jumped in. "The house has indoor plumbing. All the floors have fitted bathrooms." She grinned at the reaction of the group, most of whom used a slop bucket and a toilet down the yard. "Because it's just off the canal the house has no basement." Molly was seeing it in her mind's eye. She'd visited the house a lot in company with fellow dancers and actors. The man who owned it threw great parties. "What I'm thinking, Ann Marie, is this." Molly hoped she wasn't stepping out of order here. "The house is a big square one sitting on its own patch of land. You could lease or buy this house or one like it. The back of the house, as well as having the usual kitchen and scullery also has servants' bedrooms and a bathroom. John, Sadie and the girls could use the ground-floor bedrooms. Between the two of you, Sadie and Ann Marie, you could run the house. Sadie has the practical experience and you Ann Marie have the knowledge needed to run a house of that size." She didn't mention the baby but it too could have a bedroom near the girls who would be its sisters.

"Jaysus, woman!" John struggled to sit up on the sand. He wanted to jump to his feet. This was his life and that of his family they were arranging. "What are yeh talking about?"

"Ann Marie said she needs someone to look after her." Molly shrugged. "The woman doesn't seem to want a load of servants around her. She could live in the main part of the house." Molly closed her eyes, trying to see the building in her mind's eye. "I reckon Sadie and the girls could teach Ann Marie what she needs to know in order to survive without servants. I know a couple of local women come in, I think it's daily, to do the heavy cleaning and ironing and stuff like that. They could keep doing their jobs. You would have to see how the situation suited all of you but in the meantime Ann Marie would be mistress of her own home and John and Sadie would have a home near to their work and without steps to worry about." Molly was almost breathless when she finished speaking. The pain in her back was killing her. She couldn't seem to get comfortable on the sand.

"Jaysus, woman," John swore, "yeh might not say much but when you do talk 'tis a feckin' mouthful."

"Ann Marie?" Ivy said quietly. Her friend looked stunned.

"It is a radical solution to my problems but it could be absolutely perfect." In fact, more than anyone realised. She hadn't told anyone that the unborn child was related to her by blood – it would simply complicate matters. But, if this came off, she could see the baby daily. She wouldn't be responsible for the child's upbringing but she could be part of its life. "The Lawless family would have to receive recompense for all their work but if the idea suits them I would really like to try." With the Lawless family to help and someone to take care of the daily chores she may not need to employ live-in strangers. This could be perfection if they could all manage to work together.

Ann Marie turned to John Lawless.

"John Lawless," she said seriously, "you hold my future in your hands."

"I'm glad I'm sitting down." John didn't know what to think. He was dizzy with the change in his fortunes.

"We'll need to see the house, Sadie," Ann Marie said. "We could go together and check everything out. What do you think?"

"John?" Sadie looked at her husband. This wasn't her decision alone to make.

"I could drive both of you to the house in my automobile." Ann Marie sweetened the pot. "We need to check everything out before we get too excited."

"You wouldn't have to put up with living across the hall from Patsy, Sadie." Ivy's face was the picture of innocence.

"Ann Marie, you need to think long and carefully about this." John was trying to keep his emotions in check. "We need to think carefully about what we're all getting into. It would be a new way of living for all of us." He looked at his family, feeling emotion choke him. His Sadie called Ivy Murphy an angel. Look what was happening to his family because of agreeing to work with her! The bloody woman was a miracle worker!

"I know a good removals firm," Ivy said, tongue in cheek. "They come highly recommended."

The group collapsed into almost hysterical laughter. The noise woke Emmy up. The little girl sat up, rubbing her eyes and staring around at the laughing people.

"I'm thirsty," she whispered.

"I'm sure you are," Ivy jumped up, grabbed Emmy into her arms and began to dance around the sand with the sleepy-eyed girl in her arms.

"You doing all right, love?" Sadie whispered to her husband under the noise of the crowd.

"I'm completely drunk with the changes in our life, love. It's a bit much to take in, isn't it?"

"I'm getting used to it." Sadie grinned. "Ivy Murphy is a force of Nature. The woman is a marvel. She gets slapped back and then bounces up again. I've never been around anyone like her. She seems to attract people that don't think like everyone else. She doesn't seem to understand that some things just aren't done."

"I'd better buck up me thinking then." John grinned. "I don't want to be left behind by the women in me life."

"*Ooohhh!*" Molly fell back on the sand with a groan. She lay stunned with the sharp increase of pain, clutching her stomach.

"*It's time!*" Ann Marie yelled loud enough for the seagulls to be frightened into flight. "The baby's coming!"

"I know!" Molly gasped between gritted teeth.

"I'll drive you to the hospital." Ann Marie was trying to lift Molly from the sand.

"Ann Marie, relax." Sadie laughed. "This is not the first baby ever born, you know. There's time yet."

"But, but, you can't expect the woman just to sit here!" Ann Marie stared around her. She seemed to be the only one in a panic.

"Sit down a minute, Ann Marie." Sadie wasn't worried. She'd delivered a lot of babies in her time. She knew what to do.

"I'll boil the kettle," Ivy offered.

"She can't have the baby here on the strand!" Ann Marie screamed. "You people are mad!"

"She won't."

Sadie took Molly behind the nearby wagon. There was a private place of sorts created by the railway wall and the bulk of the large flatbed wagon they'd used to haul all the people and stuff here. First babies took their time. Sadie knew that. She was confident they had plenty of time. She lay Molly down and checked her out.

"Sweet Mother of Jesus!" Sadie yelled at the view that met her eyes. The baby's head was crowning. "You twit, how long have you been having pains?"

"What?" Ann Marie yelled in reaction to Sadie's shout. She was hyperventilating. She could not believe this was happening.

"This twit is going to have the baby now!" Sadie was horrified. "Molly! How long have you been having pains?"

"Back to calling me a twit – must be serious!" Molly panted. "Me back's been aching off and on all day." Molly groaned. What did it matter? She was being torn apart and the darn woman was yelling at her. "I thought it was just cause I couldn't get comfortable sitting in the sand."

"Is Molly going to die like my mama?" Emmy whispered into Ivy's ear.

"No, sweetie." Ivy hugged the shivering little girl. "Everything will be all right. We're going to help Aunt Sadie now, all right?"

But Ivy needed to stay with Emmy. "Vera!" she barked suddenly, making the young woman jump. "You helped deliver the pups. D'yeh feel up to helping a human into the world?"

"I'll just lie back on the sand and stay out of the way." John was pasty-faced but determined to cause no problems.

"If any of you women are wearing underskirts," Sadie's voice came from behind the wagon, "strip them off. We're going to need them. I'll need the men's shirts as well."

"Emmy, sweetheart . . ." Ivy shook the child gently, bringing her attention back to her, "I need you to run down the strand

and get your Uncle Jem and the lads. Can you do that?" Ivy put the child down on her own feet.

Emmy took off, screaming like a banshee.

"Ivy!" Sadie's head appeared over the rim of the wagon.

"Yes." Ivy stood, ready to do anything. Clare and Dora looked a bit green around the gills.

"Give my man a shovel and, however he does it, have him dig a bloody deep hole in the sand." She'd deliberately asked for John. She knew her girls could do it but John needed to know he could do whatever was necessary.

"Yes, sir!" Ivy saluted. "You heard the woman, John. Clare, give yer da a shovel then get more wood for this fire. We'll need plenty of hot water. Dora, you start getting the clothing ready. I have a slip."

Ivy took the slip from under her skirt, praying the thing would wash later. She'd paid good money for the thing.

"John, can you drag your carcass over here?" Ivy pointed to a spot well out of the tide. They didn't want this stuff to come back up. The waste from the childbirth needed to be buried deep.

"I can do it." John gritted his teeth, threw the shovel ahead of himself and dragged his useless legs over to where Ivy stood. "I can sit up," he growled, thinking about the problem. "I'll dig between me legs. That way I can use the strength in me shoulders to speed up the digging."

"Good man." Ivy patted him on the back and deliberately walked away.

"Ivy, have we anything to put this bloody hot water in?" Sadie yelled from behind the wagon. Her voice sounded a lot like the voice of God to Ivy.

"What can I do?" Ann Marie felt like some useless female, leaning weakly against the wagon, having a fit of the vapours. Everyone else was jumping into action, even little Emmy was pelting down the sand to get help. She had to pull herself together.

"This is all new to me too," Ivy admitted. "I hate to ask Sadie but she's the only one of us that knows what she's doing."

"Would yeez all stop standing around talking!" Sadie shouted. "Ann Marie, get back here and hold Molly's hand."

"Oh God!" Ann Marie groaned.

"Courage!" Ivy whispered.

"What's going on?" Jem arrived at their campsite breathless. He'd run back all the way with Emmy on his back and a full bucket of shellfish. "Emmy said there were ructions."

"Molly's having the baby," Ivy supplied.

"Did Ann Marie drive her to a hospital?" Jem didn't see the problem.

"You don't understand." Ivy laughed hysterically. "She's having the baby now, behind your wagon!"

"Sweet Jaysus!" Jem felt the blood flow from his head.

"Don't you pass out, Jem Ryan," Ivy snapped when she saw his face turn grey. "We have no time for another medical emergency right now."

"What can I do?" Jem asked.

"We need your shirt," Ivy said. "Yours too!" she snapped when Liam and Conn joined them. Ivy waited till the men had stripped the shirts from their backs then took the shirts and disappeared behind the wagon.

"You better put all of your dogs on leads, Liam," Jem ordered. The last thing they needed was dogs nosing around the women.

"I'll help!" Emmy cried.

Jem let her drop down. He hadn't even been aware the child was still clinging to his back.

"Anyone want to give a hand here?" John Lawless shouted. He needed some moral support. He thought the hole was deep enough already but he wasn't sure.

Jem nodded in approval when he saw the hole. "This is a turn-up for the books, isn't it?" he said as he dropped down beside John. "I feel like fainting meself."

"Ivy will hit you over the head if you do." John laughed. "My Sadie will help her." The two men sat side by side in horrified silence.

"Push!" The shout came from behind the wagon.

The two men turned pale.

"Vera and I were thinking of giving everyone a taste of our act," Liam said through stiff lips. "I think this beats that into a cocked hat." Conn and Liam disappeared with the dogs and Emmy.

"Good girl!" Sadie was discovering an unexpected bonus to giving birth in sand. The sand absorbed the liquid that poured from the labouring woman. That was a blessing since they hadn't much in the way of supplies here. "This baby is impatient to be born." Sadie looked at the struggling woman. Molly was doing everything she was told but the usual underlying excitement was missing. Sadie felt heartily sorry for the poor woman.

"Will it be much longer?" Molly Riordan felt as if a giant hand was tearing her limb from limb. She was never letting a man touch her again. No way was she every going through something like this again.

"A couple of big pushes now, Molly." Sadie was struck by the strangeness of the situation. It wasn't the fact that she was delivering a baby at a picnic. She was delivering a baby that was going to be hers. The child would belong to the Lawless family.

"I can't!" Molly groaned.

"You're a dancer, Molly Riordan." Ann Marie wanted to fall to the sand weeping but she knew that wasn't needed here. "You were told to push. Now push!" Ann Marie used her own body to hold Molly's body up.

"Come on, Molly!" Sadie was crying but didn't know it. This baby was the child she'd been longing for. Her baby was coming into the world. Her face and voice would be the first thing her child saw. "One more big push!" she yelled.

"Sweet Jesus," John whispered at the first baby cry. He looked at Jem. He didn't look so hot either. "Give us a hand, will yeh, Jem?" John held his arm up. He was exhausted. "Pull us over there and put me back against the wall."

"It's a boy!" Sadie screamed. "John Lawless, you have a son!"

"I have a son." John grinned at Jem with tears in his eyes. "Help me stand up, will you, please?" John was a proud man but he didn't care if he was begging. "I want to meet me son for the first time on me own two feet."

Chapter 30

"Mrs Harrington." Ivy held out her hand and waited for the woman to acknowledge her name.

"I'm Geraldine Harrington, how may I help you?" Geraldine Harrington shook hands while pricing Ivy's outfit from her hair to her feet in one brief glance. The woman standing before her belonged in one of the fashion magazines Geraldine received from Paris. She wished she could ask to examine the details of the avant-garde outfit she was wearing.

"Ivy Rose. I had my assistant call and make an appointment." Ivy tried not to hyperventilate. Image was everything. She'd learned that lesson well in the last seven months.

"Yes, of course." Geraldine glanced at her appointment calendar. She hadn't expected a woman to be the salesman she was expecting. "You have an item you believe will interest me for the Christmas trade." Geraldine took pride in having the most modern and expensive toys in the world in her Grafton Street shop.

"I believe our Baby Bundle will delight all year around." Ivy hoped her smile looked sweetly shy. She was clenching her teeth to stop them rattling. "I telephoned your shop to offer you first option on our stock. The dolls on offer are of a limited edition.

I'm afraid when they're gone, they're gone." Ivy had subtly picked Harry Green's business brain. He'd said it was usual to order your Christmas stock in July or August.

Ivy picked up the handcrafted leather case she carried her sample dolls in. The case was one belonging to Emmy's aunt. The woman wouldn't need it and John Lawless had played around with the monogram. He'd managed to turn what looked like an 'M' into an elaborate 'I'. Now, the case proudly bore the initials for Ivy Rose Dolls instead of Mary Rose Donnelly.

"I was given to understand that mine would be the first shop in Ireland offered the dolls?" Geraldine Harrington admired the carrying case. It was always nice to deal with quality.

"I admire your shop." Ivy owed this woman a lot if she but knew it. It was the prices marked on the toys sold in this shop that had given her the idea for her first big business venture. "It's one I enjoy visiting."

"Thank you." Geraldine was frantically trying to remember seeing this woman in her store before today. Her memory failed her.

"This is our Baby Bundle." Ivy removed a package from the case. "Every item worn by the doll is unique. No two dolls are exactly alike." Ivy arranged the doll still wrapped in its blanket on the high shop counter. She'd practised at home, displaying the items to their best advantage. She opened the pale smoke-coloured, hand-knit baby blanket slowly. She wanted this woman to appreciate the skill shown by the knitter.

Sadie and her family had rewound and processed the wool to thread-like strands. The lace design of the blanket, knit on thin wire needles, was a work of art. The baby doll resting on the soft cloud of blanket was dressed in a stunning full-length lace dress, the bobbin lace handcrafted by Ivy. Out of sight were the matching lace bloomers under the dress. The doll wore a hand-knit bonnet, jacket and bootees in whisper soft pale azure cashmere wool.

"Oh, my, that is adorable!"

Geraldine held her hands out to touch the blanket – it felt like velvet against her fingers. The baby doll was beautifully dressed and she knew it would look wonderful as a main feature in her shop window. Geraldine was mentally dressing the window display as she prepared to do business. She'd have preferred to remain a calm cool businesswoman. Too late now – the words of praise had been wrenched unthinkingly from her at first sight of an article she was sure would become her star Christmas seller.

"I'm proud of the work my artists do. I work only with the best." Ivy bowed her head regally. She had the sensation of standing outside herself. She couldn't believe the load of pompous blather coming out of her own mouth.

"I –" the woman started to say when the bell over the door jangled commandingly.

Ivy wanted to curse. She needed to get this woman to agree to take some of these dolls, even one. She needed the order so she could mention to others that this prestigious shop carried her dolls.

"Geraldine, I'm in despair!" The tall blonde woman striding towards the manager's counter paid no attention to anyone else who might be in the shop. "I desperately need your help!" The woman almost pushed Ivy out of her way. It was done politely but, nonetheless, Ivy was definitely given the push.

Ivy didn't mind. She was making a study of the habits of the rich. Several of the mannerisms she'd observed in others she'd adopted for herself. This woman's complete faith in her own pre-eminence was breathtaking.

"The Barton-Wallaces have had a granddaughter!" the woman exclaimed.

"Oh, how delightful!" Geraldine Harrington knew her lines.

"The gift I had my housekeeper pick up was for a boy, of course."

"After all those boys how could you know?" Geraldine Harrington was wondering how much money she could make from this new child.

"You marvellous woman!" Evelyn Moriarty clapped her hands in childish pleasure. "It's as if you knew in advance. I have always maintained that you, Geraldine, are a magician!" The woman pounced on the baby doll still on the counter.

"I'm so sorry, Mrs Moriarty, but I'm afraid Lady Barrington telephoned in to reserve that doll. I believe Lady Barrington wishes it for a gift." Geraldine Harrington knew her customers well. She had to if she wanted to maintain her lifestyle.

"Nonsense! Bettina, as you well know, will have forgotton all about this doll by now. She can always choose something else if need be. The doll is mine. First come, first served. Isn't that how business works?" Evelyn Moriarty had no intention of letting anyone else get their hands on this doll. It was perfection.

"Lady Barrington will be very disappointed." Geraldine Harrington had felt safe mentioning the fluff-head Lady Barrington – she was the vaguest person she had ever known. She prepared to gift-wrap a doll that wasn't part of her stock.

"I'm so sorry, my dear," Evelyn Moriarty said to Ivy. Now that she'd got her own way she could afford to be gracious. "I hope I haven't snatched that doll away from you? But, as you can tell, this is an emergency."

"Such a superior doll!" Ivy sighed sadly. She watched out of the corner of her eye as the very first Baby Bundle was wrapped to sell. Ivy didn't care that they hadn't sealed the deal yet. She'd made her first sale. She had to bite back her screams of excitement.

"Have we met before, my dear?" Evelyn Moriarty looked closely at Ivy now. "I feel I know you." Evelyn examined Ivy from her fashionably tousled black curls, covered by the merest whisper of a millinary creation, down to the beige boots on her feet. The young woman was beautiful and attired in the height of fashion. "If I had time I'd demand you join me for coffee. I want to know where you purchased that divine jacket."

Ivy had asked Mr Solomon to create a jacket using the remnants of the white sheets and her own handmade bobbin lace. The finished article was a masterpiece. The little matching hat was Ivy's own work.

"I'm sure I saw that jacket or something very similar on the catwalk of a Parisian designer. I had no idea that style was even available yet in Dublin. Well done for stealing a march on the rest of us, my dear!" Evelyn waited for the woman to tell her the name of her designer but she simply smiled. It was most frustrating but she was pushed for time. "I'm sure we've met before. My son may have introduced us – you must know him." Evelyn's laugh tinkled out. "Burton Moriarty – I'm afraid my son seems to know every beautiful young lady in the city."

"That will be three guineas, Mrs Moriarty." Geraldine Harrington placed the beautifully wrapped parcel on top of her shop counter. "Did you wish to take it with you or have a member of staff pick it up?"

"I'll write you a cheque and take it with me." Evelyn Moriarty opened her handbag and prepared to pay the outrageous sum mentioned without blinking. "I don't want you to be tempted to hand it over to Lady Barrington."

Geraldine Harrington watched one of her best customers waft out of the shop. Then she turned to Ivy.

"I'm so sorry about that," she said.

"That is quite all right." Ivy smiled sickly. She needed to put her head between her knees. Not only had she just met her aunt for the first time in her life but the bloody doll was worth a fortune. The woman had, all unknowingly, done Ivy an enormous favour. She'd never have dreamed of asking such an outlandish price for a feckin' doll. She rapidly revised her asking price.

"Why don't we discuss business over a cup of tea?" Geraldine wanted to make some gesture of apology. "I can send out for tea or make it myself at my own small kitchen in the back. We can sit and decide on numbers. Do you have a maximum number of dolls that may be ordered?" Geraldine Harrington knew she and her fellow independent traders could sell every doll this woman had over the Christmas period.

"We need to discuss your profit margin before we go much further." Ivy smiled. "We'll do that while the kettle boils, shall we?" She wondered if the woman kept smelling salts in the back.

"Ivy, I have a name for you!" Conn stopped his bike abruptly when he saw Ivy walking down Grafton Street swinging a case.

"What name's that, Conn?" Every atom of Ivy's body was

concentrating on putting one foot in front of the other. She needed to get somewhere private and have a nervous breakdown.

"I've got the name of the man who can order your eviction."

"Conn, give us a lift home on your crossbar, will yeh?"

"I'm going to have to get a saddle put on me crossbar one of these days." Conn was aware of the masculine gazes Ivy was attracting even if she wasn't. "Especially if I keep picking you up when you're wearing some fancy outfit."

"Me lucky outfit, Conn." With Conn's help Ivy heaved herself onto the crossbar. She leant back against him as they set off. "Oh God, Conn! I've just closed me first big business deal and I want to throw up."

"Don't throw up on me, Ivy." Conn looked down to make sure he didn't need to pull over.

"Get me home, Conn," Ivy whispered. "Quick."

"Jem!" Conn shouted from the tunnel. The sound carried out all around the lane. "Jem Ryan!"

"What's up?" Jem watched Conn spin out of the tunnel like a bat out of hell. "Jaysus, be careful, will yeh? Yeh might have hurt Ivy."

"Jem, I did it!" Ivy went boneless and would have fallen to the ground if Conn hadn't been expecting it and caught her.

"What the hell's going on?" Jem demanded of Conn.

"I don't know," Conn said. "I picked Ivy up on Grafton Street. She wasn't herself. She asked me to get her home quick and that's what I did."

"What's wrong with Ivy?" John Lawless was sitting in his wheelchair inside the open doors of the livery. Clare was standing at his shoulder.

"Who is answering the phones?" Jem snapped. The livery phone couldn't be left unattended. Clare and John had taken a course at the GPO because he'd had to get an actual switchboard installed to deal with the number of calls the business was receiving. A lot of the calls were enquiries and needed to be handled professionally.

"Jimmy Johnson has it," John said. "The lad can handle it with us all here. Clare trained him well, Jem, not to worry."

"Oh God!" Ivy hadn't really fainted but she'd been out of it for a while. "I did it!" She pushed away from Conn and began dancing around the street. She grabbed Jem and danced him around with her. "I did it! I did it! Jaysus, Jem, I did it!" Ivy laughed like a lunatic.

"Ivy." John Lawless tried to push himself to his feet. He still wasn't used to having no power in his legs. "Do you mean it? You really did it?"

"I did it, John! You should have seen me. I impressed the hell out of myself." Ivy continued to spin in place.

"Clare, love, will you make Ivy a pot of tea?" John knew what Ivy was talking about. "Conn, my Dora is over at Ivy's place – run and get her, will you? Jem, we need to have the lads get chairs, a few bales of hay and that old table of yours out here. It seems we need to celebrate."

John Lawless managed the livery. He might be sitting in a chair for the moment but everyone jumped to obey his orders.

"Tell Dora to bring one of the Baby Bundles with her, will you?" Ivy shouted after Conn. "Clare, Ann Marie and your ma were going to the new house today. They have more measuring to do or something. Give them a call, will yeh?"

"Give me your jacket, Ivy." Jem waited until the lads had carried out the beat-up old table he was using in the office at the moment.

Ivy seemed to be in a daze. Jem turned her around and held the collar of the jacket while she slipped her arms free. He threw the jacket over her empty case which was sitting upright on the cobbles. He'd learned his lesson well. Ivy would talk better with a cup of tea in her hand.

"Here, Ivy," Jem grabbed one of the chairs his lads were carrying out to the yard. "Sit down." He didn't like the look of her, she seemed in shock.

"Jem . . ." Ivy couldn't say any more. She fell into the chair he held, put her head down onto her knees and concentrated on simply breathing.

347

Jem stood guard rubbing Ivy's back gently. He watched while the young lads he was training up ran back and forth, setting up an impromptu picnic area in front of the livery. "Come on." He gently nudged Ivy upright. He carried the chair she'd been sitting on over to the table. When she was settled he turned his attention to getting everything set up.

"Right, Ivy Murphy!" Jem said when everyone was in place, gathered around the wobbly table standing on the cobbles of the lane. "You're sitting down in my private courtyard, a cup of tea in your hand," he joked. "Now tell me what the heck is going on. Poor Conn is still green from having you nearly faint on him."

"This is the first of me business ventures." Ivy took the wool package from Dora's hands. She checked the table was clean before putting the package down. She opened the incredibly soft, pale-peach, baby blanket to reveal the baby doll. "I've just sold thirty of these little darlings to that toff toy shop on Grafton Street." Ivy could hardly speak. She couldn't breathe.

"Thirty, Ivy?" John couldn't believe it. He and his family had been making the blankets and woollen garments and dressing these dolls for months. They were doing the work for nothing, having decided as a family and at Ivy's suggestion to take a cut of the profit.

"John, Clare, Dora," Ivy closed her eyes against the tears that wanted to pour from her eyes, "the woman in the shop in Grafton Street placed an order with me for thirty of our Baby Bundle Dolls, then . . ." Ivy's breath began to hitch in her chest again.

"Ivy?" John paled. God, had they lost money?

"Wait! Wait, give me a minute." Ivy sucked in a deep breath. "It's better than I ever dreamed. I'd prepared meself mentally. I thought the woman would try to talk me down on the price I wanted, maybe buy six of the dolls if we were lucky. She nearly ripped me arm off taking the very first price I mentioned. Then she asked me not to sell the dolls to the big department shops. I let her think McBirneys and Cleary's were interested. I'd planned to visit those shops later this week. This woman has independent toyshop owner contacts in Cork, Galway, Sligo and Belfast. For a percentage of the sale price she's going to contact them. John, I sold every feckin' doll we have!"

"What, all hundred and four of them!" John could feel the colour drain from his face. He wanted to know how much his family had made from their intense months of work but he could see Ivy still hadn't recovered.

"No wonder you couldn't listen to what I had to tell you!" Conn said softly.

"I'm sorry, Conn." Ivy heard the hurt in his voice. She waved her hands in the air and took some more deep breaths. "I'd just walked out of the shop when you caught up with me. I don't know how I was still standing to be honest. I wanted to fall down onto Grafton Street and put me head between me knees."

"Anyway, I got the name you need." Conn puffed out his chest. It hadn't been easy. "It's some chap called Burton Moriarty. The man who told me about him says he's not much. The chap prefers to spend his time playing rather then working."

Burton Moriary! Ivy was reeling from one more shock. Her mother's family owned the house Ivy lived in. Wasn't that a kick in the pants! Ivy wondered if her mother had known. It didn't matter. If Ivy played her cards right, her home was safe. She'd keep this information close to her chest but she'd use it if she had to.

"Is that the same Burton Moriarty who just became engaged to marry Betanne Morgan, one of the Morgan twins?" Ann Marie's voice came from behind Ivy.

Ivy almost reeled where she sat. How many more shocks could she be expected to deal with today? Betanne Morgan one of her best suppliers if she but knew it. She turned to see Ann Marie standing with Baby James in her arms. Sadie was standing at her side.

"You can trust Ann Marie to know all the gossip about the quality." Sadie grinned. "Who's going to tell me what's going on? My Clare was a bit abrupt when she telephoned."

"Tell her, John." Ivy tried to calm her wildly jumping pulse. She took several deep, deep breaths while John pulled a blushing Sadie onto his knees. Ivy desperately wanted some time alone to think of all the information she needed to process. That, however, would have to wait.

"Tell me what?" Sadie was trying to pretend she wasn't mortified. John loved to pull her onto his knees in his wheelchair.

"We got our first order, love." John nodded towards the baby doll lying in full view on the table.

"How much did you get for them, Ivy? I told yeh yeh'd never be able to pay us Lawlesss family as much as five bob for each doll. I never made as much as a shilling for each of those baby outfits I sold Maggie Wilson. How much did you settle for, Ivy?"

"Our boss – that one over there – the pale green one trying not to pass out," John nodded in Ivy's direction, "hasn't told us yet."

"Ivy, this is stunning." Ann Marie picked up the doll from the table. "Is this the big project you've all been working on?"

"Yes!" Ivy grinned like a fool. "We're celebrating because I've just taken our first order. I've sold every doll we have! Even the ones we haven't got dressed yet." Ivy beamed at Sadie sitting on John's lap. "The Lawless family will receive twelve shillings per doll, Sadie. The bloody dolls are worth a small fortune."

"I said she was an angel, didn't I?" Sadie collapsed against John's chest. Her brain couldn't handle that amount of money.

"A bloody miracle-worker, love." John hid his tearstreaked face in Sadie's neck. "We're in the money, Sadie." John had already done the maths. If they saved the bulk of this money he'd be able to offer his girls a much better life than he'd ever imagined. He felt kind of faint himself to tell the truth.

"So, Miss Murphy," Jem grinned, "would I be right in thinking you require the use of one of my premium carriages for your delivery service?"

"I'll let you know my requirements at a future date, my good man!" Ivy said in her posh voice. She had to pull herself together. She could think about all the information she'd gathered today, later, when she was alone in her bed.

The group began to drink the cups of tea sitting unnoticed on the table. Ivy removed the doll from the table, putting it carefully on a vacant chair. She didn't want to tempt faith. The Lawless family were in shock. John just stared at Ivy, unable to form a single question about this change in their fortunes. The women were making enough noise for everyone as gasps, laughs, ideas and schemes poured forth.

Conn was waiting for Ivy to question him further about his findings but nothing happened. He shrugged, sipping his lukewarm tea. Now wasn't the time he supposed. He had the information when Ivy was ready to hear it.

"I'm confused, Ivy," Ann Marie said when the excited exclamations and expressions of delight died down. "Did you intend to sell these dolls from your pram? Is that why you needed a street trader's licence?"

"Not exactly." Ivy said. "I was trying to increase my options. I want to be free to try many different things." She was having difficulty even thinking never mind speaking, at the moment. "I'd originally thought to sell hand-knit goods in the street but when my application for a street traders licence was refused I had to rethink my business plan."

"So, you intend to make a living dressing dolls in future?" Ann Marie asked.

"That will be the first of me business ventures. I have a supply of rubber dolls I need to shift as well. We have been working on dressing them alongside the baby dolls – I'm hoping to have a great many of them ready for sale to the passing trade outside the Gaiety Theatre during the pantomime season."

"The first of the dolls are being dressed as Cinderella. Sadie knows someone who might be willing to lend me his street trader's licence over the winter – for a fee of course," Ivy told the group.

"So it would appear that with a fair wind and a bit of good fortune we are all about to become successful businessmen." Jem grinned with delight.

"We're certainly on our way," Ivy smiled. "But nothing is certain in business. The money I made from the dolls I sold this morning is earmarked for business expenses. I've used up all the items I'd stored over the years in my tea chests and then some. I have to keep my company and my business partners going. The Cinderella doll is the biggest gamble and eventually, we pray, the biggest earner."

"I'll start lighting candles." Sadie was rocking her son and grinning like a bandit. Her family was flourishing. Who'd have thought it?

"I'm going to take a few days to gather me thoughts," Ivy told everyone. "I thought I'd go blind with all the work I had to do on the lace for the baby dolls. I want to step back and enjoy me bit of success." Ivy grinned. "I fancy a few more days at Sandymount Strand. Emmy is on her school holidays so that means I'll have a bit more free time."

"That sounds like a good idea, Ivy." Ann Marie was the first to say.

The others soon joined in. They all knew Ivy worked all the hours God sent.

"Right!" Ivy stood up abruptly. "I'm going to change my clothes. I want to have some fun. Conn, you up for giving me another lesson on the bike?"

Conn had been teaching her, running behind Ivy, holding the heavy bike steady while she tried to find her balance. The local kids loved to run alongside and scream advice. It was fun for everyone.

"Ann Marie, I advise you not to look! It's hell on the nerves," said Jem.

"I'd love a lesson myself." Ann Marie grinned.

"Me too!" Dora and Clare shouted together.

Jem and Conn looked at each other and shrugged.

"The world's going to hell in a hand-basket," Jem groaned, standing up. "Someone clean up these dishes while I go find volunteers to teach you mad women to ride bikes.

The screaming children, shouting men and laughing women attracted the attention of everyone in The Lane. Women came out of their homes and sat on the steps watching the show. It was better than the fillums any day.

John Lawless, his baby son in his arms, almost fell out of his wheelchair he was laughing so much.

"Maisie, are your lads home yet?" Ivy stopped her bike to shout up to her neighbour sitting giggling on her steps.

"Phil is inside washing himself, why?" Maisie shouted back.

"I wondered if he'd go to the pub and pick up beer and lemonade? The women can have shandies and the kids lemonade. The men can drink the beer or if they're good I'll get in a few Guinnesses." Ivy had to stop until the dancing screaming children calmed down. "We could have a little street party. My treat."

"Your ship come in, Ivy Murphy?" Maisie asked.

"I don't know if me ship came in, Maisie! I was out!" Ivy grinned. "I'll pay for the beer and lemonade."

"I'll pay for fish and chips!" Ann Marie cried, getting into the spirit of the thing.

"I have bread and butter!" Nelly Kelly shouted out her window.

"I'll make the tea if someone else supplies the milk and sugar!" Patty Grant shouted from her steps.

"I'll supply the milk and sugar!" Lily Connelly shouted from her steps. Things in the Connelly home had improved greatly since Alf found out how much his kids could earn from their life on the stage. "My Alf will bring out the first table. Someone else start bringing out more. Yeez all know to bring out cups and mugs. Come on, let's be havin yeez!"

By the time the lamplighter passed, The Lane was bouncing. The children were running wild. Adults were singing and dancing and everyone was having the best of times.

"Ann Marie, what's your party piece?" Jem Ryan was grinning down at her.

"I don't have one," Ann Marie admitted to hoots of derision.

"We've entertained you, Missus!" some wag shouted. "It's your turn. Up you get!"

Ann Marie was pulled to her feet. She stared mortified in Ivy's direction.

"You can just say a poem or recount a funny incident." Ivy grinned. "We're not fussy."

Ann Marie grinned and, with suitable actions and nudge-nudge jokes, gave the crowd her rendition of the Victorian saucy ditty "The Piano Lesson". The crowd roared their appreciation and clapped along every time Ann Marie sang of the twiddly bits he used to play. Ann Marie was having the time of her life.

"Alf Connelly, are you going to give us a song?" someone shouted when Ann Marie sat down to thunderous applause. "Get Alf up! We haven't heard from him yet. Those kids of his got their voices from him. Come on, Alf, up yeh get!"

Alf Connelly stood with his eyes closed, took a deep breath and opened his mouth. He delivered an operatic aria with such skill that Ann Marie Gannon almost fell off her hay-bale seat.

Ann Marie was horrified at her own snobbery. She'd no idea these people even knew what opera was, let alone how to sing it. She'd deliberately tried to find a simple song she thought they'd appreciate.

"Me da just makes noises for the foreign words," Conn informed everyone, not a bit impressed by his father's skill. He'd heard it all of his life.

"He's wonderful!" Ann Marie whispered.

"Don't tell him that, Missus." Conn sent Ann Marie a horrified look. "We'll never get him to shut up. Oh no, now me ma is getting in on the act."

Alf and Lily Connelly stood and sang their hearts out. A tenor to make the gods jealous and a soprano to make the angels weep. The Lane went quiet and listened.

They were greeted by thunderous applause and demands for more. Ann Marie knew she'd remember this night for the rest of her life. She'd heard opera performed at La Scala in Italy and this couple compared favourably to those masters of their art.

The party wound down naturally. The women went home with their children sleeping in their arms. The men carried in the tables and in time everything went quiet.

"Things are looking up for us, Jem." Ivy leaned against Jem's strong chest.

Emmy had fallen asleep earlier and Jem had carried her up to bed and returned to help with the clear up. The Lane was quiet around them. They could have been the only two people in the world.

"You're well on your way to becoming a successful businessman and I'm dipping me toes in!" Ivy laughed.

"So, yeh're not thinking of giving up your rounds to be a dollmaker?" Jem asked.

"Jem, I'll never give up me round. The round and the money I make from wandering is me bread and butter. I'd never risk that but it's thanks to me round that I can gamble with dressing dolls or whatever strikes me fancy."

"I think I'll go ask Dora to keep an ear open for Emmy. I don't expect her to wake up, she's had a busy day, but I prefer to be sure. There are plenty of people around here to take care of things." Jem looked around. "I'll go see what Ann Marie is doing. She'll need someone to walk her home." Jem disappeared into the livery.

Ivy stood staring around at her world. So much had changed in the months since her da died. A whole new world was opening up to her. She never knew she was a gambler but the chance for a better life for herself and her friends made her blood fizz.

Ivy looked across at the house her basement sat beneath. Now that she knew who owned it and had a chance of fighting for her rights she could take whatever Father Leary cared to throw at her. It wouldn't be anything new. Ivy Rose Murphy was going places. She wasn't sure where yet but she intended to enjoy the journey.

"Ann Marie wants to stay a while longer." Jem's voice appeared before he did. "Dora has agreed to keep watch on Emmy." He walked slowly over to where Ivy stood in the shadows and cocked his arm. "Miss Ivy, could I interest you in an evening stroll?"

"Mr Ryan," Ivy shoved her arm through the crook of his elbow, "I would be delighted."

Also published by Poolbeg

If you like *Downton Abbey* you'll love this

TYRINGHAM PARK

ROSEMARY MᶜLOUGHLIN

Tyringham Park is the Blackshaws' magnificent country house in the south of Ireland. It is a haven of wealth and privilege until its peace is shattered by a devastating event which reveals the chaos of jealousy and deceit beneath its surface.

Charlotte Blackshaw is only eight years old when her little sister Victoria goes missing from the estate. Charlotte is left to struggle with her loss without any support from her hostile mother and menacing nanny. It is obvious to Charlotte that both of them wish she had been the one to go missing rather than pretty little Victoria.

Charlotte finds comfort in the kindness of servants. With their help she seeks an escape from the burden of being the unattractive one left behind.

Despite her mother's opposition, she later reaches out for happiness and believes the past can no longer hurt her.

But the mystery of Victoria's disappearance continues to cast a long shadow over Tyringham Park – a mystery that may still have the power to destroy its world and the world of all those connected to it.

978-1-84223-520-1